MW00526882

THE VOYAGE THAT
NEVER ENDS

THE VOYAGE THAT NEVER ENDS

fictions, poems, fragments, letters

MALCOLM LOWRY

edited by michael hofmann

NEW YORK REVIEW BOOKS **nyrb** *New York*

THIS IS A NEW YORK REVIEW BOOK

PUBLISHED BY THE NEW YORK REVIEW OF BOOKS

Copyright © 2007 by the Estate of Malcolm Lowry
Introduction copyright © 2007 by Michael Hofmann
All rights reserved.

Published in the United States of America by
The New York Review of Books
1755 Broadway
New York, NY 10019
www.nyrb.com

Library of Congress Cataloging-in-Publication Data

Lowry, Malcolm, 1909–1957.
  The voyage that never ends / by Malcolm Lowry ; edited and with an introduction by
Michael Hofmann.
        p. cm. — (New York Review Books classics)
    Includes bibliographical references.
    ISBN-13: 978-1-59017-235-3 (alk. paper)
    ISBN-10: 1-59017-235-3 (alk. paper)
    I. Hofmann, Michael, 1957 Aug. 25– II. Title.
PR6023.O96V69 2007
813'.54—dc22

                              2007017329

                    ISBN 978-1-59017-235-3
        Printed in the United States of America on acid-free paper.

                    1 3 5 7 9 10 8 6 4 2

CONTENTS

INTRODUCTION

The Voyage That Never Ends does not exist, at least not in the terms—themselves subject to constant revision—in which Malcolm Lowry conceived it. It was to have been a cycle of three or five or seven novels built around but also in a way hoping to eclipse or efface *Under the Volcano*, Lowry's 1947 masterpiece. Lowry was after—this is the most widely used likeness—a sort of Divine Comedy in which he would pitch his Inferno, but the Dante was to be mixed with Piranesi and mixed with Pirandello. The cycle was more a spiral, a recessional, a *mise en abîme*, and finally a mirage. It was three or five or however many novels in search of an author. It would comprise books drafted though not to Lowry's satisfaction (such as *Lunar Caustic* and *Dark as the Grave Wherein My Friend Is Laid*), books barely sketched (such as *La Mordida*), books that were lost in fire (such as *In Ballast to the White Sea*—Lowry was chronically unlucky with manuscripts), and even the odd item that was practically complete, like the long story "The Forest Path to the Spring."

It has to be said, though, that *Under the Volcano* always menaced and destabilized the project: by the fact of its existence, by the immense labor it took to write it, and by the

formidable density of its achievement, which sets it apart perhaps from every other novel written (both the labor and the
density are brought out in the furious, serene, funny, and magnificent "Cape letter" of 2 January 1946, in response to the
guarded interest of the publisher, and an editor's standard—
and all the more mortifying—request for "rewrites" or "cuts").
Lowry's difficulty in the last ten years of his life, from 1947 to
1957, was how to be the author of one great book, a difficulty
he devolved upon other books he tried to write, which only
returned the difficulty to him. *Under the Volcano* was to appear
in some of the other books—now as the dream of another
"author," now as a book "by" Lowry's alter ego, Sigbjørn Wilderness, and called *The Valley of the Shadow of Death*, now in
the form of reprises of Mexican material in *Dark as the Grave*
or *La Mordida*, things he only half-jokingly referred to as
"Under Under the Volcano." Though he didn't stop working—
on the contrary, perhaps he worked too hard, too ambitiously,
and certainly on too many different projects—Lowry published
no more books in his lifetime. At the time of his death, he was
out of print: *Ultramarine*, his debut novel from 1933—wittily
and justifiably dubbed "Purple Passage" by Conrad Aiken—
was long gone, but so was *Under the Volcano* itself, the book
whose triumphant completion and subsequent *succès d'estime*
probably did as much to derail its author as anything else. It,
surely, was Lowry's Kilroy, distractingly popping up all over
the place, always there first, blocking him.

Lowry was in a double bind: having written it, *Under the
Volcano* was the only novel he cared to and knew how to write,
and at the same time its achievement was unrepeatable. It became a primary, somehow anterior fact, he himself secondary
to it. He became a sort of wandering expert on it, not so much
an author as an authority. In the words of the title of a short
story he wrote at the time, "the element follows you around,

sir." It haunted him, his albatross, or the machine that, having built—"it works too, believe me, as I have found out," he wrote to Cape—he was unable to get off. There is a rather Borgesian-sounding, but, I believe, true story, about a Latin American author (I'm afraid I don't know the name, if I ever did) who copied out *Under the Volcano* by hand. Well, a terrific choice, but in the non-Borgesian world, not one available to Lowry. ("The lightning, a good writer, did not repeat itself," runs a proud and sore little sentence from the opening chapter of *Dark as the Grave*, included here.) It's as though a whole continent had gone into the writing of *Under the Volcano*, if you like, almost literally: "you have a line there I wrote in Africa 15 years ago," a friend told him. And then, after the ranging and collecting and ordering, a ferocious—expressive—crush; first, a voracious appetence for real detail, then the application of sufficient force to make coal from forest, or diamond from coal. Both supreme, unrepeatable efforts—and by a man of whom Douglas Day, his biographer, said: "One must begin by understanding that Lowry was not really a novelist except by accident." It took ten years for him to grow and compress the novel from the original short story (included here); how many lifetimes could it have taken him to write something comparable?

In Lowry's personal reckoning, and in his efforts to continue as a writer, *Under the Volcano* somehow came to be entered on the debit side. It was in one weighing pannier; he himself, jumping up and down, was in the other. It hardly budged. The drama of its writing, and the further dramas of its selling and marketing—he was given one of the first, and most calamitous, "author tours" in 1947, that plucked him out of his almost unimaginable seclusion in a beach shanty in Dollarton, British Columbia, via a long, slow, drunken progress over and under the United States (St. Louis, Bourbon Street, Haiti—related in the excerpt from *La Mordida*, included here) to New York

City, where he was abruptly reacquainted with the obligations
and expectations of the public world—left him exhausted, and
in the original sense of the word, "effete." Nor was he even rid
of the thing, once published; whether in life or work its obses-
sions remained loyal to him: Mexico, drink, coincidences,
runic prophecies, guilt, fire, fear of eviction, a kind of traveling
that—like the machine in Kafka's "Penal Colony"—inscribed
the traveler. Here was someone who, sticking his nose out of
the door of his squat, was greeted by a red HELL across the
inlet (one presumes, certainly hopes, there was once an S). The
weakened writer must have looked out to behold a world
already written, and by himself; that nowhere had the cogency
and interest and character and amusement he had imparted to
it in his book. A story like that of the Consul—the primary
drama of a man in the world—is not quite replaced, but certainly overlaid in later writings, by the more specialized (and,
to my mind, lesser) drama of a-man-who-has-written-a-book
in the world.

The pieces assembled in this volume, then, while not identical
to Lowry's own projected *Voyage That Never Ends* (but then,
how could they be, and in any case there is not the novel *Under
the Volcano*), at least make a devout and well-intentioned
gesture in that direction. According to David Markson (who
would have known), "a novel became a kind of introduction,
for Lowry, to the author personally." That is the sort of book
this aims to be. It is for admirers of *Under the Volcano*, those
readers who are curious to read something else by the same hand,
and those who have conceived a kind of *tendresse* for Malcolm
Lowry, personally—as, to my mind, who couldn't, given that
Day ends his biography with an anonymous voice in a bar, saying (of Lowry): "The very sight of that old bastard makes me

happy for five days. No bloody fooling." He is something like an erudite Beat, a traveler with a phenomenal vocabulary and unmatched descriptive gift, a mild and sweet temperament, a man set on testing his early insight, that "you carry your horizon in your pocket wherever you are."

I have gone for variety and inclusiveness: poems, letters, short stories, long stories, chapters from novels at varying stages of completion (the passage from *La Mordida* gives a fascinating insight into the way Lowry tried to siphon fiction from his habitual note-taking—and also of the perhaps unnervingly close collaboration between himself and Marjorie, his wife). "30th June 1934"—the Night of the Long Knives in Germany, when Ernst Röhm and many others were arrested ("a gentlemanly account of a revolt in this chap Hitler's army, in which a few brownshirts or blackshirts...had been shot. Poor fellows")—is an instance of Lowry's antiphonal use of offstage history, reminiscent of the Battle of the Ebro in *Under the Volcano*. Rather than excerpting *Ultramarine*, I chose the little-known short story "China" from the same period in Lowry's life. "Kristbjorg's Story," a notably streamlined tale of alcoholic decline, is there, perhaps in place of *Lunar Caustic* which again I found hard to excerpt from, and didn't want to include whole. I chose twenty poems from Lowry's very up-and-down output; curiously, while the prose is almost entirely obsessed with movement—and I tried to choose as many forms of transport as I could find: bus, train, ferry, freighter, plane—the poems dwell in their places: "Kingfishers in British Columbia," "Happiness," "Delirium in Vera Cruz." There are long, reasonably self-contained samplings from the novels-in-progress. From Lowry's voluminous correspondence, I tried to choose letters that are arresting in different ways, but also representative: the brilliantly exuberant early ones to Aiken; the long and magisterial one to Cape; absurdly generous replies to strangers

(Derek Pethick) or anthologists (Ralph Gustafson); temporizing and exasperating ones to Albert Erskine, his American editor; delirious month-long rambles to Markson that must have cost Lowry most of his remittance in postage; late letters from England "home" to Dollarton (to Harvey Burt). When I began, I wasn't sure whether to use tiny scraps and shards of prose or longer coherent passages. Happening to read a piece by James Wood in *The New York Times* ("Virginia Woolf, in a characteristically Flaubertian moment of anxiety, said that we go to novelists not for sentences but for chapters") made me come down in favor of chapters—even though, left to myself, I don't think I belong to Woolf's (or Wood's) "we"—I think I go to novelists for sentences, and, God knows, there are enough marvelous ones here.

Michael Hofmann
Gainesville, Florida
April 2007

BIOGRAPHICAL CHRONOLOGY

1909	July 28: Clarence Malcolm Lowry born in New Brighton, England, to Arthur Osborne and Evelyn Boden Lowry
1923–1927	Attends the Leys School, Cambridge
1927	May–October: to Far East as a cabin boy on the S.S. *Pyrrhus*
1928	Father proposes diplomatic career; Lowry studies German at Weber's English College in Bonn. Overwhelmed by reading of Conrad Aiken's *Blue Voyage*
1929	Summer: studies writing privately with Aiken in Cambridge, MA. Fall: enters St. Catherine's College, Cambridge
1930	Travels in summer to Norway as fireman on Norwegian freighter; meets the writer Nordahl Grieg

1932   Graduates from Cambridge

1933   To Spain with Aiken and his wife; meets Jan
        Gabrial. *Ultramarine* published by Jonathan
        Cape in November

1934   Marriage in Paris to Gabrial, who leaves
        Lowry for New York almost immediately

1935   To New York; hospitalized for ten days in
        the psychiatric wing of Bellevue. Begins work
        on *Lunar Caustic*

1936   To Los Angeles with Gabrial; they sail from
        San Diego for Acapulco and settle in Cuer-
        navaca. Begins work on *Under the Volcano*

1937   Visited by the Aikens in Mexico. Final
        breakup with Gabrial

1938   Leaves Mexico for Los Angeles, where Lowry
        meets Margerie Bonner, a minor Hollywood
        star. Moves to Vancouver, BC, where he is
        soon joined by Bonner

1940   Moves into fishing shack in Dollarton, BC.
        Divorced from Gabrial. Married to Margerie
        Bonner. Sends the third version of *Under the
        Volcano* to his agent, Harold Matson

1941   *Under the Volcano* is refused by twelve
        publishers; Lowry begins a fourth version

1944   June 7: Dollarton shack burns down; moves
        in with Gerald Noxon, near Toronto, and
        finishes *Under the Volcano* on Christmas Eve

1945   Rebuilds Dollarton shack. Final version of
        Under the Volcano sent to Matson. In Mex-
        ico to work on *Dark as the Grave Wherein
        My Friend Is Laid*

1946   *Under the Volcano* accepted by Reynal &
        Hitchcock in New York and Jonathan Cape
        in London. Arrested and deported from Mex-
        ico. Returns to Dollarton. Takes bus to New
        Orleans and sails for Haiti

1947   Returns from Haiti. February 19: in New
        York for publication of *Under the Volcano*.
        Returns to Dollarton. *Under the Volcano*
        published by Jonathan Cape. Sails on French
        freighter from Vancouver, through the
        Panama Canal, to Le Havre. In Paris

1948   Travels in France and Italy

1949   In Dollarton. Works on *Dark Is the Grave,
        La Mordida*; begins stories in *Hear Us O
        Lord from Heaven Thy Dwelling Place*;
        writes filmscript for F. Scott Fitzgerald's
        Tender Is the Night. Breaks back falling
        from pier

1950–1954   In Dollarton. Completes filmscript; works on
             Hear Us O Lord, October Ferry to Gabriola,
             poems. Dropped by Random House in 1954.
             Leaves Dollarton for New York by way of
             Los Angeles. Sails from New York to Genoa
             on Italian freighter. Travels to Taormina,
             Sicily

1955   To London. Hospitalized for psychiatric
             treatment

1956   Moves to Ripe, Sussex

1957   Tours Lake District. June 27: found dead in
             house in Ripe

FICTIONS

JUNE THE 30th, 1934

SILENTLY THE TRAIN FOR BOULOGNE DREW OUT OF THE Gare de l'Est.

This was surprising. One had expected an excruciating din, a series of spastic propulsions, to be thrown from one's feet. The Reverend Bill Goodyear, of West Kirby, Cheshire, England, threw his suitcase on the rack and sat down behind *L'Oeuvre*. But there was nothing comprehensible in The Work so he looked out of the window.

Advertisements swam past, for Oxygénée, for Pernod Fils, for Jean Cocteau's *Machine Infernale*, at the Theatre des Champs Elysées, for Charles Boyer in *La Bataille*, playing at the Rex.

He gazed out beyond the hoardings, perforated to counter-set wind pressure, over the leaden acres of rooftops with their aerials and lines of washing dancing in the sun, to see if he could catch sight of his favorite church, at Alesia. But obviously, it was too far away. He returned to his paper in which he tried to follow an article devoted to the Stavisky case. He did not understand it at all. And what were those references to the great riots in the Place de la Concorde, and elsewhere, in February? His dog collar, glimpsed in the window, seemed like

3

a disguise, so that he felt a bit like Stavisky himself. It appeared that nothing less than another French Revolution had recently taken place without his knowing it. Nor did he quite understand why in order to promote peace it should be necessary for the French inner market to be stimulated by closer contact with the German steel cartels. But his French was bad and perhaps the writer was trying to convey something quite different.

After a while Bill Goodyear realised that he was not reading, so much as hiding himself, behind the paper. Ah, what a nuisance it was always to be so ill at ease in trains, on ships, in drawing rooms! Just as in the pulpit it took him such a long time to reestablish himself, to be aware of a new community. Perhaps it was because, believing passionately in mankind, he was afraid of superficial contacts, of the mere brushing of wings with a fellow creature. He folded his paper and looked out of the window again.

The signals saluted like clockwork, a wooden man in a box marked Paris 5 hauled on a lever and a score of rails rippled away and became one; and as if brushing away trucks bearing old wartime inscriptions, 40 hommes, 8 chevaux, buildings, elevated railways, even the Eiffel Tower itself, from its course, the train, free of the ambiguity of suburbs and junctions, swerved ahead whistling towards Boulogne and England. The black powerful engine, the determination of the thing, pleased him.

Goodyear produced his pipe and some hateful Scarfelati tobacco he had bought in Chartres. But the pipe too might at least conceal his uneasiness, which was now more like panic, a fear that at any moment the summons would come from the dark of things and his little universe be overthrown. Soon he was hidden behind a flood of vile grey air, a smoke-screen between himself and a toppling world.

But the Scarfelati was mere tinder, the pipe grew uncomfortably hot and the man opposite him proffered Goodyear his pouch.

In the pouch were little yellow ringlets of aromatic English tobacco.

While Goodyear was relighting his pipe he looked at his companion out of the corner of his eye. He was a short, bronzed man a good deal older than himself, he thought, badly but expensively dressed, with a jutting chin and steady grey eyes. He held one leg out stiffly.

But more than of any physical impression Goodyear was strikingly aware of a feeling of kinship, even in the other's silence. His uneasiness fell away.

"Thanks," he said. "This is a good deal better."

"Name's Firmin. Been in France long?"

"Goodyear. No. I was just visiting a confrère of mine at the American church in Paris. On the Quai d'Orsay."

"I don't like the French," said the other. "Too vindictive. Not enough sincerity."

"I wouldn't like to say that. I like them; a great people."

"Too much bureaucracy."

The men did not speak again until they reached Amiens, then he said:

"This was a very busy place during the war. You'd scarcely recognize it." He paused. "But you were too young for the war, I suppose."

Goodyear said nothing, ashamed that he had been too young.

"Well, how do you do."

"How do you do."

The two men shook hands. Firmin looked out.

"This is the Somme," he said.

They were silent until they had passed Etaples, when Firmin said:

"There was a lot of fighting here."

The train hurled swiftly on through peace; fields of campion, or cornflowers. The haystacks stood together in the meekness of love, like loaves. Now a boy and a girl were fishing in a canal.

Goodyear produced a notecase, from which he withdrew a photograph. He handed it to Firmin. In the photograph three children grouped themselves in a garden about a herbaceous border.

"That's Dick, there. He'll be twelve next July."

"Fine looking children. I'll bet you're anxious to see them again."

The man handed back the photograph which Goodyear replaced in his notecase. As he pocketed it he said:

"Ah well, I'm being returned empty anyhow."

Firmin nodded. Not seeming to have noticed the other's last words, he remarked:

"I once thought of marrying. But I smashed my hip to hell in the war. Doesn't interfere with my walking any longer. Still, in my job, I mustn't let it interfere..."

The two men sat smoking, looking out of the window. There were more boys fishing.

"Fishing," Firmin said. "You cast all round the fish. Sometimes after you've followed them a long way you find it's no good."

Goodyear chuckled. "That last goes for the fish too."

"There was a lot of fighting here," repeated Firmin.

Suddenly and embarrassingly Goodyear felt one of the fits of hysteria coming on which had been tormenting him on the voyage home. His lips trembled around the pipe stem. Turning his face further to the window so that Firmin would not see, he forced his eyelids against his quickening tear ducts. With his eyes queerly screwed up he was watching a labourer straightening his back as he gazed up at the roaring passage of the express. Next Goodyear tried to fix his eyes on the telegraph wires, undulating and diving after the train. This did not succeed either and he was about to give in to his emotion when he saw, among the woods they were passing, a bare-legged boy. He was running furiously and the curious thing about this boy was that he seemed to be keeping up with the train. Goodyear was so astonished that he quite forgot his embarrassment. Now the boy had fallen down. Extraordinary! He turned away and turned his thoughts away from the delusion, only for them to fasten on Firmin. He looked out of the window and there was the boy, but now—could it be? Good Lord no, impossible—there was no mistaking him, the boy *was* Dick.

It was preposterous. They were passing a river and it was Dick and no other who plunged into it joyously. And it was Dick, unmistakeably Dick, who was swimming that river. And Dick too who was scrambling up the opposite bank and running on faster than ever.

He did not say anything about it but every time he looked out of the window there was the boy.

"There was a place here called the bullring," Firmin was saying, "All sand—that was why they called it the bullring. You wouldn't think sand gets frozen. But my word, it was cold in winter."

Goodyear only looked out twice more but both times he saw his boy charging along, keeping up with the train.

Villages and war cemeteries plunged past them and were gone. They made conversation but the swaying of the train dragged their sentences apart. The wheels cried out against the iron.

Passing Neufchatel the track became smoother. Firmin said:

"This was a very busy place in the war. You'd scarcely think it now. Whew!"

Goodyear watched the sunset. A solitary street lamp was alight. A far plane flew over high-banked clouds. It looked like rain. Smoke was curling gently from peaked houses. There was a strange sadness about this journey in the train through the sunset, and a longing for comfort.

Now they were getting into Boulogne.

"The train goes right over the main street," said Firmin. As they slowed down the character of their motion altered, the train was becoming the appurtenance of a wharf, of the sea.

"That place was a terrible place over there during the war," said Firmin. "The Café Cristol."

And Goodyear peered out into the rain, which had just started to fall, over towards the once notorious café. Then they were at the wharf.

They were changing elements, but the idea struck him; no, it is more than this, something greater is being changed—

Shortly after the ship was clear of the quays the two Englishmen stood together at the rail looking into the wilderness of clay and rain which was France disappearing.

Presently there was nothing but darkness and the roar of the sea.

"It's desolate, desolate," said Goodyear.

"Ugly, ugly."

"I never felt so desolate. I don't know why," Goodyear laughed.

"Come on and have a drink, man, and cheer yourself up."

"A sound scheme."

Firmin limped before Goodyear down to the bar. It was heavy smelling and warm; the thrum of the engine was loud. They decided on Bass.

"Every time I have a few drinks I imagine I'm getting demobbed again," said Firmin, drinking.

Goodyear drank, then for some reason said a peculiar thing. "So do I!"

This was, by implication, a flat lie and he was astonished at himself.

"What! Were you in the war? Why didn't you tell me? Here I've been talking as though I fought the whole war by myself."

"I don't know. As a matter of fact I had an only brother killed." Goodyear was lying again. "We used to like to think that he's buried in France. His body was never identified and we don't care to speak of it."

Firmin was silent. Goodyear's heart beat with the beating of the engine. He wondered what had made him tell this curious falsehood. Of course he had no brother at all. Could this be himself talking? And had that been himself before who had seen the boy running? And now, coming on top of it, was this stupid lie about an imaginary brother.

He took another drink and saw, in his mind's eye, the boy running again, but now the boy was Firmin. Firmin as he had been some years before the last war, when he was about the same age that Dick was now.

But Goodyear didn't understand why he had told his un-truth. Had he wanted to be this man's comrade; to make up to him somehow, for his wounds, and had thought by his false-hood about the war, to bring himself nearer to him, and so to humanity, towards which was his responsibility, and in whose eyes—and were not these also Firmin's eyes?—his failure would seem the more excusable?

And with another part of his mind Goodyear was uneasily anticipating the questions Firmin might ask. What regiment? what platoon? do you remember Captain so and so? which he would never be able to answer.

But Firmin changed the subject.

"Mean, did I call them, the French? Perhaps I did them an injustice. They had to battle to get the crops out, they say. And for poor prices. A country of hard bargains."

"My American friend at the Quai d'Orsay was talking this morning about his country. All around them is electricity and they can't use it. Wheat fields, but nobody has bread. Clothing everywhere, they can't buy it. A terrible situation."

Through the porthole Goodyear watched the moving sea which close in under the glare of the lights was as green and fluctuant as the landscape from the train window.

"Fruit rotting, can't eat it. What they want they can't have."

"What can they do?"

"What can any of us do?"

After a pause Firmin said, "A ship's bar always reminds me of a play called *Outward Bound*. If I'm not mistaken there was a chap like you in it."

Goodyear checked himself from replying.

"I remember the play very well indeed," Firmin went on. "All the characters were supposed to be dead. It took place in a ship without a crew but it had a bar. Oh yes, it had a *bar*! I even remember the barman's name: Scrubby. The characters were dead, were voyaging out to what you might call their Last Judgement. It wasn't the sort of play you forget in a hurry. Saw it done in Singapore by an amateur company."

"Singapore, did you say?"

"Yes, Singapore."

"Was it in July, 1927?"

"Yes, it would be, July, 1927."

"Then I produced the play," Goodyear said.

"You produced it? That's funny. Seven years ago. Let me see, now, would that be after Lindbergh had flown the Atlantic?"

The two men stood looking at each other. Strange, Goodyear was thinking: the lie had begotten the truth.

"I may have met you then."

"I was doing mission work."

"I was a prospector out there."

"We may have met."

"Well, that's funny. Well, we'd better have another drink on it. No bird ever flew with one wing."

Goodyear ordered another Bass. "This one on me," he said.

"Here's," said Firmin.

"Good health."

"Ah, but the world isn't what it used to be," said Firmin. "Don't you feel something in the air yourself. If you don't mind my saying so, don't you find it difficult to keep your faith? Of course I'm not a religious man myself, but isn't it difficult?"

"I must admit," said Goodyear, "I *have* to admit that the Church has failed in many important respects." He looked helpless, obviously speaking about himself. "But it is difficult to start again."

"Yes, I know it is. Before the war I was training to be an engineer at Bradford Tech. After the war, after I'd got out of the hospital, I found I couldn't work at the Tech any more. In the first place we weren't allowed to smoke. Wasn't that funny? After the trenches—Good God! We complained to the Principal and he said, 'Well, as a matter of fact, I find it damned difficult too.' Then I absolutely broke away from it, became a prospector."

"You're on leave now: didn't you get very homesick? I did."

"That's what you read in books. No. Only the youngsters really felt that way." Firmin covered this by adding, "Anyway, I'll be glad to get back out East again. Can't stand the traffic here. It take me ten minutes to cross a street."

"Only the youngsters, eh? What about me? I'll be glad enough to get home," said Goodyear. He looked at his Bass. "And that is a fact."

"I work for a German company," said Firmin. "I'm going to London first, then to Hamburg for instructions. Then out East again. Yes, prospecting's meat and drink to me. Metal. All sorts of metal, every sort. Well, it's like fishing. You cast all round the place. Sometimes you may find it after you've followed it a long way and it's no good. It may be only a hundred yards. The great thing is you have to sell your dud ground."

From the other's words a sermon was forming itself in Goodyear's mind. "Brethren, aren't we all prospectors in life? You find the vein, you cast all round it. The fishermen among you will know what I mean." He would pause here for *smiling*... "Follow me," he said, "and I will make you fishers of men."

Still only half aware of what Firmin was saying but catching a familiar word here and there, Goodyear watched the pendulum of the clock over the bar above the bottle of Bass, Worthington, Johnny Walker; the pendulum that swung enormously over the world, that was swinging him back to West Kirby, Cheshire, and Firmin out again to Ambat and Batu, to Changkat and Jelapang, to Kuala Langkat, or to the Klang River. Changkat...Jelapang...Kampong...*Klang*, the engines said. Metal. Metal that streamed through land and sea: metal from the earth, moulded in fire, conqueror of air and water.

"Then of course they salt it," Firmin was concluding. "Three pickle earth. Why sometimes you can go on walking until you're dead. Well, I'm happy. I've been places you can't go without a gun, it isn't safe. And I've shot all sorts of animals. After you've been out there a while, you forget there ever was a place called England. But I daresay you've done all this sort of thing yourself?"

Goodyear watched the pendulum and now he thought of the restless moving finger of God. Systems were formed, were

JUNE THE 30TH, 1934   13

destroyed. At one moment a creature was set on earth to become self-evolving, at another wars were written of, and wars took place. Here a people were created, there erased.

Was there really a sort of determinism about the fate of nations? Could it be true that, in the end, they got what too they deserved? What had a given people done or not done that they should be obliterated? It struck Goodyear as odd at that moment that while he and Firmin had patronized France, while they had been dismayed over America, while they had "handed" it, sportingly, to the defeated nation, Germany, they had not said one word about England. What about England? They had not asked each other that. Nor had they considered openly that there might be anything wrong with themselves. What is wrong with *us*? They had been virtually silent on that point. And what is wrong with me? He had not asked Firmin that, and even while Goodyear put the question half-heartedly to himself he was being bothered by a sinister contradiction in Firmin's existence. Wasn't it a little ominous that Firmin, badly wounded in the war, should spend the rest of his life searching for the very metals with which Man *might* indeed construct a new world, a stellite paradise of inconceivable strength and delicacy, that would enable him, through vast windows of new alloys, to let the light of the future pour in, but with which, or so *L'Oeuvre* had assured him, Man was doing nothing of the sort, but on the contrary, with diabolical genius, merely using to prepare the subtler weapons of his own destruction? He imagined their quarreling about this obviousness and Firmin's inevitable answer, that religion had been the origin of numerous wars, and that when it was not, in some particular case, the war always masqueraded as a crusade, with God, or the Right, firmly supporting both sides, and so forth—all the wooled, unreal but inescapable facts that by repetition and repetition and repetition were enough to create a chaos in themselves—and all this while the two men stood facing each other still as death, as though an actual quarrel had taken place between them.

"I stopped for a while at Crete on the way home," Goodyear said at length, thoughtfully. "A fascinating island! Many thousands of years ago they had a civilization strikingly like our own. A sporting people, but not religious. At Cnossos, which might be compared to London, they'd reached a position where they thought the human intellect, by itself, could solve all their problems. Perhaps Adam made the same mistake! Anyhow, the barbarians came, who really had a God—an evil God but still one which was unanimously worshipped, the God of War that is—who was all their culture rolled into one, and it was all up with the Cretans! But not," he added earnestly, "with the Cretan spirit, that is, the human spirit, of which one assumes the intellect is only a part. And I believe that when that spirit, in spite of all its setbacks, has reached a point of development in its understanding and humility where the real God, the God of Life, be he ever so patient, doesn't have to feel sick at the very thought of it, then it will have already largely triumphed over the greater obstacles and we shall have a real world."

"I don't believe that bit about the development of the intellect applies to you and me though, eh," chuckled Firmin. "Eh?"

Goodyear, privately injured by this, said nothing.

The clangor of the engines filled the silence: from down below leverweight and fulcrum jangled their gongs: further away the turbines screamed in a whirlwind as the water was driven violently against the curved vanes of the wheel rims: and a hissing tangle of sound was weaving itself thickly through the low tunnel of the alleyway to the bar.

Metal...

"Well, it's a funny old world," Firmin said.

The men laughed.

"Have a drink. That's the best thing. I like to see a clergy-man take a drink."

"Many of them feel like taking to it," said Goodyear.

The drinks were brought.

"Well," Goodyear sighed, "once more, I say it. I'm being returned empty. Yes, and you're right, it seems that there *is* a great change taking place, but you can't put your finger on it."

"But you're only a young man yet."

"Thirty-four."

"You wouldn't think it, but I'm only thirty-nine. Five years can make a difference."

They drank.

"Seven years ago I thought that a missionary's was the life for me," Goodyear said, breathing the hot smells of the ship, that distilled memories of parting, "after two years I went home and married. This time I came out and I've only stuck it six months. Did you ever read a story called 'The Country of the Blind,' by Wells, I think? It's about a mountaineer who fell down the crater of a volcano to find himself unhurt but in a country where everyone was blind. The refrain 'the one eyed man is king in the country of the blind' sang in his head. He wanted to give the people sight. Then he discovered that they were happy to be blind, and so he climbed up out of the crater again before it was too late. The trouble was, they wanted to blind him too."

He watched the pendulum.

"Well, here's how," said Firmin.

"Yes, how."

Folkestone was now alongside. They climbed up on deck

into the wild weather. A freighter was passing, outward bound, its siren sounding hoarse and sorrowful. The gangway fell spastically, yawning, then banged into place.

"Clickety click," said Firmin.

Their ship, in turn, had now ceased to be a ship and had become a huge station. The passengers stood in droves, their scarves close over their mouths, passports ready, lining up for their landing cards. It had almost stopped raining, but wild drops still fell. Wet light picked out familiar advertisements; nostalgic: Carter's Little Liver Pills, Players Cigarettes, Bovril: a weeping bull looking, ironically, he thought, into a bottle of meat extract: "Alas, my poor brother!" Built on an incline above them a cinema was showing Chaliapin and George Robey in Pabst's *Don Quixote*; Walt Disney's *Three Little Pigs*.

This time, as Goodyear stepped on to the wharf, he had a curious apprehension—he couldn't say where it came from—that he was not so much changing elements as changing worlds. He passed without difficulty through the customs and then wandered, pipe in mouth, down the platform, where everyone seemed to be reading newspapers. The newsboys were shouting and Goodyear bought a *Star* from a boy who wore this announcement like an apron: *Hitler Atrocities. Germany Under Arms.*

What did all this mean? Was another war really starting already? No. Impossible. And Goodyear was reassured too by the paper, which, in spite of the headlines, merely gave a gentlemanly account of a revolt in this chap Hitler's army, in which a few brownshirts or blackshirts—or were those Mussolini's gang?—had been shot. Poor fellows. Nevertheless, he couldn't rid himself of the feeling that this was only confirmation of what he'd suspected; that a new cycle was beginning, that the face of the world was changing...

The long London boat train lay curved to the platform and already trembling to be gone. A horrible fancy struck Goodyear: the 7:30 to Cnossos—

He met Firmin in the Pullman and they sat down opposite each other.

"They're at it again," Firmin said, opening his paper. "There's something radically wrong somewhere."

"Yes, they're at it again."

"They're forcing another one on us now."

Firmin appeared ill at ease. Doubt and vexation showed in his face as he shook out the newspaper. They had a long wait for the last passengers to get through the customs.

"I never lie about what I've got," Firmin shifted irritably in his seat. "I always declare it."

"War: what price war? What's the prospect now? But I don't really think that this means war," said Goodyear, reading his paper.

"War," said Firmin unpleasantly, "there isn't enough money for war—yet."

"And every prospect pleases."

"There never is enough money, but they always find it," said Firmin.

Goodyear wondered: am I lying to myself as well? Deceiving myself, smuggling myself through the customs when there should be a price on my head, a dutiable metal.

A man passed outside, slowly, testing the wheels; the iron rang out, once, twice, thrice. Base. Metal. Counterfeit. The last passengers hurried into the Pullman. But still the train waited.

At last they started, jerked to a standstill.

"You have to strike back at the cause," said Goodyear, his voice suddenly loud in the carriage.

"What is the cause?"

"Yes, precisely, what?" he lowered his voice. "Ourselves, probably, as much as anything. It's no good meeting evil with evil."

The engine restarted, drowning the true adulterate words, stopped again with a violent, convulsive hissing. Billows of smoke rushed up past the window. Workmen were drilling. Drilling for gas; the terrible hydrocarbons drifting from crevices, expanding, possessing mankind. He peered out through the steaming glass. Poison, he thought. Chaos, change, all was changing: the passengers were changing: a sea change.

Goodyear lay back in his seat. He could feel the change within him, somehow his thoughts were becoming longer: an insidious metallurgy was in practice within him as his ores, his alloys, were isolated. The titanic thunder of the night-shift hammered on his nerves, lacerating them as though it would draw out from him the fine wire of his consciousness.

He knew that he had been altered by the true pattern, the archtype of the events, on the surface so trivial, of the journey. And he sensed that the other passengers, visible for the time being only as that deadly headline *Germany Under Arms*, had also been affected, were even at a crucial point in their lives, turning towards another chaos, a new complexity of melancholy opposites.

Sitting there, for a moment he *was* Firmin, the Firmin who had returned from the war, wounded, to discover only that he had to become somebody else. It was almost as if Goodyear had told the truth to him. And, looking at Firmin, he knew him too to be changed.

Perhaps now, as before, Firmin would have to take a different, unforeseen action.

And an expression of doubt, an hour ago only a shadow on both their faces in an idle conversation, had become part of their features, as years added to them.

Suddenly, cautiously, but with an accelerating motion, the train pulled off once more, slackened for a moment, skidded, and the wheels finding their rhythm, was finally away.

Red and green lights flicked past as the train gathered speed, metal acres stretched and contracted, dilated, narrowed. Folkestone 3 West.

...Metal, true metal, counterfeit, said the train. Changkat, Jelapang, liar and cheat. Manganese, chromium, old counterfeit. Goodyear rubbed a patch of steam from the window, peered into the dark. The train rattled over points. Not enough money, not enough money, not enough money for war. Folkestone 4 Circuit. Circuit Fund. Collection. Silver and copper, silver and gold. Suddenly there was his bare-legged boy again, running, running more furiously, more frenziedly, than ever, red and green lights falling on him, silver and copper lights, running through the metal fields with metal furrows spangled with coins of fire. Run-on-little-ghost-of-the-youth-of-the-next-war-there're-still-ox-eye-daisies-to-pick, said the train, going through a tunnel. Goodyear was weary and closed his eyes. He woke with a start. The passengers sat reading quietly or smoking. A girl was knitting in a corner. Down corridors men swayed, tottering like the blind, hands stretched out to wood or glass, men feeling their way through the world, walking in their sleep, somnambulists...

His eyes returned to the window. A man digging, sharply illumined by a shower of sparks like red blossoms, slowly raised his spade. Davies' words recurred to him: "The man who digs his grave, the girl who knits her shroud." It's never too late, never too late. To start again. You bore in the earth. Silver and copper. Silver and gold. Man makes his cross. With crucible steel. Base metal; counterfeit; manganese; chromium; makes his iron cross; with crucible steel.

The train took a hill. The boy fell in the fire. The knitting needles flashed like bayonets. Steel wool. The red lights flashed. Green lights. Knit. Socks! Knit. Shroud! Knit. Stab! Iron, steel, said the train. Iron, steel. Steel iron. Iron, tin, iron, tin. Steel and iron steel and iron steel and iron steel and iron *steeeeeeeeel!...*

Now they were going at a tremendous pace, but Goodyear and Firmin were fast asleep under the lamp as the express screamed on like a shell, through a metal world.

CHINA

CHINA'S LIKE A MUDDLE TO ME, IT'S JUST LIKE A DREAM, mostly a queer dream. For though I've been there it takes on a quality sometimes that my imagination bestowed on it before I went. But even if I lived there it would still seem to me to be unreal; for the most part I don't think of it and when I do it makes me laugh.

I live down at the docks now in Hoboken, New Jersey, and now and again I wander down there to see a ship that's crossed the Western Ocean. That doesn't make me homesick or stir up in me the old love of the sea or of memories I've got of China. Nor does it make me unhappy when I think I've been there and really have so few memories after all.

I don't believe in China.

You can say I'm like that man you may have read about who spent his life as a sailor on some vessel plying from Liverpool to Lisbon and on retiring was only able to say of Lisbon: The trams go faster there than in Liverpool.

Like Bill Adams I came fresh to sea life from an English public school where I had worn a tophat and carried a silver-topped cane, but there the resemblance ceases. I was a fireman.

There was a terrible war on in China at this time and in this

I did not believe either. Just across the river from where we were moored, China thundered her guns Doom! doom! doom! but the whole thing crashed over our heads without touching us. Not that I would have believed in it any more had we been blown all to hell: we do not associate such dooms with ourselves. But it was as if you were dreaming, as I often have, that you are standing unscathed beneath the tumult of an immense waterfall, Niagara for instance.

We were moored nose on to the English battle-cruiser, *H.M.S. Proteus.* Astern lay a high, brightly-painted Ningpo junk. Apart from this, there was little in our surroundings, before the stevedores arrived, to suggest that we were not at home: even the war, palpable as it seemed to be through the river fog eclipsing the opposite bank, did not dissipate this illusion: much might have happened for good or evil in our absence from England. And this perhaps brings me to my only real point. We are always "here." You've never felt this? Well, with me this was very cogent. In an English paper I could read about the famous city near at hand, divided against herself, tortured not only by the possibility of invasion but with threats of its own ochlocracy, but when the chief engineer forbade us to cross the river to it, I turned over and went to sleep. I didn't believe I was there at all. And when it was proposed by the chief steward that a cricket match take place between the *Arcturion*, which was the name of our ship, and the *H.M.S. Proteus* I was certain I was not. I had seen this coming, however.

They started it in the Indian Ocean.

I was coming off watch at eight bells and when I got to the galley I knew they were starting it.

The seamen were standing round outside their forecastle winding up strands of heaving line. They were like old maids, holding each other's knitting, I thought. Then I saw that they were making cricket balls. The *Arcturion* carried a spare propellor which was shackled to the break of the poop and the captain was chalking on this. A wicket!

While I was having my chow I knew they were starting it and when I finally came out, they had begun. From the broom-locker to the spare propellor along the seaman's side of the welldock was about the length of a cricket pitch and at the far end Hersey was bowling. He took a long run right down the companion ladder and then bowled. At the wicket chalked on the spare propellor trembled Lofty. He milled about in the air with a bat the carpenter had made him. The ball was returned to Hersey. Fieldmen stood round on the hatches, on the steam-piping, among the washing. Now Hersey was bowling again. Lofty had missed. Hersey had the ball once more. One or two were still winding heaving-lines.

When the seamen saw me they started to mince for my ben-efit. Oh, I say, pass the bally ball, —And so on.

I made up my mind I hated these men and then I wished I could crush them: they would never be anything but under-dogs. Unctuousness and servility flowed in their very veins and even now it seems necessary to me to say these things with mere malice. Imitating a workingman's accent, they were even more unpleasant than my own class.

Old bourgeois maidservants with mob cap and broom, that's what English steamboat sailors are.

A few blackened firemen stood around, watching and grin-ning like niggers. They wouldn't join in. They had solidarity, they had one enemy, the chief steward. The sailors and the oth-ers were petty Judases who had to keep in with both sides. They let each other down and they would steal the milk out of your tea. But the firemen were solid. We were prime. And we stood together against the chief steward because of the food.

They had begun by jeering at me: Where is Heton, Hoxford or Cambridge? But in the end they took the attitude, Eton,

Oxford, Cambridge and the fireman's forecastle. At any rate he didn't become a seaman and that's something. That was their attitude.

I was a coal passer and worked on the 12 to 4 or duke's watch, and after a while they accepted me silently as one of them. I worked hard and didn't growl. I respected them but to them that was neither here nor there. But now standing together looking at the sailors with contempt, they gave me a sidelong glance as if suspicious that I had gone over to the enemy.

Then the chief steward came out of the galley smoking a cigar, paused imperiously at the top of the companion ladder and descended slowly, puffing.

—Hello boys, give me a knock.

And Lofty handed over the bat to the chief.

Soon he was slogging the balls all over the place; he hit two into the Indian Ocean and it was very clear he fancied himself. Oh it was very clear he thought he had some class.

—Silly sailors, said the firemen in a long drawl.

That night as I was pacing up and down the poop in carpet slippers smoking, the chief steward came up to me.

—Tell me, he began. Surely you play cricket. Now I'm not *just* a chief steward you might say. I've got education. But let me see, you're not *the*—

Suddenly I felt I had to tell him that I was. I told him how I fared in the Eton and Harrow match, how I'd played against the Australians, there was nothing I didn't know about cricket. I also told him to hold his tongue, but I ought to have known better than to trust a sailor.

It was only after he'd gone that I thought of all the things I ought to have said to him.

He kept his promise as long as it suited him, only as long as it suited him. Meantime we were getting nearer and nearer to China.

And the nearer we got the less I believed in it.

What I want to convey to you is that to me it was not China at all but right here, on this wharf. But that's not quite what I wanted to say. What I mean is what it was not was China: somewhere far away. What it was was here, something solid, tactile, impenetrable. But perhaps neither one thing nor the other.

You see, I had worn myself out behind a barrier of sea life, behind a barrier of time, so that when I did get ashore, I only knew it was *here*. Even if I perked up after a few drinks, I always forgot I was in China. I was "here." Do you see that?

The first thing I knew when I got there was the extent of this mistake. I don't mean I was disillusioned, I want to make that clear. I didn't feel with Conrad "that what expected had already gone, had passed unseen in a sigh, in a flash together with the youth, with the strength, with the romance of illusions." That sigh, that flash, never happened. There was no moment that crystallized the East for me. This moment did not occur. What happened was different. I had been looking forward to something anxiously and I called this China, yet when I reached China I was still looking forward to it from exactly the same position. Perhaps China wasn't there, didn't exist for me just as I could not exist for China.

And I even began to believe my work was unreal, although there was always one voice that said: you get hold of a firebar and you'll soon enough know how real it is.

Then we were alongside and not long after the captain called for me.

—We've arranged a cricket match with the *H.M.S. Proteus* and we want to show them, he said.

—Sure, said the chief steward. We've arranged a cricket match and we'll show them foxy swaddies what we think of them.

—And you're going to play, said the captain.

—Sure, said the chief. And now you've got to titivate your-self up a bit, make yourself look a bit smart you know. You can't play with an old towel round your neck. What would they think of us?

—That's right, said the captain. The last time you went ashore with a towel round your neck, you were a proper dis-grace to the ship.

—You were the only man who went ashore without a tie, said the chief.

—I went to have a swim, I began. But what was the use of talking to these old washerwomen anyway? And I was highly amused to be looking right down once more into the corrupt heart of the life I'd left behind; I thought it extremely funny that my existence had not changed at all and that wherever I was I would be evaluated, smelt out, by my own kind.

A little later the chief steward came down to the forecastle with all sorts of fancy white ducks he'd rooted out and pretty soon I found one hanging on the curtain rail of my bunk. As I changed the firemen grinned.

—Now you'll feel at home, Jimmy.

No other fireman had been selected to play and inwardly I raged.

Outside the chief was saying: —We'll show these swaddies we can make a proper respectable turnout.

Then we strolled along the wharf towards the cricket field which was situated between a slagheap and a coaldump. A river mist was rolling thickly over towards the city, but the atmosphere was clear where we were going save for a thin rain of coal which drizzled in our faces from the tips, speckling our white trousers with dust. Now you could make a fine character study out of this. There was old Lofty and Hersey and Sparks and Tubby and the three mates and the doctor and you could make a fine description out of each one. But unfortunately I can't discriminate, maybe it's my loss, but they all looked the same to me, those sailors: they were all sons of bitches and now after so long I can only see them at all through the kind of mist there was then. So I won't bother you with that. They just looked damned funny as they straggled down the wharf. And I must have looked the funniest of all straggling along with them, all of us in the fancy white ducks the steward had given us. Some trousers far too short and some far too long, which made us look more like a bunch of Chinese coolies than a proper respectable turnout.

Then the swaddies came out of the *H.M.S. Proteus* and they hadn't bothered about any whites. Some wore khaki shorts, some dungarees, others singlets and khaki trousers. And now after so long I only see them through a kind of mist. I can't even say, Well, there was one fellow like this. Hell, they were just swaddies, misled, exploited, simple, handsome and ugly like the rest of us.

Their captain and the chief steward spun a coin. The chief steward won.

The captain of the *Arcturion*, who was not playing but who was reported to be "keen" on cricket, stood behind a godown and watched the proceedings with a heavily critical air.

—It was my call, I laughed. You should have run.

—I thought you said you could play cricket, the chief grumbled.

—I called. It was up to you to run, I laughed.

—Don't laugh, said the chief.

But I went right on laughing. Then the captain appeared and it seemed that he was damned angry too.

—What are you laughing at? I thought you said you could play cricket, he said. And you've run our best man out and been bowled yourself. Why, I thought you said—

—Firemen don't play cricket, I said shortly and walked away from the wharf.

Once I looked back. Lofty was playing hard with a cross bat, defending the honour of the welldock. Then rain sluiced down and stopped play. It was the monsoon season.

I ran for the *Arcturion* and changed quickly.

At the entrance I watched the others shuffling back mournfully into the seaman's forecastle, their white trousers clinging to them like wet rags. Doom! Doom! Doom!

Other firemen joined me at the entrance and we watched the stevedores unloading our cargo, of scouting planes, a bomber, a fighting plane, machine guns, anti-aircraft guns, 25 pound bombs, ammunition. I did not believe in all this. I was not there.

And here's what I want to ask you again. Haven't you felt this too, that you know yourself so well that the ground you tread on is your ground: it is never China or Siberia or England or anywhere else...It is always you. It is always the earth of you, the wood, the iron of you, the asphalt you step on is the asphalt of you whether it's on Broadway or the Chien Mon.

And you carry your horizon in your pocket wherever you are.

UNDER THE
VOLCANO

I

AS THEY WALKED UP THE CALLE NICARAGUA TOWARD
the bus stop Hugh and Yvonne turned to watch the marmalade-colored birds trapezing in the vines. But her father,
afflicted by their raucous cries, strode on austerely through the
blue, hot November afternoon.

The bus was not very full at first and soon was rolling like a
ship in a heavy sea.

Now out of one window, now out of another, they could see
the great mountain, Popocatepetl, round whose base clouds
curled like smoke drawn from a train.

They passed tall, hexagonal stands with advertisements for
the Morelos Cinema: Las Manos de Orlac: con Peter Lorre.
Elsewhere, as they clattered through the little town, they
noticed posters of the same film, showing a murderer's hands
laced with blood.

"Like Paris," Yvonne said to Hugh, pointing to the kiosks,
"Kub, Oxygénée, do you remember?"

Hugh nodded, stammering out something, and the career-
ing of the bus made him swallow every syllable.

"...Do you remember Peter Lorre in 'M'?"

But they had to give it up. The patient floor boards were creaking too loudly. They were passing the undertakers: *Inhumaciones*. A parrot, head cocked, eyed them from its perch at the entrance. Quo Vadis? asked a notice above it.

"Marvelous," the Consul said.

At the market they stopped for Indian women with baskets of poultry. They had strong faces, the color of dark earthernware. There was a massiveness in their movements as they settled themselves. Two or three had cigarette stubs behind their ears, another chewed an old pipe. Their good humoured faces of old idols were wrinkled with sun but they did not smile.

Then someone laughed, the faces of the others slowly cracked into mirth, the camion was welding the old women into a community. Two even managed to hold an anxious conversation in spite of the racket.

The Consul, nodding to them politely, wished he too were going home. And he wondered who had suggested making this ghastly trip to the fiesta at Chapultepec when their car was laid up and there were no taxis to be had! The effort of going without a drink for a day, even for the benefit of his daughter and her young man who had arrived that morning from Acapulco, was far greater than he had expected. Perhaps it was not the effort of merely being sober that told so much as that of coping with the legacy of impending doom recent unprecedented bouts had left him. When Yvonne pointed out Popocatepetl to him for the fifth time he smiled wanly. Chimborozo, Cotopaxi—and there it was! To the Consul the volcano had taken on a sinister aspect: like a sort of Moby Dick, it had the air of beckoning them on, as it swung from one side of the horizon to the other, to some disaster, unique and immedicable.

The bus lurched away from the mercado where the clock on the main building sheltering the stalls stood at seven minutes past two—it had just struck eleven, the Consul's watch said a quarter to four—then bumped down a steep cobbled incline and began to cross a little bridge over a ravine.

Was this the same arras, Yvonne wondered, that cut through her father's garden? The Consul was indicating that it was. The bottom was immensely far below, one looked down at it as from the maintruck of a sailing ship, though dense foliage and wide leaves partly concealed the real treachery of the drop. Its steep banks were piled with refuse, which even hung on the foliage; from the precipitous slope beyond the bridge, turning round, Yvonne could see a dead dog right down at the bottom, with white bones showing through, nuzzling the refuse.

"How's the rajah hangover, Dad?" she asked, smiling.

" 'Taut over chaos,' " the Consul gritted his teeth, " 'crammed with serried masks.' "

"Just a little longer."

"No. I shall *never* drink again. Nevermore."

The bus went on. Halfway up the slope, beyond the ravine, outside a gaudily decorated little cantina named the El Amore de los Amores, waited a man in a blue suit, swaying gently and eating a melon.

As they approached, the Consul thought he recognized him as the part owner of the cantina, which was not, however, on his beat: from the interior came the sound of drunken singing.

When the bus stopped, the Consul thirstily caught sight, over the jalousied doors, of a bartender leaning over the bar and talking with intensity to a number of roaring policemen.

The camion throbbed away to itself while the driver went into the cantina. He emerged almost immediately to hurl himself back on his vehicle. Then with an amused glance at the man in the blue suit, whom he apparently knew, he jammed the bus into gear and drove away.

The Consul watched the man, fascinated. The latter was

very drunk indeed, and he felt a queer envy of him, albeit it was perhaps a stir of fellowship. As the bus drew in sight of the brewery, the Cerveceria de Quahnahuac, the Consul, his too sober gaze on the other's large, trembling hands, thrust his own hands into his pocket guiltily, but he had found the word wanted to describe him: pelado.

Pelados, he thought, the peeled ones, were those who did not have to be rich to prey on the really poor. They were also those half-breed politicians who work like slaves to get into office for one year, just one year, in which year they hope to put by enough to forswear work for the rest of their lives. Pelado— it was an ambiguous word, to be sure! The Consul chuckled. A Spaniard whom he despised, used, and filled with—ah—"poisonous" liquor. While to that Indian it might mean the Spaniard, or, employed by either with an amiable contempt, simply anyone who made a show of himself.

But whatever it might or might not mean, the Consul judged, his eyes still fixed on his man with the blue suit, it was fair to consider that the word could have been distilled only from such a venture as the Conquest, suggesting as it did on the one hand exploiter, and on the other, thief: and neither was it difficult to understand why it had come in time to describe the invaders as well as their victims. Interchangeable ever were the terms of abuse with which the aggressor publicly discredited those about to be ravaged!

The pelado then, who for a time had been talking thickly to himself, was now sunk in stupor. There was no conductor this trip, fares were paid to the driver on getting off, none bothered him. The dusty blue suit with its coat, tight at the waist but open, the broad trousers, pointed shoes shined that morning and soiled with the saloon's sawdust, indicated a confusion in his mind the Consul well understood: who shall I be today, Jekyll or Hyde? His purple shirt, open at the neck and showing a crucifix, had been torn and was partially hanging out over the top of his trousers. For some reason he wore two hats, a kind of cheap Homburg fitting neatly over the broad crown of his sombrero.

Soon they were passing the Hotel Casino de la Selva and they stopped once more. Colts with glossy coats were rolling on a slope. The Consul recognized Dr. Vigil's back moving among the trees on the tennis court; it was as if he were dancing a grotesque dance all by himself there.

Presently they were getting out into the country. At first there were rough stone walls on either side: then, after crossing the narrow gauge railway, where the Pearce oil tanks were pillowed along the embankment against the trees, leafy hedges full of bright wildflowers with deep royal blue bells. Green and white clothing hung on the cornstalks outside the low, grass-roofed houses. Now the bright blue flowers grew right into the trees, already snowy with blooms, and all this beauty the Consul noted with horror.

The road became smoother for a time so that it was possible for Hugh and Yvonne to talk: then, just as Hugh was saying something about the "convolvuli," it grew much worse again.

"It's like a canterbury bell," the Consul was trying to say, only the camion bumped over a pothole at that moment and it was as if the jolt had thrown his soul up into his teeth. He steadied himself on the seat and the wood sent a piercing pain through his body. His knees knocked together. With Popocatepetl always following or preceding them they jogged into very rough country indeed. The Consul felt that his head had become an open basket swarming with crabs. Now it was the ravine that was haunting him, creeping after them with a gruesome patience, he thought, winding always around the road on one side or the other. The crabs were at the back of his eyes, yet he forced himself to be hearty.

"Where's old Popeye gone to now?" he would exclaim as the volcano slid out of sight past the window to the left, for though he was afraid of it, he felt somehow better when it was there.

"This is like driving over the moon," Hugh tried to whisper to Yvonne, but ended up by shouting.

"Maybe all covered with spinach!" Yvonne was answering her father.

"Right down Archimedes this time! Look out!"

Then for a while they were passing through flat, wooded country with no volcano in sight, nothing to be seen but pines, stones, fircones, black earth. But when they looked more closely they noticed that the stones were volcanic, the earth was parched looking, that everywhere were attestations to Popocatepetl's presence and antiquity.

After, the mountain itself would stride into view again, magnificent, or appearing sad, slate-grey as despair, poised over his sleeping woman, Ixtaccihuatl, now permanently contiguous, which perhaps accounted for it, the Consul decided, feeling that Popo had also an annoying quality of looking as though it knew people expected it to be about to do, or mean, something—as if to be the most beautiful mountain in the world were not enough.

Gazing around the camion, which was somewhat fuller, Hugh took stock of his surroundings. He noticed the drunk, the old women, the men in their white trousers with purple shirts, and now the men in black trousers with their white Sunday shirts—for it was a holiday—and one or two younger women in mourning. He attempted to take an interest in the poultry. The hens and cocks and turkeys imprisoned in their baskets, and those that were still loose, had all alike submitted. With only an occasional flutter to show they were alive they crouched passively under the seats, their emphatic spindly claws bound with cord. Two pullets lay, frightened and quivering, between the handbrake and the clutch, their wings linked, it seemed, with the levers. Hugh was bored with all this finally. The thought of Yvonne sagged down his mind, shook his brain, permeating the camion, the very day itself, with nervous passion.

He turned away from her nearness and looked out, only to see her clear profile and sleeked fair hair sailing along reflected in the window.

The Consul was suffering more and more intensely. Each object on which his glance fell appeared touched with a cruel, supersensual significance. He knew the very wood of the seat to be capable of hurting his hands. And the words which ran across the entire breadth of the bus over the windscreen: *su salva estará a salvo no escapiendo en el interior de éste vehículo*: the driver's round mirror, the legend above it, *Cooperación de la Cruz Roja*, beside which hung three postcards of the Virgin Mary and a fire-extinguisher, the two slim vases of marguerites fixed over the dashboard, the dungaree jacket and whiskbroom under the seat opposite where the pelado was sitting, all seemed to him actually to be alive, to be participating, with evil animation, in their journey.

And the pelado? The shaking of the camion was making it difficult for him to remain seated. With his eyes shut, and swaying from side to side, he was trying to tuck his shirt in. Now he was methodically buttoning his coat on the wrong buttons. The Consul smiled, knowing how meticulous one could be when drunk: clothes mysteriously hung up, cars driven by a seventh sense, police eluded by an eighth. Now the pelado had found room to lie down full length on the seat. And all this had been superbly accomplished without once opening his eyes!

Stretched out—a corpse—he still preserved the appearance of being uncannily aware of all that was going on. In spite of his stupor, he was a man on his guard; half a melon slipped out of his hand, the segments full of seeds like raisins rolled to and fro on the seat, yet with eyeless sight those dead eyes saw it: his crucifix was slipping off, but he was conscious of it: the Homburg fell from his sombrero, slipped to the floor, and though making no attempt to pick it up, he obviously knew it was there. He was guarding himself against theft while gathering strength for more debauchery. In order to get into somebody else's cantina he might have to walk straight. His prescience was worthy of admiration.

Yvonne was enjoying herself. For the time being she was freed by the fact of Hugh's presence from the tyranny of thinking exclusively about him. The camion was traveling very much faster, rolling, swaying, jumping; the men were smiling and nodding, two boys, hanging at the back of the bus were whistling; and the bright shirts, the brighter serpentine confetti of tickets, red, yellow, green, blue, dangling from a loop on the ceiling, all contributed a certain sense of gaiety to their trip. They might have been going to a wedding.

But when the boys dropped off some of this gaiety departed. That predominance of purple in the men's shirts gave a disquieting glare to the day. There seemed something brutal to her too about those candelabra cactus swinging by. And about those other cactus, further away, like an army advancing uphill under machine-gun fire. All at once there was nothing to see outside but a ruined church full of pumpkins, caves for doors, windows bearded with grass. The exterior was blackened as by fire and it had an air of being damned. It was as though Hugh had left her again, and the pain of him slid back into her heart, momentarily possessing her.

Buses bobbed by in the other direction: buses to Tetecala, to Jujuta; buses to Xiutepec, to Xochitepec, to Xochitepec—

At a great pace they swerved into a side road. Popocatepetl appeared, off to the right, with one side beautifully curved as a woman's breast, the other jagged and ferocious. The drifted clouds were massing, high-piled, behind it.

Everyone felt at last that they were really going somewhere: they had become self-enclosed, abandoned to the tumultuous will of the vehicle.

They thundered on, passing little pigs trotting along the road, an Indian screening sand. Advertisements on ruined walls swam by. Atchis! Instantia! Resfria dos Dolores. Cafiaspirina. Rechaches Imitaciones. Las Manos de Orlac: con Peter Lorre.

When there was a bad patch the bus rattled ominously and sometimes they ran off the road. But its determination outweighed these waverings: all were pleased to have transferred their responsibilties to it, and to be lulled into a state from which it would be pain to awaken.

As a partner in this, it was with a freezing, detached calm that the Consul found himself able to think, as they bucked and bounded over an interminable series of teeth-rattling potholes, even of the terrible night which doubtless waited him, of his room shaking with daemonic orchestras, of the snatches of fearful sleep, interrupted by imaginary voices outside which were dogs barking, or by his own name being continually repeated with scorn by imaginary parties arriving.

The camion pitched and rolled on.

They spelt out the word *Desviación* but made the detour too quickly with a yelping of tires and brakes. As they swerved into alignment once more the Consul noticed a man apparently lying fast asleep under the hedge by the right side of the road.

Both Hugh and Yvonne appeared oblivious to this. Nor did it seem likely to the Consul that in this country anyone else was going to think it extraordinary a man should choose to sleep in the sun by the side of the road, or even in the middle of the road.

The Consul looked back again. No mistake. The man,

receding quickly now, lay with his hat over his eyes, his arms
stretched out toward a wayside cross. Now they were passing a
riderless horse, munching the hedge.

The Consul leaned forward to call out but hesitated. What if
it were simply an hallucination? This might prove very embarrassing. However he did call out, tapping the driver on the
shoulder; almost at the same moment the bus leaped to a standstill.

Guiding the whining vehicle swiftly, steering an erratic
course with one hand, the driver, who was craning right out of
his seat watching the corners behind and before with quick yet
reluctant turns of the head, reversed along the dusty detour.

There was the friendly, overpowering smell of exhaust gases
tempered with the hot smell of tar from the repairs, though
no one was at work on the road, everybody having knocked
off, and there was nothing to be seen there, just the soft indigo
carpet sparkling and sweating by itself. But a little further
back, to one side by the hedge, was a stone cross and beneath it
were a milk bottle, a funnel, a sock and part of an old suitcase.

Now they could see the man quite plainly, lying with his
arms stretched out toward this wayside cross.

II

As the bus jerked to another stop the pelado almost slid from
his seat to the floor but, managing to recover himself, not only
reached his feet and an equilibrium he contrived remarkably to
maintain, but in doing so had arrived half way to the door in
one strong movement, crucifix fallen safely into place around
his neck, hats in one hand, melon in the other. He nodded
gravely and with a look that might have withered at its incep-
tion any thought of stealing them, placed the hats carefully on
a vacant seat near the door, and with exaggerated care let himself down to the road. His eyes were still only half-open, pre-

serving that dead glaze, yet there could be no doubt he had taken in the whole situation. Throwing away the melon he walked over toward the man in the road. Even though he stepped as if over imaginary obstacles his course was straight and he held himself erect.

Yvonne, Hugh, the Consul, and two of the passengers followed him. None of the old women had moved from their seats.

Half way across the road Yvonne gave a nervous cry, turning on her heel abruptly. Hugh gripped her arm.

"Are you all right?"

"Yes," she said, freeing herself, "Go on. It's just that I can't stand the sight of blood, damn it."

She was climbing back into the camion as Hugh came up with the Consul and the two passengers.

The pelado was swaying gently over the recumbent man.

Although the latter's face was covered by his hat it could be seen that he was an Indian of the peon class. There seemed no doubt that he was dying. His chest heaved like a spent swimmer's, his stomach contracted and dilated rapidly, yet there was no sign of blood. One clenched fist spastically thumped the dust.

The two foreigners stood there helplessly, each waiting for the other to remove the peon's hat, to expose the wound they all felt must be there, each checked from some such action by a common reluctance, an obscure courtesy. Each knew the other was also thinking it would be, naturally, even better still should the pelado or one of the passengers examine the man. But as nobody made any move Hugh became impatient. He shifted from foot to foot. He looked at the Consul with supplication. The Consul had been here long enough to know what could be done; moreover he was the one among them most nearly representing authority. But the Consul, who was trying to prevent himself saying, "Go ahead, after all, Spain invaded Mexico first," made no move either. At last Hugh could stand it no longer. Stepping forward impulsively he made to bend over the peon when one of the passengers plucked at his sleeve.

"Mistair, have you throw away your cigarette?"

"What!" Hugh turned around, astonished.

"I don't know," said the Consul. "Forest fires, probably."

"Better throw your cigarette, Señor. They have prohibidated it."

Hugh dropped his cigarette and stamped it out, bewildered and irritated. He was about to bend over the man once more when the passenger plucked his sleeve again. Hugh straightened up.

"They have prohibidated it, Señor," the other said politely, tapping his nose. He gave an odd little laugh. "Positivemente!"

"I no comprendo, gnadige Señor." Hugh tried desperately to produce some Spanish.

"He means you can't touch this chap because you'd be an accessory after the fact," nodded the Consul, beginning to sweat and wishing profoundly he could get as far away from this scene as possible, if necessary even by means of the peon's horse, to somewhere where great gourds of mescal crouched. "Leave well enough alone is not only the watchword, Hugh, it's the law."

The man's breathing and thumping was like the sea dragging itself down a stone beach.

Then the pelado went down on one knee and whipped off the dying man's hat.

They all peered over, seeing the terrible wound in the side of his head, the blood from which had almost coagulated, and before they stood back, before the pelado replaced the hat and, drawing himself erect, made a hopeless gesture with hands blotched with half dried blood, they caught a glimpse of a sum of money, four or five silver pesos and a handful of centavos, which had been placed neatly under the man's collar, by which it was partly obscured.

"But we can't let the poor fellow die," Hugh said despairingly, looking after the pelado as he returned to the bus, and then down once more at this life gasping away from them all. "We'll have to get a doctor."

This time from the camion, the pelado again made that gesture of hopelessness, which might have been also a gesture of sympathy.

The Consul was relieved to see that by now their presence had exampled approach to the extent that two peasants, hitherto unnoticed, had come up to the dying man, while another passenger was also standing beside the body.

"Pobrecito," said one.

"Chingarn," muttered the other.

And gradually the others took up these remarks as a kind of refrain, a quiet seething of futility, of whispers, in which the dust, the heat, the bus with its load of immobile old women and doomed poultry, even the terrible beauty and mystery of the country itself, seemed to be conspiring: while only these two words, the one of tender compassion, the other of fiendish contempt, were audible above the thudding and the gasping, until the driver, as if satisfied that all was now as it should be, began impatiently blowing his horn.

A passenger shouted to him to shut up, but possibly thinking the admonition was in jesting approval, the driver continued to blow, punctuating the seething, which soon developed into a general argument in which suspicions and suggestions cancelled each other out, to a heckling accompaniment of contemptuous blasts.

Was it murder? Was it robbery? Or both? The peon had ridden from the market with more than that four or five pesos, possibly he'd been in possession of mucho dinero, so that a

good way to avoid suspicion of theft was to leave a little of the
money, as had been done. Perhaps it was not robbery at all; he
had only been thrown from his horse? The horse had kicked
him? Possible? Impossible! Had the police been called? An
ambulance—the Cruz Roja? Where was the nearest phone?
One of them, now, should go for the police? But it was absurd
to suppose they were not on their way. How could they be on
their way when half of them were on strike? They would be on
their way all right, though. An ambulance? But here it was
impertinent of a gringo to interfere. Surely the Red Cross were
perfectly capable of looking after such a matter themselves?
But was there any truth in the rumor that the Servicio de
Ambulante had been suspended? It was not a red but a green
cross and their business began only when they were informed.
Perhaps it was imprudent of a gringo to assume they hadn't
been informed? A personal friend, Dr. Vigil, why not call
him? He was playing tennis. Call the Casino de la Selva then?
There was no phone; oh, there was one once but it had decom-
posed. Get another doctor, Dr. Gomez. Un hombre noble. Too
far, and anyhow, probably he was out; well, perhaps he was
back!

At last Hugh and the Consul became aware that they had
reached an impasse upon which the driver's horn still made a
most adequate comment. Neither could presume, from the appearance of it, that the peon's fate was not being taken care of
in some way "by one of his own kind." Well, it certainly didn't
look as though his own kind had been any too generous to him!
On the contrary, the same person who placed him at the side of
the road, who placed the money in the peon's collar, was probably even now going for help!

These sentiments got up and knocked each other down
again and although their voices were not raised, although
Hugh and the Consul were not quarrelling, it was as if they

were actually knocking each other down physically and getting up again, each time more weary than the last time down, each time with a practical or psychic obstruction toward cooperating or even acting singly, the most potent and final of all of which obstructions being that it was not their business at all but somebody else's.

Yet on looking around them they realized that this too was only what the others were arguing. It is not my business, nor yours, they said as they shook their heads, but someone else's, their answers becoming more and more involved, more and more theoretical, so that finally the discussion began to take a political turn.

To the Consul, time suddenly seemed to be moving at different speeds: the speed at which the peon was dying contrasting oddly with that at which everyone was arriving at the conclusion it was impossible to make up their minds. Aware that the discussion was by no means closed and that the driver, who had stopped blowing his horn, and was conversing with some of the women over his shoulder, would not think of leaving without first taking their fares, the Consul excused himself to Hugh and walked over to the Indian's horse, which, with its bucket saddle and heavy iron sheathes for stirrups, was calmly chewing the "convolvulus" in the hedge, looking as innocent as only one of its species can when suspected even wrongfully of throwing its rider or kicking a man to death. He examined it carefully, without touching it, noticing its wicked, friendly, plausible eyes, the sore on its hipbone, the number seven branded on its rump, as if for some clue to what had happened. Well, what *had* happened? Parable of a too late hour! More important, what was going to happen—to them all? What was going to happen to him was that he was going to have fifty-seven drinks at the earliest opportunity.

The bus was hooting with real finality now that two cars

were held up behind it; and the Consul, observing that Hugh was standing on the step of one of them, walked back shaking his head as the camion came toward him to stop at a wider part of the road. The cars, wild with impatience, thrust past and Hugh dropped off the second one. Bearing tin plates under their numbers with the warning "Diplomático" they disappeared ahead in a cloud of dust.

"It's the diplomatic thing, doubtless," said the Consul, with one foot on the step of the camion. "Come on, Hugh, there's nothing we can do."

The other passengers were getting on board and the Consul stood to one side to talk to Hugh. The periodicity of the honking now had become much slower. There was a bored, almost amused resignation in the sound.

"You'll only be hauled into gaol and entangled in red tape for God knows how long," the Consul persisted. "Come *on*, Hugh. What do you think you're going to do?"

"If I can't get a doctor here, God damn it, I'll take him to one."

"They won't let you on the bus."

"The hell they won't! Oh—here come the police," he added, as three smiling vigilantes came tramping through the dust at that moment, their holsters slapping their thighs.

"No, they're not," the Consul said unfortunately. "At least, they're just from the policía de seguridad, I think. They can't do anything much either, just tell you to go away or—"

Hugh began to expostulate with them while the Consul watched him from the step of the camion apprehensively. The driver was wearily honking. One of the policemen began to push Hugh toward the bus. Hugh pushed back. The policeman drew back his hand. Hugh raised his fist. The policeman dropped his hand and began to fumble with his holster.

"Come on Hugh, for God's sake," the Consul pleaded,

grasping him again. "Do you want to land us all in the gaol? Yvonne—"

The policeman was still fumbling with his holster when suddenly Hugh's face collapsed like a heap of ashes, he let his hands fall limply to his sides, and with a scornful laugh boarded the bus, which was already moving away.

"Never mind, Hugh," said the Consul, on the step with him, a drop of sweat falling on his toe, "It would have been worse than the windmills."

"What windmills?" Hugh looked about him, startled.

"No, no," the Consul said, "I meant something else, only that Don Quixote wouldn't have hesitated that long."

And he began to laugh.

Hugh stood for a moment cursing under his breath and looking back at the scene, the peon's horse munching the hedge, the police enveloped in the dust, the peon far beyond thumping the road, and now, hovering high above all, what he hadn't noticed before, the obvious cartoon birds, the xopilotes, who wait only for the ratification of death.

III

The bus plunged on.

Yvonne was flaccid with shame and relief. She tried to catch Hugh's eyes but he crammed himself into his seat so furiously she was afraid to speak to him or even to touch him.

She sought some excuse for her own behavior in the thought of the silent, communal decision of the old women to have nothing to do with the whole affair. With what sodality, scenting danger, they had clenched their baskets of poultry to them, or peered around to identify their property! Then they had sat, as now, motionless. It was as if, for them, through the various tragedies of Mexican history, pity, the impulse to approach, and terror, the impulse to escape (as she had learned at college), had been reconciled finally by prudence, the conviction it is better to stay where you are.

And the other passengers? The men in their purple shirts who had a good look at what was going on but didn't get out either? Who wanted to be arrested as an accomplice, they seemed to be saying to her now. Frijoles for all; Tierra, Libertad, Justicia y Ley. Did all that mean anything? Quién sabe. They were not sure of anything save that it was foolish to get mixed up with the police, who had their own way of looking at the law.

Yvonne clutched Hugh's arm but he did not look at her. The camion rolled and swayed as before, some more boys jumped on the back of the bus; they began to whistle, the bright tickets winked with their bright colors and the men looked at each other with an air as of agreement that the bus was outdoing itself, it had never before gone so fast, which must be because it too knew today was a holiday.

Dust filtered in through the windows, a soft invasion of dissolution, filling the vehicle.

Then they were at Chapultepec.

The driver kept his hand on the screaming emergency brake as they circled down into the town, which was already invested with the Consul's abhorrence because of his past excesses there. Popocatepetl seemed impossibly close to them now, crouching over the jungle, which had begun to draw the evening over its knees.

For a moment there was a sort of twilight calm in the bus. The stars were out now: the Scorpion had come out of its hole and waited low on the horizon.

The Consul leaned forward and nudged Hugh: "Do you see what I see?" he asked him, inclining his head toward the pelado, who had been sitting bolt upright all this time, fidgeting with something on his lap, and wearing much the same expression as before, though he was evidently somewhat rested and sobered.

As the bus stopped in the square, pitching Hugh to his feet, he saw that the pelado clutched in his fist a sad, blood-stained pile of silver pesos and centavos, the dying man's money—

The passengers began to crowd out. Some of them looked at the pelado, incredulous but always preoccupied. Grinning round at them he perhaps half hoped that some comment would be made. But there was no comment.

The pelado paid his fare with part of the bloodstained money, and the driver accepted it. Then he went on taking the other fares.

The three of them stood in the warm evening in the little zócalo. The old women had disappeared: it was as if they had been sucked down into the earth.

From a street near by the crashing, plangent chords of a guitar sounded. And from further away came the bangs and cries of the fiesta.

Yvonne took Hugh's arm. As they walked away they saw the driver, now ostensibly knocked off for the day, and the pelado, stepping high and with a fatuous smile of triumph on his face, swagger into a pulqueria. The three stared after them and at the name of the saloon, after its doors had swung shut: the Todos-Contentos-y-yo-Tambien.

"Everybody happy," said the Consul, the certainty that he would drink a million tequilas between now and the end of his life stealing over him like a benison and postponing for the moment the necessity for the first one, "Including me."

A bell somewhere compounded sudden wild triphthongs.

They moved in the direction of the fiesta, their shadows falling across the square, bending upward on the door of the Todos-Contentos-y-yo-Tambien, below which the bottom of a crutch had appeared.

They lingered curiously, noticing that the crutch rested for some time where it was, its owner having an argument at the door, or a last drink perhaps.

Presently, the crutch disappeared, as if it had been hoisted away. The door of the Todos-Contentos-y-yo-Tambien, through which they could see the bus driver and the pelado getting their drinks, was propped back; they saw something emerge.

Bent double and groaning with the weight, an old, lame Indian was carrying out another Indian, yet older and more decrepit, on his back, by means of a strap clamped to his forehead. He carried the older man and his crutches—he carried both their burdens—

They all stood in the dusk watching the Indian as he disappeared with the old man around a bend in the road, shuffling through the grey white dust in his poor sandals.

KRISTBJORG'S STORY:
IN THE BLACK HILLS

THE GERMAN LIVED IN THE BLACK HILLS AND HE DRANK himself to death. Apparently he wished to obliterate something. This was in 1906. At that time there were three saloons in Deadwood: The Green Front, the Topic, and Lent Morris'. The Green Front was a fancy bar and dance hall and it had a stuffed buffalo in a glass case I remember. The Topic was not so fancy, and Lent Morris' was a bare bar. Calamity Jane used to go to the Topic, a big, mannish woman. I've seen Buffalo Bill there too, but they called him something else. The German used to go to this bare bar.

In those days the bars were open twenty-four hours a day and the bartenders worked in three shifts like miners.

The German didn't seem an average person who came from a rat hole. He was about thirty-five or forty maybe, had a fair moustache, blue eyes—German physique. He would drink a bottle of whiskey in five minutes, then he'd plunk. Sometimes he'd get half through the second bottle before keeling over, and when he did this beside you, if you didn't know him and weren't expecting it, it was a shock.

But it was no shock to Lent Morris. He wouldn't leave him in front of the bar though; they'd drag him away and prop him up against the wall; or he would lay flat. After a few hours he'd come to and frisk himself, and if he had any money he'd start priming himself once more, and then keel over plunk.

He'd keep this up till he was broke, then he'd just go off.

Nobody knew his name, or where he came from. When he went home nobody knew what home he went to. When he wasn't working in the hills his only home was the bar, perhaps in an occasional flophouse. He never said a word to nobody, just drank. If you asked him how he was he'd grunt resentfully, "Ah," perhaps, that was all. He looked very solemn-like and he wouldn't take up the cudgels on no circumstances.

Yet he didn't bother you. He never bummed any money or drinks off you. He kept himself clean and he wasn't the sort of drunk that comes into a bar with ten dollars and then after an hour is bumming drinks off everybody. The German was no bum.

Wages were very low, twenty-five cents an hour—still, in South Dakota people didn't go hungry. If you proposed to go to Butte or Aladdin on foot someone would be sure to offer you their horse. "But I'm not coming back." "Never mind, leave it there. I'll collect it sometime." God help the man who lied however.

The German was not a bum, he was a bindle stiff. Bindle stiff is a more polite way of saying it. He wasn't a hobo; a hobo carries nothing, and never works. This German carried a bundle, and he worked up in the Black Hills where there were lead mines.

In the Black Hills was a town named Lead. Perhaps it was there he worked—he was a big husky man—till he had a stake to come down to Lent's and drink.

Or maybe, at times, the German did have some kind of a home in Deadwood besides the bar. That would have been in the jungle. Every town in the Black Hills had a jungle in those days. There was a town named Cyanide, with a poison mill where they crunched the mercury, and even that had a jungle.

Nemo, that had a jungle. They were some place off to the side, like the city dump, or a lot where worn out railroad box-cars were put. The hoboes and bindle stiffs lived in these box-cars and you'd be surprised to see how they fixed them up. Some of them had cut holes in the sides, and picked up panes of glass from the dump and made windows. They even had geraniums blooming in the windows. And some of them were clean and homelike as you could imagine. There were women there too. Mostly the bindle stiffs lived there in winter. But if the German had a home like this it would only been in winter.

Had he seemed hungry he would have been fed. Or in need of a bed he would have been given a bunk, be it never so lousy. Maybe people sometimes felt sorry for him when they dragged him to the wall, out of the way of the drinkers perhaps, I don't know. Perhaps not.

This particular day the German came in it was summer and we were all drinking in Lent Morris'. He come in and pretty soon he plunked as usual and we dragged him over and propped him up against the wall. Some of us went off to the Green Front, and when we got back three or four hours later the German was still laying against the wall.

"Hey," I said to Lent, "Ain't it time he waked up and primed himself again?"

"Naw," said Lent. "To hell with him."

"But he usually don't sleep more than a couple of hours."

"Hell with him. Let him lie."

"What's the matter with him," I said, "It's time he woke up and had another priming."

So I walked over to him. He was lying with his cheek sort of cupped in his hand. I gave him a shake and he fell over. And where his hand had been his face was snow white, and the rest of his face was purple.

"Hey," I said to Lent. "He's stiff."

"Naw, he's just drunk. Let him alone."

"Drunk nothing," I said. "He's stiff."

And he was stiff too. Rijer Mortes had already set in. The German had drunk himself to death, right in front of our eyes.

I knelt down and put my hand inside his coat and felt for his heart, but I couldn't feel nothing. So we called a doctor who lived across the street.

"Why hell," he said, "the guy's been dead two or three hours."

Well, that was just one plunk too many.

But nobody knew who he was or what to do with him. He had no papers on him. Nobody knew where his folks were. Nobody knew anything about him except he was German. And he'd spent his last dime.

So we laid him on an old door Lent had that had fallen off in his basement and we put him down in the cellar on this door across two sawhorses.

Then, that afternoon, we took up a collection. It wasn't much of a collection, pretty small: we got thirty-five dollars.

We knew a carpenter who said he'd make us a box that would do good enough for twenty-five dollars, and another guy who had a sort of truck and some horses who said he'd cart him up to the boothill for ten dollars.

A boothill is the back part of a cemetery, and they call it a boothill because that's where they bury the guys who die with their boots on, guys who get hung, or shot. Every town had a boothill in those days. Cyanide, Nemo, they all had a boothill.

So the next day, or maybe it was two days later, we took him up to the boothill in Deadwood and planted him. We couldn't put up no tombstone or even a marker, but unless somebody's moved him I guess he's lying there still.

And maybe after all it was a glorious death. In those days a man could get away somewhere.

THROUGH THE
PANAMA

From the Journal of Sigbjørn Wilderness

> Frère Jacques
> Frère Jacques
> Dormez-vous?
> Dormez-vous?
> Sonnez les matines!
> Sonnez les matines!
> Ding dang dong
> Ding dang dong...

THIS IS THE SHIP'S ENDLESS SONG.

This is the engine of the *Diderot*: the canon repeated endlessly...

Leaving Vancouver, British Columbia, Canada, midnight, November 7, 1947, S.S. *Diderot*, for Rotterdam.

Rain, rain and dark skies all day.

We arrive at dusk, in a drizzle. Everything wet, dark, slippery. Dock building huge, dimly lit by tiny yellow bulbs at far intervals. Black geometry angled against dark sky. Cluster lamps glowing—they are loading cardboard cartons labeled *Product of Canada*.

(This morning, walking through the forest, a moment of intense emotion: the path, sodden, a morass of mud, the sad dripping trees and ocherous fallen leaves; here it all is. I cannot believe I won't be walking down the path tomorrow.)

Primrose and myself are the sole passengers aboard the freighter. The crew are all Bretons, the ship, French, its build, American. A Liberty ship about 5,000 tons, 10 knots, electric welded hull.

Longshoremen leave, skipper comes aboard. Sense of departure increases. Nothing happens for hours. We drink rum in cabin: Chief Gunner's cabin, between skipper and wireless operator. Primrose wearing all her Mexican silver bracelets, calmly tense, electrically beautiful and excited.

Then: the Immigration officers, very courteous and cheery. All had cognac together in the skipper's cabin.

Then: bells rang, hawsers were cast off, shouts from bridge, slowly, suddenly, we were moving. The little strip of black, oily water widened...The black cloudy sky was breaking and stars were brilliant overhead.

The Northern Cross.

Nov. 8. High salt wind, clear blue sky, hellishly rough sea (zig-zagged with a lashing tide rip) through the Juan de Fuca Strait.

—Whale geometry of Cape Flattery: finny phallic furious face of Flattery.

Cape Flattery, with spume drenched rocks, like incinerators in sawmills.

—Significance of sailing on the 7th. The point is that my character Martin, in the novel I'm furiously trying to get a first draft of (knowing damned well I'd never do any work on this voyage, which is to last precisely 7 weeks), had dreaded starting a journey on the 7th of any month. To begin with we were not going to leave for Europe until January. Then the message comes that our sailing has been canceled and we'll have to take advantage of the *Diderot*'s sailing on the 6th if we want to go at all. But she doesn't—she sails on the 7th. Martin Trumbaugh's really fatal date is November 15. So long as we don't leave Los Angeles on Nov. 15 for the long haul, all will be well. Why do I say that? The further point is that the novel is about a character who becomes enmeshed in the plot of the novel he has written, as I did in Mexico. But now I am becoming enmeshed in the plot of a novel I have scarcely begun. Idea is not new, at least so far as enmeshment with characters is concerned. Goethe, Wilhelm von Scholz, "The Race with a Shadow." Pirandello, etc. But did these people ever have it happen to *them*?

Turn this into triumph: the furies into mercies.

—The inenarrable inconceivably desolate sense of having no right to be where you are; the billows of inexhaustible anguish haunted by the insatiable albatross of self.

There is an albatross, really.

Martin thought of the misty winter sunrise, through the windows of their little cabin; the sun, a tiny little sun, framed in one of the window panes, like a miniature, unreal, white, with three trees in it, though no other trees were to be seen, and reflected in the inlet, in a high calm icy tide. Fear something will happen to house in our absence. Novel is to be called *Dark as the Grave Wherein My Friend Is Laid*. Keep quiet about house or will spoil voyage for Primrose. Intolerable behavior: remember Fielding with dropsy, being hauled on board in a basket on voyage to Portugal. Gentleman and sense of humor. Had himself tapped for water every now and then. H'm.

This desolate sense of alienation possibly universal sense of dispossession.

The cramped cabin one's obvious place on earth.

Chief Gunner's cabin.

Curious agony of not having tipped steward. Whom to tip? Not wishing to insult anybody.

Strindberg's horror at using people. Using one's wife as a rabbit for vivisection. Seems more honorable to use yourself. This idea unfortunately not new either.

Fitzgerald would have been saved by life in our shack, Martin thought (who had been reading *The Crack-Up*). The Last Laocöon. Impossible to find anybody less like Fitzgerald than Martin. Sad that F. hated the English. To my mind his latter work represents essentially best qualities of chivalry and decency now too often lacking in the English themselves. This quality true essentially of soul of America. Can this be expressed without obsequiousness? Or good manners, with fidelity to the ghastly façade of Deathpic and Spaceclack, pulpy enemies of the earth and mankind. Read *Alc*, the weekly booze-magazine, etc.

—Would like to express cultural debt of England to America. It is enormous, even bigger than our national one, if possible. But what use have we made of it? Public school boys fishing vicariously for Hemingway's trout. Or Deathpic and Spaceclack talk. The English are now so loathed in Canada we are rapidly becoming a tragic minority. Starve to death in Stanley Park rather than ask for help. It happens every day. Canada, whose heart is England but whose soul is Labrador. Of course I am a Scotsman. As a matter of fact I am Norwegian.

Frère Jacques
Frère Jacques

—Played by Louis Armstrong and his orchestra. Art Tatum on piano. Joe Venuti violin. *Battement de Tambours.*

And I think of O'Neill. *Iceman* is wonderful play. Wonder if similarity to the theme of *The Wild Duck* was conscious, in which drink is justified as "life illusion." I wish O'Neill had written more plays about the sea. The Norwegian barque? My grandfather, captain of the windjammer *The Scottish Isles*, went down with his ship in the Indian Ocean. He was bringing my mother a cockatoo. Remember the story told about him by Old Hands in Liverpool. The owners loaded his ship badly: he complained: was forced to take it out. So he sailed it right bang down to the Cape, and right bang back again to Liverpool and made them load it correctly.

—"The man who went to sea because he read *The Hairy Ape* and *The Moon of the Caribbees*." (That was me twenty years ago. Accounts partly for my depression on board, *Diderot* is totally different freighter to any in my experience though. Liberty ship—but really beautiful in my opinion, if of romantic slowness. Food is superb; and great gulps of pinard at every meal. A wonderful trip, really.)

—A long black albatross, like a flying machete—strictly 2 machetes... Albatross like a distant lone left wing three quarter at rugby, practicing...

An iron bird, with saber wings. Actually *is* black albatross, though captain says no.

But the captain, for once, is wrong. It is not a shearwater, though there is a sooty shearwater behind, Primrose says. Melville's hatred of shearwaters: birds of bad omen. Nonsense. Hope we do not sail on the 15th of November from Los Angeles.

We have crossed the border and are off the state of Washington.

ALBATROSS SLAIN, BRINGS GRIEF, PAIN
(Excerpt from a fragment of newspaper,
left by steward in cabin):
Shaft Snapped, Leg Broken, Net Fouled
When Sea Tradition Defied.

Port Angeles, Wash. (A.P.)—A University of Washington faculty member who defied the tradition of the sea knows better now. His sad story came to light when the U.S. Fish and Wildlife Service's exploratory vessel put in here. The university research assistant, John Firmin, started it when he sighted a white albatross flying near the vessel, engaged in exploratory deep sea trawling off Cape Flattery. Firmin asked permission to shoot it and bring it to the university museum as the first known specimen of a white albatross seen in Washington coast waters.

Crew Horrified.

The seven crew men immediately shouted "No!" reminding Firmin of the fate of Coleridge's "Ancient Mariner" and the old tradition of bad luck which follows shooting an albatross. But because of the specimen's rarity—etc.

See, conversely, newspaper clipping I've been saving:

ALBATROSS SAVES SAILOR

Sydney, Friday. An English seaman who fell overboard from a liner owes his life to an albatross. It landed on his chest and guided a life-boat to him.

Seaman John Oakley, 53, of Southampton, fell from the stern of the 20,204 ton *Southern Cross* 10 miles off the New South Wales coast yesterday.

A little boy, a passenger, saw him fall and told the deck officer. The ship turned about and a lifeboat was lowered.

Oakley was obscured by waves until the albatross landed on his chest and served as a beacon to the rescuers.—*Reuters.*

—The albatross is one of the largest flying birds in the world with a wing span of 10 ft–12 ft and weighs about 17 lb.

Now there are three shearwaters.
Golden sunset in a blue sky.
Several large green meteors from Gemini.

Nov. 9. Primrose and Sigbjørn Wilderness are happy in their cramped Chief Gunner's cabin.
Martin Trumbaugh however is not very happy.
Trumbaugh: named after Trumbauer—Frankie. Beiderbecke, et al.
A dead storm petrel on the bows, with blue feet like a bat.
Off the coast of Oregon.
Thousands of white gulls. The crew are feeding them. Will our gulls starve without us? Incredible jewel-like clearness of some days in November in the shack, a bell ringing in the mist. Mill-wheel reflections of sun on water, sliding down the shack. Such radiance for November! And turn the pine boughs into green chenille.

Nov. 11. The dramatic diatonic booming of fog horns, bells, whistles, on Golden Gate Bridge, in the fog, warping early in the morning into cold San Francisco. Past Alcatraz. Bird watcher who lives there.
Fog lifts; to the left, Oakland is dark, cloudy, bridge disappears into low gray clouds. To the right San Francisco, the sky is tender blue, the bridge arching away, incredible, with its cables and towers.

Skipper wearing fur-lined jacket, collar turned up, blue cap, formidable, with beaky profile against the sky. He is angry with longshoremen and shouting curses and orders in French and English. Pilot amused, bored, respectful. Various mates stand around tensely.

Brilliant comment of a person to whom I once lent *Ulysses* on returning it the next day. "Thanks awfully. Very good." (Lawrence also said: "The whole is a strange assembly of apparently incongruous parts, slipping past one another.")

Leaving at night the jeweled city. Baguette diamonds on black velvet, says Primrose: ruby and emerald harbor lights. Topaz and gold lights on two bridges.

Primrose is very happy. We embrace in the dark, on deck.

Nov. 14. Los Angeles. A notice in a shed: *Watch the Hook It Can't Watch You.*

Warm blue satin sea and mild sun.

Nov. 15. Sure enough, off we go. Of course.

We have another passenger: his name? Charon. Naturally.

—Outward bound, from Los Angeles to Rotterdam, S.S. *Diderot* sailed November 15, in the evening.

(Mem. *Outward Bound*, seen at the Theatre Royal in Exeter with my mother and father in 1923. Eight bells ring up each curtain. Wonderful performance by Gladys Ffolliot.)

S.S. *Tidewater*, a black glistening oil tanker, very close, empty: red rails: *Marie Celeste?*

Description of sunset: sailing into boiling Quink. Magenta scarves to starboard, from the galley, a smell of loaves, to the right, vermilion spare ribs, aft, a sort of violet porridge.

FRÈRE *Jacques*
FRÈRE *Jacques*

Gulls blowing, silhouettes. And more shearwaters.

Sailing close into a black mountainous coast of clouds, with stars over them.

And Mr. Charon, he's there too.

Nov. 16. We have crossed the border in the night.

—At sunset, leaden clouds, black sky, with a long line of burning vermilion like a forest fire 3,000 miles long, far away between black sea and sky.

Strange islands, barren as icebergs, and nearly as white.

Rocks!—The Lower California coast, giant pinnacles, images of barrenness and desolation, on which the heart is thrown and impaled eternally...

Frère Jacques, Frère Jacques Laruelle.

Baja California. In fact, Mexico to port. Thousands and thousands of miles of it.

—But nothing equaled now the inconceivable loneliness and desolate beauty of the interminable Mexican coast (down which the freighter now slowly made its way), with the furnace of the ship saying *Frère* Jacques: *Frère* Jacques: *dor*mez-vous: *dor*mez-vous, and a single lone digarilla floating, turning, against the purple frightful coast, and the sunset of misery—

> dormez-vous
> dormez-vous
> sonnez *lament*ina
> sonnez *lament*ina
> dong dong dong
> doom doom doom

The digarilla is the bosun bird, or frigate bird, or man-o'-war bird, with a tail like a swallow; it is a bird of ill omen in *Dark as the Grave Wherein My Friend Is Laid*. It was a bird of ill omen to Primrose and me in Acapulco three years ago. Yet one week after that *The Valley of the Shadow of Death* was accepted. The book will be divided into three parts, three novels. *Dark as the Grave Wherein My Friend Is Laid*, *Eridanus*, *La Mordida*. *Eridanus* is a sort of typical intermezzo and is about a shack in Canada. *Dark as the Grave* is about the death of Fernando, who is Dr. Vigil in *The Valley of the Shadow*. *Real* death that is, we discovered. *La Mordida*, The Bite, is set in Acapulco. *The Valley of the Shadow* worked like an infernal machine. Dr. Vigil is dead like the Consul—in reality that is. No wonder my letters were returned.

Someone has written an opera about another Consul. It hurts my feelings. This sort of thing is the theme of the book too.

Nov. 17. Mr. Charon looking at Mexico.

Daemon on the job: 24 hours a day.

All noises of the engine set themselves to the tune of "Frère Jacques" (Martin thought), sometimes the words were "Cuernavaca, Cuernavaca" instead of "Frère Jacques"; the engine had another trick too, of singing

> Please go *on*!
> Why not *die*!
> Sonnez les matines...

and what's more taken up by the ventilators, it would sing in harmony; I swear it, I heard aerial infernal choirs chanting in harmony, sometimes rising to a frightful pitch... And then it would begin again, saying something quite ridiculous, instead of ding dang dong:

Sans maison
Sans maison

and when it got literally into that groove it would never stop.

—The inability to breathe almost, as the heat grows worse—your mouth too becomes a sort of perpetual pulped vise, your face swollen so that you can scarcely open it save to mutter something inane, and always unfinished, like "I thought it would be—or—ah, please dear it—"

Battement de Tambours

Dark as the Grave Wherein My Friend Is Laid. Fernando is buried in Villahermosa. Murdered. He ah drink too much mescal. Mehican whiky. Alfred Gordon Pym.

Title too long: why not just "My Friend Is Laid" (Primrose suggested).

The distant inane motorcycle of the electric fan, whose breeze does not reach you, sitting below, watching the sweat pricking your hands, and seep out of your chest.

The crew are chipping rust: hammers on the brain.

White leathery pelicans in the afternoon.

Peaks like machetes, pointing down. Inverted swordfish. Barren mountains, sharp-finned, or peaked like cones. (Yeats's *Vision?*)

Waking in the night with eyes aching and twitching vision to wonder (for Martin Trumbaugh, for the Consul, likewise named Firmin, to wonder) where did I put my shoe, did I have a shoe? I did, and the lost one seemed in the right place, but then where are the cigarettes, and where am I? etc. Surely standing now in the corridor of a train vacantly; but then again the engine with its *Frère* Jacques, *Frère* Jacques, *dor*mez-vous, *dor*mez-vous: of course, you bloody well can't dormez.

I fear that was the consequence of a case of none too good

American whisky bought in Los Angeles because I liked its name. Green River. Even so, there is not half enough for this voyage. But perhaps the captain would ask Sigbjørn Wilderness and his wife on to the bridge for an apéritif.

Nov. 18.—the long long dead cruel sorrowful uninhabited coast of Mexico.

Frère Jacques.

Wake at 3 a.m., stumble around dark cabin. Where am I?

5 a.m. Primrose goes out to watch dawn. Indigo sea, black tortured shapes of mountains and sharp-pointed islands, a beautiful nightmare against a gold sky. For two hours we pace and weave, in and out, out and in, from cabin to deck. Try to sleep and cannot. Too close to Mexico?

Day becomes stinking hot and still. Coast faded out of sight. We are crossing the mouth of the Gulf of California. The crew are painting ventilators, wearing wooden shoes.

The skipper says they are "beautying up the ship."

In his loneliness and fixedness the ancient Mariner yearneth towards the journeying Moon, and the stars that still sojourn, yet still move onward; and everywhere the blue sky belongs to them, and is their appointed rest and their native country and their own natural homes, which they enter unannounced, as lords that are certainly expected, and yet there is a silent joy at their arrival.

—at sunset, the Tres Marias Islands, two ships, three frigate birds, jet against amber sky, clouds like boiling cauliflower by Michelangelo: and later, the stars: but now Martin saw the fixity of the closed order of their system: death in short. The thought comes from Keyserling. (They are only *not dead* when I look at them with Primrose.) Wonderful truth in Lawrence about this. Somehow my life draws (he writes) strength from the depths of the universe, from the depths among the stars, from the great world! Think Primrose feels something like this. And how true was that of them in Eridanus! But he can only get the feeling vicariously on board this ship, as it takes him away inexorably from the only place on earth he has loved, and perhaps forever.

Our Mr. Charon, Mr. Pierre Charon, is a Frenchman, but acting Norwegian Consul in Papeete, Tahiti. An excellent fellow. He will take boat from Cristobal. Bon vivant. Wears shorts and high white stockings and calls Henry Miller an atom bomb. Also was in foreign legion and goose-steps on the foredeck every now and then. Also he says: Vous n'avez pas de nation. La France est votre mère. Soldat de la Légion Étrangère. Now who in the world said that before? Why no one but a character in *The Valley of the Shadow of Death*. And you know what happened to the Consul at that point, don't you, observed Sigbjørn Wilderness, helping himself to his fourth sarsaparilla.

Man not enmeshed by, but *killed* by his own book and the malign forces it arouses. Wonderful theme. Buy planchette to provide for necessary dictation.

—Death takes a holiday. On a Liberty ship.

—Or does he? All day I can hear him "cackling like a pirate." Robert Penn Warren's phrase. Charon is really a good fellow too, offers us cognac, says I look like Don José in my bandanna handkerchief tied round my head. But the Captain does not invite him on the bridge for an apéritif however *like he did us*. Case of two masters looking at each other face to face. And by the way, who is Don José? The chap who murders Carmen?

Everyone talks so fast I can't hear a word: admirable crew.

The book should not be 3 books but 6 books, to be called *The Voyage That Never Ends*, with the *Valley* in the middle. The *Valley* acts like a diabolic battery in the middle. Resolution should be triumphant, however. That is to say it is certainly in my power to make it so.

Nov. 19—or 21? The French Government falls: our little

princess is married. Gallantly, the French crew drink the health
of Princess Elizabeth. The radio reporter, Carpentier, reads long
radio report at dinner for our benefit: his English is peculiar:

"And at that moment Lord Mousebatten..."

"At *Book*ing'am Palace..."

They don't intend any offense.

These Bretons are wonderful sailors; chivalrous and kind-
hearted people to a man.

Englishmen who pride themselves on speaking French,
snazzily being great judges of wines, referring to "my friend, the
best cook in Normandy, of course," with the object of discred-
iting American salads. Did you ever meet a Frenchman who
prettied up his English or was a good judge of a tankard of bitter and a steak and kidney pudding?

—But I dream of death, a horrible dream, Grand Guignol,
without merit: but so vivid, so palpable, it seemed to contain
some actual and frightful tactile threat,
or prophesy, or warning: first there is
dissociation, I am not I. I am Martin
Trumbaugh. But I am not Martin Trumbaugh or perhaps
Firmin either, I am a voice, yet with physical feelings, I enter
what can only be described—I won't describe it, with teeth,
that snap tight behind me: at the same
time, in an inexplicable way, this is like
going through the Panama Canal, and
what closes behind me is, as it were, a
lock: in a sense I am now a ship, but I
am also a voice and also Martin Trumbaugh, and now I am, or he is, in the
realm of death: this realm is, rather
unimaginatively, entirely full of noseless
white whores and ronyons with pulpy

But the curse liveth for
him in the eye of the
dead men.

The Polar Spirit's
fellow-demons, the
invisible inhabitants of
the element, take part
in his wrong; and two
of them relate, one to
the other, that penance
long and heavy for the
ancient Mariner hath
been accorded to the
Polar Spirit, who
returneth southward.

faces, in fact their faces come to pieces when they touch them, like newspapers picked out of the sea; Death himself is a hideous looking red-faced keeper of a prison, with half his face shot away, and one shattered leg whose shreds are still left "untied" (because he apologized for this); he is the keeper of the prison, and leads him or me or it through the gates, beyond which is St. Catherine's College, Cambridge, *and the very room* (I'm not sure what he means) but Death, although hideous, has a kindly voice, and even sweet in his gruesome fashion: he says it is a pity I have seen "all the show" whereupon I remember the vaudeville show when I entered, that is to say I remember moving chairs (in the sense of moving staircases) on which one sat as at a cafeteria, and some of the ghouls were sitting on these chairs and some seemed to be performing in some way: he said this meant I was doomed, and gave me 40 days to live, which on the whole I considered very generous of him. How can the soul take this kind of battering and survive? It's a bit like the toy boat. It is hard to believe that a disgusting and wicked dream of this nature has only been produced by the soul itself, in its passionate supplication to its unscrupulous owner to be cleansed. But it has.

Must be something I ate despite eulogy to French cooking.

Martin woke up weeping, however, never before having realized that he had such a passion for the wind and the sunrise. The Mariner awakes, and his penance begins anew.

Sir, hombre, that is tequila.

(This now seems ridiculous to me, having risen early and washed a shirt.)

—I am the chief steward of my fate, I am the fireman of my soul.

Nothing can exceed the boundless He despiseth the creatures of the calm misery and desolation and wretchedness of a voyage like this. (Even though everyone is so decent and it is the nicest crew one could have encountered, the best food, etc. And the Trumbaughs were of course having a hell of a good time, etc., etc.)

A shearwater, reconnoitering doubtless.

Leviathan, by Julian Green. The short story.

Acapulco on the beam, and I recognize it immediately— before the skipper indeed. There is Larqueta, with the lighthouse going past so slowly, and it even seems we can make out the Quinta Eulalia.

Since passing Manzanillo Acapulco is the first sign of any life we have seen down the entire Mexican coast. Almost from the ship, I can hear them shouting, attracting people to the camiones: Culete! Culete!

—This, Acapulco, is the place that is the main scene of my novel that I have been writing about these past months: and this is where Martin Trumbaugh meets his nemesis. This is also where Primrose and Martin, in 1946, saw the digarilla. One week before the acceptance of *The Valley of the Shadow of Death*. Which is when "it" all began to happen. Story of a man (Man himself no less) Joyced in his own petard. A sense of exile oppresses me. A sense of something else, beyond injustice and misery, extramundane, oppresses, more than desolates, more than confounds me. To pass this place like this. Would I, one day, pass England, home, like this, on this voyage perhaps by some quirk of fortune not to be able to set foot on it, what is worse, not want to set foot on it? Acapulco is also the first place where Martin ever set foot in Mexico. November 1936. Yes, and on the Day of the Dead. I remember, going ashore, in a boat, the madman foaming at the mouth, correcting his watch; the mile-high bodiless vultures in the thunder. And all this somber horror is lying calmly to port, slowly going astern, innocent as Southend-on-Sea. That is also when the Consul began. Scene of first mescal is now abaft the beam. Intervening years spent writing it—happiest of his life so far, with Primrose in shack—and other things, mostly burned. I know what the feeling must resemble; exactly that of a ghost who revisits some place on earth to which it is irresistibly drawn. He longs to make himself seen but, poor hovering gas bag, cannot even land. (And last, at sundown, the skipper said innocently: "Look at the little Mexican boat going down the coast with all its lights on. A coastwise human soul. Isn't it pretty?") His feelings are equally compounded of a desire for revenge and an illimitable desire that can never be fulfilled. Feeling is also like excommunication. Infringement of spiritual rights of man. Where else may he pray to the Virgin of Guadeloupe? The Saint of Desperate and Dangerous Causes? Here. Filthy, mean little place. Acapulco is that. Certainly not worth throwing a tragedy at. But Martin Trumbaugh was passing the theater of his whole life's struggle, his whole future life's struggle, if any, in this endless passage down the Mexican coast. Christ how those ferociously ignorant and mean and wicked little men made the Trumbaughs suffer, though, here—would like to get them, every one. The Minister of the Interior of Death especially. Country of the Absolute Devil. Protest to the United Nations. How many Americans, Canadians, murdered there every year. Hushed up, without investigation, to save face— whose? Some Mexicans just as good as others are evil. Don José—Ah, Don José, so that was the meaning of Mr. Charon's remark?—for example, at the Quinta Eulalia. Think of the risk he took for us. His charity. Mexicans are the most beautiful people on earth, most lovely country. Mexican government seems still controlled by Satan, that's the only trouble. All Mexicans know it, fear it, do nothing about it, finally, despite revolutions; at bottom it is more corrupt than in the days of Diaz. Mem: *Juarez in exile landing secretly in Acapulco ...*

Culete! Culete! in memory. The little buses, and the shaking man and the blaze of beach at Pied de la Cuesta and the sharks and the manta ray as big as a drawing room. And the tiny brilliant tropical fishes at Culete...And Primrose's broken holiday, her first holiday in ten years. I'll get them for that, if it is the last thing I do, on paper anyhow.

Another digarilla. The bosun bird. Rapacious giant swallow of the Zapotecan Sea.

The mournful song of the crawling ship, that rose and fell; And envieth that they should live, and so many lie dead. the heartbreaking endless purple barren coast against which the great lone frigate bird, with bat's wings and a swallow tail, ceaselessly falls, silently turns, and turns, and soars again.

Nov. 20—or 21.

FRÈRE Jacques
FRÈRE Jacques
DORMEZ-vous?
DORMEZ-vous?
SONNEZ les matines!
SONNEZ les matines!
Doom doom doom!
Doom doom doom!

If these things should be survived, Martin decided, he must never forget, and write down, to the accompaniment of Frère Jacques, etc.: for they represented to his mind the bottom of all sorrow and abjectness.

God help me

Frère Jacques Frère Jacques dormez-vous?

Was it, Sigbjørn thought, that he did not wish to survive?

At the moment, it seems, I have no ambition...

Sigbjørn Wilderness (pity my name is such a good one because I can't use it) could only pray for a miracle, that miraculously some love of life would come back.

It has: apparently this retracing of a course was part of the main ordeal; and even at this moment Martin knew it to be no dream, but some strange symbolism of the future.

—The French Government falls again.

In spite of having spent the night wrestling with the torments of the d.t.'s Martin Trumbaugh put in a remarkably good appearance at breakfast, looking bronzed and hearty.

"You are in good form."

"Bon appétit."

"Il fait beau temps"... and so on.

(This gentleman with the d.t.'s is not myself. Everything written about drink is incidentally absurd. Have to do it all over again, what about conflict, appalling sadness that can lead equally to participation in the tragic human condition, self-knowledge, discipline. Conflict is all-important. Gin and orange juice best cure for alcoholism, real cause of which is ugliness and complete baffling sterility of existence as *sold* to you. Otherwise it would be greed. And, by God, it *is* greed. A good remark: Guess I'll turn in and catch a little delirium.)

A white dove comes on board.

And a jaeger flies by.

And the French Government falls once more.

The little church bells that chime the hours; for the curious thing about the ship's bells on the *Diderot*—they are slow, melancholy, like the infinitely sad bell-chimes from the cathedral in Oaxaca—Oaxaca, now to port, home of Fernando the Oaxaqueñian, and Dr. Vigil, dead, murdered in Villahermosa.

"For she is the virgin for those who have nobody them with."

"Nobody goes there, only those who have nobody with."
"For she is the virgin for those who have *nobody* them with."
Dark as the Grave Wherein My Friend Is Laid. Where is his
girl now, to whom he used to write his notes on old monastic
walls? We should have looked her up.

Song for a Marimba,
or
In the Wooden Brothel the Band Plays out of Tune

Oa-xa-ca! Oa-xa-ca!
Oa-xa-ca! Oa-xa-ca!
It is a name like
A bro-ken
A broken heart at night.
Wooden wooden wooden are those faces at night.
Wooden wooden wooden are those faces at night.
Broken hearts are wooden at night.
Wooden, are wooden, at night.

Limerick

There was a young man from Oaxaca
Who dreamed that he went to Mintaka
And dwelt in Orion
And not in the Lion
The pub where he drank, which was darker.

A Prayer

God give those drunkards drink who wake at dawn
Gibb ring on Beelzebub's bosom, all outworn
As once more through the windows they espy
Looming, the frightful Pontefract of day.

—From this you might get the impression that Martin was a

gloomy and morbid fellow. Quite the contrary. One of Martin's happiest private memories: a bit of conversation accidentally overheard about himself—"The very sight of that old bastard makes me happy for five days. No bloody fooling."

It is my impression, from maritime law, that the ship can now go anywhere the Captain—or rather Commandant—pleases. He could play Ahab and get away with it. For France has no government. The crew, happy thought, might even mutiny if they wish, and it would be difficult for anyone—say in Oaxaca—to do anything about it. But the crew don't wish to mutiny for the simple reasons (a) this is a happy ship, (b) they want to be home for Christmas. And as for the Commandant, who unlike most captains has the respect and liking of everyone, it is a matter of sublime indifference how many governments fall. She is indeed, as the chief steward (a fellow rugby enthusiast) says, a ship bien chargé. Would that the world were such. All shades of political opinion on board this ship, but I have yet to hear an unkind word. Now if we had a world governed by Bretons!

Turkish bath of the toilet, and *forgetting* where the flush handle is...

Terror, too, in the toilet, scarcely daring to stir, will the Captain object? Martin Trumbaugh wondered. Between two stools. And between two stools the breech falls to the floor.

For Captain read Commandant: the Capitaine is the first mate of a French vessel. The second mate, the first lieutenant, etc. This has a naval, rather than mercantile flavor. The Commandant uses ancient regal privilege of dining alone. Wonder if my grandfather did that. From this you'd think the ship was undemocratic, nothing could be further from the truth, though. Everyone is equally courteous—first requisite of any democracy. Primrose's presence may have something to do with obvious manifestations of this, but the thing seems innate with the

French. Nor do there seem any of the heartbreaking persecu-
tions, petty snobberies, that used to pertain in an English
freighter. As an old hand I can smell these things. I remember
the eternal argument between the bosun and the carpenter as to
who was the senior; in fact, the carpenter, though he is technically a tradesman. Also the poor fellow on his first voyage, so
persecuted by the crew, he stood on the windward side in a
storm praying to be washed overboard. To say nothing of the
apprentice they kept in the chicken coop. By the time we got to
Dairen (then Dalny and now part of Russia) half the crowd had
the pox. There hasn't been a single case of V.D. on board this
ship since it set off four months ago, says the 3rd mate, who
acts as doctor and who should know. Something worth remembering since the British have the idea the French invented it.
Still, grandmother invented penicillin. Wisdom and sanity of
having wine with meals for all hands. And same food for everybody. And wonderful it is, ten times better than on dear old
American bauxite ship we went to Haiti on, though stores on
return voyages, be it remembered, all come from America. On
English ship, though food used to be better than its reputation,
they went to endless trouble to see that we, as the crew, had
especially "worse" food than the officers. I didn't eat a hot meal
for two months on the outward voyage to China—1927. Things
are probably better now. Only advantage I can think of we had,
being a coal burner, with the aid of a tarpaulin, we rigged up a
bunker hatch as a swimming pool. There seems no way they
can do that here, and it is a pity for the crew. Stokers and trim-
mers—I have been latter—no longer suffer, to be sure: there are
none: but engineers and greasers—the machinists—do, as ever,
as a consequence of which—superb and sane compensation!—
they are allowed twice as much wine with meals. (One of the
consequences of which, we sit at the engineers' table, not without having been expressly and courteously invited, of course.)

—Who am I?—

—A great black bird sitting crucified on the cross-trees, its wings so vast it obscures the foremast light; the Captain calls us to see it, says: "I will not shoot the eagle, or anything, I never kill anything, but—" "Shoot it! I should damned well think not!" says Primrose. It is a condor (Gymnogyps Californianus) with a 10½-foot wingspread, and the sight one of the rarest in the world, for the bird, a sort of super-xopilote or vulture by Thomas Wolfe, is almost extinct; after a while it has vanished, as mysteriously as it arrived.

The Captain (the Commandant) likes cats, is a first-rate chess player, but likes to madden himself with some kind of contraption like a yo yo, drinks rum before dinner, sleeps in a hammock on bridge because his room is too hot, refuses to discuss politics, yet is in great tradition of captain who not only loves but *is* his ship; at the same time cannot escape pathetic subterfuges of men longing for their homes and wives. Gets a ton of sand for his cats, Grisette and Piyu, each voyage. Admirable fellow, has been in sail, like my grandfather. Humorous, kindly, charitable, absolutely the best kind of person.

Nov. 22. The Gulf of Tehuantepec: sapphire calm, long, almost imperceptible swells, the surface like crepe (Primrose says). Flying fish of electric blue with dragon-fly wings, skitting and flying everywhere. Their sudden swift tracery on the water, Prospero skimming winged souls, much as a boy skims stones; and indeed their brief heavenly passage through the air is like our moments of happiness on earth; old turtle breast-stroking past solemnly, turns a quizzical eye on us. Astral body of Wallace Stevens writing his wonderful poem about Tehuantepec...A flying fish skidding over the sapphire sea toward an albatross floating to meet it: ecstasy. Primrose in seventh

heaven . . . The Zapotecan Sea . . . Just under the bow a shark—
a dark, shining shape with wicked fins, turning beautifully,
swimming swiftly, then he dives, is green, blue—gone.

My faithful general Phenobarbus, treacherous to the last?
(Note for Martin.)

Nov. 23. Going down the coast of Guatemala, we crossed
the border from Mexico in late afternoon. Coast is tame here, the
mountains rounded, green and pretty, now and then a river flows.
I wish I could see it with volcanoes spitting fire into the night.

The skipper tells us a good story about his last voyage here:
sweltering in the heat below; the volcanoes above cooling their
heads with snow. The skipper, with magnificent hospitality,
invites us almost every other day to have an apéritif with him,
so that we have begun to look forward to this enjoyable inter-
lude, nearly to look on it as a right.

The skipper tells another story: he found a beautiful Medi-
terranean island where he took his wife for a holiday; everything
was perfect, a fine cheap hotel, good food, beach, swimming,
and no one else there at all! What luck! But when they went to
bed that night, they found out why: the rats. Thousands of rats,
swarming through the windows and doors all night.

Primrose tells me: "I was sitting in the sun on deck when the
skipper invited me to the lower bridge for a drink. (You were
asleep in the upper berth like the lion in the basket.) He is a
friendly man, lonely and gay, stern, eager and boyish. I have
mentioned the French crisis and he laughs and says:

" 'I never hear the news. If they make another trouble I will
run to Mexico.'

"We discuss cats. I say Piyu speaks French and he is delighted. The cats go to their box and we have a long conversation re cats' cleanliness: he points to Piyu and Grisette digging
holes, doing, and covering them up; he is like a proud parent

watching his child playing a piece on the piano, noting everything and calling for my attention and applause."

However:

*Over the freedom of all people hangs the shadow of the
Immigration Inspector*, with his little card (not always the little
card) sent you in advance (and his 5 children, his anxiety about
his wife, his inadequate income, his fear of being fired, his
allergy, and analogy, to the sprue, and his unfinished novel),
asking you questions you never can answer viz.:

Information required from Passengers in Transit through or
destined to the Canal Zone of the Republic of Panama. Infor-
macion requerida de los *Pasajeros en transito o con destino* a la
Zone del Canal or la Republica de Panama...

(1) Name

Nombre	Family (Apellido)	Given (Primero)
Sex		Race
Sexo		Raza

(2) Birth date — Place of birth

Fecha de	Lugar del nacimiento
nacimiento	
Citizen of	
Ciudadano da	

(3) Occupation — Embarkation port

Ocupacion	Puerto de Embarque

(4) Passport no. — Issued at — Visas for

Pasaporte no.	Expedido en	Visado para

(5) Arrival port — Name of vessel

Puerto de llegada	Nombre del barco
Arrival date	
Fecha de llegada	

(6) Destination — Ticket — Date of departure

Destino	Boleto	Fecha de salida

(7) Address on Isthmus   Purpose of visit
    Direccion en el Istmo   Objeto de la visita
(8) Date of last smallpox vaccination
    Fecha de la ultima vacuna contra la vizuela

(And now come the insults, to be completed by the Quarantine
and Immigration Officer.)

Reasons _____
Medical and Immunization _____
Disposition of passport _____
Remarks _____
                                  (Initials) _____
                    History after Arrival
Departed for _____
Vessel _____   Date _____   (Initials) _____

   In this subtle way, the true freedom of every traveler is lost
forever in his own world.
   A sapphire sea. Would that one were a flying fish!
   A turtle, swimming sleepily, is smacked by the boat but—he
dives...Hope he is not hurt.
   Whales spouting astern, just before sunset.
   Strange to be sitting in the very seat of one's agony the day
after, restored and in one's right mind, the miracle happened.

      Miraculous such nights as these
      Should be survived, how no one knows,
      Far less, how one reached finer air
      That never breathed on such despair.

   I know you think Tennyson wrote that, but I did.

Nov. 24. Going down the coast of El Salvador—the latter out of sight however—usual angry-looking slate elephants and jagged coasts of sunset, and the changing light on the sea, every bit like in the newest supercinema at home; fine old dirty freighter on horizon keeping up with us; at evening, suddenly, Venus...

The agony of Martin Trumbaugh is related to the agony of repeating experiences.

And ever and anon throughout his future life an agony constraineth him to travel from land to land.

Unripe bananas and porterhouse steak colored sunsets of Nicaragua.

Charon, lonely, peers with binoculars into the west. H'm...

Ahead are four storms. Thunderheads, snow white on top, becoming more dark and deep as one's eyes travel down until at a distance above the horizon the cloud bank is black, cut off sharply in a straight horizontal line, with the black sea below. Between are vertical lines, like pencil lines, of rain. The wind is blowing from that quarter and freshening.

Did I mention the new patented black oiled windlass, like a gigantic set of false teeth squatting on the foredeck?

A little albatross sitting on the mast, preening his feathers.

An elephant sitting on the horizon.

Venus swimming in a mauve cloud.

Engine that sings the "Marseillaise."

Venus, with a circle around it, like the moon...

Engine that sings "The Kerry Dancers."

Primrose...Primrose...

Nov. 25. Going down the coast of Costa Rica. Rain all day.

A plague on all Central American republics with their corruption, their cuteness, their dictators, their mordidas, their tourists, their fatuous revolutions, their volcanoes, their history and their heat!

The abomination of desolation, standing in the holy place.

Alarme

Le signal d'alarme consiste en 5 coups longs donnés par sonnerie et sifflet.

A ce signal:

—allez dans votre cabine

—couvrez-vous chaudement

—mettez votre gilet de sauvetage

—laissez-vous guider par le personnel et rendez-vous au Pont des Embarcations.

Côté à l'Abri du vent

Abandon

Le signal d'abandon est donné par 6 coups brefs suivis d'un coup long.

A ce signal vous embarquerez dans le canot No. 1. Tribord
                                                    ou 2. Babord

Selon la direction du vent.

Cie. Générale Transatlantique

Avis.   S. S. *Diderot*

(Sinister notice in saloon)

Chacun est prié d'économiser l'eau attendu que nous ne pourrons pas nous en approvisionner avant Rotterdam.

Au cas où le gaspillage serait trop grand, nous serions obligés de rationner l'eau.

Bord le 22 November 1947
le/*2ème* Capitaine
(Samuel Taylor Coleridge)

Safety

Your lifebelt is in this stateroom.

Put it on as you would an ordinary jacket
Your arms through the shoulder straps
Never wear the lifebelt without the shoulder straps
Pull the two ends of the belt together across
Your chest and tie the tapes very securely
                                    (Wilderness Carlos Wilderness)

(Mem:)—Passing San Francisco, below Mount Diablo, going down past Monterrey and Cape Saint Martin, passing San Pedro, forgetting Point Firmin (sic) down, down, at 404 fathoms at Carlsbad on November 16 at 1,045 fathoms off Cape Colnet, at midday on the 17th at 965 fathoms, still going down Lower California, on the 18th at midday, having gone past Cape St. Lazaro (?) opposite La Paz but still in the opposite peninsular Cape Falso (Cape Falso is good)—*False Cape Horn* good name for a novel—but disheartening—there *are* no False Cape Horns?—and Cape S. Lucas, going down to 1,800 fathoms opposite the Tres Marias, on the 19th, at midday on the 20th at 2,712 fathoms, below Manzanillo, by Black Head, on the 21st, just passing Acapulco, by Porta Malconda 2,921 fathoms—Acapulco!—and going out into the Gulf of Tehuantepec on the 22nd at midday 1,883 fathoms, on the 23rd—after the Gulf of Tehuantepec—opposite San José, at 2,166 fathoms, on the 24th near the Guardian Bank, having passed El Salvador, at 1,850 fathoms.

   After Acapulco: B. Dulce, Pta. Malconado, Morro Ayuca (?), Salina Cruz, Tehuantepec, La Puerta, Sacapulco—getting into Guatemala—S. Benito, Champerico, San José, and in El Salvador, Acajutla, La Libertad, La Union indeed—passing altogether the Golfo de Fonseca—Corinto, getting toward Costa Rica...

Death in Life...

Their beauty and their happiness.

He blesseth them in his heart.

—the albatross, at midnight, huddled upon the foremast, her great beak, from the captain's bridge, gold in the moving light: when her beak was there it made a third light. Finally her beak moved away and you could only see, from the port side, her tail feathers. This was the mother albatross. She stayed there all night, while on the mainmast, aft, there were 3 other young albatross, huddled together, black... The mother albatross had brought her little brood on board to rest.

Nov. 26. In the morning one of these was captured for Primrose by the crew. The baby albatross sitting on the after deck, with its red feet and blue enamel beak and soft fawn-colored feathers, hissing at us. Then, to my joy, they released it...

Frère Jacques. Frère Jacques. Dormez-vous? Dormez-vous?

The coast of Panama is like Wales. Old Charon would not come to see the albatross. After the capture of the albatross, there is further excitement, a ship on the horizon, that seems to be on fire; it is a Russian tramp, a coal burner?

Life in Death

But Life-in-Death begins her work on the ancient Mariner.

The burning ship turns out to be just some old haystack of a tramp, that passes very slow, billowing smoke from her funnel, like some sea-going Manchester, or the funereal pyre of the ship in Conrad's *Youth*, nothing wrong with her at all; I am vaguely disappointed, having visualized some rescue at sea, in which one took a heroic part.

Bad news: due to the unexpected arrival of more passengers in Cristobal, perhaps Primrose and I are to be separated, into different cabins...

Death in life.

Facts and Figures on the Canal
Atlantic to Pacific length—40 miles.
Minimum channel depth—45 feet.
Maximum elevation above sea level—85 feet.
Average time of ship transit—8 hours.
Railroad time across Zone—1 hour 25 minutes.
Canal opened to traffic—August 1914.
Total cost—$543,000,000.

(Fear of anyone seeing me write these valuable war secrets down. Giving aid and comfort to the enemy. Which enemy?)

Idea for part of a novel: Make the Trumbaughs somehow have this happen to them, in manner of the sad experience of two other people on the last trip, as recounted by skipper. Devoted married couple who fear they are going to be separated, at Balboa, into different cabins. Decide to write some of this, to take mind off possibility of its happening to us. Can't even think of being separated from Primrose.

Sailing into Balboa under a full moon against a strong ebb tide, cloud like picked mackerel bones and loomy Hercules—the disastrous alien sunsets for the alienated, of travel.

We are now approaching the Panama Canal

Francisco Pizarro, a native of Portugal who began life as a swineherd...

(Martin was so distressed at the idea of their separation that for a while, as is sometimes the case in the face of actual disaster, he lost all sense of proportion, and for a moment indeed it was as if he forgot which was the more important, the threatened catastrophe of the separation itself, or the fact that having been

I beg your pardon.

William Paterson, founder of the great Bank of England, who was on the contrary a native of Scotland, who began life by walking backwards through England, with a pedlar's pack on his back, having been impressed by the memories of a British surgeon, Lionel Wafer, who had crossed the Isthmus on the way to Peru with one William Dampier, an author and freebooter, and who had subsequently remained—like, later, William Blackstone—for some years living among the Indians, who had nursed him back to health from almost certain death, conceived, that is to say, William Paterson conceived the ennobling idea—no doubt feeling that in a vicarious sense this would be repaying the Indians' hospitality to the writer he so much admired—of capturing Havana and gaining possession of the Isthmus, and thus securing to Great Britain the keys of the universe, as they called it in those days, by which they meant that it enabled the possessor of those keys to give laws to both oceans and become arbiter of the commercial world.

unable to buy a bottle of Martell from the steward he was thus incumbent upon an invitation from the skipper for a drink which had never seemed more necessary and to which, since the skipper was the nearest representative of the company who had betrayed him, he had never felt more entitled. Primrose returned from the bridge without further news, and the prospect of the drink seemed even more remote, for the Commandant was now taking his vessel, against a strong ebb tide, under more clouds to the west like picked mackerel bones, into Balboa Harbor: in spite of this responsibility of the skipper who could not obviously be drinking himself in these circumstances—an assumption in which he was proved to be mistaken—Martin strongly resented the fact that they had not been invited: after a while Martin had an angry drink of cold water and there was something very strange now in the transformation of his emotion about the drink back to the sadness in hand: after a while too, as if this drink had miraculously been hard liquor, Martin Trumbaugh's glass of cold water began to take effect...Nonetheless long after the ship had been anchored and was lying off the lights of Balboa, and the skipper had finished fishing off the stern, and had doubtless turned in, since his was the ordeal of taking the ship through the canal early on the morrow, Martin still found himself waiting futilely for their invitation, waiting, even though he had drunk at least two quarts of pinard at dinner in the meantime, and so his passions in that respect would have been thought partly at least to have been assuaged. But no: he was still on tenterhooks for the skipper's knock on the door, more anxious for that even than for the purser's knock, which would lead to the definite news of the disposal of their plight. My God, did poor stewards wait like this for a tip? Was this how, too, with this gnawing anxiety, Mexicans waited for La Mordida? A desire to go down and tip the steward immediately even if it meant getting him out of bed, assailed him and—)

Going out on deck Mr. Charon was peering through his binoculars into the darkness, in the direction of the canal...

Nov. 27. Waked before dawn—sky still gray, with a moon—by second mate: immigration officers are in salle-à-manger and must see our papers before boat enters Panama. Dress stupidly, half asleep, myself angrily apprehensive, but really hate all immigration officers too much to fear them, and stagger down. Captain muy correcto in elaborate white

Now this Paterson was a self-made man as who shall not say—however much we may pity him—that he was soon to become a self-unmade man also.

(I am constrained to mention that the majority of the information in this commentary I have obtained from the diverting book I hold in my hands, lent us by the 3rd mate of this vessel and called *The Bridge of Water* by Helen Nicolay, published by, etc. etc. And I mention this because strange though it may seem I have never read a book about the Panama Canal before.)

Probably neither have you. It may be more intricate works on the subject are to be found in Tokyo, in Moscow—certainly in Acapulco—and even Glasgow, perhaps even at the Unesco, but the homely touch, such as evinced by Miss Nicolay, may well be rare. So my kind acknowledgements.

So at Bristol, we are

told, William Paterson embarked for the Bahamas and the West Indies, where he made friends with the natives and buccaneers alike, teaching theology to the former and learning from the latter everything he could about the strange region in which he found himself.

(such as that there were no high mountains down toward the Gulf of Darien and that it would therefore be easy to make a canal at that point.)

Having developed this plan, says Helen Nicolay, he returned to England, hoping to interest the King, but disappointed, organized the Bank of England instead, though he soon withdrew from the Bank's management—perhaps, explains our good Miss Nicolay, because he had too many novel ideas to please the more conservative directors—

dress uniform with black and gold epaulettes, etc., drinking brandy with officers. Formalities—save that we don't get a drink—over in 5 minutes and we go on deck. Make amusing scene out of this with Martin. Ha ha. Digarillas floating around Balboa motionless. Dawn behind the *Henry B. Tucker* of Luckenbach Line.

Going down, at 7 a.m., between buoys, passing, at buoy 7, going the other way, the S.S. *Parthenia*, out of Glasgow; emerald palm trees, a road house on piles blinking its light, to the right; very green to right and left; to the left an island like a cupcake, completely flat, marshy land and a stretch of emerald jungle like chicory salad, and palms, with white houses showing through and what looks like a nice beach, buoys like little Eiffel Towers—ahead, the green light marks the first écloue (lock)—really beautiful beach to the left now beneath the chicory salad round the corner; Balboa to the right as we approach first buoy, palm trees and objects that look like country clubs, golf courses; left it gets more jungly—20 or 30 frigate birds sailing motionless, circling—docks to the right, then a launch comes alongside and 20 Negroes carrying canvas bags climb up a pilot ladder.

Orion: old type American battleship and submarine.

Quite cool going through the canal—

then to the right mud flats, a beached houseboat, striped stakes of an indeterminate purpose, then something innocent like a grove of alders at home: 1,000,000 country clubs or brothels beyond these; lighthouse like a chessman, ashore snowy egrets standing on mud flats by gigantic drain-pipe with this same background of chicory salad. The Canal now looks like a narrow, casual creek with muddy banks.

Swallows twittering on our masts and round our aerials, playing on the maintop, swallows skylarking—and a long-tailed grackle.

Gigantic frigate birds—digarillas—common as vultures in Mexico here, curious sense of land, birds singing.

Locks.

The first lock: Miraflores: 1913. Gigantic iron-studded gates very high but looking too narrow for a ship to steer into—but we do. Amuse Primrose by telling her silly Punch story of two country folk in London underground for first time. "Coo, Martha, look at that, bang in the 'ole every time!"

We ascend 54 feet through double lock.

1,000 birds of bad omen.

Second lock: Pedro Miguel: 1913.

We ascend 31 feet in second, single lock (symbolic) in 10 minutes.

and raising 900,000 pounds, founded now the Company of Scotland with a sudden upsurge of patriotism perhaps, because Scotland and England were not—as now—at that time united.

So in the year 1698 William Paterson sailed with 1,000 colonists on what came to be known as the Darien Expedition, landing in this region made famous by Balboa and Pedrarias—as in a different way by Keats—where he no doubt made friends once more with the natives and buccaneers alike, teaching theology to the former and learning from the latter everything that he could about the strange region in which he found himself—another traveler in the realms of gold—and in which, to make it seem more familiar, they called their colony Caledonia (much as later they called the region that is now British

Columbia, New Caledonia), and the town they founded New Edinburgh. But the Spaniards, perhaps not approving of the theology, were unfriendly, and the Indians, perhaps not liking the name New Edinburgh, in addition to not approving of the theology, became downright disgusted.

But at this point the story becomes tragic —Fever; hundreds died, including poor Paterson's wife and child. While Panama and Cartagena gathered land and sea forces to expel the unwanted New Caledonians, and the English King, partly to placate Spain and partly the British merchants, forbade any kind of assistance whatever to the Darien colony from the Governors of Virginia, New England, Jamaica, the Barbadoes and New York.

Finally Paterson was driven almost

More salad with stuff like scarlet acacia and flamboyants. Hombres shouting, doubtless for La Mordida.

Culebra Cut.

Blackest history of canal's horror, failure, collapse, murder, suicide, fever, at Culebra Cut. Now one glides through a narrow canal, gorgeous jungle like a wall on both sides, 2 minutes lost here would mean death, or a very peculiar new life— monkeys, birds, orchids, sinister orchestrations from the jungle. Hot here as a Turkish bath in hell. Jungle has to be chopped back every day.

Memorial tablet on a rock.

Apparatus as for foghorns, remote waterfalls. Besetting fear, as a writer taking notes, of being taken for a spy. Diving floats. Gold flags, dredgers, targets, and the lonely stations with in each one a man peering through binoculars: high wiry towers: "Many bananas trees," says Charon, with his guttural Turkish laugh. "Once there were many alligators, but not now."

ROBERT CHARON
Consul of Norway
Tahiti Island   Society Islands

U.S. *Tuscada*, a dredger, visualize life on a dredger in the Panama, muddy water. Down the Panama Canal, all sorts of jungle, iguanas rattling on a rock, parrots gib-

THROUGH THE PANAMA 89

bering, a train, quite like home in England, lumbers along the side of the canal, blossoms like honeysuckle, a kind of cactus.

A ship: *The Manatee*—London.

Another ship from London, all going the other way steaming very swiftly as with current. (Bergson.)

These rude London bastards of my countrymen give the Frenchmen the raspberry! I am thoroughly ashamed. I dislike Londoners anyway, coming from Liverpool, or do at this moment.

"Courtesy is no empty form, but the assent to man's true being." The Mexicans for example...It was enough to make you weep, Martin thought. With shame, when you might have wept with joy. (Though perhaps they were only giving *him* the raspberry.)

Significance of *locks*: in each one you are locked, Primrose says, as it were, in an experience.

A buoy like a white swan and behind thick jungle, little green hills. The lighthouses like chessmen cunningly contrived to guide, the whole like a fantastic child's dream, or a sort of Rube Goldberg invention.

—Dead trees sticking right out of the water presumably on shore of old lake...

In Gatun Lake have lunch amid sense of unreality, as if on an engineless ship sailing through the jungle in a dream.

insane—and the colony forced to abandon itself—and so, says Miss Nicolay, *in mid-ocean the disbanded and half dead colonists passed a vessel westward bound going to their own relief,* who when they arrived also gave up the struggle after ten months. Today all that remains of the grandiose dream, she says, are two names on the map: Caledonia Bay, and Port Escosses. And for more than a century little was heard about an Isthmian Canal.

For a great new era of enlightenment was dawning in the world. Rousseau, Voltaire, Adam Smith, electricity, Sir Isaac Newton, Halley, Linnaeus, Herschel, Whitefield, Swedenborg, Priestley, oxygen, inoculation, the penny post, tramways and the South Sea Bubble, England with her plans to develop her American colonies and then with her efforts to subdue them. Peter the Great and Catherine the II in Russia. Frederick the Great in Prussia, the three Louis, the French Revolution and the dictatorship of Napoleon. England fighting against France. France fighting against Spain. France and Germany and Alsace. Spain fighting against Portugal. Sweden attacking Denmark. Russia attacking the Ottoman Empire. France fighting Russia. England, France, Holland, Germany fighting Spain—and then crushing Napoleon—and then England fighting Spain nearly all this time and in 1780 sending two separate fleets to the Isthmus, one against the Spanish colonies on its eastern side, the other to gain possession of Lake Nicaragua and the San Juan River on the west, and the officer commanding this second expedition

While as for poor old De Lesseps himself (Martin said—who felt himself without knowing why rather to resemble that gentleman—helping himself to pinard), seeing what nationality of vessel we are on, perhaps the less said the better.

For myself, while hereditarily disposed in favor of canals in general, while in short loving them—any child could figure one out, indeed it is the first piece of engineering a child does figure out—and in any case a canal here would have been arrived at eventually by some sort of Platonic sense of oversights— which is not to decry it as an achievement (in that sense maybe I'm a bit envious), my feeling is bugger them all if they cause that much trouble, my sympathy being 150% with the troublesome San Blas Indians, whose territory occupied by their descendants to this day remains practically unknown. But I'm not out of sympathy altogether with the two American gentlemen of wealth, George Law and William H. Aspinwall, who at length assumed responsibility for carrying the mails, if only because the latter gentleman gave his name to a town which in turn gave its name to a lighthouse which prompted a certain writer to write a story called *The Lighthouse Keeper of Aspinwall* I shall have occasion to mention later.

Other people who in the history of the Panama Canal as reported here by Miss Nicolay I find myself particularly in sympathy with in their sufferings are some 800 Chinese—who were imported here to build a railroad—in sympathy not because they were Chinese, but because they nearly all committed suicide when deprived of their customary opium, an old law being invoked "*Which forbade this on moral grounds*," as a consequence of which "they strangled or hanged themselves with their long queues (this has now become a universal habit of the English) or sat down on the beach and waited for the tide to come up and drown them."

(How long I wonder is it to Colon? Or Cristobal? Or Aspinwall? And will we be able to go ashore there and get some liquor? Have the immigration inspectors gone? Or are they starting on the second bottle?)

Which reminds me that it says here too somewhere that when the actual work of digging began on the De Lesseps Canal, "this marked a season of festivity, to which Sarah Bernhardt added brilliance by journeying all the way from Paris to perform in Panama's playhouse": while meantime some Englishman, who had evidently not lived in Liverpool, had the gall to write on arrival in Panama at

was Horatio Nelson. But despite Horatio Nelson, who reported that Lake Nicaragua was the key to the whole situation, an Island of Gibraltar, which if held by England would cut Spanish America in two, you would scarcely credit that so many people for so many years during this long era of enlightenment could be so goddamned stupid, could be so ferociously ignorant, could have learnt so little, that they went on doing precisely this same sort of bloody thing. But that is what they apparently did, for this is what it says they did in this interesting book by Miss Helen Nicolay lent me by the 3rd mate. So that I personally, although an Englishman, or rather a Scotsman, and so with a sneaking sympathy for poor old Paterson, who founded the Bank of England, am quite relieved to read what it says here, that in 1846 the United States concluded a treaty with New Granada whereby it obtained exclusively right of transit across the Isthmus from the borders of Costa Rica and down to the Gulf of Darien and promised in return for this to insure the neutrality of any canal it might establish and defend it from foreign attack which is exceptionally sporting of me since I mention nothing of an ancestor of mine who also had a plan for the Panama Canal that was very favorably received at a dinner given for De Lesseps in New York in 1884.

this period "that it would be difficult to find elsewhere on the earth's surface a place in which so much villainy and disease and moral and physical abomination were concentrated."

And that is about all—save for the persistence and foresight and skill and enterprise and heroism of its final builders, of course, which we take for granted, and La Mordida, which is always with us—save that this book tells us some things about the operations of the canal we perhaps wouldn't have known even though we're going through it at this moment. That our engines are locked and sealed. That our sailors—which is maybe why the chief engineer is on deck looking so hot and upset—are obeying the orders of the pilot. That perhaps we couldn't go through at all—for the water hyacinths would render navigation impossible—but for some dredging outfit poetically known as the "Hyacinth Fleet." That our good captain is only a decoration, temporarily, despite his epaulettes and his bottle of Martell—

—and that man over there sitting on the control tower on the central wall, has a model of the canal locks before him, carefully built, which registers electrically the exact depth of the

After lunch the jungle looks like a gigantic conglomeration of spinach against the horizon with occasional lonely wild familiar-looking trees, such as one might see in Westmorland, under a windy cloudy summer sky...

The Last Lock
Gatun Lock

We descend 85 feet through triple lock.

The Hawaiian Banker: Wilmington, Delaware: rising from a grave of lock, as from Atlantis: Americans having wonderful time on bridge.

And ourselves, watching, happy, happy at the news we won't be separated after all.

Gigantic concrete street lamps as on a great boulevard, with grass walks, a lighthouse apparently on a bowling green, the sun beating down ferociously in the foreground and beyond a little lake, entirely surrounded by jungle over which floated vultures as a black storm was gathering: little isolated palm trees blew on the bowling green, and in the immediate foreground the vast ship from Wilmington, Delaware, slowly rising, blocking the view, elsewhere other ships were rising, or sinking, Negroes were pulling ropes, and from the rising and sinking ships people were taking photos. Little electric cars were trundling along the wharf.

Where Kilroy had also been and a little American family stood, with black glasses, waving their hands (I wave too) the children eating all day suckers. A great hook dangling against the sky— three great ships on three different levels—the lighthouse now alone, the

water and every movement of every lever and thus is able— ghastly image of the modern world—to see what is happening at every moment—and has possibly even seen me taking notes— That great chain that is rising suddenly from the water, is doing so to prevent us from going too far forward, and that water swirling upwards from the opening near the bottom of the lock, is making us rise at the rate of about 3 feet a minute, soundlessly, and without orders.

That those small squat electric engines that are following us and which seem such a far cry from the camels of the Suez Canal are called "mules" and are attached by hawsers to the ship—

All in all though, gentlemen, what I would like to say about the Panama Canal is that finally it is a work of genius —I would say, like a work of child's genius —something like a novel—in fact just such a novel as I, Sigbjørn Wilderness, if I may say so, might have written myself —indeed without knowing it am perhaps in the course of writing, with both ends different in character, governed under different laws, yet part of the same community, the one end full of boiler and repair shops, and the other full of clubhouses—with the jungle on every side, with the one end copying the other's worst features, which was a town anyhow of the Middle Ages, and where at any moment one expects to see ambulances carrying yellow fever patients, or piles of coffins lying on the dock but where actually all you see are these small squat electric engines called mules attached by hawsers to the ship— for it works, God how the whole thing beautifully and silently works, this celestial meccano— with its chains that

American flag flying, and the Tricolor— and again now emerging, sun, dark clouds, concrete, the jungle and the lake disclosing itself once again: driving blackness now over the once innocent Westmorland horizon, little streetcar stations on the bowling green, and cable cars with cabins on either end (and a drum in the middle) like roller coasters—chute-the-chutes—and the xopilotes slowly slowly ascending into the tempest over the jungle—there were seagulls blowing in every direction: for we have reached the Caribbean Sea.

Danger—Capacity 4 Persons.

(Martin takes this to heart.)

An old Negro with mackintosh, solar topee and rolled umbrella and gaiters limping along the lock wharf—why are there always these poor old men limping along wharves? ME.

And a lone loon diving in the last lock.

Looking back on it—The Panama— from the Caribbean is like looking back on a fairground with chute-the-chutes and great dippers: even the lighthouses contribute to the illusion, being something like the English helter-skelter.

De Lesseps' old canal goes off to the right into a swamp, a sad monument to unfinished projects, though actually *it is worse than that.*

Hot rain, coconut palms, pelicans.

Saying good-by to Charon: dropping the pilot, after the passage through the canal.

—Whatever Cristobal may be like ashore—not a town but a dormitory as a friend of mine (J. L. D.) said—from the sea, in the rain, at 3 o'clock in the afternoon, it is one of the dreariest places, imaginable on God's earth; on one side of the harbor, a row of houses, all exactly the same type of architecture, and precisely the same in every detail, resembling square electric generators, with tin roofs, the masonry of some tanned substance, rimmed at the window lines with yellow, stand under the jungle, seemingly alone: surprised by that I turned my binoculars on Cristobal itself, where, although at first one saw what might have been an old Spanish building, with arches, suggesting arcades, I was astonished to discover that here too, lining the waterfront, were likewise these houses, row after row of them, resembling electric generators; turning my glasses now upon what, perhaps wrongly, I surmised to be Colon, I saw that this was also entirely composed of these electric generators half hidden by the murk: the only other objects of interest being a gas-works and what seemed to be a Methodist church, I now

rise sullenly from the water, and the great steel gates moving in perfect silence, and with perfect ease at the touch of that man sitting up in the control tower high above the topmost lock who, by the way, is myself, and who would feel perfectly comfortable if only he did not know that there was yet another man sitting yet higher above him in *his* invisible control tower, who also has a model of the canal locks before him, carefully built, which registers electrically the exact depth of everything *I* do, and who thus is able to see everything that is happening to me at every moment—and worse everything that is *going* to happen—

And lastly, to the right, gentlemen— Cristobal, with houses described by Miss Nicolay here as perched on concrete pillars to outwit termites—making an interesting contrast with the legs of the beds in De Lesseps' hospital, which legs were placed in little cups of water to protect the patient from the crawling insects that instead of crawling liked to breed in these little cups of water prior to flitting from bed to bed, and from person to person, thus to provide more patients for De Lesseps' hospitals. For this is the way civilization advances, so that now we have the concrete pillars of Cristobal and rows and rows of electric-lighted dry closets screened in black gauze, with their woodwork painted white, instead of the legs of the beds in little cups of water which in itself was an advance in the days when Cristobal was once criticized for having too low a death rate. And talking of little cups of water I can see without being told that one is not even going to get a little cup of water here whether this is

turned my glasses back to that section which, as if it were Fairhaven to New Bedford, I had first looked at the same generators, and leading from that, a long breakwater of broken stones with a skeletal lighthouse on it—Point Manzanillo—that now shone green (or red), later there were more passengers and farewell to Mr. Charon, "We will see each other, not in Jerusalem, but in Tahiti," he said (what does he mean by that, and what is Martin in for?)—coming on board in the rain.

I had forgotten to mention that the tragedy of the Trumbaughs' separation had now been replaced by another; they were still to have their cabin as before, but they were not, on the other hand, to be allowed to go ashore in Cristobal; instead, as has been seen, they dropped anchor well outside, the passengers were to come aboard by launch, it was rough and murky, and the skipper was planning to get away as soon as possible, as a consequence it was impossible to go ashore and get any rum or other supplies. For a moment the thought had flashed through one's mind that the American *Amberjack* (why not apple jack?), the boat manned by Negroes running alongside the most closely and dangerously, with a bunch of bananas on the bow, could possibly be countermanded to go ashore and get some liquor, but the bananas—for one dollar—having been refused by the chief steward, the *Amberjack* turned off at a tangent and dashed into the murk again; the other launches that had been following dropped behind, and likewise turned away toward Cristobal, soon our new passengers were on board, we were waving good-by to Mr. Charon, disappearing into the rain on the American *Owl*, and we were underway ourselves. Underway themselves, were the Trumbaughs, with their cabin, but no liquor.

Can it be imagined? Martin had little gratitude for this, and no sympathy either for the skipper, who had spent eight hours on the bridge: he scarcely dared let himself out of his room on to the deck lest he be asked for an apéritif, and miss the invitation. Finally he shaved, and as a final act of desperation, even, in the washbasin, washed his feet, a feat he had not attempted for many months, afterward making an attempt to cut his toenails, an even greater feat, doubtless not attempted for many years: and yet even these latter paradoxical preparations were being made, in a sense, for the apéritif to which they were not going to be invited. It was Primrose who finally broke down and suggested,

Cristobal or Colon (or even Aspinwall). Though here is a thing that is worthy of mention where Miss Nicolay says that the completion of the canal passed almost unnoticed. That plans of the United States for a naval parade were abandoned. For Nature does not celebrate her victories in noisy ways, she observes, but works silently, and when the task is done lets the consequences proclaim it. Which is something for all novelists to remember!

But I almost forgot The Lighthouse Keeper of Aspinwall. And there he is. Or rather there he once lived. In the imagination of another novelist, over there, through the hot rain, somewhere in that direction, from which direction nothing shall be provided for our own illumination, though that was the whole point about the poor lighthouse keeper of Aspinwall. That in having another kind of illumination himself, he failed to provide illumination for his lighthouse, in fact went to sleep, which no lighthouse keeper should do even if spiritually advanced enough to have an illumination in Aspinwall. And so in imagination I ask you to behold, through that hot rain, the lighthouse made famous by the famous Polish author, Henryk Sienkiewicz, whose works are probably at the moment no longer on sale in Poland, though they will be but whose great novel is even now I hear being filmed in Rome with an enormous cast of thousands and which some years from now will doubtless be seen by many in America —and appropriately I address you in America too, since it's your canal—seen not for the first time —though for the first time at such popular prices ranging I dare say from $1.25 to

as Martin gazed mournfully at a ship, on the gloomy horizon, the shape of the Empire State Building, that he should buy some wine from the steward. (Try and find reasons for Martin's inability to do this—and also for his finally sending Primrose to ask the skipper.) Sure they could buy wine. (But Martin, stingy bastard, wanted to buy pinard.) But the skipper was in the same boat as they were. Well naturally. Nor was he sure they would even be able to get supplies in Curaçao. But perhaps he would cable forward, radio forward, getting the Company to get in some stores... The long day dragged onward until dinner, at which Martin sat silent, drinking too much pinard—half hating it because he could *only* drink it at dinner—unable, almost, to speak to the poor Salvadoreans, and another gloomy personage, whom he had glimpsed through a door, putting on a pair of new wooden shoes. Was it imaginable, but even after dinner, even after the skipper must have long been asleep, that Martin should even think, still hesitating, upon his still relatively clean, if swollen, feet, upon the threshold, and still as it were waiting— God knows for what—that he distinguished, among the hoarse cossack choir of the wind, the electric fan, the engine and the sea, the word "apéritif,

apéritif," endlessly, as if to the tune of "Frère Jacques," repeated...

Silent on a peak in Bragman's Bluff.

Silent on a peak in Monkey Point.

—Keats could scarcely have written.

To the territory of La Mordida—good-by, and may Christ send you sorrow! (Well, I take this back: Christ has already sent you enough. May you live, rather, bloody Mexico, to afford to man an example of the Christian charity you profess, else the abomination destroy you!)

Nov. 27. But that was nothing to the torments (while they were almost out of the Gulf of Darien, opposite Barranquilla—the little barranca?) Martin suffered on the next day, although he rose

$2.40 or nearly an English pound, to sit in a cinema. A project that while it might in fact have benefited Henryk Sienkiewicz would certainly have astonished Mr Paterson, a Scotsman, and the founder of the Bank of England, even though he began life walking backwards through England, and who first conceived the Panama Canal— All prices include taxes of course— And of course you know the book to which I refer: QUO VADIS?

early, did his hardest Indian exercises, and cleaned his teeth—gingerly—for in the strain of creation—and also the urge toward cleanliness—of the previous almost liquorless day he had cleaned them no less than 8 times. It was a healthy day on the whole, spent mostly in the sun. On the other hand, it appearing likely that now they would stop in Curaçao in the morning, and not at night (as had been feared), but on a Sunday, Martin remembered that then all the shops would be shut, everything indeed save the church, the 4th mate inadvertently and tactlessly said "No whisky no interesting." (In actual fact this remark pertained to a bleakly uninhabited island they were passing to starboard.) Later that afternoon, trying to study French with Primrose and the 3rd mate, in the windy salle-à-manger with books of matches and cigarettes blowing about, the red-faced engineer came in, angrily helped himself, out of the frig., to 3 glasses of wine. "Hullo, Mr. Wilderness." (Earlier it had been Sigbjørn.) Later it seemed Martin heard his name being vilified: "Il fait beau temps"—"But if there is this *wind*," shouted the engineer, "then Mr Wilderness won't be able to go ashore in Curaçao and get his whisky!" What the hell. This suggested to me however to have Martin think that the story had now gone round. Later, the agony of inarticulate neuroses, the fear—perfectly imaginary—of rebuffs: they get some St. Julien (Martin still vainly tried to buy pinard off the steward, who is now going to bake a cake on their wedding anniversary. But what is that cake going to demand of the Trumbaughs? The cake itself seems a nightmare. In spite of stars, wind, and sun, Martin had almost foundered in some complicated and absurd abyss of self, could only pray for another miracle to get out of it . . .).

In fact, Primrose tells me, the Chief Engineer is furious with the wind because it may put us into Curaçao at night—where we only stop to refuel—and then *no one* will be able to buy liquor and everyone, including the skipper, is dry.

Seaweed like an amber necklace, Primrose says.

Nov. 30. Three days, plodding across the South Caribbean, off the coast of Colombia, past the Gulf of Maracaibo, the coast of Venezuela.

Situation in France is now serious, I read in Panamanian paper Primrose borrowed from our new passengers; 2 million on strike—no transportation—riots, etc.

CURAÇAO

Sailing into Curaçao in the early morning. Low, barren, tree-less, grassless hills with sideways peaks and the bright neat town. A sea wall—the Dutch just can't resist their dykes, says Primrose—like an ancient fort. But where is the harbor? The ships? Then suddenly we sail into a narrow channel, and bang! right through the main street of Willemstadt. Pontoon bridge sweeps open for us and the channel then opens out abruptly into a huge inland harbor with hundreds of ships.

In Curaçao, *Havendienst II*, a black motorboat, and the beautiful swinging pontoon bridge across the canal—which is the main street—a delightful town, very clean and neat and Dutch, pointed red roofs, like a Dutch fairy tale sitting in the tropics. Olive-green water with a film of oil. Sea breeze stinks.

Having laid in a case of rum from the ship's chandlers we went ashore: Streets: Amstelstraat: IOC store, Pinto and Vinck.

Koninklyke Nederlandsche.

Stoomboot-Maatschappy N.V.

—and

Hoogspanning
Levensgevaar
Peligro de Muerte
Electricidad
Danger

We had a happy time!

—Seamen, visit your home: Cinelandia: Klipstraat (well named?): Step into Ice Cold Beer: Restaurant La Maria: Emma Straat: Cornelis Dirksweg: Leonard B. Smith—Plein: Borraire-straat: *Jupiter*—Amsterdam...

Angel trees like flat umbrellas.

In a street of strange solid Sunday-shut banks that remind me of *Buddenbrooks*, we took refuge from a shower in the Wonder Bar—a characterless place, with an open front, 3 tables (like an ice cream parlor, Primrose says) and a 6 foot bar: 2 Negro bartenders speak English with a Dutch accent: this will be a happy memory, drinking Bols and feeling like Hansel and Gretel with the Sunday shower, the Sunday crowds out-side, held up at the scything, sweeping pontoon bridge, and the great ships hurtling down the main street.

Back at the ship in the oil dock, all colors (and all smells) are on the water: surrounding the ship are something like sand dunes at Hoylake, only infinitely more desolate, more like slagheaps in a Welsh mining town, or the worst of the desert in Sonora, Mexico, with the masts of 3 little frigates, as if wrecked, sticking up above small cliffs: the abomination of desolation. Oil tanks, the twin cupolas of a church, like Port-au-Prince, just rising over the roofs of the blue-gray-dun-colored charac-terless mud houses with windows like small black rectangles.

The entrance to Curaçao is the most dramatic in the world. Hans Andersen would have loved the town. There is a more enormous sense of sea and ships in Curaçao than in any other part of the world I know of, except Liverpool.

From where we are moored ten ships: Argentine, British, Costa Rican, Norwegian, Greek, etc., can be seen, with a wild background of oil refineries (factory chimneys) giving an effect of Detroit rather than of a remote West Indian island, beneath a rainy water-color sky, showing patches of green. *Taverns*— Torrens? English ship. *Rio Atuel* Argentine *Matilde* unspecified probably Venezuela. CPIM—on pillbox-like tank.

Dalfoun—Stavanger (Norsk): *Jagner*—Goteborg (Swedish): *Clio*—Curaçao: *Plato*—Curaçao: pink-tiled roofs on the wharf. Verboden te Ankeren: S.E.L. Maduro and Sons: *Jupiter* —Amsterdam. Highland Prince: Seaman's Home: Casa Cohen: Club de Gezelligheid: El Crystal Photo Studio: Troost Ship: Chandler: G. Troost: Kelogovia: Joyeria.

Ridiculous mass exercises, people running up and down the long bridges of ship in shorts—probably very sensible—on board the Norwegian oil tanker.

It brought back to me the horror of "crocodiles," discipline at school; I try to visualize life on an oil tanker: the pure aseptic horror of it: almost better (it seemed for a moment) the clap-stricken death of the ships of Martin's own day...

—A letter came on board causing me much anxiety: my brother reports my mother is seriously ill in England. This is the first time I shall have seen her, as I still hope to, in 20 years. Last time I saw her was at Rock Ferry Station, Birkenhead (where Nathaniel Hawthorne was Consul), when she saw me off on the London train. Where, alas, did she think I was going? Where did I go? But I never came back. Nevertheless I wrote, regularly, which was more than I did for myself very often.

Leaving Curaçao...

> Frère Jacques
> Frère Jacques
> Dormez-vous?
> Dormez-vous?
> Sonnez les matines!
> Sonnez les matines!

The entrance—now exit—of Curaçao harbor—on the Venezuela side: final impression of its sweeping pontoon bridge, its immediate sense of the character and originality of an individual people.

Now the desolate coast; a little lagoon, with a tiny church standing at the right of the entrance, a dun-colored hill behind that, wine-colored hill behind that, violet hill behind that.

A house.

On the extreme right (looking to port) are sinister lead-colored, gun-metal-colored tanks, each with a tiny polka dot in the middle (shadow like a man on one), like barrels of sawed-off guns, with oil tankers lying below, "where the goats wear green spectacles to eat the morning newspaper..." And a castle, with to the right a gigantic Montana-like bluff: more medieval castles rising up between oil tanks, a little lagoon with sailboats, going into a sort of wild Yorkshire moor...

Little shadowed islands at sunset; formations like Stonehenge.

Last sight: 3 lone angel trees on long long flat sandbar.

Reaction to magniloquent sunset.

—resolution—

Dec. 1. ... Situation now reversed: Martin wanting to invite skipper for apéritif, after getting liquor at Curaçao. Martin got a case of rum, only $20, thanks to the skipper. "But why not two cases, Monsieur? I myself shall buy two, perhaps three at this price." Why not? Because Martin wanted to appear as if he did not need two cases. How wrong he was! How right the skipper. Already he can scarcely broach the case because he is thinking of wanting the second one they don't have—the skipper knows this too, that's why he charitably dodged having an apéritif with them. Nonetheless, Martin, who has acquired a mother too, doesn't want to use her as an excuse to get drunk. This sort of absolutely bona fide excuse supplied at such a moment is the dirtiest trick of the gods.

—Resolution!—

Other passengers.

The Hungarian from Nueva Mordida boarded at Colon. As I entered the saloon he was saying in answer to the El Salvadoreans, who have just said in Spanish they think I won't understand:

"And who drove you out then?"

"The police."

"And what had you done?"

The Hungarian, spreading his hands and lowering his voice as I approached: "Nothing."

The Hungarian drinks out of a private silver tankard, looks sadly at the sea, wants to sail a small boat on it.

"I go to Soviet territory..." He shrugs his shoulders. "Under Russian rule. Of course I risk my life. But," he adds, "my family... And of course I am a sportsman."

That's right, brother.

The Salvadoreans, tiny little people, a couple and their son, about 14 years old, seem Jewish, are wholly delightful: going to Paris. New Life. But I feel they have suffered some sort of persecution too—perhaps anti-Semitic—quien sabe? Somerset Maugham would find out. But it's just curiosity that makes me loathe all writers, and incidentally prevents them from being human. Primrose and Señora Mai sitting in the sun on deck, twittering like birds and painting each other's finger nails and toe nails. Primrose chattering atrocious French and worse Spanish to the Señora, who speaks no English, and both laughing and giggling at Primrose's mistakes. (I myself speak terrible French and a sinister Spanish.) Later we play parchesi with them and like them very much. (Snobbery of novelists whose characters always speak atrocious French and drink "something that passed for coffee.")

In addition: three Dutch engineers returning to Holland from Curaçao: Mynheer von Peeperhorn, Mynheer von Peeperhorn, and Mynheer von Peeperhorn. They too are delightful and kindly, but the only way Martin can think of opening conversation is by saying: Now as we were saying about Hieronymus Bosch—so he says nothing. Alcoholics Hieronymus.

Would do for description of novels about alcoholics. Alcoholics Hieronymus. Bosh!

We are cutting due northeast across the Caribbean and tomorrow will be in the Atlantic...

Dec. 2. Our anniversary. At noon, in the distance, on the horizon, a lighthouse to starboard: Sombrero Island. (Mem: story, very pertinent, about Sombrero: in Baring Gould.) Am exceedingly grieved about my mother but it is no use thinking about it.

The Cake, survived, somehow even eaten, at lunch. Extra wine, too. Many toasts and congratulations.

We make the Anegada Passage and are in the Atlantic.

Seaweed like gold tinsel, says Primrose. Sargasso Sea directly north. Isle of Lost Ships, featuring Stuart Rome, Moreton Cinema, Cheshire, England, Matinee at 3 p.m. My brother and I missed 26 years ago. Now we enter the Western Ocean and the 4,000 miles before we sight land at Bishop's Point, at Land's End. But to what end?

The Atlantic Highlands—long deep swell. Atlanterhavet.

Montserrat not far away to starboard where I altered geography books by climbing Chance's Mountain in 1929, in company with two Roman Catholics: Lindsey, a Negro, and Gomez, a Portuguese.

One albatross.

Six bottles of beer on top of mountain.

Primrose says, I'm afraid of this boat, thrown together in wartime by makers of washing machines... But for myself, I like her, though she rolls worse than the ship Conrad loaded with one third of the weight "above the beams" in Amsterdam. It is wrong to suppose the poor old Liberty ship hasn't got a soul by this time, just because she was thrown together in 48 hours by washing machine makers. What about me?—thrown together by a cotton broker in less than 5 minutes. 5 seconds perhaps?

Another ship to starboard: Flying Enterprise. Pretty name.

Dec. 3. Great storm to leeward near sunset, sweeping diagonally past.

Commandant, meaning well, hunts out old American magazines for me. Old *Harper's.* Terrifying ancient brilliant and even profound article by De Voto on later work of Mark Twain. (Mem: Discuss this a little: problem of the double, the triple, the quadruple "I.") Almost pathological (I feel) cruelty to Thomas Wolfe. Would De Voto like to know what I think of him, in his Easy Chair, lambasting a great soul—and why? because he is a man—who, as N. might say, cannot answer? Mem: quote Satan in *The Mysterious Stranger.* And then on top of this obsession with Wolfe's weaknesses to come across a statement like: "I am (I hope) a good Joycean." Why? To keep in with whom? Coming from De Voto it's almost enough to make you hate Joyce. And indeed I do sometimes hate Joyce.

—Reason for Thomas Wolfe's lapses, De Voto himself probably analyzed perfectly elsewhere, about someone else he didn't hate, like De Voto: reason was Thomas Wolfe was in a hurry, knew he was going to die, like N., in same sort of hurry. And what about what *is* disciplined about him, his marvelous portraits, his humor, savagery, sense of *life*. There is far more sense of life actually felt in Wolfe than in all Joyce for that matter. I myself consider it unjust too to criticize Wolfe for seeming to have nothing fundamentally to say (as they say). He had not time to get a real view of life. A giant in body, he might not have really matured till he was 60. That he had not time was, for literature, a tragedy: and I myself feel that one should be grateful for what he has given us. Much to be learned in De Voto's articles however; agonizing about Mark Twain. Possibly De Voto had troubles of his own though, in that uneasy chair. Enough to give one delirium Clemens.

The sea is worse than before to me, its expanse, rough, gray blue or rainy, and without seabirds, says nothing to me at the moment: though well do I understand now Joyce's fear of the sea: (who knows what lives in it? Don't want to think about this—frightening thought occurred to me last night, when Primrose says I woke her up saying: "Would they put Mother back in the sea?" What awful thing did I mean? Belief in mermaids?). It seemed to Martin he had offended some of the good Frenchmen too—both the second engineer and the third mate stern to him, curiously more formal: La Mer Morte, a sea that comes following a day of high wind when the wind has dropped, leaving behind the great dead swell of the day before: hangover within and without.

POSITION REPORT
S.S. *Diderot*

Date: 5 Dec. 1947
Latitude: 27° 24' N.
Longitude: 54° 90' W.
Course: Rv. 45
Distance: 230 m.
To go: 2,553 m.
Length of Day: 23H. 40M.
Average Speed: 9nds 7
Wind : N. 6
Sea: Houleuse, du vent
Signed: CH. GACHET 1st Lieut.

Two squalls: cobalt thunderstorms. Wind catches spray and blows it across the sea like rain, a tiny squall of rain.

Martin was gloomy and savage, lying all day in his bunk predicting death and disaster.

During these last days, since going through the Anegada Passage, have been through some important spiritual passage too—what does it mean?

Afternoon squall hit suddenly with a million hammers. The ship shakes, shudders. The sea is white, sparkling, sequined—it is over in a flash.

Terrific squall toward sunset. Thunder. Cobalt lightnings reveal a sizzling sea... *vision of creation.*

For some reason this made Martin happy. He rose from his bunk and went down to dinner in a jovial mood. He even played games afterwards with the Mais, Andrich and Gabriel.

—am glad to be welcomed by skipper again—really believe I have now got through some spiritual ordeal... though a little hard to see what.

Dec. 6. My mother's birthday. In getting out of bed this morning I seemed to be edging out of the table after dinner.

—utter forgetfulness whether one had gone to lavatory or not.

—finally one doesn't bother; for 5 whole days—result: a pain in back: no wonder: forgetfulness of teeth, hatred of teeth, continually muttering little phrases like—I wonder... couldn't have been as if...

—Tragedy of someone who got out of England to put a few thousand miles of ocean between himself and the non-creative bully-boys and homosapient schoolmasters of English literature only to find them so firmly entrenched in even greater power within America by the time he arrived (Martin thinks), and responsible for exactly the same dictatorship of opinion, an opinion that is not based on shared personal or felt experience or identity with a given writer, or love of literature, or even any intrinsic knowledge of *writing*, and is not even formed independently, but is entirely a matter of cliques who have the auxiliary object of nipping in the bud any competitive flowering of contemporary and original genius, which however they wouldn't recognize if they saw it. What! A person like myself—Martin went on to write—who discovered Kafka for himself nearly 20 years ago, and Melville 25 years ago, when about 15, and went to sea at 17, becomes disgusted in a way not easy to explain. Kafka meant something spiritually to me then: no longer. Melville likewise: I find it almost impossible to share what they meant to me with these people. They have ruined these writers for me. In fact I have to forget that there is such a thing as so-called "modern literature" and the "new criticism" in order to get any of my old feeling and passion back. How can I help remembering that no fewer than seventeen years ago it was I myself who had to *point out* to one of the editors of the *Nouvelle Revue Française* that they actually *had* published Kafka's *The Trial*. On reading it—for no, of course he hadn't read it—the fellow said to me: "Did *you* write that book?" "What? Didn't you like it?" "Not much—the bar part was quite funny—but I got the feeling I was reading about *you*." (His boss made a play out of it fifteen years later.) Then again, fifteen years ago, I couldn't find a single book of Kierkegaard's in the New York Public Library save *The Diary of a Seducer*. (Some years later we found this book in the market in Matamoros, Guerrero, Mexico.) Now he is all the rage and there is probably even a waiting list in the best-sellers department for *Fear and Trembling*. And yet what right have these English junior housemasters of American literature to Kafka and Melville? Have they been to sea? Have they starved? Nonsense. They probably haven't ever even been drunk, or had an honest hangover. Nor did they even discover Kafka and Melville themselves . . . etc. etc.

A brilliant piece of scorn, thought Martin (who suffered slightly from paranoia), regarding what he had written, and with his mouth almost watering. Then he added:

Now you see how easy it is to be carried away by an impulse

of hatred! There is some truth in what I say (that is, it is certainly true that I hate these people) but what of this whole thing, read aright? What a testimony to my inadequacy, my selfishness, my complete confusion indeed! Worse than that. Suppose we take it to pieces, starting at the end, and see what our persistent objective self makes of such a thing. First it seems apparent that the writer feels that literature exists for his personal benefit, and that the object of life is to get drunk, to go to sea, and to starve. (As well it may be?) Moreover we feel sure that the writer wants us to know he has *had* many hangovers, *been* drunk very often, and *has* starved. (Though this last is doubtful because it is immediately qualified by the word Nonsense.) Certainly we must feel, if we read him aright, that he is a most unusually dog-in-the-manger sort of fellow, because for some undisclosed reason, among other things, he wishes to prevent the "English junior housemasters of American literature" from reading Kafka and Melville. Perhaps the writer wanted to be just such a curious junior housemaster himself, and failed (either in England, or in America, or even in both)? Mystery. Mystery too clothes the mention of *Fear and Trembling* and the *Diary of a Seducer*, though that the author evidently feels himself to be singularly misused (to the extent that it even causes him to have some sort of mystical experience in the New York Public Library), at the same time feels himself to be some sort of unrecognized pioneer, who maybe even lives himself in a state of Fear and Trembling, perhaps even is undergoing some sort of Trial at the moment, seems manifest here too. And how proud he is of being mistaken in his youth for the author of *The Trial*, though this little story looks like a lie. (Or does it? The little story in question is not a lie, Martin knows, the trouble is that he has told so many lies now he has become incapable of making the truth not look like a lie.)

—Alas, before we can arrive at any real view of the undoubted truth that seems shadowily contained in some of these damaging phrases, certain syntactical deficiencies in this first paragraph oblige us to question the writer's own "love of literature" (it looks as though it isn't very wide—perhaps he has only read the three books he mentions, though we may doubt even that)—we may wonder why, if he despises these school-masters so much he bothers himself about their "power," wonder too if he has not even secretly thought of himself as being "a non-creative bully-boy and homosapient schoolmaster," at which rate we may feel that it is no wonder if he has failed to put a thousand miles of ocean between himself and himself (however schizophrenic) and come down finally to what seems to be the one undoubted unequivocal brute fact in the whole thing, which is that it looks indeed as though some sort of tragedy were involved.

What? Neurosis, of one kind and another, is stamped on almost every word he writes, both neurosis and a kind of fierce health. Perhaps his tragedy is that he is the one normal writer left on earth and it is this that adds to his isolation and so to his sense of guilt. (But without Primrose he wouldn't be a writer of any kind, or normal either.)

Just the same it is necessary for people to stand in judgment every now and then, and not allow themselves to be crippled by such smashing self-criticism as the above, or all talent—though we note with a smile he called it genius—would be "nipped in the bud" and the world get nowhere. And this brought Martin to the business, the question rather, of equilibrium.

No one likes it (indeed it seems so intangible how can you discuss it?) and the people who recommend it, if one can so phrase it, are nearly always bastards who have never known what was more than enough anyway—(there Martin went again). And yet there has never been a time in history when there was a greater necessity for the preservation of that seemingly most cold-blooded of all states, equilibrium, a greater necessity indeed for sobriety (how I hate it!). Equilibrium, sobriety, moderation, wisdom: these unpopular and unpleasant virtues, without which meditation and even goodness are impossible, must somehow, because they are so unpleasant, be recommended as states of being to be embraced with a kind of passion, as indeed passions themselves, as the longing for goodness itself is a passion, and thus invested somehow with all the attractions and attributes of qualities rare and savage (though you personally can be as drunk as a cock on blackberry brandy for all I care, albeit your chances of equilibrium, unless you are a veritable Paracelsus, become increasingly fewer in that state). Without such equilibrium, be it then only mental, Martin thought, all reactions, public and personal, will tend to react too far. Whereas before we had sadism in literature, for instance, now an equal kindness, a distaste for cruelty in any shape or form will be envinced: but we shall not believe it presages a universal change in man, because this apparent kindness will be allied with other qualities in themselves dull or wicked—albeit so far as cruelty is concerned this is one point upon which man should allow the pendulum to swing to its furthest reach of compassion for all God's creatures, human and animal, and there remain.

And yet one should be able passionately to impugn the wanton slaughter of wild creatures as something essentially cowardly, unworthy, contemptible and even suicidal without at the same time feeling bound in the same breath to attack your Hemingway; one should realize that your Hemingway has a right to shoot wild creatures and while he is engaged in that dubiously masculine occupation he is not, at least for the moment, shooting anyone else.

Bully-boys and schoolmasters now go to church, instead of

Communist meetings, and obediently popular opinion follows, prayer book in hand. Into the church of myth go the other bloody lot—Oh shut up.

But the people really responsible for the spread of interest in Kierkegaard, stemming out of the interest in Kafka, for which they are equally to be thanked, Edwin and Willa Muir, the brilliant translators of Kafka, responsible by virtue of the preface to *The Castle*, have never received the credit. Since but for that preface Kierkegaard would no doubt have remained in oblivion, and the bully-boys and—Oh shut up. Shut up. Shut up.

When Martin starts to study French, after a difficult period of abstinence, but still with a hangover, he is confronted, to say the least, in his French grammar, with the following phrases:

Traduisez en français:

1. The man was not dead but his wife told him that he had died two days ago.

2. She dressed herself as the Goddess of Death.

3. She opened the door and offered to the drunkard a dinner that was not very appetizing—(all this stemming from a lecture on the page headed *L'Ivrogne Incorrigible*... and beginning, Un homme revenait tous les soirs à la maison dans un état d'ivresse complet—below this was a photo of La Bourse, Paris, taken circa 1900).

4. You must suffer for your vice, said she. I shall come each day to bring you the same meal.

5. The meal does not matter, but I am suffering from thirst, you must come every hour to bring me 3 glasses of wine. —On the back of this rusty-colored book an embossed cock (perhaps the one I mentioned earlier as being drunk on blackberry brandy) greeting the dawn, beneath it the words: *Je t'adore, ô soleil*, in gilt letters... *What does this portend?*

Kindly remark of Lorca's: I'd like to pour a river of blood on her head.

Dec. 9. Bloody weather! Slow, dark daylight. The salle-à-manger is depressing, porthole covers down and electric lights going at noon, and noisy, with sea thundering tons of water across foredeck.

The poor little Mais, who've huddled, arms entwined, on deck, chattering like little gibbons, are now sad and sick; they could not eat lunch and finally all lay down on bench behind table.

Only Gabriel is still gay: "I have been eating 5, 6 and 8 because I am always hungry when the sea is bad."

Crash! Coffee, milk, etc. falls into Primrose's lap and on floor. I fear she will be scalded (she was too) but she is wailing because her pretty new red corduroy slacks are stained.

Godawful storm is on the wing (a good line) unless I have been a seaman for nothing. As a matter of fact I was a seaman for almost nothing, as wages go these days.

King Storm whose sheen is Fearful.

Huge seas, snow-capped mountains, but a south wind en arrière so that the sea is following us; the *Diderot* riding it wonderfully (but rolling so everything in cabin is banging about) like a Nathaniel Hawthorne blowing along in the wind to see the devil in manuscript, or windjammer running before the wind: passed another Liberty ship, going in the opposite direction, pitching away up in the skies, could not be making more than 20 miles per day.

Our rescue ship—coming to meet us.

The crew, in oilskins and sou'westers, battling the driving rain and wind, stretch lifelines on the after deck, terrific seas beyond and astern. Beyond and astern of time.

At sunset, tremendous sight of sprays and seas breaking over ship, black smoke pouring out of galley chimney straight to bâbord shows, however, that wind has gone to west...

Dec. 10. Gale increasing. And in fact what we seem in for is one of those good old Conradian Southwesterlies, dreaded by sailors, first read about at school by torchlight, where the moon, sun and stars disappear for 7 days, and oneself finally beneath the blankets.

Primrose says: well, this is the Atlantic, the Western Ocean as I always imagined it.

Low, wild sky with now and then a muted sun; gray, gray sea with a huge roll (grosse houle), but confused and breaking in every direction, some waves breaking like combers on a beach with a crash, with curving snowy crests from which the wind lifts the spray like a fountain. Some waves collide, rising to jagged peaks high above the ship, where the top breaks, and even spouts. Most weirdly beautiful of all, once in a long time a light comes through the top: beneath the spray appears a pale luminous brilliant green like phosphorescence, as though the wave were lighted from within by a green flame.

He heareth sounds and seeth strange sights and commotions in the sky and the element.

Standing on the passerelle, Charles tells us the wind was Force 8 at 1 a.m. but has now dropped a little. There is a bad storm ahead all right but traveling faster than we are. We are making 11 knots.

Later, near sunset, the wind has risen, is still rising, and radio reports it is shifting to a southwesterly quarter. The radio operator and the 3rd engineer, on passerelle with us, obviously don't like it and mutter together, predicting a dirty night.

They have posted an extra lookout on the bridge.

Gabriel points to the #3 hatch just below, over which waves are constantly breaking (they are almost breaking over the bridge) and says: "Flour! But ze cover eez waterproof." "Why?" says Primrose. "What does he mean?"

The Commandant scampers up and looks around: "She isn't rolling—not too much. A good ship, eh?" Good, fine, we say, and he is pleased.

Le vent chant dans le cordage.

Later. The wind is now Force 9 and still rising, also has shifted, and is abeam. Wind flickering the spray like smoke along the face of the water. We are making 9 knots.

Rilke comes to Martin's aid, via *The Kenyon Review*: "The experience with Rodin has made me very timid toward all changing, all diminishing, all failure—for those unapparent fatalities, once one has recognized them, can be endured only so long as one is capable of expressing them with the same force with which God allows them. I am not very far off work, perhaps, but Heaven forbid that I should be called upon (right away at least) for insight into anything more painful than I was charged with in Malte Laurids. Then it will just be a howl among howls and not worth the effort..."

But Martin has not, as a matter of fact, read a line of Rilke, and the whole thing, on his part, is simply an illusion of grandeur.

And, "Things must become different with us, from the ground up, from the ground up, otherwise all the miracles in the world will be in vain. For here I see once more how much is lavished on me and just plain lost. The Blessed Angela had a similar experience—"quand tous les sages du monde," she says, "et tous les saints du paradis m'accablereraient de leurs consolations et de leurs promesses, et Dieu lui-même de ses dons, s'il ne me changeait pas moi-même, s'il ne commençait au fond de moi une nouvelle operation, au lieu de me faire du bien, les sages, les saints et Dieu exaspéraient au delà de toute expression mon désespoir, ma fureur, ma tristesse, ma douleur, et mon aveuglement!" This (says Rilke) I marked a year ago in the book, for I understand it with all my heart and I cannot help it, it has since become only the more valid..."

Frère JACQUES—Frère JACQUES—

Sonnez les MATINES! Sonnez les MATINES!

Dec. 11. Gale still worse. Poor Salvadoreans and Dutchmen stuck in their cabins on after-deck: seas breaking right over: they can't get to salle-à-manger. Try to help but turns out couldn't matter less, they are all seasick and it's impossible to eat anyhow with dishes jumping off table onto floor—nearly impossible to drink too, should one want to: have to brace back against wall, clutch bottle in one hand and glass in other and pour teaspoonful at a time, for Primrose too. Have to write standing up too.

STORM OVER ATLANTIS

Martin had a dream of seeing mad pictures of Bosch, in Rotterdam. Probably I have seen them somewhere, or reproductions of them, particularly the dreadful St. Christopher. Real dream was preceded by a vision of a gigantic cinema, also apparently in Rotterdam, otherwise catastrophic ruin, a great queer slim tower, at the top of which church bells were ringing ceaselessly.

Then barrel organs as big as shops, and cranked with the kind of energy one associates with a coal trimmer, i.e., myself, winding up ashes from the stokehold on a winch...I once knew a man, who in thus dumping the ashes overboard, went overboard himself with the ashcan. That chap not unlike me either.

Then the St. Christopher, carrying Christ on his back, and a fish in his right hand, a dog barking on the opposite bank, old women, cocks, and a sort of gnome house up a tree where the gnome has hung up washing in near background, someone enthusiastically hanging a bear, on the other side of another kind of river, with a background of castles, old Rotterdam, etc. (will we make it?), but rather modern; some sort of naked fiend apparently dancing by his clothes, preparing to bathe from the river bank—the general effect one of the inerrable horror, and Satanic humor. But why should Martin be dreaming about it? perhaps clairvoyant—

The Beast
—The abomination of desolation, standing in the holy place.

But the Bosch picture of most importance to *La Mordida* I might describe as follows: in the foreground there is the same detailed figure, to whom I will return, in the background is a house, with some rafters missing from the roof, panes missing in the windows, etc., but giving a sense of even greater inerrable evil and horror and at the same time poverty and utter debauchery: in the doorway a man and a woman are discussing some matter that one knows is gruesome and terrible, without being able to say quite why: on the right of this house, which also on examination shows some signs of having been recently partially burned, an old man is peeing lustily; to return to the figure in the foreground: he has the air of a pilgrim, his goods slung over his shoulder, cadaverous he is likewise, and one leg is bandaged (like Death in my other dream); up a rather nice-looking tree between him and the man peeing are various objects that turn out upon close inspection to be demons of one sort and another, the most remarkable being an extremely wide, cat-like of visage, yet seemingly bodiless creature a bit like the Cheshire Cat in the illustrations to Lewis Carroll. This should occur in *La Mordida* in Trumbaugh's dream: for the meaning of this horror—a horror this time almost without humor unless it is the pissing man—is indeed that of the Pilgrim—even Bunyan's if you like, though the imagery is far more deeply religious, the man in the foreground in fact is the Protagonist, turning his face from damnation, as he thinks, and limping off into the unknown, and leaving his poor house, though he is making a great mistake as it happens, for his poor house was his salvation—like an image of his niche in the next world he was presented with in advance—and his business was to purify it and rebuild it, before setting forth... To hell with this... I think the trouble with Martin is that Hieronymus Bosch is literally the only painter he can appreciate at all, and at that not much, because he seems vaguely to recognize—well, whatever it is he does recognize, poor devil. Or was it because he was a pre-Adamite?

—What I'm really getting at with Martin, is to try and plot his position of isolation, not merely in society, but from all other artists of his generation. Though an Englishman perhaps, in reality he belongs to an older tradition of writers, not English at all, but American, the tradition of Jamesian integrity and chivalry, of which Faulkner and Aiken, say—though both Southerners, which raises other questions—are about the last living exponents, albeit their subject matter might sometimes have scared their elders. However, Martin is quite incapable of their kind of chivalry and tolerance toward writers of that same generation, of whose souls the cover on *Esquire* might be considered the outward semblances, and who tend to divide mankind into two categories: (a) those who are regular, (b) the sons of bitches, the bloody bully-boys, who—

Bah, but what I mean is something like this. I am capable of conceiving of a writer today, even intrinsically a first-rate writer, who *simply cannot understand*, and never has been able to understand, what his fellow writers are driving at, and have been driving at, and who has always been too shy to ask. This writer feels this deficiency in himself to the point of anguish. Essentially a humble fellow, he has tried his hardest all his life to understand (though maybe still not hard enough) so that his room is full of *Partisan Reviews*, *Kenyon Reviews*, *Minotaurs*, *Poetry* mags, *Horizons*, even old *Dials*, of whose contents he is able to make out precisely nothing, save where an occasional contribution of his own, years and years ago, rings a faint bell in his mind, a bell that is growing ever fainter, because to tell the truth he can no longer understand his own early work either. Yet he still tries, for the hundredth thousandth time to grasp *The Love Song of Alfred Prufrock*, for the nine millionth time to grapple with *The Waste Land*, of which the first line—though he knows it by heart of course!—is still as obscure to him as ever, and in which he has never been able to understand why Christ should have been compared to a tiger, though this has caused him to read William Blake (he had really been drawn to William Blake in childhood because he'd read in his father's London *Times* that Blake was cuckoo) whose poem about the little lamb is perhaps the only thing in all literature that he has thoroughly grasped, and even in that case maybe he's fooling himself. I am partly joking, for in fact my writer has a thorough grounding in Shakespeare. H'm. Anyhow, when he really faces up to matters, he finds his taste has been formed not necessarily by things that he has liked, but by things that he has understood, or rather these are so pitifully few that he has come to identify the two. Is this a fantastic portrait? Because it isn't that this man is not creative, it is because he *is* so creative that he can't understand anything; for example, he has never been able to follow the plot of even the simplest movie because he is so susceptible to the faintest stimulus of that kind that ten other movies are going on in his head while he is watching it. And it is the same way with music, painting, etc. At the age of 37, having acquired a spurious fame for various pieces that, as I say, he has long ceased to understand himself, he wakes up to the fact that he has really only enjoyed with aesthetic detachment four things in his life. A poem by Conrad Aiken, a performance of *Richard II* when he was 10 years old at the Birkenhead Hippodrome, a gramophone record of Frankie Trumbauer's with Eddie Lang, Venuti and Beiderbecke, and a French film directed by Zilke (rhymes with Rilke?) called *The Tragedy of a Duck*. Despite this, he still heroically reads a few pages of William Empson's *Seven Types of Ambiguity* each night before going to sleep, just to keep his hand in, as it were, and to keep up with the times...

There is a truth contained in this portrait, for this man, while a genuine artist—in fact he probably thinks of nothing but art—is yet, unlike most artists, a true human being. For alas this is the way the majority of human beings see other human beings, as shadows, themselves the only reality. It is true these shadows are often menacing, or they are angelic, love may move them, but they are essentially shadows, or forces, and the novelist's touch is missing in their human perception. Nothing indeed can be more unlike the actual experience of life than the average novelist's realistic portrait of a character. Nonetheless Martin's blindness, isolation, anguish, is all for a reason. I can see that on that road to Damascus, when the scales drop from his eyes, he will be given the grace to understand the heroic strivings of other artists too. Meantime he must slug it out, as they say, in darkness, that being his penance.

(Note: it must be said somewhere that Martin had been on this planet for so long that he had almost tricked himself into believing he was a human being. But this he felt with his deeper self not to be so, or only partly so. He could not find his vision of the world in any books. He had never succeeded in discovering more than a superficial aspect of his sufferings or his aspirations. And though he had got into the habit of pretending that he thought like other people, this was not the case. It is thought that we made a great advance when we discovered that the world was round and not flat. But to Martin it was flat all right, but only a little bit of it, the arena of his own sufferings, would appear at a time. Nor could he visualize the thing going round, moving from west to east. He would view the great dipper as one might view an illuminated advertisement, as something fixed, although with childish wonder, and with thoughts in mind of his mother's diamonds. But he could not make anything move. The world would not be wheeling, nor the stars in their courses. Or when the sun came up over the hill in the morning, that was precisely what it did. He was non-human, subservient to different laws, even if upon the surface he was at best a good-looking normal young man with rather formal manners. How else explain the continual painful conflict that went on between him and reality, even him and his clothes. "There is a continuous cold war between me and my clothes." Like a man who has been brought up by apes, or among cannibals, he had acquired certain of their habits; he looked like a man, but there the resemblance ended. And if he shared some of their passions, he shared these equally with the animals. Describe The Getting Up of Martin Trumbaugh, in the complications, futility, complications with clothes, reality, etc. And yet, also, in his deepest self, he possessed aspirations that were neither animal, nor, alas, any too commonly human. He wished to be physically strong, not in order to defeat people, but in order to be more practically compassionate. Compassion he valued above all things even though he saw the weakness in that desire. In fact anybody who said anything like this would immediately seem to be condemned for some sort of hypocrisy in his eyes just as he felt himself condemned at that moment. That weakness of self-pity he wished to correct too. He valued courtesy, tact, humor. But he wanted to find out how these could be put into practice in an uncorrupted form. But above all he valued loyalty—or something like loyalty, though in an extreme form—loyalty to oneself, loyalty to those one loved. Above all things perhaps he wanted to be loyal to Primrose in life. But he wanted to be loyal to her beyond life, and in whatever life there might be beyond. He wanted to be loyal to her beyond death. In short, at the bottom of his chaos of a nature, he worshiped the virtues that the world seems long since to have dismissed as dull or simply good business or as not pertaining to reality at all. So that, as in his lower, so in his higher nature too, he felt himself to be non-human. And he was in general so tripped up by the complexities of his own nature that too often he exhibited no virtues whatsoever, and all the vices, once glaring but now obscure; sins, that for all her victory, Protestantism is responsible for rendering less deadly than they in fact are. And he had good cause—)

Another dream of a huge desolate cathedral, yet involved marvelously with life, pissoirs underneath it, shops living within its very architecture, the great unseen triptychs of Rubens in the gloom, and the gigantic tinkling of a huge bell...The peace, and the distant bowed priests in white, carrying ingots.

The wireless operator praying lonely in the church: and I too, am he.

—Delirium of sea under moon—

Dec. 11. Night

> Al stereless within a boot am I
> Amid the sea, betwexen windes two
> That in contrarie standen evermo

Chaucer's comment is to be taken seriously: something has gone west in our steering gear. That is what I think at least, though I can gain no information and to my humiliation I have no knowledge of the hydraulic contraption we're dependent on. But the ship did not answer her helm from the upper bridge earlier, and there is something evilly wrong. Nearly all hands seem working down blow, and I suspect the second mate of having gone down the propeller shaft, which is a bad sign... All stereless within a stormboot are we.

—Tonight, in a full gale, off the Azores, our cabin—the Chief Gunner's—being on the lee side and the wind from the southwest, with tremendous seas, but being driven down wind, it was possible to leave our porthole wide open, through which one could see, as the ship lurched down to leeward, great doctor of divinity's gowns of seas furling to leeward, the foam like lamb's wool: the wind rose to a pitch of wailing in the cordage so extreme that it sounded almost false, like movie wind about a haunted house: and indeed the whole ship sounded like an immense exaggeration of the same thing: clankings of chains, unearthly chimes, inexplicable tinkerings clinkings and chatterings and sudden horrid whistlings: from down below in the engines, there issued an unimaginable noise of battering, whistling and thumping, accompanied too, for whatever reason, and at regular intervals, and as if were concealed down there some of mystic Ahab's secret harpooners engaged in forging their weapons, a tremendous sound of hammering that always ceased after a while, and doubtless was concerned some way with the propeller but so fearsome that I could explain it to Primrose only by saying that indeed it was the custom during gales for the chief engineer to keep his intransigent greasers employed in chipping rust (she didn't believe me but nodded gravely), that they might not become discouraged or bored and lose their nerve: on top of this, and

> The Mariner hath been cast into a trance; for the angelic power causeth the vessel to drive northward faster than human life could endure.

also at regular intervals, there was the noise that seemed to come out of the wall between myself and the wireless operator's cabin, as of a jack being cranked up, which Sacheverell Sitwell has taught us to associate with the signing off or evening greeting of a poltergeist. Beneath one, lying in the bunk, when this was possible, the ship squirmed and twisted, at moments of crisis, like a woman in an agony of pleasure, and looking out at the storm, and observing the gigantic seas, rising all above us as if we were in a volcano, it seemed impossible the ship could survive the punishment she was receiving; horrible detractable noises too came from the closed galley two decks below where that day the cook had been badly burned: and yet

The supernatural motion is retarded; the Mariner awakes, and his penance begins anew.

the sea never visited us through the porthole, we were safe in the midst of chaos, the wind rose to a howl of wolves as we plunged on, leaving me not merely a feeling that it was impossible to be experiencing this but, at every moment, the feeling that one had not experienced it at all.

We have had to change our course, the skipper says, and are going by dead reckoning.

Mad game of chess with skipper in his cabin; tables and chairs are mostly anchored to deck (nearly said floor), other chairs etc. and so on are lashed, so the cabin resembles escapologist's "rumpus" room—how I hate that phrase!—everything goes over from time to time anyhow: giacomo piano opening: chessmen peg into board like cribbage board—bottle of whisky in skipper's furred sea-boot beside table, because sea-boot won't fall over, is for me, he scarcely touches it; this chess is his idea of an hour's relaxation instead of sleep—he has summoned me to play in the middle of the night as if I were a medieval courtier subject to the King's wishes: dash to the chartroom something like one of those dashes, when scrum

half on opponent's twenty-five, over the try-line—opposing XV
in this case being not human beings but objects, fortunately
static: wireless operator hasn't turned in for three days, looks
half dead, poor fellow, keeps fighting uphill into skipper's cabin
every now and then with idiotic reports of fine weather and
light winds in the Baltic, meantime the scene outside, when I
can see it, is like a descent into the maelstrom. Other, more serious radio reports, to the skipper's sardonic amusement, are
always accompanied by some such remark as "These reports
have nothing to do with navigation." We are evidently in a bad
way though skipper has no intention of telling me what is
wrong, or at least not yet; anyhow we can't hear ourselves
speak. Skipper looks damned grave, however; despite which,
after a long game, he beats me very decisively. Grisette, the little cat, is delighted with all these escapologist's arrangements,
"for her benefit." I was so concentrated on the game that I forgot to look on the bridge, which seemed unnaturally dark, to
see if there was a man at the wheel. However I tell Primrose
that there was. But so help me God, I don't think there was.

—Game of chess now seems to be utterly unreal and something like that eerie wonderful absurd scene in the French
movie by Epstein of *The Fall of the House of Usher* in which
Roderick Usher and the old doctor are reading by the fire, the
house has already caught fire, not only that but cracks are
opening in the walls and the house is in fact coming to pieces all
around them, while flames creep toward them along the carpet,
an insane electric storm moreover is discharging its lightnings
outside in the swamp, through which Mrs Usher, née Ligeia,
having just risen from the grave, is making her way back to the
house with some difficulty; nonetheless, absorbed in the story,
Usher and the good doctor go on reading: the unspeakably
happy ending of that film, by the way, Martin thought, under
the stars, with Orion suddenly turned into the cross, and Usher

reconciled with his wife in this life yet on another plane, was a
stroke of genius perhaps beyond Poe himself, and now it occurs
to me that something like that should be the ending of the
novel....

> Roderick Usher rose at six
> And found his house in a hell of a fix.
> He made the coffee and locked the door,
> And then said, what have I done that for?
> But had poured himself a hell of a snort
> Before he could make any kind of retort,
> And poured himself a jigger of rum
> Before he heard the familiar hum
> Of his matutinal delirium
> Whose voices, imperious as a rule,
> Were sharper today, as if at school:
> Today, young Usher, you're going to vote.
> Said Roderick, that's a hell of a note.
> So he packed his bag full of vintage rare,
> His house fell down but he didn't care,
> And took the 9:30 to Baltimore
> And was murdered, promptly, at half past four.

—Three flying Dutchmen.

Later. In vain attempt to get some information I am
informed by the fourth mate—the sort of information I might
have given myself in a similar situation—that all hands are
engaged in putting a ceinture around the ship to prevent its
falling apart. (Indeed this is not so funny as it sounded—get
from newspaper cuttings Pat Terry's story of the ship that used
chains in this regard: also it is an electric welded ship; danger of
breaking in two or cracking hull very real.)

Charles says, smiling, "These Liberty ships, you know, Sigbjørn, they all fell in two in the Atlantic, in the war." Then, seeing Primrose's face, he added, "Do not worry, Madame, we have put a ceinture around its middle."

Later.—My sailor's instincts tell me, all of a sudden—and it is amazing with what suddenness such a crisis is upon one—that it will actually be an unusual bloody miracle if we pull through. The worst is being able to do nothing. Worse still, can't tell what they're doing, or if they think they are doing anything, what they imagine it can be. Despite the fourth mate's joke, there is an actual sound as of the ship breaking up. On an old type of ship such as I knew, if the steering gear went, there was still an old-fashioned windjammer wheel on the poop that could go into direct action. On top of that—believe it or not—even as late as 1927, we carried sails on board; and the lamp-trimmer, one of the petty officers, and a rating they seem to have no longer, corresponded to the old sailmaker. Here there is no windjammer-like wheel, and as certainly there are no sails. But there are two wheels, one above the other, on the upper and lower bridge, and so far as I can gather, both of these are out of commission. Yet we still have steerage way, of a kind, and are not hove to. The thing to be thankful for is that we haven't lost our propeller. Yet.

—Martin took his ignorance of the nature of the crisis to heart, telling himself that it was because these Liberty ships were not like the old ships where you could see what was going on, that there was an almost Kafka-like occlusion, everything closed, ghastly, so that in the Chief Gunner's cabin, while it connected with the bridge, you might as well have been hidden away on the upper deck of one of the Fall River Line paddle-steamers for all that you were in contact; but no matter what he told himself, it seemed all part and parcel of his wider isolation, and in fact like the ultimate ordeal of—

Primrose is assured, whenever she washes up against

anyone, that everything is all right and there's nothing to worry
about. She can't possibly be fooled but pretends she is. She's a
good sailor, spends her time eating sandwiches, for there's been
no hot food for two days, and watching the storm from the
lower bridge. What else to do? Can't get into bunk or you're
thrown out. The poor Salvadoreans, the Hungarian sportsman,
and the Mynheer Peeperhorns are all half dead of seasickness
and there is nothing anyone can do to help them. Our store of
liquor, however, takes on a dimension of social utility for once.
Second mate reports all lifeboats to starboard smashed. You'd
think one would notice this, but somehow one didn't. One
lifeboat to port is still possible—Côté à l'Abri du vent...etc.
While wheel is functioning again on the lower bridge.

Later. The wind is now 100 miles an hour. Seems unbelievable but I've forgotten whether this is Force 10 or 12. Wireless
weather report: overcast sky, some rain.

Dec. 12. Position Report. S.S. Diderot. There is no position
report. (As Stephen Leacock would say.)

Dec. 13. 3 a.m. Wind is now Force 10–11. On lower bridge
with Primrose and Commandant, who says to Primrose,
laughing:

"Well, there is now nothing I can do. But if you like,
Madame, you can pray."

—The storm, paralyzing scene from bridge, of the ship in
anguish shipping sea after sea of white drifting fire, after each
smash the spume smoking mast high above the foremasthead
light.

Later. We have now had no sleep for 2 nights—I think it has
been 2 nights—impossible to lie down, or even sit down. We
stand, bracing ourselves and holding on. This desk thank God

is strongly anchored, so I hang on with one hand to desk, write with other. Hope I can read this scrawl later. Primrose spends most of her time on lower bridge. I know she is frightened but she won't say so. She comes staggering in every so often to reassure me, or give latest report. Primrose...

She tells me: Everyone is on duty except 1st mate, who is asleep! Skipper sends man to wake him. Impossible. Finally skipper himself stamps down in a rage. They shout and shake him, but, says André, "He was like a dead corpse."

Absolute blackness and wild water all around. Our rudder trouble has started all over again. Uncanny scene of completely useless wheel in bridgehouse spinning round, with the ship going like a bat out of hell. Or did I dream it?

Ship seems to jump out of water, shudder from end to end.

Sonnez les matines!

Sonnez les matines!

Back in Chief Gunner's cabin I remember Gerald once saying, "when in doubt make a memorandum." So I do...Death compared to a rejected manuscript. Am my grandfather's son, who went down with ship—do I have to do that? Ship not mine anyhow...Seems unnecessary. Would be downright awkward, in fact. Embarrassment of skipper. A short story: "The Last Apéritif."

Martin reflected that these kind of idiotic thoughts were simply a mechanism in forced inaction to short-circuit anxiety about Primrose. This anxiety, when one gives way a bit, seems less anxiety than an inoculation against intolerable and appalling grief, a grief indeed that seems exactly like this sea...

Primrose, laughing, manages to shout to me: "Do you know, I just had the most idiotic thought, if we have to take to the lifeboat I mustn't wear my beautiful fur coat—I don't want to ruin it!"

But, as a matter of fact, there are now no lifeboats.

No use trying to get into bunk—we are pitched out on the floor.

Another way of confronting death is to conceive of it as a Mexican immigration inspector: "Hullo. What's the matter with you, you look as though you'd swallowed Pat Murphy's goat and the horns were sticking out of your arse."

(That is what the Manx fisherman admirably observed to the skipper of the liner, who not only nearly ran his boat down, but started yelling at him apoplectically for not keeping out of his way. So I tell Primrose this story which diverts her a lot. In fact, it is enough to make God laugh, that story, I always think. Possibly something like this anecdote—which I had from a Manx fisherman—is the origin of someone's threat—Bildad's?—in *Moby-Dick*: "I'll swallow a live goat, hair and horns and all.")

Our house. Incredible jewel-like days in December sometimes. Such radiance for December. Celestial views. Then a bell ringing in the mist. Would like someone to have it, live in it, without fear of eviction.

> —Thou god of this great vast, rebuke these surges
> Which wash both Heaven and Hell: the seaman's whistle
> Is as a whisper in the ears of death,
> Unheard.

But one should be grateful that there are not 6 *short* whispers followed by one *long* whisper.

In fact, as I surmise, many lives have been saved by the weather's being too bad to abandon ship.

Sonnez les matines!

Sonnez les matines!

Three S.O.S. going at once. Radio next door crackling like

small storm within a storm inside. Operator tells me—how
many hours ago?—Costa Rican tanker has been sinking for
three days. A Greek and a Finn also in distress. And now a
Panamanian. Greek ship is called ΑΡΙΣΤΟΤΕΛΗΣ just to give
us our unities presumably, since Aristotle's personal destiny is
not much help. (Note: Aristotle drowned himself.) We are all
too far away from one another, all too far down the drain ourselves, to do any good. Still, it is a comfort to each other to
know we are not alone. This is apparently one of the worst
storms in living history in the Atlantic. Though messages still
come through, "having nothing to do with navigation."

Ventilators singing in wild organ harmony: Hear us, O
Lord, from heaven thy dwelling place!

—No ship would stand many more seas like that—in old
type of steamer half crew would be cut off in the fo'c'sle. Now
it is the poor passengers, the Salvadoreans, etc., who are
cut off.

Popular illusions to spike about French, officers and crew of
this ship anyhow (message in a bottle):

That they are predominantly homosexual. (There are seemingly none aboard this ship. Though a Frenchman is capable of
living a balanced and even chivalrous life with a female giraffe,
without inflicting it on you.)

That they are predominantly unfaithful to their wives.
(There is one longing in common among all the married men,
officers and sailors to whom I have spoken, to be home with
their wives for Christmas. Though this may be a virtue peculiar
to married sailors.)

That they are mean. (Your concierge may be so. Madame
P.P. is so.)

No matter what yoke they were reeling under, no matter
how starved, I believe you would never see in France, or among
Frenchmen, the appalling sights of despair and degradation to

be met with daily in the streets of Vancouver, Canada, where man, having turned his back on nature, and having no heritage of beauty else, and no faith in a civilization where God has become an American washing machine, or a car he refuses even to drive properly—and not possessing the American élan which arises from a faith in the very act of taming nature herself, because America having run out of a supply of nature to tame is turning on Canada, so that Canada feels herself at bay, while a Canadian might be described as a conservationist divided against himself—falls to pieces before your eyes. Report has nothing to do with navigation. Instead of ill this very extremity in Canada probably presages an important new birth of wisdom in that country, for which America herself will be grateful.

That they are not good sailors. (Even Conrad, in his most whiskery mood, admitted in *The Rover* that they were among the best.)

That they have no, or a prissy, or a precise or merely urbane sense of humor. (Rabelais' "roaring arm chair" has never been vacated.)

Prosper Mérimée writing on the Scots. And on the Americans placed at different tables on the Riviera (during the American Civil War) "to prevent them eating each other." Similiar illusions should be spiked re Americans, English, Jews, Mexicans, Negroes, etc., etc. An example of humor to be appreciated in any language: Grisette is now in heat.

Greatest fault of the French is that they do not listen to what each other say. No wonder their governments fall—or rather they are talking so much all at once they can't even hear them fall, perhaps.

Prayer to the Virgin for those who have nobody them with.
For she is the Virgin for those who have nobody them with.
And for mariners on the sea.
And to the Saint of Desperate and Dangerous Causes.

For the 3 El Salvadoreans. For the 1 Hungarian sportsman. And for the 3 Mynheer von Peeperhorns.

Plight of an Englishman who is a Scotchman who is Norwegian who is a Canadian who is a Negro at heart from Dahomey who is married to an American who is on a French ship in distress which has been built by Americans and who finds at last that he is a Mexican dreaming of the White Cliffs of Dover.

Mystical objection to changing one's religion. But let the whole world make a fresh start. A universal amnesty (extending even to the bullies, the Mexican immigration inspectors, the schoolmasters, and finally myself, who have never lifted a finger to speak against the death in life all about me till this moment). Society is too guilty in the eyes of God to hold any man permanently to account in a larger sense for a crime against it, no matter how wicked: collectively, who have always—these donkey, these man—done something worse.

The day in Bowen Island we found the bronze bells and saw the harlequin ducks.

Prayer for Einar Neilson, who saw us off, singing "Shenandoah."

"And from the whole earth, as it spins through space, comes a sound of singing." (C.A.)

Sonnez les matines!

Sonnez les matines!

¿Le gusta esta jardin? ¿Que es suyo?

Vanity of human beings is terrific, stronger than fear, worse than that story in Schopenhauer.

S.O.S. going on next door. Battement de tambours!

God save the Fisher King.

Can't tell what's happening on deck at all. And there is absolutely nothing, for the moment, that can be done, which is never how you visualize it. Nevertheless, Martin reflected, this is a position all novelists find themselves in eventually. Put on your life jacket, your arms through the shoulder straps. Damned if I will. Couldn't if I tried. Have always had trouble with things like that. Put life jacket on Primrose, Martin thought. But Primrose, eating a sandwich, has already decided she wants to return to the bridge. So meanwhile we manage a drink. It is a rather good, strange drink.

à ce signal:

—Go to your cabin.

—Cover yourself warmly.

—Put on your gill-netting of sauvetage, and letting yourself be guided by the personnel render yourself at the Bridge of Embarcations, on the side secluded from the wind...

The signal of abandon...Couldn't hear it given in this noise.

Chief Gunner's cabin.

Martin swore that if he survived he would never willingly do another injurious action, or a generous one for an ulterior motive, unless that were an unselfish one. But the thing to do was *not to forget this*, like the character in William March's story, if you ever got out of the jam. God give me, he asks, a chance to be truly charitable. Let me know what it is You want me to do...

—Wish old Charon was here...

The whole is an assembly of apparently incongruous parts, slipping past one another—

Something like our steering gear in fact.

—law of series.

Sonnez les matines!

Sonnez les matines!

Miraculous such nights as these...etc.

Great God—we seem to be steering again.

The second mate says to Primrose, laughing, "All night we have been saving your life, Madame."

Dawn, and an albatross, bird of heaven, gliding astern.

À 9nds. arrivée Bishop Light, Angle-
terre, le 17 dec. vers 11 H.

—S.S. *Diderot,* left Vancouver
November 7—left Los Angeles November 15—for Rotterdam.

And the ancient
Mariner beholdeth his
native country.

And to teach by his
own example, love
and reverence to all
things that God made
and loveth.

Frère Jacques
Frère Jacques
Dormez-vous?
Dormez-vous?
Sonnez les matines!
Sonnez les matines!
Ding dang dong!
Ding dang dong!

STRANGE COMFORT
AFFORDED BY THE PROFESSION

Sigbjørn Wilderness, an American writer in Rome on a Guggenheim Fellowship, paused on the steps above the flower stall and wrote, glancing from time to time at the house before him, in a black notebook:

> Il poeta inglese Giovanni Keats mente maravigliosa quanto precoce morì in questa casa il 24 Febbraio 1821 nel ventisessimo anno dell'età sua.

Here, in a sudden access of nervousness, glancing now not only at the house, but behind him at the church of Trinità dei Monti, at the woman in the flower stall, the Romans drifting up and down the steps, or passing in the Piazza di Spagna below (for though it was several years after the war he was afraid of being taken for a spy), he drew, as well as he was able, the lyre, similar to the one on the poet's tomb, that appeared on the house between the Italian and its translation:

Then he added swiftly the words below the lyre:

The young English poet, John Keats, died in this house on the 24th of February 1821, aged 26.

This accomplished, he put the notebook and pencil back in his pocket, glanced around him again with a heavier, more penetrating look—that in fact was informed by such a malaise he saw nothing at all but which was intended to say "I have a perfect right to do this," or "If you saw me do that, very well then, I *am* some sort of detective, perhaps even some kind of a painter"—descended the remaining steps, looked around wildly once more, and entered, with a sigh of relief like a man going to bed, the comforting darkness of Keats's house.

Here, having climbed the narrow staircase, he was almost instantly confronted by a legend in a glass case which said:

Remnants of aromatic gums used by Trelawny when cremating the body of Shelley.

And these words, for his notebook with which he was already rearmed felt ratified in this place, he also copied down, though he failed to comment on the gums themselves, which largely escaped his notice, as indeed did the house itself—there had been those stairs, there was a balcony, it was dark, there were many pictures, and these glass cases, it was a bit like a library—in which he saw no books of his—these made about the sum of Sigbjørn's unrecorded perceptions. From the aromatic gums he moved to the enshrined marriage license of the same poet, and Sigbjørn transcribed this document too, writing rapidly as his eyes became more used to the dim light:

Percy Bysshe Shelley of the Parish *of* Saint Mildred, Bread Street, London, Widower, *and* Mary Wollstonecraft Godwin *of* the City of Bath, Spinster, a minor, *were*

married in this Church *by* Licence *with Consent of*
William Godwin her father *this* Thirtieth *Day of December in the year one thousand eight hundred and sixteen.*
By me Mr. Heydon, Curate. This marriage was solem-
nized between us.

PERCY BYSSHE SHELLEY

MARY WOLLSTONECRAFT GODWIN

In the presence of:

WILLIAM GODWIN

M. J. GODWIN.

Beneath this Sigbjørn added mysteriously:

Nemesis. Marriage of drowned Phoenician sailor. A
bit odd here at all. Sad—feel swine to look at such things.

Then he passed on quickly—not so quickly he hadn't time to
wonder with a remote twinge why, if there was no reason for
any of his own books to be there on the shelves above him, the
presence was justified of *In Memoriam*, *All Quiet on the Western Front*, *Green Light*, and the *Field Book of Western Birds*—
to another glass case in which appeared a framed and
unfinished letter, evidently from Severn, Keats's friend, which
Sigbjørn copied down as before:

My dear Sir:
Keats has changed somewhat for the worse—at least
his mind has much—very much—yet the blood has
ceased to come, his digestion is better and but for a cough
he must be improving, that is as respects his body—but
the fatal prospect of consumption hangs before his mind
yet—and turns everything to despair and wretchedness—

he will not hear a word about living—nay, I seem to lose his confidence by trying to give him this hope [the following lines had been crossed out by Severn but Sigbjørn ruthlessly wrote them down just the same: *for his knowledge of internal anatomy enables him to judge of any change accurately and largely adds to his torture*], he will not think his future prospect favourable—he says the continued stretch of his imagination has already killed him and were he to recover he would not write another line— he will not hear of his good friends in England except for what they have done—and this is another load—but of their high hopes of him—his certain success—his experience—he will not hear a word—then the want of some kind of hope to feed his vivacious imagination—

The letter having broken off here, Sigbjørn, notebook in hand, tiptoed lingeringly to another glass case where, another letter from Severn appearing, he wrote:

My dear Brown—He is gone—he died with the most perfect ease—he seemed to go to sleep. On the 23rd at half past four the approaches of death came on. "Severn —lift me up for I am dying—I shall die easy—don't be frightened, I thank God it has come." I lifted him upon my arms and the phlegm seemed boiling in his throat. This increased until 11 at night when he gradually sank into death so quiet I still thought he slept—But I cannot say more now. I am broken down beyond my strength. I cannot be left alone. I have not slept for nine days—the days since. On Saturday a gentleman came to cast his hand and foot. On Thursday the body was opened. The lungs were completely gone. The doctors would not—

Much moved, Sigbjørn reread this as it now appeared in his notebook, then added beneath it:

On Saturday a gentleman came to cast his hand and foot—that is the most sinister line to me. Who is this gentleman?

Once outside Keats's house Wilderness did not pause nor look to left or right, not even at the American Express, until he had reached a bar which he entered, however, without stopping to copy down its name. He felt he had progressed in one movement, in one stride, from Keats's house to this bar, partly just because he had wished to avoid signing his own name in the visitor's book. Sigbjørn Wilderness! The very sound of his name was like a bell-buoy—or more euphoniously a lightship—broken adrift, and washing in from the Atlantic on a reef. Yet how he hated to write it down (loved to see it in print?)—though like so much else with him it had little reality unless he did. Without hesitating to ask himself why, if he was so disturbed by it, he did not choose another name under which to write, such as his second name which was Henry, or his mother's, which was Sanderson-Smith, he selected the most isolated booth he could find in the bar, that was itself an underground grotto, and drank two grappas in quick succession. Over his third he began to experience some of the emotions one might have expected him to undergo in Keats's house. He felt fully the surprise which had barely affected him that some of Shelley's relics were to be found there, if a fact no more astonishing than that Shelley—whose skull moreover had narrowly escaped appropriation by Byron as a drinking goblet, and whose heart, snatched out of the flames by Trelawny, he seemed to recollect from Proust, was interred in England—should have been buried in Rome at all (where the bit of Ariel's song inscribed on his gravestone might have anyway prepared one for the rich and strange), and he was touched by the chivalry of those Italians who, during the war, it was said, had preserved, at considerable risk to themselves, the contents of that house from the Germans. Moreover he now thought he began to see the house itself more clearly, though no doubt not as it was, and he produced his notebook again with the object of adding to the notes already taken these impressions that came to him in retrospect.

"Mamertine Prison," he read...He'd opened it at the wrong place, at some observations made yesterday upon a visit to the historic dungeon, but being gloomily entertained by what he saw, he read on as he did so feeling the clammy confined horror of that underground cell, or other underground cell, not, he suspected, really sensed at the time, rise heavily about him.

MAMERTINE PRISON [ran the heading]
   The lower is the true prison
of Mamertine, the state prison of ancient Rome.

The lower cell called Tullianus is probably the most ancient building in Rome. The prison was used to imprison malefactors and enemies of the State. In the lower cell is seen the well where according to tradition St. Peter miraculously made a spring to baptise the gaolers Processus and Martinianus. Victims: politicians. Pontius, King of the Sanniti. Died 290 B.C. Giurgurath (Jugurtha), Aristobulus, Vercingetorix.—The Holy Martyrs, Peter and Paul. Apostles imprisoned in the reign of Nero.— Processus, Abondius, *and many others unknown* were:

   decapitato
   suppliziato (suffocated)

strangolato
morto per fame.

Vercingetorix, the King of the Gauls, was certainly
strangolato 49 B.C. and Jugurtha, King of Numidia, dead
by starvation 104 B.C.

The lower is the true prison—why had he underlined that?
Sigbjørn wondered. He ordered another grappa and, while
awaiting it, turned back to his notebook where, beneath his
remarks on the Mamertine prison, and added as he now
recalled in the dungeon itself, this memorandum met his eyes:

Find Gogol's house—where wrote part of Dead Souls—
1838. Where died Vielgorsky? "They do not heed me, nor
see me, nor listen to me," wrote Gogol. "What have I
done to them? Why do they torture me? What do they
want of poor me? What can I give them? I have nothing.
My strength is gone. I cannot endure all this." Suppliziato. Strangolato. In wonderful-horrible book of Nabo-
kov's when Gogol was dying—he says—"you could feel
his spine through his stomach." Leeches dangling from
nose: "Lift them up, keep them away..." Henrik Ibsen,
Thomas Mann, ditto brother: Buddenbrooks and Pippo
Spano. A—where lived? became sunburned? Perhaps
happy here. Prosper Mérimée and Schiller. Suppliziato.
Fitzgerald in Forum. Eliot in Colosseum?

And underneath this was written enigmatically:

And many others.

And beneath this:

Perhaps Maxim Gorky too. This is funny. Encounter between Volga Boatman and saintly Fisherman.

What was funny? While Sigbjørn, turning over his pages toward Keats's house again, was wondering what he had meant, beyond the fact that Gorky, like most of those other distinguished individuals, had at one time lived in Rome, if not in the Mamertine prison—though with another part of his mind he knew perfectly well—he realized that the peculiar stichometry of his observations, jotted down as if he imagined he were writing a species of poem, had caused him prematurely to finish the notebook:

On Saturday a gentleman came to cast his hand and foot—that is the most sinister line to me—who is this gentleman?

With these words his notebook concluded.

That didn't mean there was no more space, for his notebooks, he reflected avuncularly, just like his candles, tended to consume themselves at both ends; yes, as he thought, there was some writing at the beginning. Reversing this, for it was upside down, he smiled and forgot about looking for space, since he immediately recognized these notes as having been taken in America two years ago upon a visit to Richmond, Virginia, a pleasant time for him. So, amused, he composed himself to read, delighted also, in an Italian bar, to be thus transported back to the South. He had made nothing of these notes, hadn't even known they were there, and it was not always easy accurately to visualize the scenes they conjured up:

The wonderful slanting square in Richmond and the tragic silhouette of interlaced leafless trees.

On a wall: *dirty stinking Degenerate Bobs was here from Boston, North End, Mass. Warp son of a bitch.*

Sigbjørn chuckled. Now he clearly remembered the biting winter day in Richmond, the dramatic courthouse in the precipitous park, the long climb up to it, and the caustic attestation to solidarity with the North in the (white) men's wash room. Smiling he read on:

In Poe's shrine, strange preserved news clipping: CAPACITY CROWD HEARS TRIBUTE TO POE'S WORKS. *University student, who ended life, buried at Wytherville.*

Yes, yes, and this he remembered too, in Poe's house, or one of Poe's houses, the one with the great dark wing of shadow on it at sunset, where the dear old lady who kept it, who'd showed him the news clipping, had said to him in a whisper: "So you see, *we* think these stories of his drinking can't *all* be true." He continued:

Opposite Craig house, where Poe's Helen lived, these words, upon façade, windows, stoop of the place from which E. A. P.—if I am right—must have watched the lady with the agate lamp: Headache—A.B.C.—Neuralgia: LIC-OFF-PREM—enjoy Pepsi—Drink Royal Crown Cola—Dr. Swell's Root Beer—"Furnish room for rent": did Poe really live here? Must have, could only have spotted Psyche from the regions which are Lic-Off-Prem.—Better than no Lic at all though. Bet Poe does not still live in Lic-Off-Prem. Else might account for "Furnish room for rent"?
Mem: Consult Talking Horse Friday.
—Give me Liberty or give me death [Sigbjørn now

read]. In churchyard, with Patrick Henry's grave; a
notice. No smoking within ten feet of the church; then:
    Outside Robert E. Lee's house:
    Please pull the bell
    To make it ring.
    —Inside Valentine Museum, with Poe's relics—

Sigbjørn paused. Now he remembered that winter day still
more clearly. Robert E. Lee's house was of course far below the
courthouse, remote from Patrick Henry and the Craig house
and the other Poe shrine, and it would have been a good step
hence to the Valentine Museum, even had not Richmond, a city
whose Hellenic character was not confined to its architecture,
but would have been recognized in its gradients by a Greek
mountain goat, been grouped about streets so steep it was
painful to think of Poe toiling up them. Sigbjørn's notes were in
the wrong order, and it must have been morning then, and not
sunset as it was in the other house with the old lady, when he
went to the Valentine Museum. He saw Lee's house again, and
a faint feeling of the beauty of the whole frostbound city outside came to his mind, then a picture of a Confederate white
house, near a gigantic red-brick factory chimney, with far
below a glimpse of an old cobbled street, and a lone figure
crossing a waste, as between three centuries, from the house
toward the railway tracks and this chimney, which belonged to
the Bone Dry Fertilizer Company. But in the sequence of his
notes "Please pull the bell, to make it ring," on Lee's house, had
seemed to provide a certain musical effect of solemnity, yet ush-
ering him instead into the Poe museum which Sigbjørn now in
memory re-entered.

    Inside Valentine Museum, with Poe's relics [he read
    once more]

Please

Do not smoke

Do not run

Do not touch walls or exhibits

Observation of these rules will insure your own and others' enjoyment of the museum.

—Blue silk coat and waistcoat, gift of the Misses Boykin, that belonged to one of George Washington's dentists.

Sigbjørn closed his eyes, in his mind Shelley's crematory gums and the gift of the Misses Boykin struggling for a moment helplessly, then he returned to the words that followed. They were Poe's own, and formed part of some letters once presumably written in anguished and private desperation, but which were now to be perused at leisure by anyone whose enjoyment of them would be "insured" so long as they neither smoked nor ran nor touched the glass case in which, like the gums (on the other side of the world), they were preserved. He read:

Excerpt from a letter by Poe—after having been dismissed from West Point—to his foster father. Feb. 21, 1831.

"It will however be the last time I ever trouble any human being—I feel I am on a sick bed from which I shall never get up."

Sigbjørn calculated with a pang that Poe must have written these words almost seven years to the day after Keats's death, then, that far from never having got up from his sick bed, he had risen from it to change, thanks to Baudelaire, the whole course of European literature, yes, and not merely to trouble, but to frighten the wits out of several generations of human beings with such choice pieces as "King Pest," "The Pit and the Pendulum," and "A Descent into the Maelstrom," not to speak of the effect produced by the compendious and prophetic *Eureka*.

> My *ear* has been too shocking for any description—I am wearing away every day, even if my last sickness had not completed it.

Sigbjørn finished his grappa and ordered another. The sensation produced by reading these notes was really very curious. First, he was conscious of himself reading them here in this Roman bar, then of himself in the Valentine Museum in Richmond, Virginia, reading the letters through the glass case and copying fragments from these down, then of poor Poe sitting blackly somewhere writing them. Beyond this was the vision of Poe's foster father likewise reading some of these letters, for all he knew unheedingly, yet solemnly putting them away for what turned out to be posterity, these letters which, whatever they might not be, were certainly—he thought again—intended to be private. But were they indeed? Even here at this extremity Poe must have felt that he was transcribing the story that was E. A. Poe, at this very moment of what he conceived to be his greatest need, his final—however consciously engineered—disgrace, felt a certain reluctance, perhaps, to send what he wrote, as if he were thinking: Damn it, I could use some of that, it may not be so hot, but it is at least too good to waste on my foster father. Some of Keats's own published letters were not different. And yet it was almost bizarre how, among these glass cases, in these museums, to what extent one revolved about, was hemmed in by, this cinereous evidence of anguish. Where was Poe's astrolabe, Keats's tankard of claret, Shelley's "Useful Knots for the Yachtsman"? It was true that Shelley himself might not have been aware of the aromatic gums, but even that

beautiful and irrelevant circumstantiality that was the gift of
the Misses Boykin seemed not without its suggestion of suffering, at least for George Washington.

> Baltimore, April 12, 1833.
> I am perishing—absolutely perishing for want of aid.
> And yet I am not idle—nor have I committed any offence
> against society which would render me deserving of so
> hard a fate. For God's sake pity me and save me from
> destruction.
>
> E. A. POE

Oh, God, thought Sigbjørn. But Poe had held out another
sixteen years. He had died in Baltimore at the age of forty. Sigbjørn himself was nine behind on that game so far, and—with
luck—should win easily. Perhaps if Poe had held out a little
longer—perhaps if Keats—he turned over the pages of his notebook rapidly, only to be confronted by the letter from Severn:

> My dear Sir:
> Keats has changed somewhat for the worse—at least
> his mind has much—very much—yet the blood has ceased
> to come ... but the fatal prospect hangs ... *for his knowl-
> edge of internal anatomy ... largely adds to his torture.*

Suppliziato, strangolato, he thought ... *The lower is the true
prison. And many others.* Nor have I committed any offense
against society. Not much you hadn't, brother. Society might
pay you the highest honors, even to putting your relics in the
company of the waistcoat belonging to George Washington's
dentist, but in its heart it cried:—*dirty stinking Degenerate
Bobs was here from Boston, North End, Mass. Warp son of a
bitch!* ... "On Saturday a gentleman came to cast his hand and

foot..." Had anybody done that, Sigbjørn wondered, tasting his new grappa, and suddenly cognizant of his diminishing Guggenheim, compared, that was, Keats and Poe?—But compare in what sense, Keats, with what, in what sense, with Poe? What was it he wanted to compare? Not the aesthetic of the two poets, nor the breakdown of *Hyperion*, in relation to Poe's conception of the short poem, nor yet the philosophic ambition of the one, with the philosophic achievement of the other. Or could that more properly be discerned as negative capability, as opposed to negative achievement? Or did he merely wish to relate their melancholias? potations? hangovers? Their sheer guts—which commentators so obligingly forgot!—character, in a high sense of that word, the sense in which Conrad sometimes understood it, for were they not in their souls like hapless shipmasters, determined to drive their leaky commands full of valuable treasure at all costs, somehow, into port, and always against time, yet through all but interminable tempest, typhoons that so rarely abated? Or merely what seemed funereally analogous within the mutuality of their shrines? Or he could even speculate, starting with Baudelaire again, upon what the French movie director Epstein who had made *La Chute de la Maison Usher* in a way that would have delighted Poe himself, might have done with *The Eve of St. Agnes: And they are gone!* ... "For God's sake pity me and save me from destruction!"

Ah ha, now he thought he had it: did not the preservation of such relics betoken—beyond the filing cabinet of the malicious foster father who wanted to catch one out—less an obscure revenge for the poet's nonconformity, than for his magical monopoly, his possession of words? On the one hand he could write his translunar "Ulalume," his enchanted "To a Nightingale" (which might account for the *Field Book of Western Birds*), on the other was capable of saying, simply, "I am perishing...For God's sake pity me..." You see, after all, he's just like folks...What's this?...Conversely, there might appear almost a tragic condescension in remarks such as Flaubert's often quoted "Ils sont dans le vrai" perpetuated by Kafka—Kaf—and others, and addressed to child-bearing rosy-cheeked and jolly humanity at large. Condescension, nay, inverse self-approval, something downright unnecessary. And Flaub—Why should they be dans le vrai any more than the artist was dans le vrai? All people and poets are much the same but some poets are more the same than others, as George Orwell might have said. George Or—And yet, what modern poet would be caught dead (though they'd do their best to catch him all right) with his "For Christ's sake send aid," unrepossessed, unincinerated, to be put in a glass case? It was a truism to say that poets not only were, but looked like folks these days. Far from ostensible non-conformists, as the daily papers, the very writers themselves—more shame to them—took every opportunity triumphantly to point out, they dressed like, and as often as not were bank clerks, or, marvelous paradox, engaged in advertising. It was true. He, Sigbjørn, dressed like a bank clerk himself—how else should he have courage to go into a bank? It was questionable whether poets especially, in uttermost private, any longer allowed themselves to say things like "For God's sake pity me!" Yes, they had become more like folks even than folks. And the despair in the glass case, all private correspondence carefully destroyed, yet destined to become ten thousand times more public than ever, viewed through the great glass case of art, was now transmuted into hieroglyphics, masterly compressions, obscurities to be deciphered by experts—yes, and poets—like Sigbjørn Wilderness. Wil—

And many others. Probably there was a good idea some-where, lurking among these arrant self-contradictions; pity could not keep him from using it, nor a certain sense of horror that he felt all over again that these mummified and naked cries of agony should lie thus exposed to human view in permanent incorruption, as if embalmed evermore in their separate eternal funeral parlors: separate, yet not separate, for was it not as if Poe's cry from Baltimore, in a mysterious manner, in the manner that the octet of a sonnet, say, is answered by its sestet, had already been answered, seven years before, by Keats's cry from Rome; so that according to the special reality of Sigbjørn's notebook at least, Poe's own death appeared like something extraformal, almost extraprofessional, an afterthought. Yet inerrably it was part of the same poem, the same story. "And yet the fatal prospect hangs..." "Severn, lift me up, for I am dying." "Lift them up, keep them away." Dr. Swell's Root Beer.

Good idea or not, there was no more room to implement his thoughts within this notebook (the notes on Poe and Richmond ran, through Fredericksburg, into his remarks upon Rome, the Mamertine Prison, and Keats's house, and vice versa), so Sigbjørn brought out another one from his trousers pocket.

This was a bigger notebook altogether, its paper stiffer and stronger, showing it dated from before the war, and he had brought it from America at the last minute, fearing that such might be hard to come by abroad.

In those days he had almost given up taking notes: every new notebook bought represented an impulse, soon to be overlaid, to write afresh; as a consequence he had accumulated a number of notebooks like this one at home, yet which were almost empty, which he had never taken with him on his more recent travels since the war, else a given trip would have seemed to start off with a destructive stoop, from the past, in its soul: this one had looked an exception so he'd packed it.

Just the same, he saw, it was not innocent of writing: several pages at the beginning were covered with his handwriting, so shaky and hysterical of appearance, that Sigbjørn had to put on his spectacles to read it. Seattle, he made out. July? 1939.

Seattle! Sigbjørn swallowed some grappa hastily. Lo, death hath reared himself a throne in a strange city lying alone far down within the dim west, where the good and the bad and the best and the rest, have gone to their eternal worst! The lower is the true Seattle...Sigbjørn felt he could be excused for not fully appreciating Seattle, its mountain graces, in those days. For these were not notes he had found but the draft of a letter, written in the notebook because it was that type of letter possible for him to write only in a bar. A bar? Well, one might have called it a bar. For in those days, in Seattle, in the state of Washington, they still did not sell hard liquor in bars—as, for that matter, to this day they did not, in Richmond, in the state of Virginia—which was half the gruesome and pointless point of his having been in the state of Washington. LIC-OFF-PREM, he thought. No, no, go not to Virginia Dare...Neither twist Pepso—tight-rooted!—for its poisonous bane. The letter dated—no question of his recognition of it, though whether he'd made another version and posted it he had forgotten— from absolutely the lowest ebb of those low tides of his life, a time marked by the baleful circumstance that the small legacy on which he then lived had been suddenly put in charge of a Los Angeles lawyer, to whom this letter indeed was written, his family, who considered him incompetent, having refused to have anything further to do with him, as, in effect, did the lawyer, who had sent him to a religious minded family of Buchmanite tendencies in Seattle on the understanding he be entrusted with not more than 25¢ a day.

Dear Mr. Van Bosch:
   It is, psychologically, apart from anything else, of extreme urgency that I leave Seattle and come to Los Angeles to see you. I fear a complete mental collapse else. I have cooperated far beyond what I thought was the best

of my ability here in the matter of liquor and I have also
tried to work hard, so far, alas, without selling anything.
I cannot say either that my ways have been as circum-
scribed exactly as I thought they would be by the Mackorkindales, who at least have seen my point of view on
some matters, and if they pray for guidance on the very
few occasions when they do see fit to exceed the stipu-
lated 25¢ a day, they are at least sympathetic with my
wishes to return. This may be because the elder Mackor-
kindale is literally and physically worn out following me
through Seattle, or because you have failed to supply sufficient means for my board, but this is certainly as far as
the sympathy goes. In short, they sympathize, but cannot
honestly agree; nor will they advise you I should return.
And in anything that applies to my writing—and this I
find almost the hardest to bear—I am met with the opinion that I "should put all that behind me." If they merely
claimed to be abetting yourself or my parents in this it
would be understandable, but this judgment is presented
to me independently, somewhat blasphemously in my
view—though without question they believe it—as coming directly from God, who stoops daily from on high to
inform the Mackorkindales, if not in so many words, that
as a serious writer I am lousy. Scenting some hidden truth
about this, things being what they are, I would find it discouraging enough if it stopped there, and were not
beyond that the hope held out, miraculously congruent
also with that of my parents and yourself, that I could
instead turn myself into a successful writer of advertisements. Since I cannot but feel, I repeat, and feel respectfully, that they are sincere in their beliefs, all I can say is
that in this daily rapprochement with their Almighty in
Seattle I hope some prayer that has slipped in by mistake

to let the dreadful man for heaven's sake return to Los Angeles may eventually be answered. For I find it impossible to describe my spiritual isolation in this place, nor the gloom into which I have sunk. I enjoyed of course the seaside—the Mackorkindales doubtless reported to you that the Group were having a small rally in Bellingham (I wish you could go to Bellingham one day)—but I have completely exhausted any therapeutic value in my stay. God knows I ought to know, I shall never recover in this place, isolated as I am from Primrose who, whatever you may say, I want with all my heart to make my wife. It was with the greatest of anguish that I discovered that her letters to me were being opened, finally, even having to hear lectures on her moral character by those who had read these letters, which I had thus been prevented from replying to, causing such pain to her as I cannot think of. This separation from her would be an unendurable agony, without anything else, but as things stand I can only say I would be better off in a prison, in the worst dungeon that could be imagined, than to be incarcerated in this damnable place with the highest suicide rate in the Union. Literally I am dying in this macabre hole and I appeal to you to send me, out of the money that is after all mine, enough that I may return. Surely I am not the only writer, there have been others in history whose ways have been misconstrued and who have failed...who have won through...success...publicans and sinners...I have no intention—

Sigbjørn broke off reading, and resisting an impulse to tear the letter out of the notebook, for that would loosen the pages, began meticulously to cross it out, line by line.

And now this was half done he began to be sorry. For now,

damn it, he wouldn't be able to use it. Even when he'd written it he must have thought it a bit too good for poor old Van Bosch, though one admitted that wasn't saying much. Wherever or however he could have used it. And yet, what if they had found this letter—whoever "they" were—and put it, glass-encased, in a museum among *his* relics? Not much—still, you never knew!—Well, they wouldn't do it now. Anyhow, perhaps he would remember enough of it... "I am dying, absolutely perishing." "What have I done to them?" "My dear Sir." "The worst dungeon." And many others: and *dirty stinking Degenerate Bobs was here from Boston, North End, Mass. Warp son—!*

Sigbjørn finished his fifth unregenerate grappa and suddenly gave a loud laugh, a laugh which, as if it had realized itself it should become something more respectable, turned immediately into a prolonged—though on the whole relatively pleasurable—fit of coughing....

THE FOREST PATH
TO THE SPRING

To Margerie, my wife

AT DUSK, EVERY EVENING, I USED TO GO THROUGH THE forest to the spring for water.

The way that led to the spring from our cabin was a path wandering along the bank of the inlet through snowberry and thimbleberry and shallon bushes, with the sea below you on the right, and the shingled roofs of the houses, all built down on the beach beneath round the little crescent of the bay.

Far aloft gently swayed the mastheads of the trees: pines, maples, cedars, hemlocks, alders. Much of this was second growth but some of the pines were gigantic. The forest had been logged from time to time, though the slash the loggers left was soon obliterated by the young birch and vines growing up quickly.

Beyond, going toward the spring, through the trees, range beyond celestial range, crowded the mountains, snow-peaked for most of the year. At dusk they were violet, and frequently they looked on fire, the white fire of the mist. Sometimes in the early mornings this mist looked like a huge family wash, the property of Titans, hanging out to dry between the folds of their lower hills. At other times all was chaos, and Valkyries of storm-drift drove across them out of the ever reclouding heavens.

Often all you could see in the whole world of the dawn was a huge sun with two pines silhouetted in it, like a great blaze behind a Gothic cathedral. And at night the same pines would write a Chinese poem on the moon. Wolves howled from the mountains. On the path to the spring the mountains appeared and disappeared through the trees.

And at dusk, too, came the seagulls, returning homeward down the inlet from their daily excursion to the city shores— when the wind was wailing through the trees, as if shot out of a catapult.

Ceaselessly they would come flying out of the west with their angelic wings, some making straight down the inlet, others gliding over the trees, others slower, detached, staggering, or at a dreadfully vast height, a straggling marathon of gulls.

On the left, half hidden among the trees in monolithic attitudes of privacy, like monastic cells of anchorites or saints, were the wooden backhouses of the little shacks.

This was what you could see from the path, which was not only the way to the spring but a fraction of the only footpath through the forest between the different houses of Eridanus, and when the tide was high, unless you went by boat, the only way round to your neighbors.

Not that we had any neighbors to speak of. For the greater part of the year we were often almost alone in Eridanus. My wife and myself, a Manx boatbuilder named Quaggan and occasionally some of Quaggan's sons, a Dane, Nicolai Kristbjorg, and a Channel Islander called Mauger, who had a fishing boat, *Sunrise*, were usually the sole inhabitants, and once we were quite alone the whole winter.

Yet for all their air of abandonment most of the little shacks were prettily and neatly painted and some had names too. Next to ours was Dunwoiken, and by the spring, on the right, the steps went down to Hi-Doubt, which, as if indeed in doubt, was not built upon piles sunk in the hardpan of the beach, but on log rollers, so that the whole could be floated away the easier if necessary to another place, and in this country it was not an uncommon sight to see a house, mounted on such rollers, its chimney smoking, drawn by a tug, sailing downstream.

The very last and northernmost shack of all, the one nearest the mountains, was called Four Bells, and was owned by a kindly engine driver, whose real home was in the Prairies.

On the opposite side, the right of the path, across the mile of water, ran the railway track along the other bank of the inlet, in the same way that the path ran along our bank, with more little shacks mysteriously under the embankment.

We always thought we could tell when the engine driver was bringing his train back with the prospect of a sojourn at Four Bells, where perhaps he could just make out over the water from his cab his sailing craft tugging at anchor like a little white goat, by the way he would sound his whistle gloriously in welcome. It was his fireman no doubt did so but Mr Bell whom one felt to be the artist. The sound after hallooing across the inlet to us would echo for fully a minute down the gorges and back and forth across the mountains and always the day after this happened, or that evening, smoke would be seen coming out of the chimney of Four Bells.

And on other days during the storms in the same manner thunderclaps would go crashing and echoing down the inlet and the gorges.

Four Bells was not called Four Bells because its owner was an old seafarer, as I had been, but because his name was Bell, his family was three, so they were indeed Four Bells. Mr Bell was a tall rawboned man with a red weather-beaten face and the quizzical poetical longing and responsible look appropriate to his profession, but no sooner was the smoke going, and himself tacking up and down in his catboat, than he was once more happy as the child who had dreamed of being an engine driver.

Deep-sea freighters came down the inlet silently to the timber port invisible round the point beyond Four Bells or with a great list, tilted like wheelbarrows, sailed outward bound, their engines saying:

> *Frère* Jacques
> *Frère* Jacques
> *Dor*mez-vous?
> *Dor*mez-vous?

Sometimes too, on the seaboard of the night, a ship would stand drawn, like a jeweled dagger, from the dark scabbard of the town.

Since we were in a bay *within* the inlet, the city, like the town—by which latter I mean Eridanus Port at the sawmill— the city was invisible to us, *behind* us on the path, was our feeling; almost opposite us was Port Boden, seen only as power lines ruled across the dawn or gentian and white smoke of shingle mills, and on the opposite bank too, though nearer the city, was the oil refinery. But the point southward blocked for us what would have been, beyond wide tide flats, a distant view of the cantilever bridges, skyscrapers and gantries of the city, with more great mountains that way too, and on this southerly point stood a lighthouse.

It was a whitewashed concrete structure, thin as a match, like a magic lighthouse, without a keeper, but oddly like a human being itself, standing lonely on its cairn with its ruby lamp for a head and its generator strapped to its back like a pack; wild roses in early summer blew on the bank beside it, and when the evening star came out, sure enough, it began its beneficent signaling too.

If you can imagine yourself taking a pleasure steamer down the inlet from the city some afternoon, going toward the northern mountains, first you would have left the city harbor with its great freighters from all over the world with names like *Grimanger* and ΟΙΔΙΠΟΥΣ ΤΥΡΑΝΝΟΣ and its shipyards, and then to starboard would be the railway tracks, running away from the city along the bank, through the oil-refinery station, along the foot of steep cliffs that rose to a high wooden hill, into Port Boden, and then, curving out of sight, beginning their long climb into the mountains; on the port side beneath the white peaks and the huge forestation of the mountain slopes would be tide-flats, a gravel pit, the Indian reserve, a barge company, and then the point where the wild roses were blowing and the mergansers nested, with the lighthouse itself; it was here, once around the point with the lighthouse dropping astern, that you would be cutting across our bay with our little cabins under the trees on the beach where we lived at Eridanus, and that was our path going along the bank; but you would be able to see from your steamer what we could not, right around the next point at Four Bells, into Eridanus Port—or, if this happens to be today, what was Eridanus Port and is now a real estate subsection; perhaps you would still see people waving at you before that though, and the man with the megaphone on your steamer who points out the sights would say contemptuously, "Squatters; the government's been trying to get them off for years," and that would be ourselves, my wife and me, waving to you gaily; and then you would have passed our bay and be sailing directly northwards into the snow-covered mountain peaks, past numerous enchanting uninhabited islands of tall pines, down gradually into the narrowing gorge and to the uttermost end of that marvelous region of wilderness known to the Indians as Paradise, and where you may even today, among the advertisements for dyspeptic soft poisons nailed to trees, have, for the equivalent of what used to be an English crown, a cup of chill weak tea with a little bag in it at a place called Ye Olde Totemlande Inne.

This side of Four Bells were two nameless shacks, then Hangover, Wywurk, Doo-Drop-Inn and Trickle-In, but no one lived in these houses save in summer and they were all deserted for the rest of the year.

At first, rowing past it—for the names appeared on the side of the houses facing the water—the majestic name Dunwoiken had struck my imagination and I thought it must have been built by some exiled Scotsman, remembering his former estate, fallen on evil days, yet living amidst scenery that reminded him of the mountains and lochs of home. But that was before I understood its name was cousin-german to Wywurk and that both words were, in a manner of speaking, jokes. Dunwoiken had been built by four firemen—that is to say city firemen, not ship's firemen, as I had been—but immediately they built it they lost interest and never came back to the beach, though they must have rented or sold it, for over the course of years people came and went there.

Having once seen the joke about some of these names—and intended timbre of pronunciation, more sinister than at first met the eye—they began to irritate me, especially Wywurk. But apart from the fact that Lawrence wrote *Kangaroo* in a house called Wyewurk in Australia (and he was more amused than irritated), though I did not know this at the time, the irritation itself really springs I now think from ignorance, or snobbery. And in these days when streets and houses are mere soulless numbers is it not a survival of some instinct of unique identity in regard to one's home, some striving with ironic humor and self-criticism of this very estate of uniformity, for identity itself, in however bad taste. And even were it not, were they any more pretentious or unimaginative than the lordly sources they parodied? Is Inglewood a more imaginative name than Dunwoiken? Is Chequers? Or The White House? Is Maximilian's Miramar to be preferred to Maple View? And is Wuthering Heights not merely weathered out of its cuteness? But irritate me they did then, and most especially Wywurk. The holophrastic brilliance of this particular name, and more obvious sympathetic content, never failed to elicit comment from the richer passersby in motorboats, who, having to shout in order to make themselves heard on board above the engine, could be very well overheard on shore. But in later years, when we lived nearer to it, I soon learned to be grateful for the distraction this name provided.

For the sea-borne comments, carrying to our ears and which were invariably hurtful or cruel and cut us to the heart before the motorboats reached Wywurk, never failed to be appreciative on their passing Wywurk itself. First there was the brilliance of the pun to be discussed as it dawned upon them, then its philosophic content to be disputed among the boat's occupants, as a consequence of which they would disappear round the northward point in that mood of easy tolerance that comes only to the superior reader who has suddenly understood the content of an obscure poem.

Hangover—no doubt simply a statement of fact commemorating some cherished and even forgotten or perhaps permanently catastrophic state of mind, for we never saw anyone enter or leave this house and have not till this day—rarely inspired more than a passing chuckle. While Four Bells, whose name had been chosen with love, rarely excited comment either.

Eventually I realized that the hamlet was really two hamlets, that it was divided almost precisely into the houses with names, and the houses without names, though these two hamlets, like interpenetrating dimensions, were in the same place, and there was yet another town, or sort of town, by the sawmill round the northward point sharing our name Eridanus, as did the inlet itself.

The houses with names—with the exception of Four Bells, for Mr Bell's sojourns were any season—Hangover, Wywurk, Hi-Doubt and so on, belonged to people who just came to Eridanus for the week-end in summer, or for a summer holiday of a week or two. They were electricians, loggers, blacksmiths, mostly town-dwellers earning good salaries but not sufficient to afford summer houses at one of the settlements further up the inlet where land could be bought if, which was a point indeed, they would have cared to buy it; they built their little shacks here because it was government land and the Harbor Board, upon whom I often felt must have sat God Himself, did not object. Most of these summer people had children, most of them liked to fish for sport, and to do what they felt they were supposed to do on a summer holiday. When they came most of them had a wonderful time doing these things and then they went away again—I regret to say much to the relief of ourselves and the sea-birds—in some few cases no doubt to turn into the very sort of people who later would make cruel remarks, as from the superior vantage of their motorboats they observed the lowly homes of the squatters who still actually lived in such places.

The others, who lived for the most part in the houses without names, were all, with one exception, deep-sea fishermen who had been here many many years before the summer people came, and who had their houses here by some kind of "foreshore rights" allowed to fishermen. The exception was the Manx boatbuilder whose boat shed was large as a small church and built of hand-split cedar shakes, and whose floating pier bisected the bay and constituted its own general landing, the only thing perhaps that made the little impromptu port an entity, and he seemed to be the father or grandfather of most of the other fishermen, so that, in the way of Celts, it was a little like a big family the entrance to which, for an outsider, I was to find by no means easy.

Sometimes when it was stormy, in the later days, we used to sit in his shack strewn with a litter-like neatness, with bradawls and hacksaws, frows and nailsets and driftbolts, and drink tea, or when we had any, whisky, and sing the old Manx fishermen's hymn while the tempest howled across the inlet and the water, scarcely less loud, rushed with a mighty enthusiasm down his hemlock flume.

Because we were drinking tea or whisky inside while his sons, the fishermen, were outside—and moreover the strange life we were leading had made my wife and me by this time have an aversion even to fishing—now and then we sang it a bit ironically. Nonetheless in our way we must have meant what we sang. I had a guitar salved, not from my days as a jazz musician, but an older one from my days as a ship's fireman, my wife had a beautiful voice, and both the old man and I had not bad bass voices.

There is no hymn like this great hymn sung to the tune of Peel Castle with its booming minor chords in which sounds all the savagery of the sea yet whose words of supplication make less an appeal to, than a poem of God's mercy:

> Hear us, O Lord, from heaven Thy dwelling place,
> Like them of old in vain we toil all night,
> Unless with us Thou go who art the Light,
> Come then, O Lord, that we may see Thy face.
>
> Thou, Lord, dost rule the raging of the sea
> When loud the storm and furious is the gale,
> Strong is Thine arm, our little barks are frail,
> Send us Thy help, remember Galilee . . .

When the wild roses began to blow on the point by the light-house in June, and the mergansers swam in and out of the rocks with their little ducklings perched on their backs, these fisher-men went away, sometimes singly, sometimes in pairs, some-times three or four boats joined together, like proud white giraffes their newly painted fishing boats with their tall gear would be seen going round the point.

They went to sea, and some of them never returned, and as they went to sea, so Eridanus was taken over by the summer people.

Then on Labor Day, as if swept away by the great wash of the returning fishermen's craft wheeling across the bay and breaking all along the length of the beach, reaching within the bay at last with the successive thunder of rollers, the summer people would depart, back to the city, and the fishermen, their boats singly or in pairs, would have come home again.

They were only a bare half-dozen fishermen all told who lived in Eridanus so that one stormy equinox, when Kristbjorg, who had been sailing alone up to Alaska, in his sturdy snub-nosed old tub painted green, to differentiate it from the others, had still not returned, he left a gap.

Quaggan, my wife, and myself, were repairing Quaggan's iron stove with a mixture of wood ashes, asbestos and salt, and at the same time singing the fishermen's hymn, when Krist-bjorg, a bald strong wide but childish-faced Dane, who lived as he fished absolutely alone too, walked right in. Soon we were all singing something very different—a Danish song of his, his translation of which may be written as follows:

> It blew a storm in the red-light district
> It was blowing so hard that not a sailor
> Was blown off the sea but a pimp was blown
> Off the street. It blew through the windows,

And it rained through the roof—
But the gang chipped in and bought a pint.
And what is better
When a bunch of soaks are together—
Even when the roof is leaking?

Kristbjorg always came round to say good-by with solemnity before he sailed for the summer, as if for the last time. But we found that he sometimes liked to delay his return beyond the period necessary so that he would be missed by us, and missed indeed he was.

"We were anxious about you, Nicolai, we thought you were never going to get back in this weather."

But it would turn out that he had been back and had been lurking in the city for a week.

"... In the city got a little exercise. Been sitting humped up in the old boat so long. I never saw a street flusher. They just letting the old grime go. The streetcars are getting so humpy and dumpy!—I ran into a couple of bottles of rye.... I thought a little walking would speed the old ticker...."

Quaggan loved all kinds of wood and did not care much to fish (save locally, off the end of his pier, just before he went visiting his grandchildren). "Hemlock is very sweet that way," he would say tenderly of his doughty flume that had survived a quarter of a century without decay.

There was another lonely man from the Yorkshire moors, who lived quite alone down beyond the lighthouse, and though he seldom came up to our little bay we saw him, from time to time, when we walked down to the point. It was his joy to make sure that the automatic lighthouse was working, he told us, and in fact he would start to talk, as if half to himself, as soon as he saw us approaching.

"The heagles, how they fly in great circles! Nature is one of the most beautiful things I ever saw in my life. Have you seen the heagle yesterday?"

"Yes, we did, Sam—"

"Why the heagle went round to get his bearings, to look over the country. Two miles wide, hin great circles...Pretty soon you'll see crabs under these stones, and then it will be spring. They're some crabs in spring no bigger than a fly. Now have you ever seen how an elephant was constroocted? And where did those old Romans get them shields but from the rooster's wings?"

"Roosters, Sam?"

"Aye. And take in the desert now—the Sahara—where camels stamp with hooves like great spittoons upside down. One day they build a railroad—" he would lean against his lighthouse, nodding his head, "—but *hin*sects heat up all the wooden ties. Aye. So now they make the ties out of metal shaped like camels' hooves....Nature is one of the most beautiful...And soon the birds, and pretty soon the crabs will bring the spring, my dearies, and the deer swimming right across the bay with their hantlers, beautiful, sticking up like branches on a floating tree, swimming, swimming across to this here lighthouse, right here, in spring....Then you'll see dragonflies like flying machines back-pedaling...."

The summer people rarely saw the fearful depredations their houses had to suffer in the winter, nor knew, during those hard months, what it was like to live in them. Perhaps they wondered why their summer homes had not been swept away by the storms they had heard shrieking and whipping against their city windows, the timbers they could imagine striking the piles and foundations of their shacks, the tempest, always the worst since 1866, that they read about in the city paper called the *Sun*, bought at a time of day when the real sun had gone down without, for that matter, sometimes ever having come up: the day after that they might motor out, leaving their cars—for unlike us they had cars—up on the road, and shake their heads to find their houses still there. How well we built, they would say. It was true. But the real reason was that there was that about Eridanus, existing by grace of God and without police or fire or other civic protection, that made its few inhabitants thoughtful. And a spirit would have seen that the fishermen during the winter had protected those summer houses as their own, but by the time summer arrived the fishermen had gone, not asking or expecting thanks. And while the fishermen were away it is also true that the summer people would not readily see damage happen to a fisherman's house, if they had lived long enough on the beach to think about it, that was, or happened to have been fishermen themselves, as was sometimes the case, or were old people.

This was Eridanus, and the wrecked steamer of the defunct Astra line that gave it its name lay round the point beyond the lighthouse, where, its engines failing, it had been driven ashore in a wild foehn wind decades ago, carrying a cargo of cherries-in-brine, wine, and old marble from Portugal.

Gulls slept like doves on its samson posts where grasses were blowing abaft the dead galley, and in early spring pecked their old feathers off to make room for their new shiny plumage like fresh white paint. Swallows and goldfinches swept in and out of the dead fiddley. A spare propeller blade upright against the break of the poop had never been removed. Down below lever weight and fulcrum slept in an eternity of stillness. Grass grew too from the downfallen crosstrees, and in the dead winches wildflowers had taken root—wildflowers, spring beauties and death camass with its creamy blooms. And on the stern, seeming to comment on my own source, for I too had been born in that terrible city whose main street is the ocean, could still be almost made out the ghost of the words: *Eridanus*, Liverpool—

We poor folk were also Eridanus, a condemned community, perpetually under the shadow of eviction. And like Eridanus itself, in its eternal flux and flow, was the inlet. For in the heavens at night, as my wife first taught me, dark and wandering beneath blazing Orion, flowed the starry constellation Eridanus, known both as the River of Death and the River of Life, and placed there by Jupiter in remembrance of Phaethon, who once had the splendid illusion that he could guide the fiery steeds of the sun as well as his father Phoebus.

Legend merely states that Jupiter, sensing the danger to the world, shot a thunderbolt which, striking Phaethon, hurled him, his hair on fire, into the River Po, then that, in addition to creating the constellation in Phaethon's honor, in pity he changed Phaethon's sisters into poplar trees that they might always be near and protect their brother. But that he went to all this trouble suggests that he, even as Phoebus, was impressed by the attempt, and must have given the whole matter some thought. Recently our local paper, showing a surprisingly sudden interest in classical mythology, has claimed to see something insulting in the name of our town of a political, even an international nature, or as denoting foreign influences, as a result of which there has been some agitation, on the part of some distant ratepayers, with I know not what motives, to change its name to Shellvue. And undoubtedly the view in that specified direction is very fine, with the red votive candle of the burning oil wastes flickering ceaselessly all night before the gleaming open cathedral of the oil refinery—

II

It was on Labor Day, years ago at the beginning of the war, just after we had been married, and thinking it would be both our honeymoon and our first and last summer holiday together, that my wife and I, strangers from the cities, myself almost from the underworld, came to live in Eridanus. But we did not see it at all then as I have described it now.

The beach was crowded, and when we first came down to it from the road, after having taken the bus from the city, and emerged on it from the cool green benison of the forest, it was as if we had suddenly stumbled upon a hidden, but noisy popular resort. Yet it must have been the garishness and strangeness of daylight and the sun itself which gave it to me, long used to the night and sleeping fitfully during these daylight hours, the quality of a nightmare.

It was a scorching hot afternoon and seven Scots were sitting inside the tiny cabin we'd been told we might rent for a small sum by the week, with the woodstove going full blast, and the windows shut, cackling, and finishing, as their last holiday meal, some sort of steaming mutton broth.

Outside the mountains were covered with heat haze. The tide was out—so far out it did not occur to me it would ever come in—the foreshore, along the whole length of which people were digging for clams, was stony, or covered with huge barnacled rocks, that made me fear for my young wife's feet, for which, since they were so small and delicate, I had a special feeling of protection. Further down by the water's edge the beach was strewn with seaweed and detritus and didn't even look like a possible place to swim.

Nor was anybody in swimming, though children shouted and squealed, paddling in the mud, among the tide-flats, from which arose the most impressive and unusual stink I ever smelt in my life. This archetypical malodor on investigation proved partly to emanate from the inlet itself, which was sleeked as far as the eye could reach with an oil slick I quickly deduced to be the work of an oil tanker lying benignly at the wharf of the refinery I have mentioned opposite the lighthouse, so that now it looked as though one certainly could never swim at all; we might as well have come to the Persian Gulf. And to add to the heat, which further suggested the Persian Gulf, as we crunched thoughtfully over the barnacles and exoskeletons of crabs, or avoiding the deposits of tar or creosote, sank up to our ankles instead in slippery reeking slime, or splashed into pools themselves preened with peacock feathers of oil, came, from high up the beach, a blast of hot breath and ashes from a dozen clambakes, round the fires of which, it seemed to us, hundreds of people were howling and singing in a dozen languages.

As human beings we loved no doubt to see people enjoying themselves, but as a honeymoon couple seeking privacy we felt increasingly we had come to the wrong place, all the more so since it began to remind me of arriving in some fifth-rate seaside resort for a one-night stand.

That is how selfish lovers are, without an idea in their heads for anyone save themselves. As against this the worthy Scot from whom we rented the cabin, though poor himself and clearly struggling with that thrift in his own nature which so long supposed to be traditional had now become a fact, was extremely generous. He saw at once that we had come because it was all we could afford and before he and his fellow Scots had departed the shack was ours for the month at a rental of twelve dollars, he having lowered this from fifteen himself.

"But do ye ken boots, young man," he asked sharply.

"Boots?"

"Aye, lad, I'm fussy about me boot."

So the Scotsman's boat was generously thrown in. I had once been a ship's engineer, I explained, not caring to say ship's fireman.

But could you rent Paradise at twelve dollars a month? was our thought, the next morning, as from the porch of the shack, gazing on the scene of absolute emptiness and solitude, we watched the sunrise bringing the distant power lines across the inlet at Port Boden into relief, the sun sliding up behind the mountain pines, like that blaze behind the pinnacles of a Gothic cathedral, hearing too, from somewhere, the thrilling diatonic notes of a foghorn in the mist, as if some great symphony had just begun its opening chords.

From the oil company's wharf just visible down the inlet the oil tanker had vanished, and with it the oil slick; the tide was high and cold and deep and we swam, diving straight off the porch, scattering into dividing echelons a school of minnows. And when we came up, turning round, we saw the pines and alders of our forest high above us. To us lovers the beach emptied of its cheery crowd seemed the opposite of melancholy. We turned again and there were the mountains. After that we swam sometimes three and four times a day.

We rowed the Scotsman's boat down the inlet and picnicked on an island, uninhabited, with a deep cover where we drew up in the boat, among wild asters and goldenrod and pearly ever-lasting. The further reaches of the inlet, under the soaring snow-capped mountains, were now in September a deserted heaven for ourselves alone. We could row all day and once beyond Eridanus Port scarcely see another boat. One day later we even rowed to the other side of the inlet, across to the rail-way. This was partly because right under the railway embank-ment on the opposite side were dimly to be discerned, as I said, some more little shacks, scattered and smoke-blackened, but above which sometimes a strip of the metals themselves at noontide would seem to be rippling in motion with the inlet sparkling just below; still, we used to wonder how ever people could live so close to the noise of trains. Now our curiosity would be satisfied. The row over toward the railway, that had promised to be anything but picturesque, grew more beautiful by the minute as we drew out of our own bay. For these peo-ple—a few old pioneers and retired prospectors, maybe a hand-

ful of railroadmen and their wives who didn't mind the noise
—poor like ourselves but whom we had patronized in our
minds for being yet poorer, were richer in that they could see
round the point of the inlet and right down it, could see beyond
the timber port of Eridanus, the very highest mountains of all,
the Rocky Mountains themselves, that were for us hidden by the
trees of our forest, though both of us saw range beyond range
of the Cascades—the great Cordilleras that ribbed the continent from Alaska to Cape Horn—and of which Mount Hood
was no less a part than Popocatepetl. Yes, fine though our view
was, they had a finer, for they saw the mountains to the south
and west too, the peaks beneath which we lived, yet could not
see at all. As we rowed along the shore in the warm late afternoon light these great peaks were reflected in and shadowed
the flowing water, and seemed to move along with us, so that
my wife spoke of Wordsworth's famous peak, that strode after
him; this was something similar, she said, though very different, because there was nothing threatening about this apparent
movement; these peaks that followed us were, rather, guard-
ians. Many times were we to see this phenomenon, as of a
whole mountainside or ridge of pines detaching themselves and
moving as we rowed, but never did it, or they, seem "after" us:
it seemed a reminder of duality, of opposing motions born of
the motion of the earth, a symbol even while an illusion, of
nature's intolerance of inertia. When we finally rowed back the
sunset light was falling on the tiered aluminium retorts of the
oil refinery, so that it looked to us, so infatuated were we
(though this was before the time I would have thought it
looked like an open cathedral at night, for the flickering candle
of oil waste wasn't there), like a strange and beautiful musical
instrument.

But still we did not see Eridanus as a place to live. The war
was on, many of the ships that passed and sent the commotion

of their washes over the beach were cargoed with obscenities toward death and once I had found myself saying to my wife:

"It's a hell of a time to live. There can't be any of this non-sense about love in a cottage."

I was sorry I'd spoken like that for I seemed to see a trembling hope die out of her face, and I took her in my arms. But I had not intended to be cruel; nor was she a sentimentalist, and anyhow we hadn't got a cottage, nor much hope of having one in the foreseeable future. The shadow of the war was over everything. And while people were dying in it, it was hard to be really happy within oneself. It was hard to know what was happy, what was good. Were we happy, good? Or, being happy at such a time, what could one do with one's happiness?

One day when we were out rowing we came across a sunken canoe, a derelict, floating just beneath the surface in deep water so clear we made out its name: *Intermezzo*.

We thought it might have been sunk on purpose, perhaps by two other lovers, and it was this that kept us from salving it. And we reflected, yes, that was perhaps all our lives here would be, an intermezzo. Indeed we had not asked for, or expected, more than a honeymoon. And we wondered where those other lovers were now.

The war? Had the war separated them? And would the war separate us? Guilt and fear came over me and anxiety for my wife, and I began to row back gloomily and in silence, the calm sunlit peace of the inlet turned for me into the banks of some river of the dead, for was not Eridanus also the Styx?

Before I had married, and after I left the sea, I had been a jazz musician, but my health had been ruined by late hours and one-night stands all over the hemisphere. Now I had given up this life for the sake of our marriage and was making a new one—a hard thing for a jazz musician when he loves jazz as much as I.

At the beginning of the war I had volunteered. I had been rejected, but now, with my new life, my health was beginning vastly to improve.

Even now, as I rowed, sluggishly and unhappily though I was pulling, I could feel the improvement. Little by little self-discipline, a sense of humor and our happy life together were wreaking a miracle. Was this effort toward life and health merely to be a probationship for death? Nonetheless it was a matter of simple honor to attempt to fit myself for the slaughter if humanly possible, and it was as much this as for my marriage that I had given up my old life of night clubs, and incidentally nearly my only means of making a reasonable living, though I had saved enough for us to live on for a year and possessed a small income from royalties on records, for a few of which I was part composer.

What if we should continue to live here? The idea did not strike me seriously, or from any considered depths of my mind, merely flickered across my horizon like one of those sourceless evanescent searchlight beams that used occasionally to flash over the mountains from the vague direction of the city, "where they were probably opening a grocery store," as my wife laconically used to observe. Cheap it would certainly be. But then honeymoons were surely not events that by their nature were supposed to continue. And far worse than the notion of "intermezzo" was that, on one plane, it would be like living on the very windrow of the world, as that world had not hesitated to remind us.

And while a summer holiday, even a protracted summer holiday, was one thing, how hard it would be to actually live here, for my wife to cope with the old cookstove, lack of plumbing, oil lamps, no ordinary comforts of any kind in cold weather. Ah yes, it would be too hard for her, even with my help (for though I had a sort of slow-witted strength, I did not have the coordinated handiness and practicality usually native to the sailor). It might be fun for a week, even a month, but to live here meant accepting the terms of the most abject poverty, would be almost tantamount, I thought, to renouncing the world altogether, and when I reflected in what dead earnest we would be playing the game in winter, I simply laughed: of course it was out of the question.

I backed water with my oars, turning the boat round. High up the alders and the pines swayed against the sky. The house stood prettily on its simple lines. But below the house, underneath it, on the beach, were its foundations of piles and wooden stringers and its interlaced tracery of cross-braces, like the frozen still machinery between the two paddleboxes of a paddlesteamer.

Or it was like a cage, as I rowed nearer, where one-by-twos, through which I saw the machinery, were nailed vertically to the stringers of the front porch, acting, one might explain, remotely like a train's cowcatcher, to prevent timbers at flood tide from drifting beneath the house and undermining the foundations.

Or beneath, it was like a strange huge cage where some amphibious animal might have lived, there on the beach, when often at low tide, resetting a cross-brace, amidst the seaweed smells, I felt as if I were down in the first slime, but in which work I delighted as I delighted in the simplicity of the stresses of the foundations I was looking at, that unlike most foundations were of course above ground, as in the most primitive of all houses.

It was simple and primitive. But what complexity must there have been in the thing itself, to withstand the elemental forces it had to withstand? A ton of driftwood, launched with all the force of an incoming high tide with an equinoctial gale behind it, the house would thus withstand, and turn aside harmlessly.

And suddenly, as I helped my wife out and tied up the boat, I was overwhelmed with a kind of love. Standing there, in defiance of eternity, and yet as if in humble answer to it, with their weathered sidings as much a part of the natural surroundings as a Shinto temple is of the Japanese landscape, why had these shacks come to represent something to me of an indefinable goodness, even a kind of greatness? And some shadow of the truth that was later to come to me, seemed to steal over my soul, the feeling of something that man had lost, of which these shacks and cabins, brave against the elements, but at the mercy of the destroyer, were the helpless yet stalwart symbol, of man's hunger and need for beauty, for the stars and the sunrise.

First we had decided to stay only till the end of September. But the summer seemed just beginning and by the middle of October we were still there, and still swimming every day. By the end of October the glorious Indian summer was still golden and by the middle of November we had decided to stay the winter. Ah, what a life of happiness had now opened before us! The first frosts came, and there was silver driftwood on the beach, and when it grew too cold to swim we took walks through the forest where the ice crystals crackled like rock candy under our feet. And then came the season of fogs, and sometimes the fog froze on the trees and the forest became a crystal forest. And at night, when we opened the window, from the lamps within our shadows were projected out to sea, on the fog, against the night, and sometimes they were huge, menacing. One night, coming across the porch from the woodshed with a lantern in one hand and a load of wood under the other arm, I saw my shadow, gigantic, the logs of wood as big as a coffin, and this shadow seemed for a moment the glowering embodiment of all that threatened us; yes, even a projection of that dark chaotic side of myself, my ferocious destructive ignorance.

And about this time we began to reflect with wonder: this is our first home.

"Moonrise of the dying moon."

"Sunrise of the dying moon, in a green sky."

"White frost on the porch and all the roofs...I wonder if it's killed poor Mr McNab's nasturtiums. It's the first heavy frost of the year. And the first clear sunrise in a month."

"There's a little flotilla of golden eyes under the window."

"The tide is high."

"My poor seagulls, they're hungry. How cold your feet must be down there, in that icy water. The cat ate all your bones—I found them on the floor—the wretch. The bones I saved from the stew last night."

"There's a raven sitting on the top of the big cedar, and a fine, foul, fearsome creature he is too!"

"Look—now! The sunrise."

"Like a bonfire."

"Like a burning cathedral."

"I must wash the windows."

"Part of what makes this sunrise so wonderful isn't just pure nature. It's the smoke from those wretched factories at Port Boden."

"The sunrise does things to these mists."

"I must put out some breakfast for the cat. He'll come in very hungry from his dawn prowl."

"There goes a cormorant."

"There goes a great loon."

"The frost sparkles like diamond dust."

"In a few minutes now it will melt."

So each morning, before the really cold days when I got up myself, I would be awakened by my wife's comments while lighting the fire and making the coffee, as if now upon a continual sunrise of our life, a continual awakening. And it seemed to me that until I knew her I had lived my whole life in darkness.

III

Now the great tides and currents in their flux and flow fascinated us. It was not merely because of the exigencies of our boat, which was not our property, which we could not anchor, and which it was not always possible to keep on a float, that it was necessary to watch them. In the great high tides of winter, with the Pacific almost level with our floor, the house itself could be in jeopardy, as I have said, from the huge timbers or uprooted trees racing downstream.

And I learned too that a tide which to all appearances is coming in may be doing so only on the surface, that beneath it is already going out.

Quaggan, the Manx boatbuilder whom we had now met, told us, rocking under our windows in his boat one warmer evening when the settlement was like a minuscule Genoa or Venice in a dream, of the Manx belief that at the new moon the birds on the ninth wave out from the shore are the souls of the dead.

Nothing is more irritating and sorrowful to a man who has followed the sea than the sound of the ocean pounding mercilessly and stupidly on a beach. But here in the inlet there was neither sea nor river, but something compounded of both, in eternal movement, and eternal flux and change, as mysterious and multiform in its motion and being, and in the mind as the mind flowed with it, as was that other Eridanus, the constellation in the heavens, the starry river in the sky, whose source only was visible to us, and visible reflected in the inlet too on still nights with a high brimming tide, before it curved away behind the beautiful oil refinery round the Scepter of Brandenburg and into the Southern Hemisphere. Or, at such a time of stillness, at the brief period of high tide before the ebb, it was like what I have learned the Chinese call the Tao, that, they say, came into existence before Heaven and Earth, something so still, so changeless, and yet reaching everywhere, and in no danger of being exhausted: like "that which is so still and yet passes on in constant flow, and in passing on, becomes remote, and having become remote, returns."

Never was the unfortunate aspect of the beach on that first day exactly to repeat itself. If oil sometimes appeared on the waters it was soon gone, and the oil itself was oddly pretty, but in fact the discharge of oil by tankers into the harbor reaches was about that time put a stop to by law. But when the law was broken and the oil slicks appeared it was miraculous with what swiftness the flowing inlet cleansed itself. It was the cleanest, the coldest, freshest, most invigoratingly beautiful water I have ever swum in, and when they spoke of damming the inlet, when a British brewery interest later talked of turning the whole place into a stagnant fresh water basin, perverting even those pure sources and cutting it off from the cleansing sea altogether, it was as if for a moment the sources of my own life trembled and agonized and dried up within me. Tides as low as those on that first day, also, were of course exceptional. And at low tide the mud flats themselves were interesting, seething with every imaginable kind of strange life. Tiny slender pale turquoise starfish, fat violet ones, and vermilion sunstars with twenty pointed arms like children's paintings of the sun; barnacles kicking food into their mouths, polyps and sea-anemones, sea-cucumbers two feet long like orange dragons with spikes and horns and antennae, lone strange wasps hunting among the cockles, devilfish whose amours sound like crackling machine-gun fire, and kelp, with long brown satin streamers, "when they put their heads up and shake them, that means the tide is slackening," Quaggan told us. Round the point northwards beyond the seaport were indeed miles of muddy flats at the lowest tides with old pilings like drunken giants bracing each other up, as if staggering homeward evermore from some titanic tavern in the mountains.

At night, sometimes all seemed still, at rest on the beach and the flats, wrapped in a quietude of reflection. Even the barnacles slept, we felt. But we found we had never made a greater mistake. It is only at night that this great world of the windrow and tide-flats really wakes up. We discovered that there were little shellfish called Chinese Hats that only walked at night, so that now when night fell, we had a standing joke, and would turn to one another laughing to say in sepulchral tones:

"It is night, and the Chinese Hats are on the move!"

And equally the rocks on the beach that at first had seemed only to threaten my wife's tiny feet became a factor of delight. The difficulty of walking over them at half tide down to swim was simply overcome by wearing old tennis shoes. And in the morning when one got up to make the coffee, with the sun blazing through the windows so that it was like standing in the middle of a diamond—or looking out through the windows into the inlet where in the distance the struggling sunlight turned a patch of black water into boiling diamonds—I began to see these intermediate rocks as with Quaggan's eyes, the eyes of a Celt, as presences themselves, standing round like Renan's immutable witnesses that have no death, each bearing the name of a divinity.

And of course we got much of our wood from the beach, both for making repairs round about the place and for firewood. It was on the beach we found one day the ladder that was later to be so useful to us and that we had seen floating half awash. And it was also on the beach that I found the old cannister that we cleaned and that in the end I used to take each evening to the spring for water.

The Scot had left us two small rain barrels for rain water, but long before I found the cannister drinking water had begun to constitute one of our most serious problems. On the highway beyond the forest was a general store and garage with a water tap next to the petrol pump and it was in every way possible, though tiresome, to take a bucket and obtain water from this source and bring it down through the forest, and most of the summer people would do just this. But we discovered that where possible the real beach dwellers avoided doing so, though this was largely a point of honor, for the storekeeper, a good man, did not mind, and the beach people provided him a major source of revenue. But he paid taxes and we did not, and also the rate-payers in the district were in the habit of using the slightest excuse to make a public issue of the existence of the "wretched squatters" at all upon the beach, whose houses, "like malignant sea-growths should be put to the torch"—as one city newspaper malignantly phrased it. What use saying to such as they: "Love had he found in huts where poor men lie." For these reasons the permanent residents, or even the summer people who had been there for some time, preferred to obtain their water from a natural spring or source. Some had sunk wells, others, like Quaggan, had flumes which conducted water down from the mountain streams flowing through the forest, but we did not find that out until afterwards, for at this time we had scarcely met those who were to become our neighbors and friends, and a good quarter of a mile separated us from each of our two nearest ones, from Quaggan to the north, and Mauger to the south. The Scotsman had left us a small barrel filled with fresh water and told us that he always replenished this by rowing to a spring about half a mile away, round the point with the lighthouse, and beyond the wharf of the barge company. So every few days I would load the barrel and a bucket into the boat and my wife and I rowed there with them. This stream ran all the year round but was so shallow you couldn't scoop your bucket into it. You had to fill it where a waterfall, about a foot high, poured through rocks, where you could put your bucket under.

The beach here, in a no man's land between the barge company and the Indian reserve, was very flat and low, not sandy, but covered with a deep slimy ooze and growths of seaweed: when the tide was low the boat was grounded about a hundred feet from the waterfall on the shore, and you had to wrestle the barrel back from the creek over the ooze and through shallow water, sinking in the muck. On the other hand at high tide the sea came right up over the waterfall covering it completely, though afterwards it was pure again. So that you had to time it exactly at half tide when you could come in fairly close with your boat or it was an all but impossible task. Even at best it is difficult for me now to see how we got so much fun out of that particular chore. But perhaps it just seems like fun now because of the memory of our despair on the day when we found we couldn't go there any more; for the moment it seemed that on this account we would really have to leave Eridanus altogether.

It was by now late in November, and less than a month to the winter solstice, and we were still lingering on; the sparkling morning frosts, the blue and gold noons and evening fogs of October, had turned suddenly into dark or stormy sunrises, with sullen clouds driving through the mountains before the north wind. One morning, in order to take advantage of the half tide, I, having taken over from my wife, rose well before sunrise to make the coffee. Jupiter had been burning fiercely and when I rose, though it was eight-fifteen, the waning moon was still bright. By the time I'd brought my wife her coffee there was a dawn like china, or porcelain. Earlier there had

been a black mackerel sky with corrugated rose. Always my
wife loved me to describe these things to her, even if inaccu-
rately, as was more often the case, as she would describe them
to me when she got up first in warmer days.

But apparently I was wrong about the sunrise, as I had been
wrong about the tide's incoming, because later, toward ten
o'clock, we were still drinking coffee and still waiting for the
sun to come up and the tide to come in. It had become a calm,
rather mild day with the water like a dark mirror and the sky
like a wet dish clout. A heron standing motionless on a stone by
the point looked unnaturally tall, and for a moment we remembered we had seen men working out there with lanterns the
other night: perhaps the heron was some kind of new buoy. But
then this tall buoy moved slightly, mantling itself in condor
wings, then stood motionless as before.

All this time, though, the sun actually had been rising, had,
for other people beyond the hill across the water, already risen.
I say the hill, for no longer as in September did the sun rise in
the east, over the sea, over Port Boden, with the power lines
ruled across it, or in the northeast where the mountains were,
but ever more toward the south, behind this wooded hill above
the railroad tracks.

But now suddenly an extraordinary thing happened. Far
south of the power lines, directly above the invisible railway,
above where the blackened shacks under the embankment
were, the sun struggled up, the only live thing in a gray waste,
or rather it had abruptly appeared, the sun, as a tiny circle with
five trees in it, grouped round its lower rim like church spires in
a teacup. There was, if you shut your eyes and opened them
wide again hard, no glare, only this platinum circle of sun with
the trees in it, and no other trees to be seen for fog, and then
clouds minutely drawn over the top, the sun taking in more

trees along the hilltop as it slanted up. Then for a moment the sun became suffused, then it looked like a skull, the back of a skull. We shut our eyes and opened them again and there was the sun, a tiny little sun, framed in one of the window panes, like a miniature, unreal, with these trees in it, though no other trees were to be seen.

We took the boat and rowed to the creek and found a new notice:

PRIVATE PROPERTY KEEP OFF

But we decided to fill the barrel anyhow this last time. Someone came running down the slope gesticulating angrily and in my haste to get the boat away, which was hard aground with the increased weight of the barrel, one of its hoops became loosened, and by the time we'd got home not only was the barrel nearly empty but we had nearly sunk the Scotsman's boat too. My wife was crying and it was now raining and I was angry; it was wartime and we could scarcely buy another barrel, and in the quarrel—one of our very first—which ensued, we had almost decided to leave for good when I caught sight of the cannister on the beach left by the receding tide. As I examined it the sun came half out, casting a pale silver light while the rain was still falling in the inlet and my wife was so entranced by the beauty of this that she forgot all the harsh things that had been said and began to explain about the raindrops to me, exactly as if I were a child, while I listened, moved, and innocently as if I had never seen such a thing before, and indeed it seemed I never had.

"You see, my true love, each is interlocked with other circles falling about it," she said. "Some are larger circles, expanding widely and engulfing others, some are weaker smaller circles that only seem to last a short while.... The rain itself is water from the sea, raised to heaven by the sun, transformed into clouds and falling again into the sea."

Did I know this? I suppose so, something like it. But that the sea itself in turn was born of rain I hadn't known. Yet what she said was uttered with such inexpressible wonder I repeat that, watching, and listening to her, it was like the first time I'd witnessed the common occurrence of rain falling into the sea.

So terrible and foreign to the earth has this world become that a child may be born into its Liverpools and never find a single person any longer who will think it worth pointing out to him the simple beauty of a thing like that. Who can be surprised that the very elements, harnessed only for the earth's ruination and man's greed, should turn against man himself?

Meantime the sun was trying to burst forth again and we knew that its showing itself as a skull had been a pose. As if it were the beam from that lighthouse at Cape Kao that they say can be seen seventy-six miles away, so we saw spring. And that I think was when we really decided to stay.

As for the cannister it was of a kind that I had seen on shipboard used in the bosun's or engineer's mess as a filter in those days when I had been a fireman and I surmised that it had been thrown overboard from an English ship. Whether it was my imagination or not, it smelled of lime juice. Such filters are intended for water but it used to be common practice to put lime juice in them. Now the lime juice that is standard for the crew on English ships is so strong undiluted that they used to use it for scrubbing the mess tables white—a few drops in a bucket of water would do the trick—but on metal it can have a corrosive as well as a cleansing effect and it struck me that some green mess boy had possibly put too much lime juice in this filter by mistake, or with insufficient dilution, the bosun had come off duty thirsty, drawn himself a draught of nice quenching rust, torn the filter off the wall, threatened to crown the unfortunate mess boy with it, and then thrown it overboard. Such was the little sea story I made up for my wife about it as I set about converting it into a good clean water container for ourselves.

Now we had a cannister but still no honorable place to get water. The same day we met Kristbjorg on the path.

"—and there's your wand," he said.

"What?"

"Water, Missus."

It was the spring. Wand, or a word like it, though not pronounced the way it looks, was apparently either the Danish or Norwegian for water, or if not the word Kristbjorg sometimes used. It had been there all the time, not a hundred yards from the house, though we hadn't seen it. No doubt because it had been an extremely dry and protracted Indian summer, it had not started running till late, by which time we had got used to its not being there, so we hadn't seen it. But for a moment it had been as if Kristbjorg had waved a magic wand and suddenly, there was the water. And the kind soul went and brought a bit of iron piping to make it easier to fill our cannister from it.

IV

Nor shall I ever forget the first time I went down that path to the spring for water. The evening was highly peculiar. In the northeast a full moon like a burning thistle had risen over the mountains. Mars hovered over the moon, the sole star. On the other side of the water a bank of fog stretched along the coastline the length of the inlet, luminous in the east opposite the house, but becoming black toward the south and west to the far right beyond the trees on the headland—that was, from our porch, from the path, the headland with the lighthouse was behind me, but it was such a strange evening I kept turning round—through which the fog showed like spirals and puffs of smoke, as though the woods were on fire. The sky was blue in the west, shading down to a pastel-like chalky sunset against which the trees were etched. A spindly water tower stood out above the fog over there. It had been dark inside the house but now I was outside on the path it was light. This was six o'clock and in spite of the blue sky to the west a patch of moonlight was reflected in the water by a diving float. The tide was high below the trees. In one instant, however, when I reached the spring, the moon went behind a cloud and it was dark: the reflection disappeared. And when I got back there was a blue fog.

"Welcome home," my wife smiled, greeting me.

"Ah yes, my darling, it really *is* home now. I love those curtains you made."

"It's good to sit by the window and look when it's beautiful outside, but when it's a gloomy twilight I like to pull the curtains, and feel from the dark night withdrawn, and full of lamplight inside."

"None of this nonsense about love in a cottage?"

I was lighting the oil lamps as I said this, smiling as I reflected how this unprophetic and loveless remark had become a loving catchphrase, and enchanted now by the golden color of the flame of the lighted oil lamps against their pretty blue holders backed with fluted tin brackets like haloes, or a monstrance.

"But now it's night, and the Chinese Hats are on the move!" We laughed, as I turned down the flame of a wick that was smoking the chimney.

And outside the tide was sweeping in still further from the Pacific until we could hear it washing and purling under the house itself. And later we lay in bed listening to a freighter's engines as they shook the house:

Frère Jacques
Frère Jacques
Dormez-vous?
Dormez-vous?

But the next morning when the gulls sailed outward bound to the city shores the clear cold sun streamed right into the two rooms of our house filling it with brilliant incessant water reflections and incandescence of light as if it knew that soon the world would start rolling through the mountainous seas of winter toward inevitable spring. And that evening after the last gulls had come to rest, when the moonlight came in there was time for it to embroider the waving windows of our house with their curtains on the unresting tide of Eridanus that was both sea and river.

Thereafter at dusk, when the gulls came floating home over the trees, I used to take this cannister to the spring. First I climbed the wooden ladder set into the bank and made into steps that had replaced the Scotsman's old broken steps, that led up from our porch to the path. Then I turned right so that now I was facing north toward the mountains, white plumaged as gulls themselves with a fresh paint of snow; or rose and indigo.

Often I would linger on the way and dream of our life. Was it possible to be so happy? Here we were living on the very windrow of existence, under conditions so poverty stricken and abject in the eyes of the world they were actually condemned in the newspapers, or by the Board of Health, and yet it seemed that we were in heaven, and that the world outside— so portentous in its prescriptions for man of imaginary needs that were in reality his damnation—was hell. And for these illusory needs, in that hell of ugliness outside Eridanus, and for the sake of making it a worse hell, men were killing each other.

But a few evenings later, returning homeward along the

path, I found myself possessed by the most violent emotion I had ever experienced in my life. It was so violent it took me some time to recognize what it was, and so all-embracingly powerful it made me stop in my tracks and put my burden down. A moment before I had been thinking how much I loved my wife, how thankful I was for our happiness, then I had passed to thinking about mankind, and now this once innocent emotion had become, for this is indeed what it was, hatred. It was not just ordinary hatred either, it was a virulent and murderous thing that throbbed through all my veins like a passion and even seemed to make my hair stand on end and my mouth water, and it took in everyone in its sweep, everyone except my wife. And now, again and again I would stop on the path as I came back with water, putting down my burden as I became possessed by this feeling. It was a hatred so all-consuming and so absolutely implacable that I was astounded at myself. What was all this hatred? Were these really my feelings? The world, surely, one could hate the world for its ugliness, but this was like hatred of mankind. One day, after I had been turned down again for the army, it occurred to me that in some mysterious way I had access to the fearful wrath that was sweeping the world, or that I stood at the mercy of the wild forces of nature that I had read man had been sent into the world to redeem, or something that was like the dreadful Wendigo, the avenging man-hating spirit of the wilderness, the fire-tortured forest, that the Indians feared and believed in still.

And in my agonized confusion of mind, my hatred and suffering *were* the forest fire itself, the destroyer, which is here, there, all about; it breathes, it moves, and sometimes suddenly turns back on its tracks and even commits suicide, behaving as though it had an idiot mind of its own; so my hatred became a thing in itself, the pattern of destruction. But the movement of the forest fire is almost like a perversion of the movement of the inlet: flames run into a stand of dry inflammable cedar, yellow flames slice them down, and watching, one thinks these flames will roll over the crest of the hill like a tidal wave. Instead, perhaps an hour later, the wind has changed, or the fire has grown too big for itself, and is now sucking in a draft that opposes its advance. So the fire doesn't sweep up the hill, but instead settles back to eat the morsels of the trees it felled during its first rush. So it seemed was the hatred behaving, turning inward and back upon myself, to devour my very self in its flames.

What was wrong with me? For nearly all was unselfishness in our little settlement. Like benevolent mountain lions, I had discovered, our neighbors would wait all day, only to perform an unselfish act, to help us in some way, or bring a gift. A smile, a wave of the hand, a cheery greeting was a matter of great importance here too. Perhaps they thought us a bit shiftless but they never let us know it. I remembered how Mauger, the Channel Islander, would reconnoiter in his boat, looking at our house, trying to pick the best time to bring us some crabs, or salmon, without inconvenience to us, for which he would accept no payment. To the contrary, he would pay us for the privilege of giving us the crabs by enriching us with stories and songs.

Once he told us of a salmon he saw drown an eagle. The eagle had flown away with a salmon in its claws that he had not wanted to share with a flock of crows, and rather than give up any part of its booty it had allowed itself finally to be dragged under the waves.

He told us that in the northern regions where he fished there were two kinds of ice, blue and white: live and dead. The white was dead so could not climb. But the blue ice would come and calmly ravish an island of all her beauty of trees and moss, bleed her lichen to the rock, and leave her bare as the Scotsman's door he had come to help us mend.

Or he would tell us of Arctic visions, of winds so strong they blew in the outgoing tide in which were found strange fish with green bones—

When he came back in September he loved to sing:

> Oh you've got a long way to go
> You've got a long way to go
> Whether you travel by day or night
> And you haven't a port or a starboard light
> If it's west or eastward ho—
> The judge will tell you so—

Or he would sing, in his curious jerky voice with its accents of the old English music hall, and which was more like talking:

> Farewell, farewell, my sailor boy
> This parting gives me pain...

And we too had grown unselfish, or at least different, away from the tenets of the selfish world. Eternally we watched Quaggan's float to see that it was safe and if it broke away without his knowledge, or when he was in the city, we brought it back, no matter how bad the weather, honestly hoping he would not know it was us, yet proud that it had been ourselves, for had it not been, it would have been someone else.

No one ever locked their doors, nobody ever discussed anyone else meanly. Canonical virtues must not be assumed for the inhabitants of Eridanus however. Though one point should be made in regard to the womenfolk of the fishermen. With the exception of those who were married, there never were any women. The unmarried fishermen often lent their shacks to their friends in the summer, but they were sacrosanct when they returned. What they did in the city was their own business, yet they never brought whores, for example, to their shacks. The attitude of the solitary fisherman toward his shack, and his boat, was not dissimilar. In effect his love for the one was like his love for the other. Perhaps his shack was less a part of him than his boat and his love for his shack was more disinterested; I think one reason for this is that their little cabins were shrines of their own integrity and independence, something that this type of human being, who seems almost to have disappeared, realizes can only be preserved without the evil of gossip. And actually each man's life was in essence a mystery (even if it looked like an open book) to his neighbor. The inhabitants varied in political and religious beliefs and unbeliefs and were certainly not sentimental. There was at one time, in later years, a family with three children living in Eridanus by necessity and not by choice and they were indeed convinced that it was "beneath them," and that the true values were to be found in "keeping up with the Joneses." They let themselves sink into degradation, as seeming to be the conventional counterpart of poverty, without ever having looked at a sunrise. I recall that their dishevelment and general incapacity caused some rather sharp comment among the fishermen and everyone was relieved when they left, to move into a slum in the city, where they certainly did not have to carry their water from a spring and where their only sight of a sunrise was behind warehouses. And even ourselves were not entirely absolved from identifying such a life with "failure," something we certainly should have outgrown. And I remember very well how we used to drift along in our little boat in the sun, or sit by the fire in the gentle lamplight if it was night and cold weather, and murmur together our day-dreams of "success," travel, a fine house, and so on.

And everything in Eridanus, as the saying is, seemed made out of everything else, without the necessity of making anyone else suffer for its possession: the roofs were of hand-split cedar shakes, the piles of pine, the boats of cedar and vine-leaved maple. Cypress and fir went up our chimneys and the smoke went back to heaven.

There was no room for hatred, and resuming my load of the cannister, I resolved to banish it—after all it was not human beings I hated but the ugliness they made in the image of their own ignorant contempt for the earth—and I went back to my wife.

But I forgot all my hatred and torment the moment I saw my wife. How much I owed to her! I had been a creature of the night, who yet had never seen the beauty of the night.

My wife taught me to know the stars in their courses and seasons, and to know their names, and how she always laughed like a peal of merry little bells telling me again about the first time she made me really look at them. It was early in our stay at Eridanus while I, used to being up all night and sleeping during the day, could not accustom myself to the change of rhythm, and the silence, and darkness all around us. Because I found it hard to sleep, in the small dark hours of one moonless night she took me walking deep into the forest; she told me to put out my electric torch and then, in a moment, she said, look up at the sky. The stars were blazing and shooting through the black trees and I had said, "My God, I never saw anything like that in my life!" But I never could see the patterns she pointed out and she always had to teach me afresh each time, until one late autumn night there was a brilliant full moon. That night there was frosted driftwood and a slow silver line of surf on the beach. Above the night itself flashed with swords and diamonds. Standing on the porch she pointed out Orion—"See, the three stars of his belt, Mintaka, Alnilam, Alnitak, there's Betelgeuse above in his right shoulder, and Rigel below in his left knee—"and when I saw it at last she said, "It's easier tonight because the moonlight drowns all but the brightest stars."

I reflected how little I had known of the depths and tides of a woman until now, her tenderness, her compassion, her capacity for delight, her wistfulness, her joy and strength, and her beauty, that happened through my wild luck to be the beauty of my wife.

She had lived in the country as a child and now returning after her years in the cities it was as if she had never left it. Walking through the forest to meet her returning from the store I would sometimes come upon her standing as still and alert as the wild creature she had seen and was watching, a doe with her fawn, a mink, or a tiny kinglet on a bough over her head. Or I would find her on her knees, smelling the earth, she loved it so much. Often I had the feeling that she had some mysterious correspondence with all nature around her unknown to me, and I thought that perhaps she was herself the eidolon of everything we loved in Eridanus, of all its shifting moods and tides and darks and suns and stars. Nor could the forest itself have longed for spring more than she. She longed for it like a Christian for heaven, and through her I myself became susceptible to these moods and changes and currents of nature, as to its ceaseless rotting into humus of its fallen leaves and buds— nothing in nature suggested you died yourself more than that, I began to think—and burgeoning toward life.

My wife was also an accomplished cook, and though the woodburning cookstove we had reminded us of Charlie Chaplin's in *The Gold Rush*, she somehow turned our limited and humble fare into works of art.

Sometimes, when we were most troubled in heart because of the war, or fear we would be separated, or run out of money, she would lie in bed laughing in the dark and telling me stories to make me laugh too, and then we would even make up dirty limericks together.

We found we could rarely do any outside work together, like

splitting wood, or making repairs, or especially when we built the pier, without singing; the jobs begat the songs, so that it was as if we had discovered the primitive beginnings of music again for ourselves; we began to make up our own songs, and I began to write them down.

But it was the accompaniment of her speech, of her *consciousness* of everything that impressed me then, half absurd, wholly perceptive, it intensified our whole life.

"See the frost on the fallen leaves, it's like a sumptuous brocade." "The chickadees are chiming like a windbell." "Look at that bit of moss, it's a miniature tropical forest of palm trees." "How do I know the cascara from the alder trees? Because the alders have eyes." "Eyes?" "Just like the eyes on potatoes. It's where the young shoots and branches drop off." "We shall have snow tonight, I can smell it on the wind." Such was our small talk, our common gossip of the forest.

My old life of the night, how far away that seemed now, my life in which my only stars were neon lights! I must have stumbled into a thousand alcoholic dawns, but drunk in the rumble seat I passed them by. How different were the few drinks we drank now, with Quaggan or Kristbjorg, when we could afford it or when there was any. Never had I really looked at a sunrise till now.

Once or twice on Sundays some of the boys who'd played with me came out to see us, when they happened to be filling a week's engagement in the city at the Palomar Dance Hall, or on the stage at the Orpheum cinema. Many combinations had been broken up during the war and my old band was not the same now, but whatever the world may think jazz musicians not merely possess unusual integrity but are among the most understanding and spiritual men and they did not tempt me back to my old life, knowing that would kill me. It was not that

I imagined that I was transcending jazz: I could never do that or wish to, and they wouldn't have let me get away with that illusion either. But there are some who can stand the racket and some who cannot. No one can be fool enough to think that Venuti or Satchmo or the Duke or Louis Armstrong have "ruined their lives" by living what I have pretentiously called "a life of the night." For one thing it is their lives and it has for me the aspects of a very real glory, of the realest kind of true acceptance of a real vocation. On one plane I can see them laughing their heads off at this kind of language. But they would know that what I say is true.

I belonged, somehow, way in the past, to the days of prohibition—as a matter of fact I have still not quite lost my taste for bootleg booze—and Beiderbecke, who was my hero, and Eddie Lang who taught me to play. Jazz had advanced since those days and Mr Robert Hackett is capable of flights that would have been difficult even for Bix. But I was attached romantically to those days as I was to the obsolete days of stokeholds. I had never been able to play sweet music, and I had rarely been able to play very sober either, and I was in danger of worse when I quit, and all this my colleagues, filled with grave polite wonder at this extraordinary life I was leading, and on whose hangover-concealing faces the pieces of plaster betrayed the heroism and decency of their visit at all, thoroughly appreciated. They had brought me an old gramophone which could be wound by hand, since of course we had no electricity, and a collection of our old recordings, and I understood too, through the familiar jargon into which we all would familiarly fall, that their serious impression was that I would have to do something creative with my life if I did not want somehow to go to pieces, for all my happiness.

One bitter gray day with the north wind shrilling through

bare iron trees and the path through the forest almost unnego-
tiable with ice and frozen snowdrifts, there was a sudden commotion outside. It was some of the boys from my old band and
they had brought me a small, second-hand cottage piano. Can
you conceive of the self-sacrifice, the planning, the sheer *effort*
inherent in this act? They had taken up a collection, had somehow found the instrument, and since it was only on Sunday
they could visit me, and being Sunday they could not hire anyone to help them, they had hired a truck and driven out, and
finally brought this piano to me through the frozen forest, over
that all but impassable path.

After this my friends sent me from time to time many hot
arrangements to work on for them. And they also made it possible for me to supplement my income in a manner that gave
me great pleasure and is besides, so far as I know, unique. That
is, I was able to provide on many occasions the titles for certain
hot numbers, when it came to recording them, that had grown
out of improvisation. In the old days such titles would seem to
grow out of the number itself, and in this category are the titles
for such numbers as For No Reason at All in C, and the piano
solos In a Mist, In the Dark, of Beiderbecke. Walking the Dog
is the title of an unknown masterpiece of Eddie Lang's, Black
Maria is another. Little Buttercup—the tune so far as I know
having nothing to do with the air in H.M.S. *Pinafore*—and
Apple Blossom are two of Venuti's in a poetical vein, and
Negroes have always been particularly good at titling such
numbers. But latterly despite some brilliant titlings in bebop,
and some superlative efforts such as Heavy Traffic on Canal
Street (a swing version of Paganini's Carnival in Venice) and
the Bach Bay Blues by the New Friends of Rhythm, even the
genius of our brother race has begun to fail in this respect. One
day my friends got stuck for a title in San Francisco and half

joking, half serious, asked my advice on a Christmas card for a number they were recording with a small combination shortly after the New Year. We wired them: Suggest Swinging the Maelstrom though cannot be as good as Mahogany Hall Stomp God bless you happy new year love.

Thereafter I received many inquiries of this nature and most of my suggestions being used, half joking but wholly considerate, I would receive a sum of money out of all proportion to what I would ordinarily have earned from any royalties on the sale of the record in question. Some titles which I supplied and you may recognize are, besides Swinging the Maelstrom—Chinook, Wild Cherry, Wild Water, Little Path to the Spring, and Playing the Pleiades—and I did a variation on Bix that I worked out on the piano, calling it Love in a Mist.

Little Path to the Spring! In this extraordinary manner I had earned enough, the way we were living, to keep us for the next two or three years, and to provide some reassurance for my wife were I eventually to be called up. And all these things I used to think of on the path itself while I was getting water, like some poverty-stricken priest pacing in the aisles of a great cathedral at dusk, who counting his beads and reciting his paternoster is yet continually possessed by the uprush of his extraneous thoughts. Ah, little path to the spring! It struck me that I must be at bottom a very humble man to take such creative pleasure from such an innocent source, and that I must be careful not to let my pride in this humbleness spoil everything.

That first winter in Eridanus was a difficult one for us, in many ways; used as we were to city life our primitive existence here on the beach—simple enough in summer and warm weather—propounded problems every day for which we had no answer, and yet always we solved them somehow, and it forced upon us feats of strength or endurance which we often performed without knowing how or why; and yet looking back on it now I remember much profound happiness.

V

In our part of the world the days are very short in winter, and often so dark and gray it is impossible to believe the sun will ever shine again; weeks of icy drenching rain, interspersed by the savage storms that sweep down the inlet from the mountains when the sea roared around and under us and battered our shack until it seemed sometimes January would never end, though once in a long while would come a day of blinding sunlight and clarity, so cold the inlet fumed and the mist rose from the water like steam from a boiling caldron, and at night my wife said of the stars, "Like splinters of ice in a sky of jet."

The wintry landscape could be beautiful on these rare short days of sunlight and frostflowers, with crystal casing on the slender branches of birches and vine-leaved maples, diamond drops on the tassels of the spruces, and the bright frosted foliage of the evergreens. The frost melted on our porch in stripes, leaving a pattern against the wet black wood like a richly beaded cape flung out, on which our little cat tripped about with cold dainty paws and then sat hunched outside on the windowsill with his tail curled round his feet.

One dark windy day deep in January, when there seemed no life or color left in a sodden world and the inlet looked like the Styx itself, black water, black mountains, low black clouds shuddering and snarling overhead, we walked down to the lighthouse.

"—And soon the crabs will bring the spring—" Sam called to us. "But crabs...I had a friend, a diver—thief he was in private life, never come home without somethink, even if it was only a nail. Aye. Basement like a junkyard...Well, this time he goes down, down, down, you know, deep. Then he gets scairt.—

Why? Migrations of billions of crabs, climbing all around him, migrating in the spring, aclambering around him, aswallering and stretching their muscles."

"!"

"Aye. Perhaps they see somethink *else* down there—who knows? Because he was so crazy scairt he wouldn't speak to no one for two weeks. But after that, he sings like nightingales, and he'd talk the head off any wooden duck. . . . And soon the crabs, my dearies, and soon the birds will bring the spring. . . ."

It was about this time we began to read more. I went to the city library and took out a "country card" which entitled me to take away a shopping bag full of books at once. The city, that already, in a few hours, had begun to render our existence an almost impossible fable, so that I seemed to know with sad foresight how even its richest comforts that one day we might in cowardice yearn for, and finally have, would almost suffocate all memory of the reality and wealth of such a life as ours, the city, with its steam heat, its prison bars of Venetian blinds, its frozen static views of roofs and a few small dingy gardens with clipped shrubs that looked, in the winter dusk, like chicken croquettes covered with powdered sugar. And ah, after being away from my wife for all these hours, to return from the city to discover the house still in place and the inlet sleeked and still, the alders and the cedars high, the pier there—for we had built a little pier—the sky wide and the stars blazing! Or, making my way down the sodden slippery path with the trees tossing and groaning about me in the tempest and the darkness, to make again the port, the haven of lamplight and warmth.

But then at night sometimes the elemental despair would begin again and we would lose all hope for terror at the noise, the rending branches, the tumult of the sea, the sound of ruination under the house, so that we clung to one another like two little arboreal animals in some midnight jungle—and we were two such animals in such a jungle—until we could laugh again at the very commotion, the very extremity of duty to a house filled with an anxiety of love like that of officers for a sailing ship in a gale. Though it was in the early mornings of high tide when getting breakfast that this wild elemental menace often proved the most unnerving, with the gray sea and white caps almost level with the windows, and the rain dashing against them, the sea crashing and hissing inshore under the house, causing horrible commotions of logs, jarring thunders dithering the whole little shack so that the lamp brackets rattled with the windows, past which a drifting timber sailed threatening the pier, and beyond the smoke of the factories in Port Boden was just a rainy gray, while leaves were falling into the sea; then our boat hurling itself about down below would seem in jeopardy, at the same time there would be the sound of breaking branches in the forest, the great maple tree would seethe and roar, while the tossing floats squealed piteously, and the loops of Mauger's fishing nets hung on the porch would flap like mad ghosts; and then be motionless; and all the anxiety that had been stretched to its utmost tension repeating, would the poor boat be hurt, the pier against which a thud was like a blow at the heart, relaxed too: though only an instant, the next moment it had all started again, so that what with the wind, the thunderous boomings, the delight in the swiftness outside, the anxiety within and without, the pride that one had survived, the sense of life, the fear of death, the appetite for breakfast as the bacon and coffee smells went singing down the gale every time one opened the door—I was seized sometimes with an exuberance so great that I wanted to dive swiftly into that brimming sea to acquire a greater appetite still, either that or because the sea seemed safer than the house.

But then we went out to a morning of wild ducks doing sixty downwind and golden-crowned kinglets feeding in swift jingling multitudinous flight through the leafless bushes, and another day of winter companionship would draw down to an evening of wind, clouds, and seagulls blowing four ways at once, and a black sky above the trembling desolate alders, the heart clothed already in their delicate green jewelry I had never really seen, and the gulls whitely soaring against that darkness, where suddenly now appeared the moon behind clouds, as the wind dropped, transillumining its own soaring moonshot depths in the water, the moon reflected in the half-moonlit clouds in the water down there, and behind, in the same translunar depths, the reflection of the struts and cross-braces of our simple-minded pier, safe for another day, disposed subaqueously in some ancient complex harmony of architectural beauty, an inverse moonlight geometry, beyond our conscious knowledge.

With February the days were noticeably longer and brighter and warmer, the sunrise and sunset were sometimes bright and beautiful again, there would be a sudden warm bright noon, or even a whole day that melted the ice in the brooks and set them running, or a day of sunlight where one could look through the trees at heaven, where luminous Aconcaguas sailed God's blue afternoon.

In the evening when I went for water, which I always liked to time to coincide with the seagulls' evening return over the trees and down the inlet, the twilight was growing longer, and chickadees and kinglets and varied thrushes flitted in the bushes. How I loved their little lives, now I knew their names and something of their habits, for my wife and I had fed them all winter and some were even quite tame, regarding me fearlessly near at hand. Just past Dunwoiken the path took a sharp dip down toward the beach, at a steep gradient, then it turned to the left, up a small slope, and there was the spring that came down from the mountains, where I filled my cannister. Ah, the pathos and beauty and mystery of little springs and places where there is fresh water near the ocean.

We called it the spring though in one way it was not. It was a lively little brook but it was called the spring because it was only a little further up that it emerged from underground. It was a source of water, a source of supply; that is why it was called the spring; it is a nuisance, but not insignificant, that I have to use the same word for this as for the season.

One evening on the way back from the spring for some reason I suddenly thought of a break by Bix in Frankie Trumbauer's record of Singing the Blues that had always seemed to me to express a moment of the most pure spontaneous happiness. I could never hear this break without feeling happy myself and wanting to do something good. Could one translate this kind of happiness into one's life? Since this was only a moment of happiness I seemed involved with irreconcilable impulses. One could not make a moment permanent and perhaps the attempt to try was some form of evil. But was there not some means of suggesting at least the existence of such happiness, that was like what is really meant by freedom, which was like the spring, which was like our love, which was like the desire to be truly good.

One cold rainy day I met Quaggan, a wiry homunculus, in a Cowichan sweater knitted by Indians in a series of friezes; he was in the path, cutting cascara bark.

"Proteus path," he said musingly.

"Proteus?"

"Aye. The man who cut this trail. Blacksmith, lives in the city now. We used to call it the Bell-Proteus path, for 'twas Bell helped him," said the old man, scuttling off into the dusk with his bright purgative load.

When I returned home I looked up Proteus in the dictionary which had been left behind by the Scotsman (who with uncanny insight had not returned it for twenty years to the Moose Jaw Public Library) together with some essays on Renan and a Bible, the loan of one Gideon, which was in the woodshed, and discovered—though I can't say I didn't more or less know it before—that he was a prophetic sea-god in the service of Poseidon. When seized, he would assume different shapes.

But how strange this was, I thought. Here Proteus was a man, who had given his name to this path. But he was also a god. How mysterious! And Eridanus too, that was a ship and the name of our hamlet and seaport, and inlet, and also a constellation. Were we living a life that was half real, half fable? Bell's name had no meaning I knew of. Neither had Quaggan's. Kristbjorg might have Christ-like virtues but he was anything but Christ-like. And yet I could not help remembering Hank Gleason, the bull fiddle's, pronouncement on Eridanus that Sunday. "Out of this world, brother," he had said. It gave me an uneasy feeling for a moment, like seeing one of those grotesque films in which they use animated cartoons with real figures, a mixture of two forms; it was also the feeling, though I couldn't put my finger on it, such as I had about Wywurk or Hi-Doubt. And yet did the confusion come from pinning the labels of one dimension on another? Or were they inextricable? As when, just about this time, the oil refinery decided to put a great sign over the wharfs, as an advertisement: SHELL. But for weeks they never got around to the s, so that it was left HELL. And yet, my own imagination could not have dreamt anything fairer than the heaven from which we perceived this. (In fact I was even fond of the evil oil refinery itself that at night now, as the war demanded more and more lubrication, was often a blaze of lights like a battleship in harbor on the Admiral's birthday.) But these problems I could never solve: if I could even state them in my "music"—for I had taken to bouts of composition on the cottage piano—I would be doing well.

And then, before I had time to think, I would seem to be getting water again, walking as if eternally through a series of dissolving dusks down the path. And at last the night would come like a great Catherine wheel.

It was a very still evening, and I had gone later than usual. There were quiet lamps already gleaming in Quaggan's shack, in Kristbjorg's, and on the point in Four Bells, though I knew none of their owners were at home for I had just seen all three of them through the trees going to the store. I think it was the stillness, the quietude, with the tide in, and the fact of the lamps burning in the empty houses by the sea that must have reminded me of it. Where had I read of the Isle of Delight—in Renan of course—where the birds sing matins and lauds at the canonical hours? The Isle of Delight, where the lamps light of themselves for the offices of religion, and never burn out for they shine with a spiritual light, and where an absolute stillness reigns, and everyone knows precisely the hour of his death, and one feels neither cold nor heat nor sadness nor sickness of body or soul. And I thought to myself, these lights are like those lights. That stillness is like this stillness. This itself is like the Isle of Delight. And then I thought to myself, stopping in the path: what if we should lose it? And with this thought of all-consuming anxiety I would always pause with a sigh. And then came the season spring and I forgot this anxiety too.

VI

Ah, not till that year had I observed a spring!

We went out on the porch and looked at the spring stars: Arcturus, Hercules the giant, the Lion and the Sea Serpent, the Cup, the Crown, and Vega in the Lyre.

One morning we saw our two great loons in their black and white high plumage, diving and calling softly to each other with low clear whistles, and that day the first bright leaves of the green dragons came thrusting through the earth on the path near the spring.

We were speaking together of these things that evening when suddenly we stopped talking at an apparition of terrifying beauty: in the darkness, in the northeast sky, within a circular frame, appeared the crosstrees of a windjammer on fire: the blazing crosstrees of a windjammer in port, no sails, just the masts, the blazing yards: a whole blazing Birkenhead Brocklebank dockside of fiery Herzogin Ceciles: or as if some ancient waterfront scene of conflagration in neighboring old windjammered Port Boden had been transported out of the past, in miniature, into the sky: now, to the right within the miniature frame, turned blackened crumbling yards: and now one lone silvery mast, ash-gray, with its naked canted yards, a multiple tilted cross, chording it perpendicularly, sinking below the circular frame, ascending, of blazing gold; we laughed out of sheer joy, for it was just the full moon rising clear of the pines behind the mountains, and often it must do this, but who looked at it? Who could see it? Could anyone else see it? I had never seen it. Why had God given this to us?

—And often I was to ask this: My God, why have You given this to us? But when the moon waned, rising further and further south, the sun would rise further and further north. And the truth of this simple fact, learned also from my wife, for the first time the following morning, confronted in the sky, not by a blazing windjammer, but by a spectacle such as might have been beheld by a shipwrecked seaman on a spar, seeing, at sunrise, the becalmed ship of the Ancient Mariner. Through the window the sea was so calm in the mist it rose up steep as a wall. Mr Bell's float seemed above us, halfway up the window, with far below that—a little later—divided not by sea or reflected mountains but by what seemed space itself, the orange sun rising still, barred with angry clouds. But the windjammer stood broadside in the sun; three masts, sad in the doldrums, tilted yards. And then the next moment had turned so that there was just this one gigantically tall mast, cross-boomed, coming towards us, changing into the tallest pine on the hill, as the rising sun left it behind. And I thought of my grandfather, becalmed in the Indian Ocean, the crew dying of cholera, my grandfather giving orders finally, at the beginning of wireless, to the oncoming gunboat, to be blown up himself with the ship.

That night there were two evening herons in the moon at high tide, the herons projected large and primeval before it, the one flapping high, blocking a moment the moon itself, the other, engines switched off, gliding low an inch above the moon-struck swelling water to land noiselessly on the float; a *squark* when they met, the one waiting for the other, and then flying off together: the bat turned into a firefly before the moon, and the cat's magical rites: and the tide full and high beneath the window: the swim at high tide, and love at high tide, with the windows liquescent on the floor: and waking again the next moment to the full tide again in the dawn, and the lights of the oil tanker still on alongside the oil-refinery port: and waking to the sudden O'Neillian blast of a ship's siren taking your soul to Palembang in spite of yourself, and again, the swim, the swim at dawn! And the shell-pink chiffon, my wife probably said, of factory smoke far in the northeast at Port Boden, and the four aluminum gas tanks, that later would come out in all their ugliness, like four golden pillars (because each was left half in shadow) to a Greek temple, and behind the old chemical factory like a ghost of a Grecian ruin and behind the four golden pillars a silent climbing train like a chain of golden squares: and the wash of a passing motorboat under the window like carved turquoise in onrushing movement toward you: and then the oil tanker lying under the pillars and retorts at the refinery like Troy, the pillars reflected in the water: the wonderful cold clean fresh salt smell of the dawn air, and then the pure gold blare of light from behind the mountain pines, and the two morning herons, then the two blazing eyes of the sun over the Cascade foothills, and the five gaunt growing pines caught tall in the circular frame, and then with such a blast of light it seemed to cut a piece out of the hill, the herons flying, the oil-tanker sailing with the morning tide—

Oh, what light and love can do to four gas tanks at sunrise over the water!

And how different the forest path was now, in spring, from the other seasons we had known it: summer, autumn and winter. The very quality of the light was different, the pale green, green and gold dappled light that comes when the leaves are very small, for later, in summer with the leaves full out, the green is darker and the path darker and deeply shady. But now there was this delicate light and greenness everywhere, the beauty of light on the feminine leaves of vine-leaved maples and the young leaves of the alders shining in sunlight like stars of dogwood blossoms, green overhead and underfoot where plants were rushing up and there were the little beginnings of wildflowers that would be, my wife said, spring beauties, starflowers, wild bleeding hearts, saxifrage and bronze bells. Or on some cool still mornings came the mysterious fogs: "Anything can happen in a fog," she said, "and just around the next corner something wonderful will happen!"

And now it was spring and we had not lost our way of living; in fact, with the money I'd earned we had bought a little house further up the beach between Kristbjorg's and Four Bells under a wild cherry tree for a hundred dollars. No one had lived in this house for years and it was badly in need of repairs and of cleaning so that we did not move into it until May and we worked very hard to make it clean and sound and beautiful.

In early spring we had not yet moved into our second house and this is the time I am really thinking of when I say that each evening at dusk I used to go down the path for water. Carrying my cannister I would pass along the back of Dunwoiken, descend the sharp gradient toward the beach, then turn left again, up a little slope, to the spring. Then I set the cannister under the iron piping Kristbjorg had put there and waited for it to fill. While it filled I watched the gulls coming up the inlet or gazed up the trunks of the trees to the highest pinnacles of the smallest branches trembling like a moonsail, and breathed the scents of evening: the rich damp earth, myrtle and the first wild crabapple and wild cherry blossoms, all the wild scents of spring, mingled with the smell of the sea and from the beach the salt smells, and the rasping iodine smell of seaweed.

But one evening I forgot to do this and found myself to my surprise not looking at anything nor smelling anything. And now, all of a sudden, very different seemed the journey back. Though the cannister only held four gallons, and since I had become stronger, the task ought to have seemed much lighter than before, yet on this evening it began to weight a ton and it was just slip and slide, one foot after another. I found myself stopping for breath every moment. The worst part was the dip down which on the way to the spring I had run so gaily, but which had become a veritable hill of difficulty on the return journey, so that I had to drag rather than carry my cannister up it. And now I stopped and cursed my lot. What had happened now? Now that the spring we had so longed for had come, now that our life on the beach seemed doubly secure with our new house—what was I bothering about now? It seemed to me as though all our prayers having been answered and myself for once having nothing in the world to worry about, for the moment, I had to find something to irk me in this chore. It was as though man would not be contented with anything God gave him and I could only think that when God evicted him from Paradise it served him right.

And now no matter how happy I had been all day the awe-inspiring thoughts were as if waiting for me here at the spring. Somehow I always made it back, but somehow too, for the first time, I came to dread this simple little chore. It wasn't as if this were a mere malaise of self-centeredness. Each of us thought more of the other than of himself. Nor was it a matter of mutual self-absorption. Sincerely we considered our neighbors. Quaggan had indeed grown so fond of us he made a red mark on his calendar every time we went to see him.... One day I saw an old frayed but strong rope on this path, cast away on a tree stump, and I thought: yes, that is the awful end of such thoughts. Had I actually been tempted to kill myself? Aghast at the thought I took the rope back and reaved it up for use.

But at the same time that I dreaded it I was also aware that I looked forward to it, looked forward to the walk to the spring, which was like going toward the future, toward our new little house. It was a sweet time of the day when the sun sank and the only part of the day in which I was really apart from my wife, unless I counted my "work." I did not look forward to it because I would be separated from her but precisely because I was then able to enjoy the pleasure of returning to her, as if after a long journey. The journey might be, or had become, a sort of anguish, but we always met again with cries of joy and relief after this interminable separation of not more than twenty minutes.

But again, I thought, was the chore even anguish? In the surroundings there was everywhere an intimation of Paradise, in the little job, so far from mechanical, a sense of simple human accomplishment. I thought of the old ladder we had salved from the beach. This too was an accomplishment. At first we had pushed it away, but it had drifted back again and this seemed like a sign to use it. And I reflected: yes, and like this vermiculated old ladder, stinking with teredos and sea-worms, washed down from the sawmill, this sodden snag, half awash when I first saw it, is the past, up and down which one's mind every night meaninglessly climbs!

But I had salved this ladder last autumn, in the days when I used to lie awake brooding in the night, which now I never did. And the ladder no longer stank, or smelled of teredos. Much of it was good, and hacking out the rotten wood, I had put its frame to use, and indeed converted it into these very steps I was even now climbing down to greet my wife on the porch, with joy after my gloomy thoughts, carrying my burden, the same steps up which I had set forth twenty minutes ago on my path to the spring.

Yet a ladder was a ladder, however transmuted, and the past remained. It was in this way I came to the conclusion that it was not the chore itself, because it was heavy, but something to do with my thoughts, something that was always elicited on my return journey, especially when I came to the hill, that I really dreaded. Though I did not understand this until after I had met the mountain lion, and shortly after I had met the mountain lion something else happened that put it right out of my mind for many years, until, in fact, the other day.

The cougar was waiting for me part way up a maple tree in which it was uncomfortably balanced, to one side of the hill section of the path, and what is strange is that I should have met it on the return journey without having noticed it, just as I hadn't noticed the rope, if it was there, on my way to the spring.

A logger had once told me that if you set fire to your mittens and throw them at a mountain lion that would take effect, and I know that bears are often very susceptible to human laughter.

But this folklore—and there is a great deal about mountain lions in these parts—did not help. All I immediately knew was that I had no sort of weapon, and that it was impractical as well as useless to make any movement of running away. So I stood traditionally and absolutely still. Then we simply waited, both of us, to see what the other would do, gazing straight into each other's eyes at short range; in fact it was only his gleaming topaz eyes and the tip of his tail twitching almost imperceptibly that showed me he was alive at all.

Finally I heard myself saying something like this to the mountain lion, something extraordinary and absurd, commanding yet calm, my voice as unreal to myself as if I'd just picked myself up from a lonely road after falling off a motorcycle and in shock were adjuring the wilderness itself to aid, a fact one half recalls under chloroform afterwards. "Brother, it's true. I like you in a way, but just the same, between you and me, get going!" Something like that. The lion, crouched on a branch really too small for him, caught off guard or off balance, and having perhaps already missed his spring, jumped down clumsily, and then, overwhelmed, catlike, with the indignity of this ungraceful launching, and sobered and humiliated by my calm voice—as I liked to think afterwards—slunk away guiltily into the bushes, disappeared so silently and swiftly that an instant later it was impossible to believe he'd ever been there at all.

At the time I completely forgot the rest of my return journey, though ludicrously it turned out I had not failed to bring the cannister with me, nor do I have any recollection at all of coming down the steps. I had to warn my wife not to go out, then row round to warn the neighbors and see that the alarm was given to the forest warden; I rowed, close inshore, straining my eyes through the gloom to warn anyone else I might see on the forest path. But night was coming on and I saw no one.

I didn't even see the lion again, which, when he ran off, according to later reports, did not stop until ten miles away when he jumped right through the glass window of a trapper, who offered him his elbow to eat while with the other hand, I truly regret to say, the man reached for a carving knife to cut the beast's throat, after which the trapper was obliged to row for several hours, as penance, to get aid in his underdrawers; when we heard this we mourned the animal a bit, in our way.

But that night as we lay in bed, and the moon shone through the window, with my arms around my wife and our cat purring between us, I saw that the only reason I had not been afraid of the mountain lion—otherwise I must have been a fool and I do not for this reason escape the charge—was that I was more afraid of something else. It was true, though this was less due to courage than a naïve ignorance, that I was not very afraid of mountain lions even when there was a report of them. But then I did not really believe in them. I must have been afraid—I mean I must have been afraid in some way of the lion—but at the hill on the spring path have been already gripped by the anticipation of a so much greater fear that the concrete fact even of a lion had been unable to displace it. What was it I feared? Lying in bed with my arms around my wife, listening to the roar of the surf we couldn't see, for it was a fierce low tide—I felt so happy that all of a sudden I could not for the life of me give it a name. It seemed something past, and that was what it was, though not in the sense in which I was thinking. Even when one is happiest it is possible to entertain, with one section of one's mind, the most ghoulish reflections, and so I did now, before I went to sleep, but now as at a distance, as if in retrospect. It was as though I had entered the soul of a past self, not that of the self that merely brooded by night, but an earlier self to whom sleep meant delirium, my thoughts chasing each other down a gulf. Half conscious I told myself that it was as though I had actually been on the lookout for something on the path that had seemed ready, on every side, to spring out of our paradise at us, that was nothing so much as the embodiment in some frightful animal form of those nameless somnambulisms, guilts, ghouls of past delirium, wounds to other souls and lives, ghosts of actions approximating to murder, even if not my own actions in this life, betrayals of self and I know not what, ready to leap out and destroy me, to destroy us, and our happiness, so that when, as if in answer to all this, I saw a mere lion, how could I be afraid? And yet mysteriously the lion was all that too.

But the next night, and upon nights after, something even more curious happened, as I say, that caused me to forget this till now.

The next evening when I went for water all I can remember is that on my way there, or on setting out, I was certainly prepared for another encounter with the mountain lion, of whose sad demise we had not yet heard, and prepared to be conventionally afraid of him, I suppose, though I went unarmed (it was because I didn't have a gun) and my wife, who had no fear of anything on earth save spiders, was curiously unapprehensive about it and had implicit faith in me. Actually, at the bottom of her mind, so great was her love of wild animals and her understanding of them, a love and understanding I came to share, I felt sometimes she may have wished I had charmed the animal home for a companion instead of scaring him away.

Something about the aspect of the mountains that evening distracted me from the lion. Though it was a warm evening, it was windy, and the mountains were wild with chaos, like an arctic island seen through snow. And indeed it had snowed far down on the mountains in the last three nights, though I was not reminded by this snow that it was this changeable weather that had driven the cougar down to the warmer regions in search of food. The wind roared and howled through the rolling treetops like an express train. It was a chinook— the kind of foehn wind that years before at night had driven the S.S. *Eridanus*—Liverpool—ashore with her cargo of old marble, wine, and cherries-in-brine from Portugal. The further mountains grew nearer and nearer until they looked like the precipitous rocky cliff-face of an island gashed with guano. The nearer hills were very light but their inner folds grew ever darker and darker. In the chaos high up there appeared a church of blue sky by mistake, as if put in by Ruysdael. A gull whose wings seemed almost a maniacal white suddenly was drawn up, driven straight up perpendicularly into the tempest. One of Quaggan's sons passed me running on the path:

"It's blowing real hard. I'm just dashing madly to see how things were."

I remember this Celtic way of expressing it delighted me: maybe his boat, or more likely Kristbjorg's, who was in the city, was dragging its anchor, and I said to give me a shout if he wanted any help. I remember filling the cannister with the cold mountain water pouring down. Gulls were blowing backwards above the trees and one came to rest on the roof of Hi-Doubt. How touching the gull, dovelike there, with his white blowing feathers! But the next thing I remembered was that I was singing and had passed the hill without remembering a single step I had taken or with any recollection of its difficulty; and the next thing I was down the steps, cannister and all, with no clear vision once more of how this had been managed, and my wife was greeting me as usual, as if I'd come back from a long journey. To the mountain lion I had given no thought at all. It was like a dream, with the difference that it was reality.

The next time I set off with the cannister I recall almost a precisely similar thing happened, though this was just a quiet spring evening, the mountains remote and still, muffled at their base by a great scarf of mist that rose without division from the calm reflecting sea. The journey to the spring seemed much the same, though even this seemed more dreamy, mysterious, and accomplished in a shorter time. But once more, on the way back, I was only conscious of the hill when I realized that I had traversed it without effort.

At the same time I became conscious of my gloomy thoughts again, but in a quite different way: how can I say it? It is as if I saw those thoughts at a distance, as if below me. In one sense I did not see them but heard them, they flowed, they were like a river, an inlet, they comprised a whole project impossible to recapture or pin down. Nonetheless those thoughts, and they were abysmal, not happy as I would have wished, made me happy in that, though they were in motion they were in order too: an inlet does not overflow its banks, however high the tide, nor does it dry up, the tide goes out, but it comes in again, in fact as Quaggan had observed, it can do both at once; I was aware that some horrendous extremity of self-observation was going to be necessary to fulfill my project. Perhaps I have not mentioned my project, or rather what I conceived my project to be.

VII

Though this may at first seem inconsistent with my dismissal of this project as "my music," "my bouts of composition," or "my work," I had been haunted for months by the idea of writing a symphony in which I would incorporate among other things, for the first time in serious music (or so I thought), the true feelings and rhythm of jazz. I did not share, among other perplexities of my vocation, the vocation that I had not yet discovered, the common romantic conception of the superiority of music over words. Sometimes I even thought poetry could go further, or at least as far, in its own medium; whereas music, destined to develop in terms of ever more complex invention (I knew this because I had mastered, almost accidentally, the whole-tone scale), seemed to me then to have its unconscious end in silence, whereas the Word is the beginning of creation itself. Despite this I always felt, as a practicing jazz musician, that the human voice managed to spoil a given instrumental record. To contradict this again, my wife and I loved to sing, and sometimes I felt our life together to be a kind of singing.

How well I recall struggling through all these, and many more, contradictions and perplexities. I finally even prayed, and the other day, looking through some scraps of early work saved from our fire, I encountered, half burnt, the edges scorched and crumbling, the following, written as it were over a score: *Dear Lord God, I earnestly pray you to help me order this work, ugly chaotic and sinful though it may be, in a manner that is acceptable in Thy sight; thus, so it seems to my imperfect and disordered brain, at the same time fulfilling the highest canons of art, yet breaking new ground and, where necessary, old rules. It must be tumultuous, stormy, full of thunder, the exhilarating Word of God must sound through it, pronouncing hope for man, yet it also must be balanced, grave, full of tenderness and compassion, and humor. I, being full of sin, cannot escape false concepts, but let me be truly Thy servant in making this a great and beautiful thing, and if my motives are obscure, and the notes scattered and often meaningless, please help me to order it, or I am lost....*

But despite my prayers my symphony refused to order itself or resolve itself in musical terms. Yet I saw what I had to do clearly. I heard these thoughts ordering themselves as if pushed off from me: they were agonizing, but they were clear, and they were my own, and when I returned home I tried again to put them down. But here I was beset by further difficulties, for when I tried to write the music, I had to put it down first in words. Now this was peculiar because I knew nothing about writing, or words, at that time. I had read very little and my whole life had been music. My father—who would have been the first to laugh at this way of putting it—had played French horn in the first performance in 1913 of Stravinsky's Sacre du Printemps. My father was with Soutine too, and knew and respected Cocteau, though he was a very proper kind of Englishman in some respects. Stravinsky he worshipped, but he died at about the age I am now, before the Symphony of Psalms at all events, so I had many lessons in composition and was even brought up, though I had no formal musical education, on Stravinsky's children's pieces. I grew to share my father's wild enthusiasm for the Sacre but to this day I believe it to be in one important respect rhythmically deficient—in a way I won't go into—and that Stravinsky knew nothing at all about jazz, which also goes for most other modern composers. I reflected briefly that though my unconscious, and even conscious, approach to serious music had been almost entirely through jazz, nonetheless my rhythmical touchstone had proved an uncanny method of separating the first-rate from the not quite first-rate, or of differentiating the apparently similar or related in merit and ambition: on this view, of modern composers, both Schönberg and Berg are equally first-rate: but as between Poulenc and Milhaud, say, Poulenc is somewhere, but Milhaud, to my ear, nowhere at all. What I am really getting at is probably that in some composers I seem to hear the very underlying beat and rhythm of the universe itself, but to say the least I am, it is admitted, naïve in expressing myself. However, I felt that no matter how grotesque the manner in which my inspiration proposed to work through me, I had something original to express. Here was the beginning of an honesty, a sort of truthfulness to truth, where there had been nothing before but truthfulness to dishonesty and self-evasion and to thoughts and phrases and even melodies that were not my own. Yet it is queer that I had to try and put all this into *words*, to see it, to try and see the thoughts even as I heard the music. But there is a sense in which everybody on this earth is a writer, the sense in which Ortega—the Spanish philosopher whom I have recently read thanks to one of the summer people, a schoolmaster, and now one of my best friends, and who lent me his books—means it. Ortega has it that a man's life is like a fiction that he makes up as he goes along. He becomes an engineer and converts it into reality—becomes an engineer for the sake of doing that.

I am bound to say that even in the worst of my struggles I did not feel like Jean Christophe; my soul did not boil "like wine in a vat," nor did my "brain hum feverishly," at least not very loudly: though my wife could always judge the degree of my inspiration by the increasing tempo of my sniffs, which, if I was really working, would follow a period of deep sighs and abstracted silence. Nor did I feel "This force is myself. When it ceases to be I shall kill myself." As a matter of fact I never doubted that it was the force itself that was killing me, even though it possessed none of the above dramatic characteristics, and I was in every way delighted that it should, for my whole intention seemed to be to die through it, without dying of course, that I might become reborn.

The next time I went for water, despite the fact that I had forearmed myself consciously against any illusion, almost exactly the same thing happened; this time indeed the feeling came more strongly than ever, so that it seemed in fact, to me, as if the path were shrinking at both ends. Not only was I unconscious of the hill, and the weight of the cannister, but I had the decided impression that the path *back* from the spring was growing shorter than the path *to* it, though the way there had seemed shorter too than on the previous day. When I returned home it was as if I had flown into my wife's arms, and I tried to tell her about it. But no matter how hard I tried I could not express what the feeling was like—beyond saying that it was almost as if a "great burden had been lifted off my soul." Some such cliché as that. It was as if something that used to take a long and painful time now took so little time I couldn't remember it at all; but simultaneously I had a consciousness of a far greater duration of time having passed during which something of vast importance to me had taken place, without my knowledge and outside time altogether.

No wonder mystics have a hard task describing their illuminations, even though this was not exactly that; yet the experience seemed to be associated with light, even a blinding light, as when years afterwards recalling it I dreamed that my being had been transformed into the inlet itself, not at dusk, by the moon, but at sunrise, as we had so often also seen it, suddenly transilluminated by the sun's light, so that I seemed to contain the reflected sun deeply within my very soul, yet a sun which as I awoke was in turn transformed, Swedenborgwise, with its light and warmth into something perfectly simple, like a desire to be a better man, to be capable of more gentleness, understanding, love—

There has always been something preternatural about paths, and especially in forests—I know now for I have read more— for not only folklore but poetry abounds with symbolic stories about them: paths that divide and become two paths, paths that lead to a golden kingdom, paths that lead to death, or life, paths where one meets wolves, and who knows? even mountain lions, paths where one loses one's way, paths that not merely divide but become the twenty-one paths that lead back to Eden.

But I did not then need the books to be deeply conscious of this mysterious feeling about paths. I had never heard of a path that shrank before, but we had heard of people who disappeared altogether, people who are seen walking along one moment, and then the next have vanished: and so, overlooking the fact that the experience might have some deeper significance, and solely with the purpose of deliciously making our flesh creep, we made up a story along those lines that night in bed. What if the path became shorter and shorter until I should disappear altogether one evening, when coming back with the water? Or perhaps this story was a means of propitiating fate for the miraculous fact that we had not been separated by not assuming it to be a smug certitude, a form of inoculation, since we still might be separated by the war (I had been rejected a second time by then, probably for being half-witted), against such a separation, and at the same time a kind of parable of the "happy ending" of our lives come what might—for no matter what we might make up about the character on the path, I myself was certainly going to come back from the spring and that journey to end in, for us, a glorious lovers' meeting.

But in fact the path did seem in effect to get shorter and shorter, if the impression was never again to be accompanied by quite the same sense of incommunicable experience. No matter how consciously I determined to remember on the outward journey, it always turned out that I had climbed the hill coming back without giving it a thought. And so realistic had our little story become that not many evenings after when I came back with water at dusk my wife came running to meet me, crying:

"Oh my God! I'm so glad to see you!"

"My darling. Well, here I am."

So genuine was the relief on my wife's face, and so genuine was my own feeling at meeting her again, that I was sorry we'd ever made up such a story. But it was a wonderful and profound moment. And just for an instant I felt that had she not come down the path to meet me, I might indeed have disappeared, to spend the rest of my extraterritorial existence searching for her in some limbo.

Up above the topmasts of the trees swayed against the April sky. Suddenly the gulls appeared, as if shot out of a catapult, hurtling downwind above the trees. And over my wife's shoulder, coming across the inlet toward the lighthouse, I saw a deer swimming.

This reminded me that despite the wind it was warm enough for me to start swimming again—I had virtually given up in December—so I went straight in, and it was as though I had been baptized afresh.

It was soon after this that we moved into our little house under the wild cherry tree that we'd bought from the blacksmith.

This house burned down three years later and all the music I had written burned with it, but we built another house ourselves, with the help of Quaggan, Kristbjorg and Mauger, out of driftwood and wood from the sawmill in Eridanus Port, which was now being torn down to make way for a real estate subdivision.

We built it on the same spot as the old house, using the burned posts for part of our foundations that now, being charred, were not susceptible to rot. And the music got itself rewritten too somehow, in a way that was more satisfactory, for I had only to come back to the path to remember parts of it. It was as if the music had even been written during some of those moments. The rest, as any creative artist will understand, was only work.

But I never could recapture my symphony after losing it by fire. And so, still struggling with words as well as music, I wrote an opera. Haunted by a line I had read somewhere: "And from the whole world, as it revolved through space, came a sound of singing," and by the passionate desire to express my own happiness with my wife in Eridanus, I composed this opera, built, like our new house, on the charred foundations and fragments of the old work and our old life. The theme was suggested probably by my thoughts of cleansing and purgation and renewal and the symbols of the cannister, the ladder and so on, and certainly by the inlet itself, and the spring. It was partly in the whole-tone scale, like *Wozzeck*, partly jazz, partly folk-songs or songs my wife sang, even old hymns, such as Hear Us O Lord from Heaven Thy Dwelling Place. I even used canons like Frère Jacques to express the ships' engines or the rhythms of eternity; Kristbjorg, Quaggan, my wife and myself, the other inhabitants of Eridanus, my jazz friends, were all characters, or exuberant instruments on the stage or in the pit. The fire was a dramatic incident and our own life, with its withdrawals and returns, what I had learned of nature, and the tides and the sun-rises I tried to express. And I tried to write of human happiness in terms of enthusiasm and high seriousness usually reserved for catastrophe and tragedy. The opera was called *The Forest Path to the Spring*.

VIII

Our first little house we had rented from the good Scotsman passed into other hands on his death, though sometimes we used to go down the path by the spring and look at it, and it was only the other day that we did this again. Many years have passed.

Mauger was dead: Bell had gone, and old Sam by the light-house; but Kristbjorg and Quaggan, now seventy-five and a great-grandfather, were still very much alive, and living in the same place. As usual people were threatening to throw us off the beach but somehow we were still there. Mauger's shack toward the lighthouse with its newly shingled roof stood desolate, but we did not feel sad to look at it. His life had been too well accomplished and he died saying, "I never felt better in my life."

We happened to be completely broke when he died but someone had sent some laurels in the shape of an anchor to his funeral where, in the funeral parlor, a woman sang Nearer My God to Thee through a grille and the minister read the Twenty-third Psalm in an improved version. Our suggestion that this be followed by Hear Us O Lord from Heaven Thy Dwelling Place having been abandoned, since no one save ourselves and Quaggan could sing it, our suggestion was likewise neglected. That almost anything be substituted for Nearer My God to Thee, a hymn he hated since his father had been a stoker on the *Titanic*.

There were huge pretentious faked marble Corinthian pillars in the undertaker's parlor on either side of the minister as he read and I kept seeing these change before my eyes into the stanchly beautiful lousy old wooden piles covered with blue mussels on which Mauger's house (and I doubt not more likely, in heaven, should it stand, St Peter's too) stood. Another fisherman, his brother, was taking the house with its green reticulated nets hanging out to dry. And I thought how selflessly, taking time from their own work, and accepting no money for it, Quaggan and Kristbjorg and Mauger had helped us build our new house, helped us, though all old men, with the cruel work of putting in our foundations, in fact supplied half the foundations themselves. Mauger must have been grateful there were so many who loved him and I was surprised how many at his funeral were summer people we didn't know. Kristbjorg, one of his best friends, had his own ideas about death and had not come at all. Still, he seemed to be there too. When we stopped on the way out to look at Mauger in his coffin he seemed to be smiling, with a twinkling look beneath his heavy mustaches, even mysteriously to be singing to us under his breath:

Still you've got a long way to go
You've got a long way to go
Whether you travel by day or night...
The judge will tell you so...

Our hamlet on the beach had scarcely changed. On the front
of our first house where we had been so happy was a large
wooden plaque bearing a name that perhaps had no merit even
according to the special categories of waggery through which
one was obliged to perceive it: Wuzz-it-2-U? But otherwise it
had been improved. The porch had been widened, it had a
wireless aerial—maybe someone even listened to our opera
upon it, but we hoped not. For the local authorities on hearing
rumors of an opera by a local composer had seen an excellent
instrument with which to belabor our position on the beach
again, so that for a while such embarrassing headlines as OPER-
ATIC SQUATTERS ENDANGER DIGNITY OF CITY—WE NEED
SEWERS NOT SYMPHONIES—RICH COMPOSER PREFERS RATS-
NEST OF PERVERSION were not uncommon, until another four-
teen-year-old taxpayer's son committed a sex crime, and the
next mayor committed a murder; so that fortunately we did not
have long to wait. The house now had a roof ladder, though my
old ladder still did duty as steps. There was a new roof-jack and
a new chimney. Feeling like thieves we peeked in the window.
But where else could all nature look in too, and the house still
have privacy? For it did. It was not merely that the sunlight
came in, but the very movement and rhythm of the sea, in
which the reflections of trees and mountains and sun were
counter-reflected and multi-reflected in shimmering movement
within. As if part of nature, the very living and moving and
breathing reflection of nature itself had been captured. Yet it
was built in such a cunningly hidden manner that no one could
see into it from a neighboring house. One had to peek in like a

thief to do that. A tree we had planted in the back was now the height of the shack, a dogwood clustered like white stars, another wild cherry that had failed to blossom for us was a snow of blooms, while our own primroses we had left for the Scotsman were in flower: fireweed too had sown itself from the seeds of that beautiful willow herb, our unbidden guest, blown downwind from our second house. Once during a winter, when we were in Europe, a child had been born there in a snowstorm. There was a new stove, but the old table and two chairs where we ate in front of the window were still there. There was the bunk where we had spent our honeymoon—and what a long honeymoon it had turned out to be—and desired each other and anguished at the fear of losing each other and our hearts had been troubled, and we had seen the stars and the moon rise, and listened to the roar of the surf on the wild stormy nights of our first winter, and the grandmother of the cat that accompanied us now had slept with us and pulled our hair in the morning to wake us up—Valetta, long since gathered to the rest of her strange moonkind. Yet who would think, to look at the place idly, with its ramshackle air, its sense of impermanence, of improvisation, that such a beauty of existence, such happiness could be possible there, such dramas have taken place? Look at that old hut, the passerby shouts in his motor launch above the engine, laughing contemptuously: oh well, we'll be pulling down all those eyesores now. Start here, and keep going! Autocamps for the better class, hotels, cut down all those trees, open it up for the public, put it on the map. Nothing but receivers of stolen goods and a few old pirates live in the ratsnests anyway. Squatters! The government's been trying to get them off for years!

It was there that our own life had come into being and for all its strangeness and conflict, a pang of sadness struck us now. Longing and hope fulfilled, loss and rediscovery, failure and accomplishment, sorrow and joy seemed annealed into one profound emotion. From the porch where we stood we could see dimly—for there was suddenly a spring fog billowing in across the water—right across the arc of the bay to where our next house had burned down and there was no tragedy about that either. Our new house stood clearly visible in its place, though as we watched it began to be swallowed up by the fog.

As the mist rolled up towards us, beginning to envelop us, the sun still trying to maintain itself like a platinum disc, it was as if the essence of a kind of music that had forever receded there, that seemed evoked from the comments of my wife as she looked through this window, out on to this porch in the first days when we'd just meant to spend a week, or in the autumn when we still stayed on, while she was making the coffee, talking to herself partly for my benefit, describing the day to me, as if I had been like a blind man recovering his sight to whom she had to teach again the beauties and oddities of the world, as if it became unlocked, began to play, to our inner ear, not music but having the effect of music, not sentimental at all, but fresh and innocent, and only moving because it was so happy, or because happiness is moving; or it was like a whispering of the ghosts of ourselves. "Sunrise of the dying moon, in a green sky... White frost on the porch and all the roofs, the first heavy frost of the year... There's a little flotilla of golden eyes under the window, and the racoons have been here during the night, I can see their tracks... The tide is high. My poor seagulls, they're hungry. How cold your feet must be down there, in that icy water... Look—now! like a bonfire! Like a burning cathedral. I must wash the windows. There's a wash from a fishing boat like a strand of silver Christmas tinsel. The sunrise does things to these mists.... I must put out some breakfast for the cat. He'll come in very hungry from his dawn prowl. There goes a cormorant. There goes a great loon. The frost sparkles like diamond dust. I used to think it was fairy diamonds as a child. In a few minutes it will melt and the porch will be wet and black, with a sprinkling of harlequin leaves. The mountains look very hazy and far away this morning, that's a sign it will be a good day...."

Strange magnificent honeymoon that had become one's whole life.

We climbed the steps—they were the same steps made from my ladder and they still held—and began to walk into the mist and down the path to the spring. The fog was thick in the forest, like smoke pouring toward us as from a funnel beneath the bushes, in which it was curious to hear the intermittent insulated twitterings of birds gradually hushing. Talking of those first days, my wife remembered how once for nearly a month there had been a fog so thick we couldn't see across the inlet, and what boats went by unseen, only known by a mournful continued hooting of foghorns and lonely bells. Sometimes Kristbjorg's boat had appeared dimly as it did now and the point ahead would fade in and out and sometimes we could scarcely see beyond the porch, so that it had been like living at the edge of eternity. And we remembered too the days when it had been dark and freezing with a film of ice on the blackened porch and the steps, and the lamp going until ten o'clock in the morning. And the ships that would steer by dead reckoning listening for the echo of their hooters from the bank, though we could hear their engines, as we heard a ship's engine now, going very softly:

> Frère Jacques
> Frère Jacques
> Dormez-vous?
> Dormez-vous?

And the snowstorms in which there was no echo. And the sense of the snow driving on the night in the world outside too, and such a storm as would yield no echo. And ourselves seemed the only lamp of love within it.

Or there would seem something about these little shacks, as there did now, as mysterious and hidden as the never-found nest of the marbled murrelet, that also haunted these shores.

The path had scarcely changed; nor, here, had the forest. Civilization, creator of deathscapes, like a dull-witted fire of ugliness and ferocious stupidity—so unimaginative it had even almost managed to spoil the architectural beauty of our oil refinery—had spread all down the opposite bank, blown over the water and crept up upon us from the south along it, murdering the trees and taking down the shacks as it went, but it had become baffled by the Indian reserve, and a law that had not been repealed that forbade building too near a lighthouse, so to the south we were miraculously saved by civilization itself (of which a lighthouse is perhaps always the highest symbol) as if it too had become conscious of the futility of pretending that it was advancing by creating the moribund. And it was the same way to the north, where battles between real estate sharks over the living and dead body of Eridanus Port had resulted in the return, little by little, of the jungle itself, and vines and thimbleberry already covered the ill-surveyed lots of the subsection among the few trees that had been left. But some people lived happily there after all, who could afford it. And even beautifully. For man—whose depredations, where they did not threaten the entire country with drought and desolation, sometimes by accident provided a better view—had not succeeded yet in hacking down the mountains and the stars.

The bells of a train, slowly moving northward along the coast tracks, began to sound through the fog across the water. I could remember a time when these bells had seemed to me exactly like the thudding of school bells, summoning one to some unwelcome task. Then they had seemed like somber church bells, tolling for a funeral. But now, at this moment, they struck clear as gay chimes, Christmas bells, birthday bells, harbor bells, pealing through the unraveling mist as for a city liberated, or some great spiritual victory of mankind. And they seemed to mingle with the song of the ship now distant, round the point—but so great a conductor of sound is water that its engines thudded as if at a fathom's distance:

> Dormez-vous?
> Dormez-vous?
> Sonnez les matines!
> Sonnez les matines!

And ourselves? How had we changed? We were many years older. We had traveled, been to the Orient, and Europe, grown rich and poor again, and always returned here. But were we older? My wife seemed young and beautiful and wild as ever, far more so. She still had the figure of a young girl and she had the wonder of a young girl. Her wide frank long-lashed eyes still changed color from green to yellow like a tiger cub's. Her brow could become chaotic with frowns and it is true that despair had once carved lines of suffering on her face, though I thought these signs vanished or came at will with her moods; they vanished when she was alive and interested, and she was uniquely alive, vivid and exciting.

"He no longer loves the person whom he loved ten years ago," said gloomy old Pascal. I quite believe it. "She is no longer the same, nor is he. He was young, and she also: she is quite different. He would perhaps love her yet, if she were what she was then." So gloomy profound old Pascal, the unselfish helper of my youth in other ways, had once seemed to threaten our future age. And yet not so. Surely I loved her now much more. I had more years to love with. Why should I expect her to be the same? Though she was the same in a way, just as this spring was the same, and not the same, as the springs of years ago. And I wondered if what really we should see in age is merely the principle of the seasons themselves wearing out, only to renew themselves through another kind of death. And indeed the seasons themselves in their duration and character had changed, or seemed to have changed, much more than she. Our winters came more forthrightly down from the arctic now, in the East they were getting our old Western winters, and this winter had been the longest and gloomiest we had ever known, and one had almost seemed to feel the onset of another ice age, another search for Eden. So much more welcome and sweeter the spring, now it had come. I myself however had aged in appearance. I had even quite a few white hairs, on one side, and our latest joke was that I was "graying at the temple." On the other hand I did not feel older, and bodily I was twice as strong, and I was in every way full of health. The port of fifty now seemed to me quite blithe, and as for old Pascal, he had died younger than I was now. The poor old chap would not have said such things if he'd only lived a bit longer, I thought.

"I wonder where Kristbjorg is, these days."

"There he is."

And here he had just appeared, stepping out of the mist. He had been fishing up the Fraser River, because he was "in death" as he said, his more than explicit phrase for "in debt." But the cold for the first time had caused him to move into the city for a while last winter, though he had left his boat for Quaggan and ourselves to look after. He was getting on for seventy, and was much thinner, but hale and hearty, and many lines seemed to have been smoothed from his face. He no longer sang the song about the storm in the red-light district but he still wore the same lumberjacket and good Irish tweed trousers he had worn in his fifties when not ten years older than I was now and I had thought him an old man, though now I thought him nearer my own age.

"Why there you are, Nicolai, we missed you."

"Ah well, this weather's changing, Missus.... Been in town... The streetcars are getting so humpy and dumpy, I never saw a street flusher. They just letting the old grime go.... I ran into a couple of bottles of rye...."

He passed into the mist and we continued along our path, the Bell-Proteus path, that on the reverse journey had once long since seemed to get so much longer, and then so much shorter. The fog was lifting and I thought:

How wrongly we interpreted that whole strange experience. Or rather how was it that it had never occurred to us, seriously, to interpret it at all, let alone to see it as a warning, a form of message, even as a message that shadowed forth a kind of strange command, a command that, it seemed to me, I had obeyed! And yet, all my heeding of any warning it contained would not have averted the suffering immediately ahead. Only dimly, even now, did I understand it. Sometimes I felt that the path had only seemed to grow shorter because the burden, the cannister, had grown lighter as I grew physically stronger. Then again I could become convinced that the significance of the experience lay not in the path at all, but in the possibility that in converting the very cannister I carried, the ladder down which I climbed every time I went to the spring—in converting both these derelicts to use I had prefigured something I should have done with my soul. Then of course, and pre-eminently, there was the lion. But I lacked spiritual equipment to follow such thoughts through. This much I understood, and had understood that as a man I had become tyrannized by the past, and that it was my duty to transcend it in the present. Yet my new vocation was involved with using that past—for this was the underlying meaning of my symphony, even my opera, the second opera I was now writing, the second symphony I would one day write—with turning it into use for others. And to do this, even before writing a note, it was necessary to face that past as far as possible without fear. Ah yes, and it was that, that I had begun to do here. And if I had not done so, how could we have been happy, as we now were happy?

How could I have helped you, I seemed to be saying to my wife, in the deepest sense even have loved you? However would we have found strength to endure the more furious past that was then ahead of us, to endure the fire, the destruction of our hopes, our house, to be rich and poor, known and unknown again, to endure the fear, the onset and the defeat of disease— even of madness, for to be deprived of one's house may, in a sense, be said to be like being deprived of one's rational faculty. How else have survived the shrieks of a dying piano, even, as a matter of fact, have come, somehow, to see something actually funny about all that? And how, above all, have found strength to rebuild on the same spot, right in the teeth of the terror of fire that had grown up between us and that had also been defeated? And I remembered the time when, homeless, having lost everything we had in the world, we had been drawn, not many weeks after the fire, to the still malodorous ruin of that house, before dawn, and watching the sun rise, had seemed to draw strength out of the sunrise itself for the decision once more to stay, to rebuild that haunted ruin we loved so much that we created our most jubilant memory that very day, when careless of its charred and tragic smell we wonderfully pic- nicked within it, diving off the blackened posts into the natural swimming pool of our old living room and frightened away I have no doubt the devil himself, who, the enemy of all humor in the face of disaster, as of all human delight, and often disguised as a social worker for the common good—for that we had saved the forest was not so important as that we had seemed to threaten some valuable potential real estate—wants nothing so much as that man shall believe himself unfriended by any higher power than he.

And yet, on the other side, else life would be composed of mere heroics that were all vain gestures to oneself, it had been necessary to go beyond remorse, beyond even contrition. I have often wondered whether it is not man's ordeal to make his contrition active. Sometimes I had the feeling I was attacking the past rationally as with a clawbar and hammer, while trying to make it into something else for a supernatural end. In a manner I changed it by changing myself and having changed it found it necessary to pass beyond the pride I felt in my accomplishment, and to accept myself as a fool again. I'm sure that even old Hank Gleason, though he would put this into better English, or different English, would see my point. Nothing is more humbling than the wreckage of a burned house, the fragments of consumed work. But it is necessary not to take pride in such masterly pieces of damnation either, especially when they have become so nearly universal. If we had progressed, I thought, it was as if to a region where such words as spring, water, houses, trees, vines, laurels, mountains, wolves, bay, roses, beach, islands, forest, tides and deer and snow and fire, had realized their true being, or had their source: and as these words on a page once stood merely to what they symbolized, so did the reality we knew now stand to something else beyond that that symbolized or reflected: it was as if we were clothed in the kind of reality which before we saw only at a distance, or to translate it into terms of my own vocation, it was as if we lived in a medium to which that in which our old lives moved, happy though they were, was like simply the bald verbal inspiration to the music we had achieved. I speak in terms of our lives only: my own compositions have always fallen far short of the great, indeed they will never perhaps be anything more than second-rate, but at least as it seemed to me there was room for them in the world, and I—and we—had happiness in their execution.

We were still on earth, still in the same place, but if someone had charged us with the notion that we had gone to heaven and that this was the after life we would not have said him nay for long. Moreover if we had been charged with formerly having been in hell for a while we would probably have had to say yes too, though adding that on the whole we liked that fine, as long as we were together, and were sometimes even homesick for it, though this life had many advantages over the other.

Still, indeed, we had the hellish fear of losing our third little house but now the joy and happiness of what we had known would go with us wherever we went or God sent us and would not die. I cannot really well express what I mean but merely set this down in the Montaigne-like belief—or as someone said, speaking about Montaigne—that the experience of one happy man might be useful.

The fog began to lift and we saw the train, it was drawn by a diesel engine of sinister appearance (the first one I ever saw in my life but I recognized it from the photogravure pictures in the *Sun*) departing quite silently now into the future to become obsolete and romantic in turn. Men could not do altogether without the nostalgic mountain-borne wailing of the old steam engines it seemed, so it had been equipped with a device, a touching compromise, that mooed like a cow intermittently as it slid along into the mountain pines.

But even in that moo, of nautical timbre, as it slid into the great Cordilleras, among these northern cousins of Popocatepetl, so that those working on the lines must think that a freighter approached, it was possible to detect I thought, that note of artistry which denoted Mr Bell, a signal to his old home, and the good people, English immigrants, an electrician and his family, who now inhabited it.

The wash from the invisible freighter, the wash still invisible itself from where we were on the path, could be heard breaking all along the curve of the beach as it approached us, and simultaneously it began, slowly at first, and gently, to rain, and as the wash of undulating silver rippling into sight transversely spent itself against the rocks we stopped to watch the rain like a bead curtain falling behind a gap in the trees, into the inlet below.

Each drop falling into the sea is like a life, I thought, each producing a circle in the ocean, or the medium of life itself, and widening into infinity, though it seems to melt into the sea, and become invisible, or disappear entirely, and be lost. Each is interlocked with other circles falling about it, some are larger circles expanding widely and engulfing others, some are weaker, smaller circles that only seem to last a short while. And smiling as I remembered my lesson I thought of that first time when we had seen the rain falling into a calm sea like a dark mirror, and we had found the cannister and decided to stay.

But last night I had seen something new; my wife had called me out of bed to the open window to see what she first thought was a school of little fishes breaking the still water just beneath, where the tide was high under the house. Then we saw that the whole dark water was covered with bright expanding phosphorescent circles. Only when my wife felt the warm mild rain on her naked shoulder did she realize it was raining. They were perfect expanding circles of light, first tiny circles bright as a coin, then becoming expanding rings growing fainter and fainter, while as the rain fell into the phosphorescent water each raindrop expanded into a ripple that was translated into light. And the rain itself was water from the sea, as my wife first taught me, raised to heaven by the sun, transformed into clouds, and falling again into the sea. While within the inlet itself the tides and currents in that sea returned, became remote, and becoming remote, like that which is called the Tao, returned again as we ourselves had done.

Now, somewhere in the unseen west where it was setting, the sun broke through the clouds, sending a flare of light across the water turning the rain into a sudden shower of pearls and touching the mountains, where the mist rising now almost perpendicularly from the black abysses fumed heavenward in pure white fire.

Three rainbows went up like rockets across the bay: one for the cat. They faded and there, in the east, a widening rift of clouds had become a patch of clear rain-washed sky. Arcturus. Spica. Procyon overhead, and Regulus in the Lion over the oil refinery. But Orion must have already set behind the sun so that, though we were Eridanus, Eridanus was nowhere to be found. And on the point the lighthouse began its beneficent signaling into the twilight.

And the spring? Here it was. It still ran, down through the jack-in-the-pulpits, down toward Hi-Doubt. It purified itself a bit as it came down from the mountains, but it always carried with it a faint tang of mushrooms, earth, dead leaves, pine needles, mud and snow, on its way down to the inlet and out to the Pacific. In the deeper reaches of the forest, in the somber damp caves, where the dead branches hang bowed down with moss, and death camass and the destroying angel grow, it was haggard and chill and tragic, unsure measurer of its path. Feeling its way underground it must have had its dark moments. But here, in springtime, on its last lap to the sea, it was as at its source a happy joyous little stream.

High above the pine trees swayed against the sky, out of the west came the seagulls with their angelic wings, coming home to rest. And I remembered how every evening I used to go down this path through the forest to get water from the spring at dusk.... Looking over my wife's shoulder I could see a deer swimming toward the lighthouse.

Laughing we stooped down to the stream and drank.

POEMS

Byzantium

—Don't come any of that Byzantium stuff
On me, me fine young toff! Just plain Stamboul
Is good enough for me and Lamps and Bill.
Constantibloodynople's right enough—
Used to be, eh? Eh? Don't give me that guff
Like that wot you said about the ideal
—In a blind eye socket! But a girl's a girl
And bobhead tigers here'll treat you rough,
And give you ideal!...I bid you adieu,
The siren moos; oh whither where away,
The engine stampedes: more fool you, hee hee.
And ukuleles mourn a ululu,
The iron groans: every dog will have its day,
And stars wink: Venus first then Mercury.

The Days Like Smitten Cymbals of Brass

When I was young, the mildew on my soul,
like Antipholus, it chanced to me,
or Melville's Redburn, to take that soul to sea
and have it scoured.
Ah! the days like rust smitten from iron decks
were beaten into one deafening roar
of sunlight and monotony.
I had expected the roar of the sea,
and of tempest,
not this sullen unremitting calm,
this road of concrete to the Antipodes,
where thunder was gunfire behind the hull....
This was not the heroic working class
where men love, looking to the future,
but petty squabbles, jealousies,
a hatred of bosuns, of Mr. Facing Both Ways,
one green eye the mate's and one the men's.
For which now's sprung for man ashore
such fierce black loathing hatred and contempt
it lives on writhing like a Kansas whirlwind
between me and these panic ports I make.
When I returned I boasted of typhoons
Conrad would not have recognized.
But to have possessed a unique anguish
has been some solace through the years.

For Under the Volcano

A dead lemon like a cowled old woman crouching in the cold.
A white pylon of salt and the flies
taxiing on the orange table, rain, rain, a scraping peon
and a scraping pen writing bowed words.
War. And the broken necked streetcars outside
and a sudden broken thought of a girl's face in Hoboken
a tilted turtle dying slowly on the stoop
of the sea-food restaurant, blood
lacing its mouth and the white floor—
ready for the ternedos tomorrow.
There will be no morrow, tomorrow is over.
Clover and the smell of fircones and the deep grass,
and turkey mole sauce and England
suddenly, a thought of home, but then
the mariachis, discordant, for the beaked bird
of maguey is on the wing, the waiter bears
a flowing black dish of emotion,
the peon's face is a mass of corruption.
We discard the horripilation of the weather
in this ghastly land of the half-buried man
where we live with Canute, the sundial and the red snapper,
the leper, the creeper, together in the green tower,
and play at sunset on the mundial flute and guitar
the song, the song of the eternal waiting of Canute,
the wrong of my waiting, the song of my weeping,

betrothed to the puking vacuum and the unfleshible root
and the rain on the train outside creeping, creeping,
only emptiness now in my soul sleeping
where once strutted tigers lemonade scruffy green lepers
liquors pears scrubbed peppers and stuffed Leopardis;
and the sound of the train and the rain on the brain...
So far from barn and field and little lane—
this pyre of Bierce and springboard of Hart Crane!
Death so far away from home and wife
I fear. And prayed for my sick life—

"A corpse should be transported by express," said the Consul
mysteriously, waking up suddenly.

Xochitepec

Those animals that follow us in dream
Are swallowed by the dawn, but what of those
Which hunt us, snuff, stalk us out in life, close
In upon it, belly-down, haunt our scheme
Of building, with shapes of delirium,
Symbols of death, heraldic, and shadows,
Glowering?—Just before we left Tlalpám
Our cats lay quivering under the maguey;
A meaning had slunk, and now died, with them.
The boy slung them half stiff down the ravine,
Which now we entered, and whose name is hell.
But still our last night had its animal:
The puppy, in the cabaret, obscene,
Looping-the-loop and soiling the floor,
And fastening itself to that horror
Of our last night: while the very last day
As I sat bowed, frozen over mescal,
They dragged two kicking fawns through the hotel
And slit their throats, behind the barroom door. . . .

The Volcano Is Dark

The volcano is dark and suddenly thunder
Engulfs the haciendas.
In this darkness, I think of men in the act of procreating,
Winged, stooping, kneeling, sitting down, standing up,
                             sprawling
Millions of trillions of billions of men moaning,
And the hand of the eternal woman flung aside.
I see their organ frozen into a gigantic rock,
Shattered now....
And the cries which might be the groans of the dying
Or the groans of love——

In the Oaxaca Jail

I have known a city of dreadful night,
Dreadfuller far than Kipling knew, or Thomson....
This is the night when hope's last seed is flown
From the evanescent mind of winter's grandson.

In the dungeon shivers the alcoholic child,
Comforted by the murderer, since compassion is here too;
The noises of the night are cries for help
From the town and from the garden which evicts those who
destroy!

The policeman's shadow swings against the wall,
The lantern's shadow is darkness against the wall;
And on the cathedral's coast slowly sways the cross
—Wires and the tall pole moving in the wind——

And I crucified between two continents.

But no message whines through for me here, oh multitudinous,
To me here—(where they cure syphilis with Sloans liniment,
And clap, with another dose.)

Delirium in Vera Cruz

Where has tenderness gone, he asked the mirror
Of the Biltmore Hotel, cuarto 216. Alas,
Can its reflection lean against the glass
Too, wondering where I have gone, into what horror?
Is that it staring at me now with terror
Behind your frail tilted barrier? Tenderness
Was here, in this very bedroom, in this
Place, its form seen, cries heard, by you. What error
Is here? Am I that rashed image?
Is this the ghost of the love you reflected?
Now with a background of tequila, stubs, dirty collars,
Sodium perborate, and a scrawled page
To the dead, telephone off the hook? In rage
He smashed all the glass in the room. (Bill: $50.)

No Company But Fear

How did all this begin and why am I here
at this arc of bar with its cracked brown paint,
papegaai, mezcal, hennessey, cerveza,
two slimed spittoons, no company but fear:
fear of light, of the spring, of the complaint
of birds and buses flying to far places,
and the students going to the races,
of girls skipping with the wind in their faces,
but no company, no company but fear,
fear of the blowing fountain: and all flowers
that know the sun are my enemies,
these, dead, hours?

Thirty-Five Mescals in Cuautla

This ticking is most terrible of all—
You hear the sound I mean on ships and trains,
You hear it everywhere, for it is doom;
The tick of real death, not the tick of time;
The termite at the rotten wainscot of the world—
And it is death to you, though well you know
The heart's silent tick failing against the clock,
Its beat ubiquitous and still more slow:
But still not the tick, the tick of real death,
Only the tick of time—still only the heart's chime
When body's alarm wakes whirring to terror.

In the cantina throbs the refrigerator,
While against the street the gaunt station hums.
What can you say fairly of a broad lieutenant,
With bloody hand behind him, a cigarro in it,
But that he blocks a square of broken sunlight
Where scraps of freedom stream against the gale
And lightning scrapes blue shovels against coal?
The thunder batters the Gothic mountains;
But why must you hear, hear and not know this storm,
Seeing it only under the door,
Visible in synecdoches of wheels
And khaki water sousing down the gutter?
In ripples like claws tearing the water back?

The wheels smash a wake under the jalousie.
The lieutenant moves, but the door swings to....
What of all this life outside, unseen by you,
Passed by, escaped from, or excluded
By a posture in a desolate bar?...
No need to speak, conserve a last mistake;
Perhaps real death's inside, don't let it loose.
The lieutenant carried it into the back room?
The upturned spittoons may mean it, so may the glass.
The girl refills it, pours a glass of real death,
And if that death's in her it's here in me.
On the pictured calendar, set to the future,
The two reindeer battle to death, while man,
The tick of real death, not the tick of time,
Hearing, thrusts his canoe into a moon,*
Risen to bring us madness none too soon.

(1937)

---

*Author's note: Soma was mystically identified with the moon, who controls vegetation, and whose cup is ever filling and emptying, as he waxes and wanes.

Eye-opener

How like a man, is Man, who rises late
And gazes on his unwashed dinner plate
And gazes on the bottles, empty too,
All gulphed in last night's loud long how-do-you-do,
—Although one glass yet holds a gruesome bait—
How like to Man is this man and his fate,
Still drunk and stumbling through the rusty trees
To breakfast on stale rum sardines and peas.

England

Cold Roast Hamlet Blues, Blubberhouses Blues, Ugley Blues,
Hard to come by Blues, Make-em Rich Blues,
Tadley God Help Us Blues, Little in sight blues,
Wide-Open Blues, King Edward Horsenail Blues,
Shippobottom Blues, Wig-wig Blues. Leaping Wild
Blues. Penny-come-quick Blues.

Nocturne

This evening Venus sings alone
And homeward feathers stir like silk
Like the dress of a multitudinous ghost
The pinions tear through a sky like milk.
Seagulls all soon to be turned to stone
That seeking I lose beyond the trail
In the woods that I and my ignorance own
Where together we walk on our hands and knees
Together go walking beneath the pale
Of a beautiful evening loved the most
And yet this evening is my jail
And policemen glisten in the trees.

Happiness

Blue mountains with snow and blue cold rough water,
A wild sky full of stars at rising
And Venus and the gibbous moon at sunrise,
Gulls following a motorboat against the wind,
Trees with branches rooted in air—
Sitting in the sun at noon with the furiously
Smoking shadow of the shack chimney—
Eagles drive downwind in one,
Terns blow backward,
A new kind of tobacco at eleven,
And my love returning on the four o'clock bus
—My God, why have you given this to us?

Men with Coats Thrashing

Our lives we do not weep
Are like wild cigarettes
That on a stormy day
Men light against the wind
With cupped and practised hand
Then burn themselves as deep
As debts we cannot pay
And smoke themselves so fast
One scarce gives time to light
A second life that might
Flake smoother than the first
And have no taste at last
And most are thrown away.

Epitaph

Malcolm Lowry
Late of the Bowery
His prose was flowery
And often glowery
He lived, nightly, and drank, daily,
And died playing the ukulele.

Kingfishers in British Columbia

A mad kingfisher
rocketing about in the
red fog at sunrise

now sits
on the alder
post that tethers the floats
angrily awaiting his mate.
Here she

comes, like a left wing
three quarter cutting through toward
the goal in sun-lamped
fog at Rosslyn Park at half
past three in halcyon days.

The Wounded Bat

...on a summer's afternoon, hot
and in the dusty path a bat,
with injured membrane and little hands,
a meeting that would have knocked young Aeschylus flat,
its red mouth helpless, like a mouse or cat,
a buzzing, like a buzzer, electric,
pathetic crepitation in the path.
She hooked to the twig, I laid her in the shade
with compassion, yet with blind terror
praying that not too soon
death might care to do for me as much.

After Publication of Under the Volcano

Success is like some horrible disaster
Worse than your house burning, the sounds of ruination
As the roof tree falls following each other faster
While you stand, the helpless witness of your damnation.

Fame like a drunkard consumes the house of the soul
Exposing that you have worked for only this—
Ah, that I had never suffered this treacherous kiss
And had been left in darkness forever to founder and fail.

And yet I am of England too; odi et amo—
I have known her terrible towns in peace.
Was it yet your left eye or your right was blinded
Idiot England bidding the world to anchor.
My faith in you as home ended
In Badajoz and Salamanca.
And the muted voice of England long asleep
Was heard then.
We may not speak of islands.
England is like a ship in the sea
Who's moored fore and aft. The crew changes
And the terrible boatswains yell
The derricks down her deck. Cluster lamps
At night light the hold. What's in it?
A few old tragedies and tales, histories
Of famous men. The deceitful picture of her past.
With bowsprits stuck into the wharf of God.
England is the ultimate blockade.
It is not a matter of war or prophecy
What I say.
May she disown the hypocrites who sailed her
Since this time, she's not wounded.

Lament in the Pacific Northwest

They are taking down the beautiful houses
                                         once built with loving hands
But still the old bandstand stands where no band stands
With clawbars they have gone to work
                              on the poor lovely houses above the sands
At their callous work of eviction that
                                    no human law countermands
Callously at their work of heartbreak
                             that no civic heart understands
In this pompous and joyless city of
                       police moral perfection and one man stands
Where you are brutally thrown out of beer parlors
                               for standing where no man stands
Where the pigeons roam free and the police listen
                                 to each pigeon's demands
And they are taking down the beautiful homes
                             once cared for with loving hands
But still the old bandstand stands where no band stands.

FRAGMENTS

FROM **DARK AS THE GRAVE WHEREIN MY FRIEND IS LAID**

CHAPTER 1

THE SENSE OF SPEED, OF GIGANTIC TRANSITION, OF going southward, downward, over three countries, the tremendous mountain ranges, the sense at once of descent, tremendous regression, and of moving, not moving, but in another way dropping straight down the world, straight down the map, as of the imminence of something great, phenomenal, and yet the moving shadow of the plane below them, the eternal moving cross, less fleeting and more substantial than the dim shadow of the significance of what they were actually doing that Sigbjørn held in his mind: and yet it was possible only to focus on that shadow, and at that only for short periods: they were enclosed by the thing itself as by the huge bouncing machine with its vast monotonous purring, pouring din, in which they sat none too comfortably, Sigbjørn with his foot up embarrassedly, for he had taken his shoe off, a moving, deafening, continually renewed time-defeating destiny by which they were enclosed but of which they were able only to see the inside, for so to speak of the streamlined platinum-colored object itself they could only glimpse a wing, a propeller, through the small, foolish, narrow oblong windows. Nonetheless, the sense of adventure, if Sigbjørn participated in it mostly for Primrose's sake, was tremendous, too, and now, as they sat hand-in-hand, Primrose ecstatic at the window (the thunderous, dumbfounding voice of the plane), the sense of relief, of joy, they were through, yes, they were beyond the barrier—or one barrier, this much was certain—they were through the customs, they were away, they were in America; to the left was Oregon, to the right the Pacific coast ranges, but the sense of joy did not wholly mitigate those other gnawing feelings, which Sigbjørn took care to keep out of his face, of sorrow, of crashing failure, and, even now, when there seemed little to worry him at the moment, of blind and all-possessing, of permanent panic.

Leaving Oregon at sunset, clouds carved out of black basalt, and a rim of turquoise-jade-green—did they have jade mines in Oaxaca?—and light flowing pure gold-orange: "You never saw such a sunset on earth," Primrose said, and indeed you did not, Sigbjørn thought, so dark and terrible, this great black basalt sunset over the burned forests of Oregon, the burning gold and great shafts of burning light against ten-mile-high piles of black clouds shot through with these shafts of unearthly light and unearthly foreboding. "We're through!" Primrose said. "Now do you see how wrong you were!"

"We're late too," Sigbjørn said, glancing at his new French antimagnetic wristwatch, a pre-wedding-anniversary present from Primrose.

"But we're in America, and you said you'd never be able to go to America again."

"In America, but not in Mexico yet," said Sigbjørn, and Primrose Wilderness laughed. "Still I imagine Fernando can wait another week or so, having waited more than seven years," he added. "But it's true. Here we are, and I never thought we would get through, even to America."

"And we're on our honeymoon."

"We're always on our honeymoon."

"Five years—"

They sat at the back of the plane (at the back so that no one would see *him*) and Sigbjørn kissed her.

To their right a star shone out in the western agony on the horizon. "Altair," Primrose said.

"And soon we'll see the Southern Cross."

"Tomorrow perhaps...*and* all of Eridanus."

And it was true, they were through, beyond the barrier, or the first barrier, and there away to the right stretched the Pacific coast ranges and the sea, the same ranges in whose shadow, back in Canada, they lived, which ran right down to Tierra del Fuego itself, to Cape Horn, the same sea on which they lived too, and which lapped on the shores of Acapulco Bay, of dubious memory, and of what promise for the future?

It was as if, since that day of ruination on June 6, 1944 (tomorrow would be December 7—December 7!—1945), that Sigbjørn had, little by little, let slip his hold on his life: in a subtle sense both of them had: they had not let go, altogether, but they had fallen, and they were now on a lower ledge than before: their marriage, and their life even, was in danger, and he knew it, and was doing nothing about it (his marriage in fact was an almost exact counterpoint of his house: it had fallen asunder and had not yet properly been put together again); he was using his wife's necessity and the fact that she had never visited a foreign country as an excuse for indulging his own necessity—for what, was it—what was it but death? Or was this trip, ostensibly for Primrose, something that nature, destiny, was giving him, in return for the loss of his book...?

Just as he had taken his first drink for three years on June 6, 1944, now today—after another period of abstinence—he had begun drinking, a little, not much, to celebrate. Why had he been so disappointed that they had some kind of prohibition in

Portland? What did San Francisco mean to him but another drink? this time of Scotch, which he couldn't get in Canada. Why had he used Fernando Martinez of all people, as a kind of excuse for going to Mexico? What did his friend, his character Dr. Vigil, mean to him, but a nostalgia for delirium? Or oblivion. And his meeting with him another excuse, even such as the Consul liked to find, for "celebration."

Nonetheless, Sigbjørn had a sense of hope: or at any rate, after his illness, and his wife's, a sense of it, not great, rather poignant, as if one had risen one winter morning and looked out into the garden to see a wild apple tree in bloom.

It had been a day of darkness and murk and rain. By the time they started for Vancouver airport it was drizzling rain, and when their plane finally took off, it was a blizzard: swirls and lashes of rain across the Seattle airport, Customs inspectors in pools—Sigbjørn shuddered. Customs inspectors! How afraid of such creatures he was—would he ever get over it? And the memory of that morning more than six years ago when he had been turned back to Canada at the American border came heavily and clammily about him once more. That was September, 1939, and he had been trying to enter America by bus through Blaine, Washington, in order to see Primrose herself at San Francisco—"for the last time," as he had tactlessly put it to the Immigration inspectors. And now here they were anyway, over that border, beyond it, and a great sense of freedom possessed him at this idea, of flying right down America, right down the western side of the map, over this once forbidden territory (ravaged here by fire too as far as the eye could reach), forbidden not only because he had been designated as a person liable to be a public charge upon it, but because the territory itself was at that time neutral, and he proposed crossing it in order also to fight in a foreign war in which, incidentally, he

had not finally participated in any capacity whatsoever; so it
was true that that misfortune could be seen as having saved his
life, something for which he forgot too often to be grateful—
was he ever really grateful save when he read this as "our lives
together"?—down, down over the western ranges, beating the
sunset; but down into complete darkness now, flying into
Frisco spitting fire, lights like a bowknot, cities like rock candy,
lights like a question mark, a bus station of pearls—they got
out to have a drink. It was fine weather at the San Francisco
airport, with the stars clear. "Alis volat propriis," Sigbjørn remarked, turning, for a moment toward the faithful plane in its
more unfamiliar mood of being stationary and silent, a meek
appurtenance of a field.

"What does that mean?"

"Does an Englishman have to tell you your own state motto?
She flies with her own wings, unlike the nonexistent bird with
one. Well, it's either Oregon or California's."

"It isn't California's. So you've made San Francisco at last."
Primrose could laugh now.

"Is this your first trip by air?" a fellow passenger was asking
them.

"No, but it's our first decent drink of Scotch in half a decade,"
Sigbjørn said, though now he had it, it tasted rather medicinal,
and far from ordering another, he gave Primrose half his.

"You folks from Seattle?"

"Canada.... That is, my wife's American. I'm — well—
anyway."

"Fifty cents for a snort," Primrose was saying. "It certainly
costs."

"And how. On holiday?"

"We're on our honeymoon."

"Ah..."

"We're off to see a pal of mine in Mexico if he's still there. . . . We've been married for five years, but we're still on our honeymoon," Sigbjørn explained hastily. "Only," he added a little later, "our house burned down but we saved the forest."

Though this latter event had taken place eighteen months ago, the Wildernesses still evidently had to talk about it. But had that anything to do with why he, Sigbjørn, felt such a ridiculous need to give an *account* of himself? And why had he brought in that honeymoon, an intimate little joke between Primrose and himself? Why did he do such things? And what the devil was everybody still so suspicious for? What bloody right had they to question one? Sigbjørn wondered as they boarded the plane again, wishing now he hadn't mentioned Mexico either, which might seem suspicious in itself. And at that, three months after the war was over. Perhaps it was Primrose's Arctic skunk coat, his own preanniversary present to her, that was the trouble: people might think she was a Russian spy. There was a spy scare in Canada just now, and to judge from all accounts, an even worse one in America. In fact merely to have come from Canada, with its relative proximity to Russia, might seem even more suspicious than to be going to Mexico. Sigbjørn was so absurdly shaken, though in all seriousness, by this, that he now wished he had not given half of his drink to Primrose; he was finding difficulty with his safety belt, and after the new stewardess had admiringly hung up the beautiful coat, Primrose had to adjust the strap for him. They were soaring above San Francisco; he leaned over to see the lights again behind and below in the distance, and Sigbjørn thought of the diatonic booming of the foghorn in the great bridge. That time he had been turned back at the border he had been visualizing walking over the bridge with Primrose. He couldn't bear even now to think of her waiting vainly for him in this city, for waited she had. His first messages had somehow miscarried.

Still, it all worked to a joyous ending; Primrose instead came to Canada; and now, happily married for years, they were flying over the bridge, had literally risen above it, as she would say. When they had unfastened their belts, Primrose prepared to sleep on Sigbjørn's shoulder, while Sigbjørn wondered if he had sufficient courage to take his shoes off. He decided, despite their seat at the back, that he had not. Refraining from smoking for fear of disturbing her, Sigbjørn contrived somehow to keep his right foot up: both feet were still swollen slightly, the right was the worst one. Five hundred miles to go for the next stop, Los Angeles. And, overpraised method of travel though flying might be, this was at least better than sitting with both those feet in a bucket of hot water, five minutes after a bucket of cold water, in their poor beloved rainy house in Eridanus, British Columbia, that they had been building on what remained of their old burned site, between the forest and the inlet—better, certainly for poor Primrose, who had had, now their well was dry, to drag down the water herself from the store, and this after having not long recovered from a dangerous infection herself.

"Come over here, son, you can get a better view." The passenger who had spoken to them in the bar was leaning over the aisle, and Sigbjørn, seeing there was now a vacant seat beside him, smiled at Primrose, and went over and sat down in the other place, wondering at the same time why he had allowed his will to be presumed on. Perhaps it was the "son" that did it; somehow it moved him, not unnaturally, for Sigbjørn was thirty-six, a fact that he immediately remembered when the man added: "A lot of water has flowed under that thing since I was last here."

The remote lights of the bridge were now almost immediately beneath them, their plane was circling for height. "We've got a very beautiful one in Vancouver too, not so big as this of course. Unfortunately people are always jumping off it," Sigbjørn said.

"Ever been to San Francisco before?" asked the man, who had a rather deep voice.

"Yes," answered Sigbjørn. "As a matter of fact I have. Twice, to be exact. I went to Mexico from here once before. That was in 1936, September, 1936, when I was about twenty-seven. Panama Pacific. On the *Pennsylvania*. We sailed right down under that bridge to San Pedro, and then down the Lower California coast past Mazatlán to Acapulco, where we landed."

"Oh, you've been to Mexico before too? What did you do there?"

"Drank, mostly," Sigbjørn answered, after taking some thought.

"Oh yes, we can all do a bit of that, ha ha."

"Well, I was a journalist at times," Sigbjørn thought of saying, though it would have been almost a lie, and kept silent, though not for that reason.

"Will you have a snifter?" The man produced a flask, as the plane roared on southward through the night.

"No thanks.... Though I will have a smoke. Thanks. Thanks a lot."

"Fire is a very terrible thing," said the other, blowing out the proffered match.

Sigbjørn went on after a pause: "My mother often spoke of my grandfather sailing from San Francisco. That was in England, of course. My grandfather was a skipper in sail, he was wrecked, and drowned in the Bay of Bengal. Actually, his ship was blown up. He had a rather heroic death.... It became quite a legend. They were in the doldrums. The crew had cholera." Sigbjørn stopped. "But that would be before the bridge was built," he added.

"Were you insured?"

"You're talking about our house? No, it was just a cabin on government land we'd bought for a hundred dollars from a blacksmith," Sigbjørn said shortly. "But it was our first home and we loved it. We've been building another one now on almost the same site, not quite the same, unfortunately. We've built it mostly out of the lumber from a dismantled sawmill." Sigbjørn thought of the big windows they'd wangled from the machine shop and how proud Primrose was when, with Mauger's help, they had finally fitted them into their frames. *Nine-light windows that never saw the sun. Now face the east in a house that's scarce begun. Who once lent grudging day to a machine, what joys and agonies would they someday light within?* Too many days, too much light. Or it was, could be, almost, a poem. "We've been working on the place since last March, and we hoped to get it finished for this winter," he continued. "But we had accident after accident, and the going got too tough for us all round. We really had to put yet another roof on the place to make it habitable, and the weather's just been too bad to do it. I would say altogether it was too hard on my wife." Sigbjørn looked round to see if this well-intentioned half-lie had reached Primrose's ears for if truth were told it had more than equally proved too hard on him.

"You don't mean to tell me that you were doing this work yourselves?"

"Who else would do it? But it's a fishing village, and the fishermen gave us help, when they were there." But if he thought of the unfinished house with sadness, it was also with pride. Yes, frightened though he had become at almost everything now, they together had been courageous, though he said it himself, with their everlasting terror of fire, and considering everything that had happened, to rebuild there, in that place. And considering everything that had gone on happening, to go on rebuilding. To have done this with their own hands was the least thing about it. And especially had it been courageous of Primrose, who in her own way had become more frightened than he. The difference between them was that it was possible that Primrose had left her fright behind in Eridanus and he fervently hoped he could help, by this trip, for this to remain so, never to be assumed when they returned: for her, much depended on him, but his own road was more complicated.

"What's the name of your village?" his companion was inquiring. "Perhaps I know it. I've hunted up in British Columbia once or twice."

"Eridanus. It's down an inlet of the same name fairly near Vancouver. But that doesn't mean anything, for there's every kind of wilderness fairly near Vancouver, come to that."

"I've done a little navigation in my day. Am I wrong, or isn't Eridanus the name of a star?"

"It's the name of a constellation, the one south of Orion. It looks like a river and to the ancients was identified with the River Styx. That's about all I know about it, except that it's also been called the river of youth, possibly because it was associated with Phaeton, a man who insisted on driving the chariot of the sun against his father's orders, and as a consequence burned the earth up. Thus it's been called both the river of death and the river of youth. You can't see the whole constellation up north where we are and we were hoping to see the rest of it in Mexico. The inlet got its name from another windjammer belonging to a company that liked to christen its ships after the constellations and she was apparently driven ashore in a violent chinook. Some of the very old-timers claimed to remember when parts of the wreck were still on the beach and she was said to have carried a very pleasant cargo of marble and cherries-in-brine and wine from Portugal."

"How did your first house catch fire?" the persistent fellow was asking him, when Sigbjørn excused himself and returned to his seat by Primrose, who was now fast asleep, breathing gently like a child, with her head cushioned on her arm. God, how innocent and beautiful, even angelic she looked, with her lips slightly parted and the lamplight falling on her face like that. You would not have thought she had ever suffered. And you would have thought she was at least fifteen years younger than he was, whereas in fact she was slightly older—thirty-nine. Nor had the light anything to do with it. She looked younger still by daylight. In fact Sigbjørn had been at pains to bring his marriage license with him, not merely lest he be impeached in America under the Mann Act, the white slave traffic ruling, that must be so baffling to Frenchmen, which forbids your taking a woman not your wife across any border, under pain of hanging or electrocution, but—talk about freedom from fear— under the California law that would have baffled his own father and mother, which forbids a man's cohabitation with any woman below the age of consent, under pain of ninety-nine years' incarceration for rape. Or so, quite seriously, these laws had taken form in his mind. Sigbjørn switched his lamp off, as he did so noticing that his fellow passenger had done the same. Suddenly what remained of the feeling of pride and pleasure that he had had while talking about the house, as well as his feeling of tolerance for the man, was succeeded by one of violent shame. Idiot! Buffoon! Oaf! Here he had been maundering to himself about people's inquisitiveness, and what precisely had this damn fellow drawn out of him! Everything, or almost everything. And what had he, Sigbjørn, whose business it might be considered so to glean, learned about the man? Nothing, or almost nothing. Why, he could not now—the man was slightly ahead of them, he was dozing and had turned the light off, and Sigbjørn saw only the vague shape of his back—he could not now have told what sort of clothes the man wore,

how tall he was, though he had seen he was taller than himself
in the bar, whether he was fat or thin, whether he was an American or a German or even an Armenian. He was not even a face.
He was nothing but a voice, a rather deep voice, and what was
so awful, Sigbjørn was content that he should be so, he had no
curiosity about him in the slightest. The only thing he remembered clearly, or perhaps had looked at, was the flask and now
he wished he'd accepted a drink from it, just as he had wished
earlier that he had not only not given Primrose half his whiskey
at the bar, but ordered another one. Perhaps he'd only refused
the drink because of the flask itself, which was one of those yellow leather-clad contraptions he particularly disliked, whose
declining contents were marked by pictorial gradations: Half
full, Quarter full, a little man becoming more and more borracho, with at the bottom a picture of a pig, labeled Damn Fool,
which hinted (though what Sigbjørn possibly despised most
about them was that they always held less than a pint) that
those contents might be as cheaply unamusing as its exterior;
and that was all, absolutely all—unless you counted that the
man had once hunted, or said he had once hunted, in Canada,
and once done a little navigation, or said he'd done a little navigation—that Sigbjørn knew about him. Nor could you build
the man up from the synecdoche of the porcine flask, which
most likely had been given him as a parting present, as some
gag at the airport, and had little bearing on his character at all.
One had been presented to Sigbjørn himself years ago with
conceivably better reason. But if he had not learned anything
whatsoever about him, by this very defection was not so much
more revealed about Sigbjørn himself to himself? For Sigbjørn
had not quite given away the most salient point, that he was, if
a monumentally unsuccessful one, and of late silent, a writer. It
was thus that their positions were, so to say, reversed; the voice
having behaved as a writer was supposed to behave, and him-

self as his potential subject. And how easily he had fallen into
the trap! He had been enticed into it like a son, and then had
found himself talking like a father, or as a father might, were
his intention less to instruct than to make himself important, or
to justify himself. The immature father and the inquisitive son.
The subject and object. Yes, to justify himself. Why? For it
seemed to him now that it was not only that he hadn't grasped
the opportunity to learn anything about this individual, it was
almost as if he'd felt obliged—and this went far beyond his former thought of the necessity of giving an account of himself—
to make some excuse or explanation for being on earth at all.
Or was this in his imagination? First he was as much secretly
flattered, whatever his later reactions, as outraged, at being
spoken to in the first place. Yet while he was glad that the man
was interested in his life, since this was indeed interest in his
work at one remove, nonetheless he was very much afraid that
he would be asked embarrassing questions, which was why he
had to talk, to supply even symbolical answers to those questions in advance to forestall their being asked, such questions
as: "Were you in any of the services?" He still felt that at this
point of history in this hemisphere, to the greater part of
humanity, even if its immediate representative had never been
within a thousand miles of a war, a man simply possessed no
cognizable value whatsoever who had not been precisely in one
of those services. Sigbjørn lit a cigarette and kicked off his
shoes angrily. *Al stereless and in a boot am I, amid the sea,
between windes two, that in contrarie standen evermo.* And
those contrarie windes, what were they? Were not those
improbable winds, the subjective wind, and the objective wind,
that blew out of who knew how much more improbable
immensities? Objective wind indeed! Sigbjørn now went back
over his shameful recital, as it now seemed to him, and if for no
better reason than it had been made at all, and tried to imagine

what he himself would have learned from it, had he been in the other's place.

He could not help laughing at himself. And all that because he had not said he was a writer. Take that away, and his life, objectively considered, seemed to have no meaning at all. Did all creative writers, in one way or another, suffer from this ghastly alienation? If they did, they certainly tried their best these days to keep it dark. On the face of it, you would think they—and by "they" he meant all the better writers in his own language he could think of at the moment—were the kind of people who rose early and shot pheasants boisterously out of the sky, were capable of gigantic feats of farming or engineering or even stone masonry, had muscles like barbellmen, hurtled through Belgium on motorcycles, fought in wars like young Charlemagnes, were traitors, or became heroes of the people, like Erikson, with equal zest, and even when they were geniuses, like Daniel, turned out their work as easily as if it came out of some celestial sausage machine. And they had one thing in common: with very few exceptions they all seemed, at bottom, to be incorrigible optimists, even when their works were most despairing. Or this was what they took care to have known. Such people might go into exile, forcibly or as a protest, but you could never think of them being turned back from a border as a person likely to be a public charge. No, you felt that the very exuberance of their bloody optimism would carry them through any border, if necessary, without a passport. Sigbjørn had scarcely ever read a genuine book about a writer. Usually if the writer wanted to talk about his own struggles, he disguised them as those of a sculptor, or a musician, or of any other character, as though he were ashamed of his profession. It was a pity. For to learn something of the mechanics of his kind of creation, was not that to learn something of the mechanism of destiny? There was even a sort of unwritten law about it. Indeed it was the first thing you learned: the reader does not want to hear about your rejected play. That was true: still, why not? Half the world was like a writer who has had his play rejected. In fact the world at times seemed very like a rejected play itself. Or a rejected novel, like for instance, *The Valley of the Shadow of Death*, by Sigbjørn Wilderness. A world in suspense, a world in delirium, a drunken world in fear. But fear, that was another thing. With him there were too many fears, so that the word too, like himself, was liable to lose all meaning—it was high time he categorized them.

At this moment there was a brilliant flash throughout the plane, the machine gave a lurch upward, bounced, lurched upward again, and simultaneously with the appearance of the sign ahead bidding them fasten their safety belts, there was a single tremendous thunderpeal. But the lightning, a good writer, did not repeat itself. The plane roared on.

A ballet, yes. Such form, through his half closed eyes, Sigbjørn could now almost imagine he perceived hovering above the passengers all sitting bound to their seats under the ceiling lights, as though the plane had suddenly been invaded by sky-way robbers, like a ballet, or something in some old morality play, or a ghostly animated cartoon. There was a dancer, (a) alpha for acrophobia, the fear of heights, whose white mask was set in a fixed muted yell, as if perpetually contemplating a vast drop below him; there was a dancer (b), the fear of discovery, a jester—for even Sigbjørn could not bear that he be wholly serious, yet with an implacable mask who carried newspapers under his arm with such headlines as Wilderness's Works Written by Erikson, or Writer Confesses Old Murder, or Wilderness Admitted Liar; there was (y), a grinning witless mask, but more familiar than any of the others, for he had perhaps been with him the longest, the fear of disease; and dancer (z), with a mask that wept, the fear of losing Primrose; there was the fear of Primrose's fear, with a mask that screamed; and with Wilderness's own face streaming with blood, the fear of himself, and with his head turned always Dantesquely facing backward, with a sombrero, and a bottle of mescal in his hand, who was fear of Mexico; there was the motor face of fear of accidents and traffic, and the frenzied roaring face of fear of fire whom he could not contemplate for a second; and all of them were chased about, herded, ordered, and finally set to dance together by a master choreographer, a giant in the brutal boot-faced mask of an Immigration officer, or a border official, or a Consul, or a policeman, though his mien was military and he wore a uniform covered with medals, with two guns at the hip, who was fear of authority. One dancer who did not seem to be present was the fear of death, which was an odd thing, but perhaps he was not so much a fear as a medium in which one lived. Or possibly he was disguised as the fear of losing Primrose or the fear of sorrow. Though in another sense the fear of death in so far as it existed was his one unselfish fear, for it was the fear of Primrose's sorrow. A ghastly alienation indeed! Did any hint appear in his face that such appalling tableaux were invariably shaping themselves before his inner eye, even at his happiest moments? And was this the real reason why he had been selected all those years ago as the person to turn back from the border? The sign went off, and Sigbjørn unfastened their safety belts, and though they seemed to have come out of the storm the plane still rocked and bounced. They could not be more than an hour now from Los Angeles. Would there be any formalities to go through there? For the stewardess had said that it was not certain in this weather that the Los Angeles–El Paso–Monterrey flight would be "on," in which case they might have to go straight down through Mazatlán, and Los Angeles would be their port of exit. This would mean delay too, for he had tried for that flight, as being the more exciting of the two, but had failed to get tickets. Oh well, throw away your mind, as dear old Fernando would say. It was not easy. According to some Scandinavian writer, you always remember the moods when you were thinking hardest.

A scene that had taken place just this morning at the Vancouver airport came back to him vividly. When their airliner limousine had drawn in at the airport entrance, a police car had been standing in the rain outside, and possibly it was this that had put him off. Sigbjørn had fumbled and dropped his tickets, forgotten to give one bag in to be weighed, and become covered with confusion, and it was not until Primrose and he were seated finally on a bench waiting for the southern flight to be called that it occurred to him that the presence of the police car was probably a matter of course. Then he seemed to remember that police cars nearly always were to be found standing outside airports, a war measure that no doubt someone had forgotten to cancel, or was still in operation, for the very good reason that peace had technically not yet been signed. With this realization Sigbjørn sighed with relief and was able to give himself for a while wholly to Primrose and their excitement. Meantime they had watched, through the French windows of the waiting room, a big plane arriving from Seattle. It maneuvered for position, the ramp was wheeled up, and the passengers began to hurry down it through the downpour, over the tarmac, and toward the wicket, where their tickets were taken by cloaked officials. Sigbjørn now suddenly became aware that he was watching these passengers narrowly, that the whole process of their arrival had become something of extraordinary importance to him. Many of these passengers were obviously American and thus were landing in what was, for them, a foreign country. How would they, his cousins, his brothers from across the border, meet the ordeal of examination on this side? Well-dressed for the most part, cheerful, exhibiting an unusual patience despite the weather, they gave in their tickets and passed through the gate as thoughtlessly as though they were going into a cinema. And now here stepped one young fellow out onto the ramp, who evidently regarded his ordeal with such indifference he hadn't even bothered to shave or comb his hair. Here now, he approached hatless, chewing gum, the wind blowing his fair hair about, whereas Sigbjørn for fifteen minutes prior to landing would not have had a moment's peace about his hair; he would have been dodging in and out of the lavatory and plaguing Primrose as to whether he looked "all right" (as only too soon now, as they came ever nearer to Los Angeles, he would begin plaguing Primrose) and as this man drew closer, sauntering nonchalantly across the tarmac with his friend, and then past the gate, a minute or two later, was to be seen just as nonchalantly going through the Customs, even daring to smoke, Sigbjørn discovered that his whole mind had become focused upon him, that for a moment he filled his world, blotting out all else. For that moment the man seemed to him the epitome of everything that he would like to be, and in being that, he *was* him. It was precisely the reverse of what had just taken place on the plane between himself and his fellow passenger. So absolutely did his being seem to enter into that of this other totally different and carefree person that it was like one of those identities of subject with object that are the end of certain mystical disciplines and Sigbjørn almost had the feeling that if he did not hold on to himself he would disappear altogether. This man also, it now struck Sigbjørn, resembled in that respect one of those optimistic writers he had been thinking about, a person who would get through any Customs, any border, do what he would, by virtue perhaps of his very volition, of the impossibility of any idea of any hitch entering his head.

Was this a good sign? Sigbjørn now wondered. Certainly it

was rather a second-rate ambition to be an optimist, but was there a suggestion, in all this, that some part of him at least felt capable of writing again? Had he not once, he now recalled, transcended his own experience of having been turned back at the border by writing about it? Or if not transcended it, turned it to account, made it *work*. He had. He had, once, written a poem about it, and though he had not thought of this poem, which he had never sold and had lost completely in the fire, for years, it now, queerly, began to come back to him:

> *A singing smell of tar, of the highway,*
> *Fills the gray Vancouver Bus Terminal*
> *Crowned by dreaming names, Portland, New Orleans,*
> *Spokane, Chicago—and Los Angeles!*
> *City of the angels and my luck—*

How did it go on? If he had the energy, he would write it down, if he could remember any more. How pleased Primrose would be with him! But now he felt sleepy, and besides there was another obstruction against writing anything down. *A singing smell of tar, of the highway.* Then that would seem to mean also that he too had once been as carefree, so far as any trouble at the border was concerned, as that tousled fellow landing from the Seattle plane. His longing to see Primrose, and his joy at the expectation of meeting her again, had been so great that it had even wiped out the fear that, for all he knew to the contrary, even when he did see her, he would have to part from her again soon.

Yes indeed. His joy had been great. What kind of poem, though, had he been trying to write? A kind of sestina, though more elaborate than a sestina, of eight verses, of ten lines each with, to begin with instead of the end words being repeated, the last line of the second verse rhyming, or rhyming falsely, or striking an assonance with the first line of the first. But what had been his general purpose in choosing such a form? Sigbjørn remembered that he had wanted to give the impression of the bus going one way, toward the border and the future, and, at the same time, of the shopwindows and streets flashing by into the past: he had wished to do that, but something more: since the poem was to be about his being turned *back* at the border, these shopwindows and streets that he was so glibly imagining in the past were in the future too, for tonight and at the end of the poem he would have to return *from* the border by a similar bus along exactly the same route, that is, in both an opposite direction, and an opposite mood. But he hadn't got to the border yet so he set out afresh to do the same thing as before with another unit of two verses. How did it go on?

Primrose was shaking him, to put on his safety belt. My God! Here they were at Los Angeles itself. Lights were all round them and he was not going to have time to comb his hair. But there was no need, Primrose was saying. The El Paso flight was on.

CHAPTER V

THEIR BUS TO CUERNAVACA, WITH OPEN CUTOUT AND A noise of tearing canvas, made little spurts of speed in its last attempts to shake off the city, like Nietzsche's outworks of the ideal (though Mexico City was far from being an ideal), its outer garb (of ugsome Parisian suburbia), its masquerade (of pulquerías), and its temporary hardening (of the plaster of new apartment buildings), stiffening as of skeletal structures never to be finished, and dogmatizing Aleman-Moralización. And now the bus began its weary circling up toward the Tres Marías through scenery that was not unlike that of New Hampshire or the Cotswolds; jammed in the second-class bus and scarcely daring to breathe, the thought struck him that their journey might have a larger meaning, for them, if he reflected upon it. Was it not as if they themselves were making a pilgrimage? As if almost to the shrine, or to the oracle of miracle, to place their ignorance at the foot of the cross in humility and ask if there was any meaning, after what had happened, in their lives? Strange things had happened to them with such frequency during the past years it was almost as though a force were trying to din some matter of import into their minds. But the fact remained that something almost imperceptible had altered in

both of them. He thought back over the last week. They had
begun to haunt churches, and even today before setting off
with their bags and hangovers for the Plaza Netzalcuayatl, in
the Church of Isabel la Católica they had made a devout prayer
to the Saint of Dangerous and Desperate Causes. But what, Sigbjørn, too hypocritical to put anything in the collection box,
asked himself, as once more they changed gears and began
slowly to round another hairpin bend, past the familiar sign,
Euzkadi, another Vulcanización—was dangerous or desperate
about it all? What indeed was the cause or causes? A partial
answer to his question seemed to arise from the road before and
above him winding up ever higher and higher to the mists and
chevals de frise of the Tres Marías. No wonder it was like coming home. For had he not lived in Cuernavaca before, and made
this journey, backward and forward, many times before, both
in happiness and sorrow, and then later, in absolute crushing
despair, going to and from Acapulco, shunning his eyes from
Cuernavaca every time he came to it as if his soul, as he had
written, had been tied to the tail of a runaway horse? That last
grim time he had come back from Acapulco with Stanford—
no, he would not think of it: perhaps that had not been quite
the last time: at any rate he did not want now to make sure
which was the very last time. And yet he had the mysterious
feeling that this road from Mexico City to Cuernavaca had
something to teach him—alas, or thank God, them too; for better or worse, Primrose was caught up in it—some obscure lesson that he had not, when he was here before, succeeded in
learning, and that he must traverse this route many, many times
again, backward and forward, before it was learned to the satisfaction of whatever force moved his ways. But after all—dangerous and desperate cause.

Partly due to his stubbornness they were on a second-class
bus and not in a turismo. This time the trouble had begun in

the Plaza Netzalcuayatl by a misunderstanding on Sigbjørn's part. While he had not wanted to take the Flecha Roja, or simply the Flecha, the second-class bus, for they had too much luggage and were unlikely to get a seat, he *had* wanted to get a bus, namely the first-class one, the Estrella de Oro, for which, just as in the old days, you booked your seat and then, since passengers were not allowed to stand, were entitled to that seat and sat upon it. It was a good arrangement. Nonetheless having booked such a seat he was told—which was an evident lie; before he had finished his argument the Estrella de Oro came and departed without them—that the first-class bus was not going, and that he must take a touring car, a turismo: the price was legally not much more but what with their luggage, and the portentous presence of Primrose's fur coat—now upon their lap; they were almost glad of it for they were reaching the Tres Marías—it came to three times as much. Almost immediately another half dozen pesos or so were added, to be paid in advance. Though it was merely a question of sixty cents, American or Canadian, Sigbjørn refused, and this time Primrose herself was the more indignant.

"Pero, señor, nosotros no somos americanos ricos," she said excitedly, and Sigbjørn added, "No—nosotros somos canadianos *pobres*."

Although two expensively dressed Mexicans, an almost Italian-looking man and a woman with marmalade-colored hair, had risen courteously to their defense, their luggage—fortunately Sigbjørn held on to his guitar—was rudely thrown off the car and two other Mexicans took their places. Meantime the dispatcher for the Flecha, which started from the opposite side of the street, who'd been having a lemonade next door, apparently on hearing the word *canadianos*, strolled over to see what was going on.

"Winnipeg—you know Winnipeg?"

292 THE VOYAGE THAT NEVER ENDS

"Sí, sí, conozco Winnipeg un poco": they had visited that strange mirage of a city on the way to see the Reids after the fire. That was the extent of their conversation, but he had taken pleasure in seeing them on his own bus (the number of which Sigbjørn was too exhausted to notice) even suggesting that two other passengers, these were Indians, give up their seats, which they did with graciousness, and in a manner brooking no denial, and to make even more certain that they would not be further embarrassed, the dispatcher who had been to Winnipeg wrote down the price, including that of the extra luggage, which came to about a third of the other, upon a piece of paper that he handed to them through the window, exhorting them to pay precisely that and no more. And at this moment their fares were taken, from outside, just as in *The Valley*, he paid that and no more, the man gave him a torn ticket with a print of a huge stone god on it.

Meantime, they were going to Cuernavaca.

The bus journey from Mexico City to Cuernavaca was deceptive, as Sigbjørn knew of old. Although it was only forty or fifty miles, this gives little idea of its nature. A long, dreary, dusty road leads out of Mexico City itself, and then, half an hour later, the long circuitous climb to Tres Marías begins. Having started at an altitude of eight thousand feet you ascend to an altitude of ten thousand. At the highest point of the route, a desolate clapboard of decaying huts named Tres Cumbres in the Tres Marías, where you may encounter a blizzard, you begin to descend, unwinding, by a similar circuitous road, until, in Cuernavaca, you find yourself at an altitude of some three thousand feet, that is at a point rather lower than the one in which you have started; in this regard the journey had always struck Sigbjørn as rather like life itself. Repeat the journey many times and you have the eerie sense of repeating an existence over and over again, which, although perhaps true of any journey, seems for some reason particularly true of this one. One is liable because of the altitude and abrupt change of temperature, to feel exhausted, and when one arrives finally in Cuernavaca, quite worn out. But Primrose and Sigbjørn, if not for travel, shared, other things being equal, a love of bus journeys, which was all to the good.

And Sigbjørn could feel Primrose was enjoying herself, taking in the beautiful scenery, the flowers, the straggling adobe villages, the little pigs, the delicate ankles of the Mexican women. A vast shrouded slope loomed before them, the Tres Marías. They reached Tres Cumbres, where they stopped briefly and Sigbjørn without any haggling at all, of which he was beginning to have a dread, to her delight secured her a torta, through the window from a scolding old woman. This, for him, was a feat as well as being unselfish: for there was something in his nature that loathed to break the rhythm; only more than stopping at all did he hate to move on, lulled into a certain mood. To the right there was a signpost pointing down a windy road: *A Zampoala*. It was a lake, very high in the mountains, which Sigbjørn remembered he had never seen and he made up his mind to take her there. It was a possible happiness for Primrose over there, lakes, heights, choices, superterrestrial or sublacustrine.

As they rolled forward again, Sigbjørn remembered the visit they had made to the basilica at Guadalupe a few days earlier. They had taken the bus by Bellas Artes, and at the basilica Sigbjørn had been delighted by the sideshow: *La Maldición de Dios... ¡No deje de ver este asombroso aparato de óptica! La cabeza que habla su cuerpo fue devorado por las ratas*. The malediction of God! Step up ladies and gents and see the spectacle of the head who has his body devoured by rats. Primrose had been enchanted with the women, however poor, who wore exquisite silver earrings, and had lovely ankles and hands and often gorgeous rebozos, and carried themselves like queens, and the dancers: one man in fringes of scarlet with feathers two feet high on his head, the other wearing a horrible grinning mask on the back of his head.

They drank marvelous beer in a little booth at one side facing the basilica: the figurine of the Virgin looked like a model in an American department store window of 1917 or so, dressed in bright print and carrying in one hand a lamp—a boy of sixteen or so stood by her, leaning on her shoulder. They watched the little families sitting under trees with their sweet quick smiles, and then they wandered through the basilica of Guadalupe—they who had not been in a church in twenty years. Sigbjørn felt the sense of complete faith when Primrose knelt and prayed at the altar, and he watched the expression of passionate sincerity on people's faces, the father with the little girl, showing her how to cross herself, the old woman touching the glass case and rubbing the baby's face with it, Mexican babies, aware of man's tragic end, do not cry: "I slept here once," Sigbjørn did not say, meaning on the floor of the basilica itself, tight, in a borrowed mackintosh, in December, 1936. They smelt the smell of Mexico City, the familar smell, to him, of gasoline, excrement, and oranges, and drank beautiful Saturno for forty-five centavos.

Then something happened, or nearly went wrong, wrong enough at all events, wrong enough, so that, had he been writing about it, he would have preserved it as the "first bass chord." They were wandering, mingling with the crowd at Guadalupe, scarcely knowing where they were going; such a crowd indeed that unable to make any progress they turned into a little tiendita in which as in many such, they sold beer and spirits. People were drinking and talking at the counter, but way was courteously made for them. They ordered Carta Blanca and were drinking happily but watching the scene outside, rather than inside. A blind woman tottered past carrying a dead dog. A borracho, in a state of drunkenness almost unique, carrying a stick, and so far as Sigbjørn could see without the slightest provocation suddenly began striking her brutally with the stick and then struck the dead dog, which fell to the pavement with a horrible smack. The blind woman, furious, with obscene grief, groped, felt for the dead dog, and finding it, clutched it to her bosom again. Meantime the crowd had turned as a body from the counter and pressed toward the open doorway to watch what was happening, in the course of which Primrose's bottle of Carta Blanca, which had been standing on the counter, was knocked over by a whiskerando Indian and smashed. This Indian generously apologized and began to pick up the pieces, Sigbjørn helping him, and then, because of the chaos, thought that for Primrose's sake it was time to pay the bill.

"Nosotros no somos americanos ricos," Sigbjørn began, since by the price list on the wall they were being charged a peso a bottle more for seventy-five-cent beer. This, however, was the signal for the borracho to turn on Primrose and him. The broken bottle etc., they must pay. Americanos! Abajo los tiránicos americanos! Sigbjørn refused but seeing that the whiskerando was offering to pay, offered to pay himself. But now, the borracho insisted that five extra pesos be paid, and there were cries of "Policía!" The police already had arrived for that matter and were talking angrily to the blind woman. And while everyone was arguing they made their escape as best they could.

"It's our fault," Primrose said. "The Americans come down here and throw their money around. What can you expect?"

"Pero nosotros no somos americanos," Sigbjørn said gently, at which moment also noticing he had been robbed of his tobacco, someone doubtless having mistaken it for his notecase.

"Nosotros somos canadianos *pobres.*" In spite of his calm however, now they were safe, even if in another tiendita, the cruel and bestial little scene had made a fearful impression on him. He knew only too well to what such things could lead in Mexico. And their crime would have been that they were not being muy correcto, and behaving like Americans, in drinking at a lowly cantina. In fact, in a subtle manner, they had not even any right to have a look at the image of the Virgin of Guadalupe at all. Sigbjørn didn't like the dead dog any better, which itself seemed exhumed out of *The Valley of the Shadow of Death*. It was an incident at least such as he might have used and perhaps it was not too late to use it.

The tumultuous scene about the basilica was very curious: the merry-go-rounds and obscene or gruesome sideshows, and yet tents of shade in the tremendous heat (he had only visited the basilica before at night) with the shouts of "Step up ladies and gentlemen and see the amazing spectacle of the head that has his body devoured by rats," the wild pagan dances, the sense of freedom and confinement at once, and the feeling of definite *pilgrimage* toward the basilica, and yet the virtual impossibility of moving a step, or one found that one was only going round and round the square, the sense of sacred miracle preserved in the midst of all this chaos, the contrast of the bishop speaking, or rather mutely opening and closing his mouth, so that he might have been Mynheer Peeperkorn prior to his suicide making his final speech before the clamor of the waterfall in *The Magic Mountain* for all one heard, and yet pronouncing in the midst of all this his benediction, almost as it were his encyclical to a closed order, on all present, even Sigbjørn and Primrose, as the yelling jukeboxes shrieked and whinnied in English louder and louder, "I'm dreaming of a white Christmas"—all this had an absurdity and horror, would have been justified as an experience simply by its overwhelming effect of absurdity and ugliness, but for the equally overwhelming sense of something sublime everywhere present, of faith.

You could not say it was a simple faith, omnipresent as the jukeboxes and a curious sign that he had observed, *Kilroy was here*; you could not pin it down at all. For that matter even a devout Catholic—Primrose was descended from a Catholic-burning bishop and Sigbjørn from practicing Manx sorceresses—of the usual Western type would have been equally disgusted, and have been far more critical than he of the tasteless votive symbols of that belief, while in Sigbjørn himself—probably far more highly superstitious and less skeptical a person, and yet reluctant to submit himself to the discipline of any church, disbelieving indeed in public worship—he might have detected an element of pride, in many respects humble indeed as Uriah Heep, humble though he was, that would have immediately placed him among the damned. And yet again, there was the overpowering sense of something irrefutably sublime, of faith, or a complex faith.

Now as they commenced the unwinding descent to Cuernavaca, Sigbjørn could not help reflecting on the strange vagueness of their plans. They had, in fact, no plans at all, unless Sigbjørn's to have a drink as soon as possible could be called such; perhaps Primrose imagined that he had, but he had not thought of where to put up in Cuernavaca and for all he knew all the hotels would be full, or prohibitively expensive. They were drawn on as by an invisible cord. But these thoughts were held in abeyance for the moment by the wild excitement at seeing the volcanoes again, for Primrose loyally wanted to see them exactly as they appeared in his book. If this feeling were indeed to be compared to anything whatever, Sigbjørn thought, it would strangely be to reading a book. Yes, precisely a book that, while the terrain is so vividly communicated that it seems familiar, that indeed has become, even as we read, familiar, is exasperating in that we are being held up continually by the notion (conviction) that we can do it better ourselves. In this case, he supposed, it was, if inexactly, as though in part this book were his own, and the passages in question equivalent to that village here, or that mountain peak there, were conjured up by either a sense of their omission or ineptitude, or even a phrase of the flowers, a straggling village, the novelty of the tortas, a little pig. I didn't get that! Damn it, how could I have missed that? If he felt at this moment any clear belief that he would write again, he would have spoilt his enjoyment by making notes in the margin, or in the notebook that, alas, he carried no longer.

On the other hand, and far more powerfully, this book that he was reading was like a book that, paradoxically, had not yet been wholly written, and probably never would be, but that was, in some transcendental manner, *being* written as they went along. Viewed in this light by Sigbjørn what he read was more enthralling still. The temptation here, however, was, due to the anxiety as to what was going to happen to the protagonists, to skip ahead and see. Since this was impossible, and at least in part up to fate, and since they themselves were the protagonists, although self-absorption could perhaps not go much further, what actually seemed to happen was that from time to time they seemed on the point of disappearing altogether, a sensation so pleasurable that one forgot that one had a hangover and wished to protract it forever.

Coming back to earth at this moment with the realization however of this hangover, with which simultaneously came, once more, terror (perhaps one deliberately courted hangovers because it was the closest analogy of the feeling inspired by helpless love), it was to realize that a drink at the earliest possible moment was the best manner to protract this sensation. More or less in this way, at all events, just as he could explain his reluctance at making any move at Tres Cumbres, even to buy a sandwich for Primrose, Sigbjørn could explain to himself the vagueness of his plans. On the most obvious level of thinking anyhow it certainly was extremely odd to be going back to this town, so odd that Sigbjørn would have been quite at a loss to interpret these thoughts logically, which perhaps were so weird indeed that Sigbjørn began to find that the drink was their only essential feature. But those thoughts were held in abeyance anyhow for the moment by Primrose's loyal yet genuine wild excitement at the prospect of seeing the volcanoes again in what Sigbjørn had assured her was their most admirable setting, exactly that was, as they had appeared in his book. "Look, no, there, no there," she was searching as excitedly as she had done in the plane. They were hidden, however. It perhaps, he thought, emphasized the shadow-line quality in both their lives: both were leaving their youth behind. Nothing, however, could be more deceptive than this gloomy and logical notion, because just as in the song in *The Maid of the Mountains*, it is at this moment that perhaps your youth opens up before you all its possibilities that you were not mature enough to see before. Far more often is it than in adolescence we experience the stultifications we associate with old age. And in old age itself recapture the wonder that is popularly supposed to be correlative of childhood, when in fact we often, still as blind as starved kittens and still as unwanted, are in danger of being sent down to the bottom of the ocean with a stone in the sack. It was hard to explain this to Primrose. How often do you read: "She was a woman of middle age" or approximately forty. Have we noticed this, the more often perhaps as approaching forty, ourselves, and never without a shudder. Take heart! It is not true, for this at least is one way in which the world has advanced. Ten years ago it was sufficient for a protagonist to be approaching thirty. With the Victorians "She would never see twenty-five again" was sufficient to suggest that the apple was about to fall off the tree. As for himself, in his mid-thirties, Sigbjørn thought: if ever he should write an autobiographical novel he would begin it: "I was now approaching the critical age of five."

Although Cuernavaca itself was now clearly to be seen far down below them at regular intervals as they rounded the corners, a sort of violet haze hanging over the whole valley obscured the volcanoes from sight, and although it was a fine hot day, becoming ever hotter as they descended, it did not seem to Sigbjørn from what he could remember of the climate that this haze would lift in time for them to see the mountains before sunset. Still it was not far from the full moon, and perhaps Primrose would see them tonight by moonlight, which would be still better. To Sigbjørn's eye a suggestion of bulk in the distance, an inkling of a sloping shape within the haze, gave a hint as of some great presence there, rendered them to him even more impressive in their defection.

Now the road straightened out and they began to pass through the outskirts of Cuernavaca itself and a little later, opposite a large barracks that had not been there before, appeared a sign *Quauhnahuac*, Cuernavaca's Aztec name, with its translation in Spanish, Near the Wood. This was an innovation. Nine years ago Sigbjørn, who had not then read Prescott, had been at pains to discover what this Aztec name was and had thought, by using it, that the fact that the scene of his book was largely in Cuernavaca would be thereby disguised. Now in the event of that book coming out, and in spite of the delay in his hearing from England, and the disappointing reports from America, his hopes were not yet altogether dashed, anyone who had visited Cuernavaca recently would know. They would suppose too that he had got the geography wrong due to his lack of observation, whereas in truth this was because that part of his terrain that was not wholly imaginative was equally based upon the city of Oaxaca and sus anexas. The bus passed, still going down, the Cuernavaca Inn, to which they were making certain obscure additions. Yet hideous buildings were going up everywhere, Bebe Coca-Cola, the huge stone statue; the new bus stop—his old Terminal Cantina was no more; and where would Señora Gregorio be?—was below Cortez Palace, so that almost immediately on getting out, they were confronted with a view of the Rivera murals that he had described in his Chapter VII of *The Valley*. The wall below Cortez Palace was being reinforced, however, and the path that the Consul and Yvonne had taken when she returned to him through the rubbish heap was no more; they would now have had to come down some stone steps.

After some difficulty they checked their bags at the bus stop, with the exception of Primrose's fur coat, and on Sigbjørn's suggestion strolled up to the square. They paused by Cortez Palace to look once more in vain for the volcanoes. He guided their steps to a cantina called La Universal, which he had immediately noticed was still there, and where he once knew the proprietor, a Spaniard with whom he played dice and who always "bumped the dice" on his head. Jukeboxes, at least twenty of them apparently, kept up an endless caterwauling. La Universal was where, inside, he had obtained some of the dialogue that he had put in his Chapter XII, which he made actually take place in an awful place called the Farolito in Oaxaca—it was partly the Farolito and partly another place in the city of Oaxaca called El Bosque, that also meant The Wood.

The Universal always had been a sidewalk café and it was still. They sat down, tired, at a round table, and Sigbjørn having ordered two beers draped Primrose's coat upon a neighboring chair. With the forethought that had often been lacking during the many years he had not been drinking, he had insisted that she bring it, for it had struck him that it might be some time before they left the Universal, and the nights were cold, and the checking room at the bus station might be shut. The beer was black and delicious; they toasted each other, and ordered another one. Every now and then the cathedral let loose a jangling gaggle of bells. "I wish Juan Fernando would just happen by." He had meant to add, then we wouldn't have to go to Oaxaca, but refrained for that would hurt Primrose, who said something of the sort and Sigbjørn said, "Well, we'd go to Oaxaca anyhow. Perhaps with Fernando."

In the square, as Primrose pointed out, there was even a Ferris wheel and a few roundabouts not in use, to welcome him; although this Ferris wheel had the air of a permanent feature rather than an appurtenance, as it was in his book of a fiesta, it was swarming with Americans, in every kind of costume and all with the air of having a great deal of money. Many were in uniform. Many, however, paused at the Universal; they seemed to favor it and another little sidewalk café between theirs and the Hotel Bella Vista. Luxurious American cars made their way slowly past and occasionally an isolated tourist, or a couple, in shorts, with packs upon the backs and looks of wonder: if he could only be like that, Sigbjørn thought. Still, perhaps, why not, since doubtless he had more wondrous things to look upon than any tourist. The jukeboxes bellowed.

The second beer arrived and they waited for fate to step in. Meantime, however, the aspect of things seemed to change for Sigbjørn. He began to feel excited. How on earth could one communicate—or for that matter, excommunicate—the extraordinary drama of all this to him? There must be some way: but how do it. Then again, perhaps it was not interesting, save to him. All these thoughts that had been amorphously in his mind before now, with the proximity of their realization, took concrete shape. Every now and then the little Chapultepec bus drove up, stopped, drove away. That was the bus in his book that went to Tomalín. Before him, on that park bench, was where the Consul had sat. And down beyond Cortez Palace, in a direction that he scarcely had let himself think about, down that street at the end, lay, would it be there, that madhouse of M. Laruelle's, which even Yvonne actually *forgot* was there when Sigbjørn had caused her to return? Would it still be there? And would the writing on the wall still be there, *No se puede vivir sin amar*? And would the Calle Humboldt be the same as Yvonne had found it? And would the Consul's house at number 65, which had once been his, Sigbjørn's and Ruth's, still be there? Good God! Laruelle's house, where the Consul had made his act of will.

Sigbjørn went inside to find out what the price of beer was—Nosotros no somos americanos ricos—and when he returned, it was to find the marmalade-haired Spanish woman and her man seated with Primrose. They had seen the Wildernesses deceived in the Plaza Netzalcuayatl. "We are ashamed of my country."

They began to have a party and the day became triumphant. Señor Kent, the proprietor of the café, came by and was introduced. "Haven't I seen you before?"

Sigbjørn had stood up politely. "Why yes..."

"Don't you remember me?" Señor Kent gave him his card, but at the moment simultaneously his attention was called by someone in the road and Sigbjørn, catching the table in imbalance, spilled the tequila in the Mexican's lap, and the next moment, he dropped the card. They were helped by a rather slovenly waitress, who later charged them too much. Quite apart from anything else, what was continental in Sigbjørn required, even as Don Quixote, a café of some sort as a center of his circle, this was a necessity of travel to him, if he must travel, and La Universal—which so to speak was a divided character leading a double life, Dr. Jekyll outside and Mr. Hyde within, while sometimes at night the two would mix, clearly would not do. Things began now to happen very swiftly in Sigbjørn's mind.

"Do you know what, Sigbjørn," Primrose said excitedly, "he says he thinks he knows of an apartment to let in the Calle Nicaragua—I mean the Calle Humboldt."

"In the where!" Sigbjørn's heart began to thump loudly. "Good heavens. Well, there usen't to be any apartments there in my day. They're all private houses." Sigbjørn was feeling very strange indeed.

Primrose went off and returned, enchanted with everything she had seen, the masses of flowers, the men on horses and burros, the terrific loads that they carried.

And then, Primrose was saying even more excitedly, "I've been to the Calle Humboldt and it's still just like you describe it.... And do you know what, Mr. Laruelle's tower's still there—it's just like you say only there're not so many gewgaws on it, and there's no writing outside on the wall. But it's wonderful inside."

"I've never been inside. I made it all up."

"And do you know, I was so excited I almost forgot to tell you. It's been turned into apartments and we can have one there. There's a swimming pool and an enormous garden and it's called the Quinta Dolores."

"Are you quite sure?"

"Sure about what?"

"Sure that there's no writing on the wall."

"Perfectly sure."

"It's all right. It's only my joke."

But Sigbjørn had never been inside it. Good heavens, what a thought! What if he were, after living in it, so to speak, so long, to go inside it, to live *in*side the tower, now, if this tower should become, for a while, their home, and this again, by simply what was known as coincidence, for he had not moved a muscle in that direction, had not, apart from vaguely having moved them—the most obvious, the most logical, the, indeed, almost inevitable move to anyone who is acquainted with Mexico at all and cannot bear the city and does not have the most specific plans—toward Cuernavaca itself made any move at all. What if this were to happen? What would that be like? Surely it bankrupted the imagination, or at least invested it with powers that were normally held to be beyond it, unless they were in truth so far below it and behind it, that it had the same effect: it was enough to drive you crazy, or make you think that you were on the track of some new truth that everyone had some-how overlooked and yet was somehow bound up with some fundamental law of human destiny.

The Quinta Dolores itself was largely a garden that stretched right down from the Calle Humboldt to the barranca. It was uncultivated on the slope and where the declivity began, on level ground, was a swimming pool. The nearest approxi-mate to the establishment in America or Canada was indeed one of those "drive-ins" or "auto camps of the better class" that had threatened and were threatening Primrose and Sig-bjørn's existence in Eridanus. This however was unfair to the Quinta Dolores. Grotesque in design, as it was deficient in plumbing, roomy yet uncomfortable at the same time, the whole place nonetheless had a beauty, not to say splendor, usu-ally quite lacking in its more efficient American counterpart.

They settled for one hundred and five pesos a week, and afterward Sigbjørn took Primrose for a walk up the Calle Morelos, down which they had come early that afternoon on the bus: the glimpse through the archway of the old man and the boy on the bench, the cobbled court and stone building at right, then rolling hills and fields and sense of light and space with low afternoon sun and marvelous piles of clouds: later, the black horses running across the tilted fields, Popo in magnificent form, a cloud like a hat turning into a cloud streaming off the top as though erupting, then the barranca!—*the* barranca: just as he had described it.

Primrose said, "Is it? I must know."

"It's not *the* place, of course."

Though this was not *the* place, it was vast, threatening, gloomy, dark, frightening: the terrific drop, the darkness below. They lingered long on the scene, and Primrose beautifully remarked: roads that are laid straight east and west, those get the sun all day, but roads that go north and south get the sun later, and lose it by three o'clock in the afternoon. It was like a poem. It was difficult to see how any happiness could come—for the Consul, his hero, it would not—out of this but so it did, floating like an essence. It was the happiness engendered, strangely enough, by work itself, by the transformation of the nefarious poetic pit into sober or upright prose, even if jostled occasionally by Calderón, or it was the happiness engendered by the memory of work finished, of happy days, other evening walks, or rather, more accurately, of the memory of their escape—from some or other part of that transformation, after tea, when they discussed it to some sort of conclusion, and in this respect purposely of turning evil into good—to see Mauger, the fisherman with his tales of salmon drowning eagles, or of how the wind blowing wildly seemed to keep the tide high up a whole day, or of beaked fish with green bones.

And of other walks in Eridanus, the time they had called on old William Blake, for instance, an Englishman too, who was making a garden by the forest. His house was very clean, with fresh shingles and scarlet sills. "It is the best built house on the beach," he said proudly. "Aye, and the inside's good too. On the shore," he added, "'ave you seen them? They're *crabs wot*

jump!" His speech was such, or so he persuaded himself, as
Wordsworth dreamed to record, humble and good as plates on
a farmhouse shelf. He fed the chipmunks, then showed them
the spring where the deer came down to drink. "The deer come
right down to the lighthouse, swimming right across the
sound." In winter time they were tame, you could feed them.
Then, because it was the beginning of their life in Eridanus, and
Primrose and he did not know the way well, he showed them
their trail, the trail now widened by loutish loggers, loutish not
for being loggers, but because they practiced high rig logging,
who had left nothing but a vicious slash behind. "Keep to the
left," he said, "and you can tell when you are almost home,
because the trail bends, and where you look out to sea the trees
are thinner, where you can see the light in the sky." Then there
was the time, long before their own fire, and there was even
happiness in this memory, because it *was* at that time, when
they stumbled on a burned house in the wood. The eaves lay to
one side: a smashed barrel-tree the owners had planted, and
smashed pint bottles in a pool, limp dungarees, the washing
pole overgrown with vine. Thus was disaster's message without
word.

Now they walked higher up into the town for a view of
moonrise over the volcanoes, meaning to drop in afterward to
the Cuernavaca Inn, which was kept by a Señor Pepe, who
should have known Sigbjørn of old. As they approached the
inn the full moon, seen over an orange junkyard filled with broken and rusted tin cans, was already rising above Ixtaccihuatl.
At her summit a veil of cloud was billowing in the moonlight.
Entering the inn, Sigbjørn said:

"This is the place where Hugh really used to offer the Consul strychnine. However that's a long story, I don't know if I've
ever told you."

But all Don Pepe could say was "Mucho tiempo, mucho

tiempo"; he didn't really remember after eight years and Sigbjørn was more than half relieved. The inn was much changed,
the old swimming pool now hidden by a huge wall, no one
lived in the ramshackle old building.

When Sigbjørn and Primrose came out, it was to see an
extraordinary sight. Over Ixtaccihuatl the moon was in eclipse,
which, as they walked to the Quinta Dolores, catching strange
glimpses of the ever-increasing horrendous shadow of Tellus,
the earth, on the moon between houses, became total. They had
mysterious glimpses of it down narrow streets, and as they
walked watching, little by little the shadow of the old earth drew
across the moon; everybody else ignored it save one Chinese
boy in the zócalo with opera glasses and a man carrying a baby
down the Calle Humboldt, which was his old Calle Nicaragua.
How sinister and yet exciting in this shadow blacker than night
had Laruelle's house, had the Quinta Dolores seemed then.
What sinister omen did it hold for them, going groping into the
grounds of this house on this day, and afterward what glorious
silver portent? They heard the pure voice of a Mexican singing
somewhere on a balcony, as if rejoicing that the world had
relinquished its shadow and the moon was with them again.
And after the eclipse, standing on the roof balcony, the sense of
space and light, of being almost up in the sky. Long vines were
waving and making shadows on sun blinds. Stars were winking
like jewels out of white fleecy clouds, silver clouds; and the
wide *near* sapphire-and-white sky, a white ocean of fleece, and
the brilliant full moon sliding down the sapphire sky.

FROM **LA MORDIDA**

THE DREAM
—FROM HAITIAN NOTES

FOR A DREAM—INDUCTION IS "WE'LL HAVE A PLATE OF beans in New Orleans." Perhaps not mention Louisiana— just "somewhere down south" though this is very good. Hangover on Christmas morning, sense of slowness, the pleasure in other people's hangovers—the negro waitress standing outside the kitchen chewing gum, who seems to be "talking," though in fact she is saying nothing; passing the church, the essence, sunny, of Oaxaca, and the sense of personal filthiness. Tombeau de Rosémonde Bertonnière...décedée le 12 Novembre 1838 à l'âge de 57 ans...

Sigbjørn and Primrose were going down Basin Street to the New Orleans cemetery, with the western sun in their eyes, drifting through the evening sunlight past voodoo square, where a policeman, with a wheel on his arm, evidently from St. Catherine's College, Cambridge, was standing, chatting under the magnolias, and a man was selling hot roasted peanuts, and then they were in the cemetery, kneeling images against a rose sky, a little plane above, bowed little images, and a bearded man with keys, the sexton. There were strange names on graves: Eulalie Aarang. Ici repose Antoine A. Piccaluga: Ci Git Faustin Joe de Gruy Décédé 3 Juin 1846: For a time they were shut up in the cemetery: then they climbed over the wall, and saw, at the end of Dauphine Street, against the sunset, Christ received them with his spreading arms. They went to the Haitian Consul, who was surrounded by doves, they received a visa: they had a drink where there was a man, groaning on a manhole, the word Oh, but whinneying it like a horse, the secret manhole underneath the bar, and they were on a ship, totally unlike any other ship he had been on, with what looked like a great iron perpendicular centipede on top of the fore-mast, the mainmast looked like a telegraph post, and what seemed to be motorcar headlamps dangled from the mainmast, like the vizored helmeted heads of mediaeval warriors: there were things like macintoshed tennis rackets squatting on the bridge, on which the captain never came at all, spending all his time below decks in an inferno learning how to typewrite, and the crew apparently never did any work at all, signboards appeared suspended by hooks to the taffrails abaft the bridge and running from fore to aft with the name of the ship on it, gave the whole the appearance of a railway station, than which it seemed rather more noisy: the lost first night of sailing and the hallucinatory mountain of the sunset, changing into ladders of gold chiffon: the sun, a pendulous vermilion drop: sun sink-ing behind a cloud that looked like a horse riding across it; then becoming just a tiny little scalloped rim of vermilion against slaty clouds: chamois clouds: going on the bridge deck at 8 p.m. the Donald Wright sailing smack at Orion: the brilliant first crescent moon following us, flat on its back, slicing through some moon clouds, like a bright silver machete.

An unyielding iron ship, infernally hot and ugly, difficult to walk on. Such a sea too on the moon. Caribbean means sea of the winds. The stars of the Caribees. Though a small sea, it seems bigger than the Pacific. Few flying fish—and where are the porpoises in this sea. It seemed inhumanly broad and long and blue and monotonous. And the nearness of the stars and their wild brilliance made it all the more inhuman and unearthly. No wonder Hart Crane committed suicide here—in any other ocean there would be a hope—but in this moonlit empty maniacal immensity none: that is, of being picked up. Sigbjørn seemed now to hear a voice as if dictating to him: With a bad hangover your thoughts are often incredibly brilliant but you can't put them down because you cannot believe yourself capable in such a state of doing a single constructive thing, least of all what your higher self wants to do. One of the fatal deceptions of drinking: if you took a drink then you would want to put your thoughts down again—but the last state of that man would be worse than the first. When you start putting your thoughts down again, that means you are getting over your hangover. But by this time the thoughts are no good. The brilliant wild thoughts and inspirations have gone. I think that is another deception. The sea rushing through your soul in great cold waves of anguish. Muttering words: any words, bits of phrases—why? Psychology of remorse. The horror and dreadful importance of sex at such moments: boiling erections. Horror of reading magazines, particularly with pictures of happy and pretty women, all invested with this boiling, this cold rushing of disastrous, important, vascular oceanic remorse. Hallucinations in regard to words: the mistaken words sometimes make strangely good sense such as moonaridity for moribundity—the curtains craning forward, for the curious craning forward out of a bus window when there is a smashup. A vast hangover of sea. Mer de mort. Hallucination: someone coming up the companion-ladder in the darkness in the half moonlight. Repeated several times with a twitch. The psychology and horror of the shakes. The real horror is in the hands. All the poison—mental and physical—seems to go down into the hands. Burning hot, there seems almost a

buzzing *inside* your hands. Fear of going into dining room with
shakes, especially with captain present. Why are shakes sometimes controlled when no one is present? Beer hangovers.
Enjoyable hangovers. Other hangovers. Anatomy of the sense
of shame—of persecution in relation to the shakes. But why
should one be afraid even of going to the lavatory, even of
cleaning one's teeth. Question: Can a writer write anything
really great, finally, without a home, or having had his house
where he once wrote a great work burn down, in a house he is
continually in fear of burning down? Fear of going upstairs.
Conversely, fear of going downstairs. Psychology of sadness.
The face of yourself as you were in the past, hovering in the
room, your passport picture.

Going up on bridge-deck later with Margie on same night,
at 4 bells, Eridanus spread down all the sky on the starboard
side to Archanar, always due south, on the starboard horizon,
Orion way up there too, Regulus was rising just on the port
bow, and then below, the V of Virgo with The Retreat of the
Howling Dog—way on the port side the Great Dipper was
raised from the sea as if clutched by some hand below the horizon about to crown some celestial second cook, the Pleiades
straight overhead, the moon now sinking fast in Aquarius
astern but a little to starboard, like a Persian melon, a hanging
basket. Strange behaviour of Sirius, framed by a gadget on top
of the funnel, and blurred by its steam: it was not twinkling and
seemed about to explode.

Drama of mate who left the bridge completely to show us
the chartroom: and when skipper objected "We've got a million dollars worth of cargo and we're on one of the most
crowded sea lanes in the world" (though Sigbjørn had not seen
a ship for hours): "Some of these old skippers think their chartroom's their cathedral."

Death of a sense of fun, ditto humour, ditto of sense. Death.

How do you recover from this? If what you fear is being found out why do you always give yourself away? If you really want to hide why do you always go out and make an exhibition of yourself? How to conquer the death of the rebellion against this cowardice? And if it is oblivion that you seek, why do you drink in such a way as will inevitably cause the most agonized kind of remembrance in such a way in short as you will ever have to stop. The Donald S. Wright sounds astern like a very very slow freight train, chuffing...Justification of fear of what other people think. Remembrance of the awful Spanish moss on the poor trees, millions of acres of death under the moon of Louisiana...I, too, have the Spanish moss upon my soul. (Mildew) Why did you take books like Julian Green's Dark Journey on a trip like this? Leviathan. But the terror of reading sad tragic books. Bloat. A man so superstitious that when a fortune teller had told him the new moon was lucky for him, every time the full moon approached he expected disastar. Ah, but we are having a rebirth! We have rounded the Cape of the cross, and we land in Haiti on New Years Day. (This is the engine at the Quinta Eugenia) New Years Eve. Ship. Still crashing into the seas at 4 A.M.: the Southern Cross appeared tilted in the sky, as if an invisible priest were holding it up, to ward off evil: up at 7 into a blue sea-drenched morning: rounding the Cape of Our Lady: Haiti right in the sun, mysterious, folds of hills, gigantic shadows on wave, like shadows of rain, and sheets of silver, and blue, blue...The American flag flying (bravely) why do all flags fly bravely?—(as we approach Haiti) against white clouds; its blue scarcely more dark than the sea, its stars scarcely less bright than the stars last night.

Rolling into Port-au-Prince, the mountains of Haiti in sunlight, the bowwave leewarding into silver as far as the land, opposite Jéremie. The Île de la Gonâve to port, Haiti to starboard: woke to a vast flat blue broiling misty calm, as if sailing into the widespread jaws of some sea animal (Conradian) The crew busying themselves, though not seriously, on the derricks, playing about somewhat foolishly on the yardarms of the mizzen. Île de la Gonâve, weird desert, Haiti like an abstract Scotland, the sense of sailing on and on and in and into some strange vague mystery: and now mysterious almost motionless black sailed boats put out—barren mysterious hills seemingly endless, easy to believe anything may go on there. The steward's "You won't like it there. All them niggers and half breeds running around. I was there 37 months. General Smedley Butler, under his command...They got a dictator there. Steal Christ off the cross." Arrival New Years Eve at Port-au-Prince: apparently a town of the dead: a few feeble lights gleaming. Something that might be a train, then stops. Something that might be half an hotel. Lanterns hoisted, our riding light. Blow whistle to no avail. Drop gangway. In the gloom, on the fore deck, sailors tell stories of drunks and fights, hopefully. The skipper went up topside to fish with little pieces of salami. And then they came, silently, the boats: a native fishing smack comes by without any lights at all, slipping by slowly, noiselessly, with a sinister black sail. A few Roman candles half explode feebly and soundlessly in one corner of the dark abysm of the town and people look at them with yearning. A strange New Years Eve but what a feeling of good resolutions and a sense of rebirth on the morrow. Contrast of the veiled mystery of approach and this darkness. The noise of waiting at night for customs officers that never come aboard is the noise of an electric fan in a hot ship's cabin. Nobody comes: Not even ship's agent. The captain takes off his shirt and puts on a singlet and retires to cabin with a cup of tea and a cheese sandwich. And we prepare to celebrate New Years Eve reading O. Henry Memorial Prize Stories of 1919 from the American Merchant Marine Library Association, eating nuts and drinking icewater.

Then on deck with the captain's binoculars and now without
having another drink they have the most miraculous N.Y.E. of
their married lives. Previously there had been the strange little
sailboats passing, so silently, without lights, from which ema-
nated a curious gnat-like singing, or wailing, very few notes,
repeated again and again, various voices, one high and always
cracking on same note, tune like part of an ill-remembered
Guadalajara. Boats like wings, boats like bats, stealthily, silent,
lightless, from which this singing and again—could it be?—or
was that from afar or rowlocks, came for the first time the
sound of drums. The terrible sound of drums. Battement de
tambours! Now they saw the boats, in the moonlight, through
the binoculars. A boat with a little jib made a sound of snoring
as though the boat itself were asleep.

Sea near at hand, through powerful binoculars wrinkled like
the moon, with millions of little moons reflected on it, but on
this surface, in motion, to the horizon, to the rim of the world.
A bat boat, imprisoned in an icefield. The great frozen lake of
the moonlight on the sea. The binoculars gathered light so even
otherwise invisible boats would take shape. Under the huge silver slice of the wrinkled moon itself. Port-au-Prince through
the binoculars seems [to have] no sky signs, a square building
picked out in colored lights, other odd lights that may be ships,
away to the right an hotel—shadowy something behind square
building which may be a church. Someone in Port-au-Prince
singing Tipperary very loudly at one point: but that was the
only noise. It's a long long way to Guinea, and death will
take you there. First mate and Sparks sit glumly in his room.
Third mate says he's going to blow all the sirens, ring all the
bells, and even send up a spare rocket he has. At midnight no
sirens blow, no bells ring, not a sound, but one soft rocket
finally does whoosh off the stern past our open porthole, the
torch of the third mate, Bergson, staggering back, the quiet and

beautiful and strange end to the year, I thank God and the Blessed Virgin and pray to her that the next year may be a real New Year of goodness love and happiness for Margie and myself and acting as a man and bring a real change of character for the better.

Next morning—New Years Day, I get up bright and early, on bridge look at first disappointedly at a few things like factory chimneys and oil refineries from the porthole.

Port-au-Prince is smack in the sun in the morning from the sea consequently difficult to make out: strangely beautiful houses of pointed roofs and of seemingly Norwegian design, church spires here and there rise vaguely in the sun giving it a look of Tewkesbury, while to the right mist lay in pockets of rolling mysterious mountains like Oaxaca, this truly resembling Mexico, for in Mexico too is that sense of infinite mystery as to who lives up in the mountains—who can possibly live there?—what voodoo, what mysterious rites, which does not pertain. Futile invitation to see non-existent shark playing about the bows. After breakfast, in the mid-morning, a boat puts out from shore. They came aboard, "What are they like?" All black as coal. After ordeal of medical inspection, nice doctor with open coat, pale blue and white tie, and stethoscope— he feels our pulse, someone hands a letter. It was from his English publishers, saying that his book will come out the next month, and everyone believes in it as a book of importance. Ordeal then in skipper's cabin—by that time, strange, Sigbjørn can scarcely sign his name, police etc: "You're free" finally, he says: I manage anyway and get back with feeling of relief. But no sooner have I got back to the cabin than the fellow appears again. I have not signed my name hard enough to make any impression on the carbon. I do it this time on the bunk very steadily by pressing the pencil hard against the yielding surface:

the yielding surface is an excuse for any illegibility—the ruse
works. They go: we warp in. Approaching it looks more like
Tewkesbury than ever but also something like Africa and we
try to recognize some of the landmarks of the night before. As
they approached the wharf they saw bales and sheds, negroes
smoking pipes, or resting on their oars below, and a mangrove
swamp to the left what looked like a Mexican freighter went on
ahead. A gangway at a fantastic angle, impossible to go down,
yet it is done, and a fantastic beautiful city of mangroves and
tin roofs. Here nightmarish architecture has been turned into
bizarrerie and good taste—a credit to the mores. An hotel—
Dominicans with Goering trousers, ambassadors from a neighbouring state, and medals like the inside of fantastic watches.

"You like egg?"

"Oui. Sí."

"What egg?"

Loathsome American playing dice—for whose dead bodies:
yet it is Acapulco in reverse. A fairy in a blue seersucker suit,
blue shoes with bulging eyes, like one always suspects the original of the cover of Esquire, turns out to be a Protestant Bishop.
The honor of "Esquire." Making love in a mosquito net is like
making love in a gossamer handsome cab. Mosquito net, cas-
ket, coffin-shaped. Think of the handsome cat, says Lewis. Out
to the top of the hill with Lewis, a strange language spoken,
"Coté route ça aller?" "Route ça rivé la kay de Senator Erikson." "Est-ce-que même route ça rivé la key de Senator Erikson?" "No." "Est-ce-que on connais route laqui aller la kay de
Monsieur Erikson?" "No."

"You like egg?" "Sí. Oui." "Whose egg will you have?"

"You like egg?" "Sí. Oui." "What egg will you have?"

"You like egg?" "Sí. Oui." "Which egg will you have?"

—I recognized, behind green curtains, her sniff.

What about an author, who after, like Milton, having finished his masterpiece, threw his inkpot at the wall, threw the author after it.

Woman in a poinsettia dress against green palms.

A man with a face like a boot.

Windy privacy—breezy pioneer!

A rainbow that lasts for ten minutes, blowing colour, still high, multicolored comet, in the red sunset, they say it swallows the rain—arc du ciel.

—hot tambours—

cocks that bark and dogs that crow, *all night*.

the abyss behind the eyes, and the hand that forgets to shake, on the glass

—trumpet trees—

beautiful women with black hair, Cuban: why cannot I look at same: but I *know*—

losing my dangerous cigarette: out for 2 minutes. But what if it were not out? and where?—horror of people talking about you in hotel, everyone talks about one. Fear, therefore, of getting even a drink—(is this a help?) One at last with the great lunge and perfect final equilibrium of the perfectly possessed. Battement de tambours!

The fear beyond the fear of the fact that your cigarette has not gone out, but still is somewhere: the fear that you think yourself damned clever for this, but what is worse, the fear that you do not finally fear anything of the sort, and even that that fear is dishonest, which it is, finally the acknowledged comment that this comprises no fear at all: and no hope either (O Primrose)

Palms like women with multitudinous fans, in the wind.

the blind staggers: unique hangovers.

The sea rushing through your soul in great cold waves of anguish.

The effort—is it really being made, or is it itself the result of fear, fear of going out, fear of staying in, fear of the servants, the dining room, of the look of shame?

wild tragic beautiful and somehow boiling importance of sex in such states of mind—

the eyes

the shakes

—This is a story without any characters

doves with ruby eyes

doves with only eyes

—toy cemetery with cages and open graves (and the shadow-filled green hills behind with an iceberg sitting on top)

(When self-sacrifice becomes absurd it is at about three o'clock in the morning, when, after a late night and just upon the point of discovering the riddle of the universe, cowardly, you begin to fear reproach less, unfortunately, for not being in bed, than for drinking all the rum, and possibly beyond that, simply for staying up beyond dinner time)

Panpan, on a grave and a hansom cab (real) behind distant trees, slowly moving, tottering in the hot afternoon...

—a pregnant negro woman in sky blue, with a scarlet sash, sauntering through the cemetery.

—a handsome cat

—What about waking up in the morning and just *thinking* you have no hangover for nearly two hours, and still the hand does not shake (the shrunk trousers, the disastrous laundry in the mind) when will it hit you?

Ma femme desire la toilette: c'est une complication universelle.

—Take ½ an inch as truth (ref. drink low) moral for drunkards and prostitutes.

Sigbjørn hears whispering

—This man, friends of friends of mine, coincidence piled on

coincidence, rationalizes it all: a moral forest: stamps past door with whittled stick, shouting Men of Harlech—Cricket bat out of hell.

—all the lads that come from Norway
sticking peas up a nanny goat's doorway
—The horse, loaded with great stones, panting and sobbing, through the awful sun, its poor legs giving: hauled up by a black fury. He whipped it, too. Self-pity.

toy tin houses, with peaked roofs. A house like a child's toy, made of lace paper, beaming flamboyant trees, leaning flamboyant trees, made of ferns, made of fears.

—the dark man that follows us behind graves—
—cure hangover with Enos Fruit Salts.
—leaning flamboyant trees—trees that will never be written: dt's ditto ... leaving flamboyant trees
Paracelsus?
—the tragic swim at dawn
the awful awful American whose house had also first burned down and who played Cricket. Would you like to wear my cricket cap? Broke.

Tragedy of money gone in the real lost weekend—but the humour of it.

—I won't let Primrose take photo in cemetery—tragedy of this
—an invisible whispering voice from behind a wall: Gimme five cents please. It is a boy, up a trumpet tree.
—healthy and swimming at midday, normal, wondering how soon crisis was going to hit again, servants chuckling: "Fou" "Bouveur"
a thunderous cat
being constructive
being conclusive

—the tumultuous sobbing behind the eyes—watching yourself shake;

the progression again into the cold still sad misery

the terrible passion in the midst of the misery

but in spite of the resolution, all over again;

Rhum Barbancourt. Distillé et mis en bouteille par Sucrs. de Paul Gardère and Co. Port-au-Prince

clouds like pink ice cream Hills like Zapotecan gods, filled with shadow, purple.

—terrible scarf of black smoke, from factory chimney, across purple hills at evening.

Tragedy of Oaxaca, repeating itself. People going to the sweet little church with candles at twilight—of the dead? but no, it is the feast of—(St. Peter?)

negroes playing ping pong before front doors in houses like England.

scarlet runner beans like England ... horror of cleaning one's teeth (Dentiste)—food like England, roast beef and Yorkshire— the whole thing like England, can I make it? Oh Jesus, can I make it? Can I make her happy and still make it? And still drink?

The little boats—the pathos of the little boats—nostalgia for little silver sober moment.

Oh Jesus Christ and Baron S. deliver me from this torment for it is all about nothing.

But this, of course, you knew. At night, just a little bit of lighted streets, hooded street lamps like bended women.

The horrible bright line of the streets, in the night, silent, and the dogs crowing.

Marcellin and I shouting at each other across an abyss, under the stars. A desire to die for Haiti overcome in an ecstasy. A feeling of never having loved anything so much overwhelms, not even his father or brothers (I never had any) It will beach me to leeward. But it won't kill me just the same. It will beach me to love and work and help. M. did that. He is my father and brother. That is why we cannot comprehend each other. But there is something even greater in man than what I have conveyed, and this greatness alone can save the world from when he is living too close, I mean the devil.

Put your back into it, old fellow. Fight the bastard down. All right, dark, houses just sitting there curved, like assorted sweets. ...searchlights on the pool...

Behind my elbow, at night, the street we should have taken ...Bending elbow. Insects, the sound of them—onomatopoeia for insects: klang-maleri. Quatamapoeia for noises of cocks that begin to crow at midnight. Clip-clop-te-whit-Ic-whoooo! It'sjusthurra! Eeeeee! Booooot! Wooowowwoowowwoooo! Amesalfabor! Oh Oh Oh Oh Yapyaydedyup! Cockkkor! (Excrucior!) Yapayapadooo! Oooo! Ahahahahaha! Bab bah!

A man who tried to combine in himself all the good and bad qualities of all men. A psychoanalyst who put God into a lunatic asylum. Missing numbers of the pages, waiting for the page to turn over. "Desperate dooms of down valley," says the man, whose house burned down.

"Where's Mummy in the shower?" The day in the cemetery...Dove with vermilion eyes. Cloud like iceberg. House like toys, woven out of lace. Woven out of love. Houses like tin toys... 105 du code penal, staring at him from pack of Chesterfield... Sinking feeling when he saw it was six o'clock; only an hour till dinner—Or had he again turned his watch on...turning the watch toward five, the hour of drink. Avance ses montres—the hour of—? Man singing Rock of Ages, cleft for me, and the water and the blood, passing one on the porch...Turns out his house has burned down. "I'm going to write a story about that, feller," he says, meaning me...

Significance of soldier—bought—Kansas City watch.

Bousfield again! I would meet you here. Moves into same hotel...Has handkerchief embroidered with Spanish obscenities...He moves into our hotel. This is the end. (This Bousfield theme is most important in relation to Dark as the Grave)

Voodoo—the club?

In the streets, the devil, with a tail, huge, smeared with axle grease and waving a long wand—putting out his tongue. "H'mmm—a wild man." (says our wild driver, who is mad as a hatter himself.)

The awakening, the 5 giant Haitians with the stretcher... Hospital Notre Dame...The clinic: a long corridor of tall grey blue doors with a lattice work at the top...Jesus being crucified high up at one end of corridor by my room, a little virgin below, crowned and porcelain...At the other end: light, a kind of porter's lodge on a slope, and a telephone...Usual history of the hangover...only this time it was a cough. Outside my mosquito window carmine poinsettia and a leaning forest of small green nameless trees: crowned by a very little sweet tree, blowing. A mocking bird, a bird that pipes...A bird that makes a noise like a soft kiss...A high room with a high bed and high grey open windows. On the wall, set on a climbing incline, three small pictures: (a) a reproduction of Andrea del Sarto's La Charité from the Louvre. (b) Une robe longue, by Albert Guillaume, Paris, Salon 1929, I won't describe this, cut out of a mag, I think. (c) Lady Hamilton, by George Romney.

The man next door who has been castrated (?) *moos* with pain. Bloodstained cloths or bedclothes piled in bathroom, something like part of something human, peeping from among them, gives me a bit of a shock. I say to Phito he has been deraciné. Phito is shocked. Phito (Phaeton) who stays with me all day on first day "The suffering will pass," and on the fourth day, sure enough, the little pink grasses waving in the wind and bending so shyly cause me no pain...

Onomatopoeia for poor man moaning next door: Ezshy! Avor! gesahund! uueieeeee! oooooasigesiahinnashee! Aaaa-aaahmoooshanaahmoooo!—

man who comes one day, brother of doctor proprietor, advises me to live in Haiti, buy a bee farm—"You will have 1500 little employees out working for you (while you do your work) Honey fetches high price now. Life in the United States is horrible." I agree.

Emanuel comes to talk about Malraux.

Phito comes bringing younger brother, a handsome hypnologist, who once, on finding he had syph, shot himself right through the body, just missing his heart, and felt fine ever after...

Primrose comes to talk about a new life: perhaps this time we will win through.

When I look out of my window in the hospital into the garden, there are the sweet trees and bending grasses before me, to the left, between bougainvillea and a house, the mountains with their tilted trees on top, to the right, beyond the poinsettia bush that grows outside the patio—and why am I always looking out of hospitals, out of windows, but more especially out of hospital windows?—stretches upwards a kind of wasteland of grey purple and white stones, and rubbish heaps, with a lone coconut palm waving like a God half way up; beyond the garden a trail follows the gradient of the slope, with glimpses of thatched huts climbing, and sounds of voodoo drums.

"It only looks like spring, that's all."

swifts that dart, little goats that bleat, pigs that crow, and play the sousaphone. The swifts that dipped their wings into the Hotel Olaffson swimming pool.

When I asked for more macaroni and a little butter to help down the bread, why did I not have the courage to ask for more soup too?

The creole lessons—un—deux—trois—in creole, lampe etc (goes on half the night, shouting, good for the nerves) the negroes that sleep beside me in long chairs—afraid of the dark? Amelie brings me more soup anyhow... Amelia, (I am Amelia) who offers me more and more in honour of the Virgin of Guadalupe when I say: "But I shall become an elefant." "Ah no, no, charmant."

I get to like my room in the clinic: I can stand about on one foot, dream, work, have a shower—I almost said swim—and look out of the window, and I don't give a thought for a drink, except when I think of coming out: reason is partly due to fire: old house was Paradise but also monastic death surrogate (Huxley)—I needed such to do my work then, and seeking it in vain elsewhere, see death itself instead: idea, go and work in monastery. Impulse doubtless due to pictures of monks getting gloriously plastered. Fear of fire in monasteries? Suddenly I have a conception for a great novel: can I get away with it. Why does not Primrose come? Am lonely. Desolation without Primrose.

Food in hospital; a kind of tasteless gruel for a sweet always dry bread: cold soup: and then sometimes in the middle of that, a really good steak. No salt. A couple of things that might have been bantam eggs for breakfast once.

Damn it, they have forgotten all about me. Am I dead? Is no one here? This is an observation ward: where I observe myself.

Man next door is dying, I think family gathers round: ah, mon famille! Tragedy of little words, little things.

A small spider, seen close to, though supposedly distorted vision, in a Haitian lavatory, that seemed like a ballet dancer, a negro cricketer, a Will Rogers ropetrickster, a boxer, doing all these things furiously and *clicking*. (Delirium when sober—without hangover—and quite happy)

—fear of seeming to stay too long in lavatory is doubtless fear of being thought masturbating: but why should a pretty nurse think that W. was masturbating, especially when that was precisely what he was doing?

Everyone has forgotten about me in the whole clinic: I ring my bell in vain, thinking I should drink more liquids: But nobody comes. Dying of t.b.

At night, lying down, the little trees make a citadel with horns and God's bowing, or a kind of Olympus.

A tree with horns—clock strikes twelve, like our old clock at home—pretty girl gives me tea—goat bleats—man suddenly howls—I cannot even say Vous etes belle to pretty girl.

Surprised to find the notebook in right place, like Consul's whisky bottle: eyes? I am full of hallucinations and the crickets are singing—I write this in the dark.

Next morning I seem to have been alone for an age: five days in the tomb seems a bit much, but I'm beginning to like this little room. How I see why! Like Philoctetes, I shall be sorry to leave it. Tell Phaeto this. Good title: Batterie de tambours.

Frankly I think I have no gift for writing. I started by being a plagiarist. Then I became a hard worker, as one might say, a novelist. Now I am a drunkard again. But what I always wanted to be was a poet. (one ending) (This relates too to his being sorry to leave the ship in Ultramarine, the ward in Lunar Caustic, and the Chief Gunner's cabin in the dream...)

A bottle blue fly, basking in the air, motionless...

A deracinated matchbox, sitting on a palm frond

A soft voice at the gateway: five cents please.

The five funerals.   Battement de Tambours.

Another ending to this dream section might be, most effectively, the Spanish moss. The Spanish moss might represent, in one sense, American civilization, in another, the madness that threatens Wilderness;—"I have become a tree, dying, and already hung with the mourning of Spanish moss, in a Louisiana bayou, under the terrible moon." (Mem: the Louisiana bayous might also suggest Edgar Allen Poe... This certainly was where Poe had put his terrible House of Usher... The slow accretion of Spanish moss upon the trees, is like the slow giving in to drink, once more, the stealthy inroads of madness.)

On that last morning they had been passing through strange scenery in Mississippi, slightly rolling, not flat. They wake up feeling they are in Dollarton. Red line of dawn on left, it seems beyond swamps. Pine, pine, pine, sometimes tall and lone, others just Christmas trees, an earthly sense. A pine suddenly seems growing taller and taller in the dawn. Tierra Colorada too. And some of the houses seemed snow-covered, tin roofs—this was the first chord of Haiti—unearthly scenery. Red grass, red earth, and a deceptive sense of being high up. Yellow roads leading through the forest and grass roads. "He married one of these gypsy yallers, one of them over there somewheres." Golf course, green against red grass. Frazier's Grocery. Magnolia, a beautiful town, just over the line in Louisiana. Some even quite respectable houses have tin roofs. Superb trees. Scenery supernatural, but as it were, kindly. A sense of autumn. Bayous. Swamps, and swamp things growing in them along the road. The first sight of Spanish moss. Makes a tree look like old Chinese. Autumn landscape through Louisiana. But mixed with other exotic trees that have kept their leaves, so that they are glossy and green, and it's like autumn and spring at the same time. Pines, pines, pines, but with a faery land of delicate copper-leaved bushes beneath them. But not too much undergrowth. A sense as of the heavenly enchanted forest, such as you get in England. Land of Christmas trees and swamp adders! But instead of feeling at low level, you feel again as if on a plateau, with all these pines. Some little pines stand up very queer and abstract, with twigs and needles like rudimentary hands, like a contraption of Calder's, or a figure of Paul Valdes. Dapple shadowed gold of the forest, red berries, swamp

full, almost to top of low wire fence below road. It was here
that one first encountered the Spanish moss. At first this Spanish moss gives trees a waggish rather than a sinister air, contrary to everything one has heard, as if someone had hung them
with false beards, or as if nature had playfully added to them
some arboreal equivalent of the beards children add to pictures
of people: if they are sad, you think, they are sad in the way of
last year's Christmas decorations, or to be more precise old
decorations that are left up after Christmas, and now are to be
taken down, for never is there Spanish moss that has the air of
recent growth. On the contrary, in spite of its vitality, it seems
grey and moribund. Luziane coffee. Street scene through windows (in pantomime) Smartly dressed negro and his gal standing on pavement. Double breasted suit in good taste, dark
brown shirt, and spanking bright tie. They are laughing and
talking, she jerking her knee out rhythmically from time to
time. He is anxious to know if he is well shaved and dressed
well, strokes his cheek: she looks. She is satisfied, he evidently
not, for he goes on stroking his cheek and yawning. She makes
gestures and movements with the lapel of her own garments so
that you know she is praising his suit. He makes several attempts to button his double breasted coat on the inside button;
gives up, yawns. Formerly she had leaned a moment, affection-
ately against him, even done a little dance about him. He smiles
and yawns and finally yawns cavernously. Previously to this
nice looking negro, shortish, in green neatish suit, with brief-
case, possibly a lawyer, had left these two, who were possibly
waiting there for our bus to draw away, for he was about to
board it. He continued to smile to himself after leaving them
for many paces—the universal free-wheeling of the smile—
until he reaches the small line up before the bus door, then two
enormous frowns appear, his face becomes serious and studied,
half contemptuous and yet wary of possible insults, but at the

same time as wary of giving cause for them. All gestures in former scene are dramatic and significant: you know what they
are saying: in similar scene in Canada, none of the gestures
would have been significant, if you had known what they were
saying it probably wouldn't have been worth hearing, and the
gestures, if any, would have been unnecessary, and signified
nothing, or little: to the negro, life is a dance, slow or fast, sad
or tragic, or despairing, it never seems to be without rhythm.
Going into New Orleans, glorious morning, green swamp followed the road full of water hyacinths; but here the Spanish
moss really began to show its sinister quality. It is as ubiquitous
as cactus and ten times more sinister. In one place a whole
tragic forest of pines is killed off by it. The trees stand tragic,
desolated, ravaged, shrouded—beyond imagination. In other
places it is as if, again, they had been hung with the moss, as if
decorated for Xmas in some ghastly black magical celebration
of it. Strange shapes appear in the moss draped, moss-shrouded
pines in eternal mourning. Strangely mostly that of a ghostly
Christ crucified. But elsewhere a whole tree will be reduced to
nothing but a pillar of Spanish moss, resembling a thin abstraction of a negro, with a death's head, holding a ghostly head-
dress, or bouquet. Twisted horrible woman of a tree with hair
blowing back. Draped skeletons in every attitude of supplication. A tragic slow shrouded delirium of trees. Black water in
the swamp now following us, with gold leaves reflected in it:
pampas grass. When the moss has killed the tree, the needles
remain, but burn red, look as though they are burning. The
tragedy of the trees gets worse as you approach New Orleans.
Ah, it looks so delicate, this moss, as it starts. It gets worse, so
much worse, becomes heartbreaking, unimaginable, terribly
beyond belief. Spanish moss has done to the trees what a blitz
would do to a city and with the same beauty, (this is dubious,
now I have seen bombed cities. St. Malo, perhaps) Occasionally

a not yet killed tree holds up despairing arms, as yet some of its limbs unkilled, it seems to be crying. The Heart is filled with pity at the sight. The beautiful trees finally reduced to attenuated delirious shapes of cactus. Even the young beautiful healthy trees growing along the creek by the roadside live in this continual shadow of death—proof that while man might not be able to prevent death, he could certainly make anything he wished out of it—Death that now takes these shapes: Bats, old men creeping. Beaked shapes of the damned. The Virgin Mary appears too again from time to time, seeming to be lost forgotten gods and stricken spirits of the forest who have died with them but yet preserve their shape. Mississippi appears a moment widening on the horizon. Dead trees now right to the horizon, trees with no hope of life. Worse than a forest fire. Ah, now to think of the naked and clean and living trees some way back. The tragedy of the trees began physically to upset him. Think of these shrouded figures for hundreds and hundreds of miles, it seems to the horizon, as far as the eye can search. Think of them under the moon. It is a country far stranger than Africa. The bayou full of water hyacinths. Thirdly, didn't someone do something at the very beginning about the Spanish moss. Never were the vital powers of life and death so contiguously violently exampled. Cabins along the bayous, path cleared in the water hyacinths. Sunlight on the water hyacinths. The final lap through the forest is so absolutely different from anything one ever saw that it is difficult to believe our bus has penetrated it. But even New Orleans could not escape the suburban horror. Burma Shave comes on scene again. Doctor said, It was a boy. The whole durned factory jumped for joy. Burma shave. Trees leaning back in supplication. Others resembling Druids pointing: knights of the Orders that even Alexander Nevsky never saw. Horrid festoons. Some trees seem to have emerged, dripping from the weeds, or actually trying to extricate themselves. Hollywood Tourist Cabins. Royal Tower Cola. For a good nite rest. Metry Tourist Court. Reasonable rates. But strangely enough the suburbs seem to fade out and the Spanish moss begins again. Gigantic tortured snails and giraffes made by moss. This is the Garden of Memories Cemetery. Individual never disturbed resting places...Drink Dr. Nut. It's delicious. Royal Crown Cola (the cola that now defaced the Western Hemisphere) Scoffy Auto Store. Drink Jax. Bottled Beer. Fresh up with 7 Up. 7! Kilroy was here. We waited for a long train of oiltanks at a level crossing rolling by like great plump boloneys, rattling and chinking past, at first with a sound as of castanets, then with a clashing dancing noise like the sound of the feet and swords in a Mexican fiesta when the music has ceased. Louisiana Hatcheries. Pelican Football Stadium. Welcome to New Orleans. The Air Hub of the Americas. An interesting point: would jazz rhythm at its best be inconceivable at least before the days of trains. The washboard beater's slashing chuffing rhythm of a train at night. Sigbjørn was haunted by the conviction that there was a hidden meaning in all this. American civilization itself, might be a sort of Spanish moss...

Credit Dentist—Gas Given. Think! When working in the square or on the apron, watch the hook, it can't watch you! S.S. Aristotelis, bound for Buenaventura, Colombia.

But it was into this realm that Sigbjørn's soul now seemed to go. Why not, had not Juan Fernando Marques said that he would meet him there...

SEATTLE TO NEW ORLEANS
MARGIE NOTES & MALC NOTES

Sat. Nov. 30 we leave Vancouver—plane late, have a few beers

—wait as usual in airport, but uneventful trip, munching sand-wiches. Arrive in Seattle, decide to take midnight bus to Port-land, drink sherry in nice pub—1911 Tavern—dinner in strange cafeteria where we are floored by prices but food is superb. Frightful night on bus due to getting back seat, very bad, draughty, uncomfortable and no sleep. We wrap ourselves in my coat and curl up together and night passes somehow with great feelings of adventure and love. The skiers standing in for-mation in the bus line-up, going to ski in the Government Camp.

Breakfast in Portland and off at 7. A cool, cloudy morning with very grey dawn just breaking as we leave but this time good seats and full of love and joy despite exhaustion. Leaving P. the usual shambles of suburbs but suddenly without warning between the dreary houses I see a great cold white and grey remote peak that vanishes behind rows of flats and stores so I can hardly believe I've really seen it. Presently Malc sees it also and there we are, out of the city, on a long straight highway running between neat farms and there it is: Mt. Hood, so like Popo we are both aghast, even with the jagged bit on one side that saves it from complete perfection. Now on the other side Rainier, pure, pure, dim, white in the far distance, pure and perfect. The sky was clotted silver, the two volcanoes were whitely silver, Hood splashed and gashed with leaden grey—all the landscape colors muted and with winter and the grey cloudy morning—save in the east where there was a long gash of saffron and gold. As sometimes happens on grey days the visibility was excellent. Rainier wheeled and sank away till it became a white muffin behind a hill and was gone. Hood grew nearer and clearer, then was lost as we entered the Columbia River Gorge. This is magnificent, with waterfalls dropping from sheer cliffs around every curve. One fall so delicate, so fine, drops from 600 feet and is swept away by the wind, trans-formed into a spray a cloud of mist half way down the sheer face of the black cliff and drifts away in dissolving puffs and wisps—vanishes!

Multnomah Falls at about 10 A.M. for 10 m. stop. Grey skies still and tearing wind. The falls crashing 620 ft. and we stand, shouting and exultant at the foot for a moment, then run back to the bus. No one else on bus goes up path—all are drinking coffee in station or huddled against the wind. There is a trail to the top and Malc says it would be like climbing Tepoztlan. The picnic tables there below, and we think of people there in summer.

(MALC NOTE: From Portland to Salt Lake strange noises on board bus: I actually thought the brakes were equipped with some kind of musical instrument: they blew little trumpets and horns of their own every time we rounded a corner: whatever it was blew actual notes and kept up a continual whining but not altogether unpleasant musical accompaniment: though sometimes they wailed and even screamed.)

Then on, on up the Gorge, cliffs, mountains, and always waterfalls—then the long unexpected stretch of desert. Cliffs as flat as houses, and walls, sagebrush, mesquite, and tumbleweed then a whole valley of black broken stones like a stormy sea, no soil, no anything, a few leafless willows along the river but nowhere else—a monotone of grey and sand-color and black rock. Lunch at Arlington and foul it was and expensive and hurried—Umpatilla was cold and windy but dry frosty mountain air. Pick me up cocktail guaranteed advertised in stupid little station but no cocktail since Oregon only sells beer and wine at bar. (only beer)

But now we really begin to climb; as we climb frost grows thicker until all is covered with delicate feathery crystals, the bushes of mesquite and mountain laurel are lilac colored, the sage white, the grass whiter still. Now we plunge into a misty fog and all is ghostly with wispy streamers flowing and drifting down the canyons. Then the mist begins to thin out somewhat and through it is a smoky rose sunset, more like the smoke of a distant fire at twilight. In a slanting field a few patient ponies stood hunched with cold against the sunset, the mist puffing round them. Then suddenly the mist is gone, it is below us, and we look down on lakes, flowing rivers and a vast sea of clouds, sometimes calm and flowing, in other places storm swept, dashing against cliffs and throwing up spume and wisps like cotton. Behind this the sunset, a strip of the strange burning orange only seen from a plane or very high altitude, with distant peaks and piled clouds of violet and royal purple—that which below is gold and blue, here is intensified to orange and purple. It was like being on top of the world, vast sense of seeing the curve of the earth. Wasatch—name of the range.

The wonderful driver—"O.K. folks, tighten up your cinches and put on your spurs and get out your cigarettes, we're in Wyoming." But Cheyenne!

MALC NOTES: Tremendous Oaxaquenian sense of rolling distance unwinding and unravelling upon distance; not so much space, but just pure distance—lone tumbleweed at Multnomah falls, sagebrush like flocks of sheep. Sagebrush grazing among the rocks—rock falls look man-made: dead country, treeless to the east, save an occasional line of birches in an oasis at the mountain's foot, their filigree sliding across white Mount Rainier.

Between La Grande and Union, the bus rises above the clouds in a manner suggesting E. M. Forster's Celestial Omnibus: clouds like lakes in the valley below, very much as from plane entering Mexico City: beyond insane tremendous sense of distance, hills meadows farms rays of light, endless Oregon: a red sunset crumbling and blazing away almost behind: ponies standing in a field of crystal frost, mist swirling around them, against the silver sky with blowing rose in it and the sunset behind them: lilac colored bushes...snowy mesa, high up in Wyoming. White sun and white sky mesa, nothing but mesa, giving the effect of prairie, but without either the yearning boundless quality or that of infinite boredom of Saskatchewan or Kansas: high ranges way over on the right don't look high because we are so far up ourselves; a cheery driver makes the whole trip delightful. Soon as we are in Wyoming every one lights up their cigarettes. Fort Bridget and Church Butte and a cowboy in a horse and buggy: exciting ranges very far away to left beyond ranges. Diesel engined monsters puff past: a few sheep, no cowboys, nothing just moribundity, though Wyoming is somehow impressive: difficult to (Wyoming—moon-aridity) understand how anyone wrote anything so social as a waltz about it: but leaving Salt Lake City the mormon table like the Teeters. Wonderful beginning: Folks, you've had your town, now it's mine. The state law of Utah prohibits smoking in the coach, but in about 2 hrs we'll be across the border in Wyoming, then you folks can smoke all you want. I'd just like to ask you one thing. There is no law prohibiting it, but please, no pipes and cigars. If you want a sick driver, just light a cigar and I'll have to get out and walk. There'll be a rest stop of 10 minutes at Evanston and we stop for half an hour for lunch at Rock Spring. Be careful stepping from your seats into the aisle because you can twist your ankle mighty easy and there's just one thing more. If anybody's got a bottle keep it in your case—or keep it out of sight. I don't even want to see it.

Each state has its own characteristic: customs men and gloom of Seattle: drunken GI's and tarts—even a drunken colored tart: fantastic necking of a sergeant and a Waac in the 1911 bar: the mild mannered barkeeper who'd locked his help in the privy: the long lines outside the garish movie on the slope, waiting to see The Killers. Tense and terrific: Beer and Wine: the endlessness of Oregon, sadness of its wilderness, surprise of its

336 THE VOYAGE THAT NEVER ENDS

waterfalls: on and on: Beer only in Oregon, and your last chance for Strong Beer at Shell station, just before Snowfields. Note: I forgot Idaho.

Leaving Salt Lake—cold noli me tangere of Utah—a sense that everything important is enclosed, insulated: beauty of farms, houses seen sunk in the ground: but fine Tlaxcala feeling is Hotel Marion; chill of Mormon religion but moving story about the sea gulls: beer only—and liquor stores few and far between sordidity of beer joints and contrast between this and Moroni on the dome: few people smoke and you're told not to in restaurants this undoubted survival of tenet in Mormon religion. Going out of Salt Lake City great factory chimneys twinkling, look like obsolete steamers or Mississippi river boats lying alongside wharf. Sudden Oaxaquenian clarity on mountain tops, clear and near: then lost in haze. Venus swimming among pink clouds. White frosty salty look of ground, white light in salt white house, salty snow on top of salty mountains. a frosty dawn. a frosty little cemetery with frost all over the gravestones, closely cropped grass, neatly tended. A canyon. Weeper Canyon. Devil's Gate. Frosty seats under the grey-white willows—the High Sierras (?) huge oblique breakers of rock over to right. Sunrise on a corner of rock, sudden vermilion hymn of praise way off there. The sun rises again. Devil's slide: going down to Echo City. 290,000,000 years old. Wasatch range of the Rockies. Willow and osier and birch along frozen stream. After Echo City Elephant Rock—

Between the frost-painted hills to the right, young birches marching down a defile, from a platinum sun. Birches seem like a kind of blooming sagebrush. White maned train, the Challenger, advancing behind one platinum eye:

In Wyoming we see what looks like a forest fire, a gigantic pillar of smoke: we approach it with evil feelings of excitement but it is a train with a terrific head of steam, smoke seems issuing straight out of a hole in the boiler: soon we see more of these gigantic pillars of smoke, very exciting—in this desolate rocky landscape; then we see what looks like a huge black bar of iron with a white wake of smoke above it. This too is a train: Little America, which has been pursuing us, since Oregon, turns out to be a roadhouse with a bar, rooms in the middle of frozen waste, with penguins bought from Byrd's Expedition, Wyoming begins to be a disappointment at Rock Springs, a horrible soulless bituminous mining town, where we have a grim class-conscious lunch. Free Souvenir Penguins. Little America. STOP: live penguins from the frozen south. Post Cards. Little America. Idaho: wildly hot music coming out of a night-club on the first floor at 1 A.M.

MARGIE NOTES: Dinner in Union was hurried but delicious and we slept most of the way to Boise. 40 min stop. It is now midnight and then our wedding anniversary. Meet strange man in tan overcoat who invites us to his club and buys drink of fine Scotch. Club was like speakeasy, little orchestra, small bar and few people gambling. Back aboard bus and finally settle down and sleep right through to Burley, where breakfast at 5:40 and then off the last lap to Salt Lake City.

As we leave Burley the first faint green light in the sky to the east where Venus, the morning star, shines, between Antares and Jupiter. A clear cold exquisite dawn with splashes of salmon-colored light on the high peaks all around us. Mist is rising from the icy ground as the sun rises 3 times, distorted into a vermillion egg, swallowed by mist, rising again. Then we are all swallowed by fog or a cloud, nearly into Tremonton and now we have crossed from Idaho into Utah and soon are in Ogden, and then S.L. City.

MALC NOTES: Thence (after Rock Springs) into primeval country at Medicine Bow a pub called Old Diplodocus. Telegraph poles combing the crests of the plains, literally like combs. And further on, a dinosauria. The swinging red-lighted signals, pendulums, at level crossings. Another tremendous sunset—red astern. Black swordfish like clouds, very pale primrose sky to the right, in the south, with the Dali cliffs along the horizon. The south-eastern horizon, on our right front, powdered with mauve or magenta, like a fire running down its length. The silhouette of an irregular ridge near at hand was that of an embankment, which sneaked and writhed along against the further horizon. The funnels of two freight trains appeared from time to time just above this embankment as they raced along in a sunken track. Grimness of Laramie, but once houses on outskirts; old frontier town. Christmas trees between Laramie and Cheyenne. Cheyenne itself appeared as lights racing and twinkling disappearing and commingling on the far horizon of yet another plateau. It rather resembled Hoylake as seen from Moreton in Cheshire—and we passed Moreton-like towns. The lights of Cheyenne would drop out of sight for a time in the road then jump up again like a jack in the box. Chill, drear, inhospitable feeling of Cheyenne: worse than Huehuepan de Leon. The Albany Hotel and Richelieu Burgundy. Such American capitals are so soulless one thinks of them in terms of their individual liquor laws. Here they have packaged liquors i.e. a combination liquor store and bar, every one a Farolito. Meet man coming out carrying glass of beer on to the street. Is this against the rules? Margie sick. A horrible night and a bad drop in the holiday. Up betimes and set off for Denver— bad news of coal strike. Fields the color of rye crunch. Endless potato fields. Ranges follow on right like Wales. Snow turns fields into fens and inlets of snow. But I am thoroughly tired and abysmally depressed. Margie admires the red barns. Birches and locusts. Suburban horror—the eternal suburban horror of the motel horror, the tur-o-tel horror, the Bar B.Q. horror, the liquor store Plates put up horror, and again, the motel, the Texaco, the horror of a soulless nothing ness. Ridiculous system of numbers delays us for Kansas bus. Denver is entirely, is almost entirely, a suburban horror—but some of its Kansas side out-skirts are pretty: houses of sandstone. The suburban houses of chiropractors horror. The mountains all round the horizon must give you (I even half recall it) a feeling of hope when you're approaching it. We are leaving them behind. A holy atmosphere in the bus: the reluctance to get out once you're in —though why ever get in? Movement of trees when bus is going is interesting, their differing motions rather. The further world of fields moves round in a circle but a tree stands still. Trees that seem to be sliding across you as if in grooves. The curious craning forward and eagerness when there is a smash up. I look round in time to see the result of a villainous collision of two cars, smashed windshield, and an old lady, evidently seriously injured, being helped up a bank, among numerous hens: were the hens in the car?

The horrors of:

U-Smile—Steam Heated Cottages

Mobilgas

Ace of the Hi-way

Wimpy's Modern Garage

Burma Shave: Big mistake, use your horn and not your brake.

Well-come Cottages

Coca-cola

Hardware Auto Store

Wizard Furniture Company.

Wonderful breakfast in Kansas. Leaving Kansas, Missouri, sweet little valley with a stream going through it: dawn again, and Venus swimming in rose. Tires and Accessories: Old Friends are the best—Falstaff: Budweiser: Pete's Cafe: New and Used Pipes: Jack's Lantern: Dine and Dance: maples, oak willow;

sage-green grass by the roadside, the filigree of apple trees against a blue-shafted grey-white sky: little maples behind a cottage against a cream sky. All States Village Mizzu Motel

> When the stork
> Delivers a boy
> Our whole darn factory
> Jumps for joy
>   Burma Shave

> Car in ditch
> Driver in tree
> Moon was full
> So was he
>   Burma Shave

> I use it too
> The bald man said
> It makes my chin
> Feel like my head
>   Burma Shave

Boonville Flying Service. Crossroads Missouri. Phillips 66. Removes the goo. Improves the go. Literature at roadside never lets you alone.

> That she could cook
> He had no doubt
> Until she creamed
> His brussel sprout
>   with Burma Shave

Auto-Lite Spark-Plug. Leaning telegraph poles and corn shocks of Missouri. King Edward Cigars. The Tetrach Coca Cola and Kozy Kottages. Need seat covers? Balz label. Hotel Tiger, Air Cooled, $1.75 and Up. Columbia—operator in charge. Max Crawley safe, reliable, courteous: he had all his virtues down. The difference in, importance of—even the metaphysical importance of—ever changing driver.

A store station, like a bridewell in Columbia, with, hewn into its facade, the one dignified word: Wabash.

MARGIE NOTES: In Kansas City at 5 A.M. weary and excited we don't make the most of our time there but Malc has wonderful huge breakfast of hash, egg, potatoes, toast, jelly and coffee for 40¢ and we are happy and prices are coming down.

There is a fine sunrise, Venus wrapped in a rosy veil and now, in Missouri, there are trees again and how they delight the mind and senses after the endless white Siberia-like plateau of eastern Colorado and Kansas—or worse, without snow, in some places, due to the strange warm spell which the Kansas City Morning Star claims is God's answer to Lewis' coal strike, the plains this time of year are the color of death and are as endless and boring. So that the lovely rolling landscape of Missouri with fat farmland and everywhere brooks and streams bordered by birch and willows and charming old brick farmhouses surrounded by elms and locusts and great oaks are like a bath to the spirit, however badly the body needs one. The corn shocks are fine and here and there gold spills of corn lie in the fields or pass by in open trucks (much nicer than the trucks and fields of turnips in Wy. and Colo). In the meadows is a kind of copper-colored grass blowing in the breeze and some fields are emerald green (winter wheat?). One thinks how marvellous this country is in other seasons when it is so beautiful in bare winter.

Well, in St. Louis we pass Mound City Dye Works and enter the city over a long, rolling road of old red brick with the afternoon sun intensifying the color so that this street (actually

rather sordid and the usual stupidity of suburbs of large cities)
shines ahead like a road of glory.

The bus station is crowded and foul but we walk through a
market to get out of it that is stupefying to anyone who has
coped with Canadian shortages. What, we think, are these stories about shortages in the States? My God! Cheese! Wonderful
cheeses of all kinds (we buy Liederkranz) tinned and bottled
delicacies we've forgotten ever existed. The delicatessens
crammed with mouth-watering sausages and meats and the fruit
and vegetable counters overflowing with avocadoes and pine-
apples and grapefruit, besides all the green fresh vegetables.

Malc goes to find hotel while I send wire and see to tickets
and meets me looking alarmed, saying the only hotel for blocks
around is foul and I better come and see it. Up 2 dingy flights in
a filthy little lobby an old Jew tries to make us register before
we see the room. But we see! The stench nearly knocks me over
and I open the window, only to find the smell comes largely
from the stinking court just below about 2 feet where everybody has been throwing garbage and general refuse for a century. The bathroom—why a bathroom in a place like this?—is
filthy! painted dark red over plaster slapped on anyhow, with
floor, walls and ceiling all one swab and a tub that looks like a
child's—about 3 ft. long. We left and walked down the street
where, in the next block, we passed a large department store,
obviously one of the best in the city, with such clothes in the
windows as I haven't seen since New York. Then Malc sees a
small sign over a dark doorway in the block beyond (we are
walking round the block so are near the station again) and goes
up to inquire while I wait below in case it is just too fuerte. We
are here in a very old section of town with ancient brick buildings walling a narrow street, I wait, watching people pass:
negroes, tarts, clerks from dept. store, clerks from office buildings, tramps, people—I look through dirty glass door and see

M. coming downstairs looking joyful. The room, 3 floors upstairs, is ancient, high ceilinged, somehow reminiscent of Mexico and fantastically, sordidly, romantic. Peeling wallpaper,
narrow windows to the high ceiling with shrunken lace curtains are on 2 sides, bed with only one sheet, large electric fan
(not working) closet door firmly locked, mirror so old and
clouded you can't see at all, but all this somehow romantic
instead of hideous. We are delighted and get bags from station,
then buy cheese, burgundy and sausage and repair to room to
luxuriate and ah! bathe. But there is no hot water.

To Your Health!

Our bathrooms are sanitized daily with Bac-Trol... This
process, insuring freedom from bacteria, is another feature of
our efforts to provide you with immaculate surroundings.

The Management—Delmar Hotel.

MALC NOTES: Entering St. Louis, on a bright winter after-
noon warm as summer, down a stone pavement of gold. Mound
City China Co. Gast Beer. Stag Beer. Stemerick Supply Co.
Leaving St. Louis on a glorious day, past the glass foundry and
the advertisements: Smooth as silk but not high hat, and the
Russ Barber Shop, Baders Ford Inc. past the S.S. Peter and Paul
Catholic Church, going down 7th, crossing Russel Blvd, past
Allis Chalmers, Cooke Tractor Co., Syers Truck-Lettering. The
leafless sycamores. Slow. Approaching Fire Lane my Thirst
mate, Dr. Pepper. Phillips 66—whole town built of red bricks,
past Pestalozzi street, the whole town glowing, roseate, past
Mobilgas, Groceries and Meats, brick pavements, we give eagle
stamps. Star Athletic Club. Puzzel Inn Down Missouri, U.S. 67,
past the Western Last Company, rosy pavement, beautiful
herring-bone sidewalk, Fine Wines since 1873, BELZ, lovely
lovely red brick alleys, red in middle of streets, asphalt on
either side, ruby red, soft Indian red, queerly beautiful old city.
Goffs Confectionery. High adventure at going off to Memphis.

Caution, Slow Down. Topmost American Lady Prune Juice down the wine-colored streets, streets of claret, my ancestors were stuffed with Taystee Bread, past Peopping Street, rose-red factory chimney. Voochook Company Inc, entering St. Louis County, past the Heine Meine Liquor Store, Lemay Grill, Plate Lunch, W. C. Sullentrop, Home Appliances Store, past the Ideal Roller Rink, and now the physicians and surgeons again, the Shell, the stop, the Sinclair H.C. Gasoline, Shellubrication. Tell him O.K. he's got a new Nash, the Nic-Nac Tavern. Beautiful Mount Hope Cemetery Valley of Peace, past beautiful cemeteries, and a lone thick ochre factory chimneys belching cream fur against a vague turquoise sky, by Melville, the way the St. Louis man went when he done left this town, Tampa Nugget Good as Gold, Campho-Phenique, Join our Brushless happy throng, 100,000 Users can't be Wrong, a pretty red Lutheran church with a bow-backed fence, paradisal rolling country of Missouri, like Devonshire near Hartland, Your Operator G. C. Chroeister. Safe—Reliable—Courteous. Strong copper leaves on the oak trees, some amethyst and garnet, and copper-colored grass, the rosy theme of St. Louis repeating itself in the country. Imperial City, of Imperial, says the operator, when we stop at a little village where soldier, going home from the war, gets out, carrying blue suit, freshly-pressed in St. Louis, on a hanger.

"Thanks a lot."

"Thank you," says Mr. Chroeister.

—Safe reliable courteous—(all the bus drivers were; that was on the plate, it was only the name that changed.)

Cinnamon-brown cat tails (bulrushes) growing along the streams, the creeks tumbling down—did we cross the Mississippi?

Peaceful country that demands little of you.

Landing in St. Louis. Go to Bus Tavern to decide plans: Tavern is sensible kind of place, something like a cafe, with red tables, and booths, and wonderful meals at cheap prices, braised sweetbreads only 40¢ for example: I have seen a hotel opposite advertising rooms for $1 Up: annex of St. Francis Hotel: go through brothel-like entrance, climb bleak stone stairs like 113 Bucarelli to first floor, where find a scene at first somewhat resembling Gorki's Lower Depths. Beaky Jew bawling man out, gives me, suspiciously, key to look at room—"just as I'll know you're satisfied." Horrible sordidity of room 109. Smell as of sulphur and smoke. Heat is working. Stinking bathroom, window upon garbage heap. Presence of dark filthy bathroom, even though there is hot water, yet it seems to make it more sordid. He wants $2.80 for room, obviously can't ask Margie to face it, but it seems the only one. Margie can't: so we look for another. Find the Delmar and spend a glorious evening drinking claret and eating liederkranz and looking out over gloomy St. Louis. In top room across the street opposite doves are living. Though our own hotel room is unbelievably filthy and the hot water utopian,—none the less it occurred to me what a good thing one had done in having had the strength of will to *search* still further (after 48 hours in the bus) for it brought such happiness;—however, here is the beautifully deceptive card of the New Delmar, complete with an embossed stencil of a negro carrying three bags, two as black as he SPECIAL RATES BY WEEK   REASONABLE PRICES   PHONE GARFIELD 9651. NEW DELMAR HOTEL 712 North 7th St. (at Delmar) In the Heart of the Business, Shopping and Theatre District. Running Hot and Cold Water in every Room. For Good Eats visit Brussel's Restaurant 608 Delmar Blvd. St. Louis. Mo.

Three beautiful names—also for hot tunes—of towns: Herculaneum Junction, Golden Rule Tavern, Festus Crystal City Junction.

Trunks of jet, and leaves of copper, copper and bronze trees, and copper grass. Muted color of autumn. A jade creek with white reflections—copper corn and pale gold corn.

Gravel being spewed out the maw of a dilapidated but Wagnerian looking machine. Innumerable streams and creeks of every kind. Going further south: Oshkosh B'Gosh, World's Best Overalls.

A scene, as follows: something like a screen, with so and so in so and so advertised (Gary Cooper) therein, in front, a notice Rummage Sale Saturday, a white dovecot rising behind the screen, and an iron swing—a white dismal house, a weeping willow. Opposite a car, resting on its axles, smashed to hell in garage, result of frightful accident, rusted, peeled, a horror, but with the numberplates quite clear and bright and new.

Our lunch stop: a town with vast heaps, resembling sand.

Last morning, strange scenery in Mississippi. Slightly rolling not flat. But wake up feeling we are in Dollarton. Red line of dawn on left, it seems beyond swamps. Pine, pine, pine, some tall and lone, others just Christmas trees—an unearthly sense, etc. See page 181 to 186.

GOING DOWN THE MISSISSIPPI—Afternoon trip.

—Los Angeles, with steam up.—Cape Archway; Brazilian ship, the Comte Ligra, flying its green Brazilian flag; a ship like a great black long shoe s.s. Lucano N. Barrios: Iriona—Tela (this ship from Honduras); Snakehead—Savannah, little funnel, it seemed, set slightly to starboard, red stripes and blue stars on funnel; William B. Travis (Am) grey, black, squat funnel, red lead; Platano—Panama, white and buff—black top funnel—yacht-like, "the banana": bananas conveyors, all kinds of American landing war vessels L.C.Y. Grande Victory, black ochre funnel, bring tobacco and sisal; Chinese characters of Plimsoll line;—the load line; ships in salt water, which has greater buoyancy, would ride higher; S.S. Oregon Fir—yellow, queer funnel, with black twisted tip like a shoe horn.

The President goes first upstream past the steamship docks, the Porto Rican docks, Banana docks, Army Store Houses, Industrial Canal, levee, Jackson Barracks, Sugar Refineries where about opposite the Chalmette Battlefield it turns and proceeds back down the other bank, past the truck gardens, U.S. Immigrant Station, U.S. Naval Station, and the dry docks (where it blows its whistle) crosses to other side of river again past the place where she docked, ocean vessels, cotton docks, and grain elevators, round again and home via the other bank again, truck farms, molasses plant, oil docks, cotton-seed oil-mills, Gretna, Sulphur Docks, salt docks, crossing over again here back to foot of Canal St. Later, lock gates rise, from one angle, look like fallen factory chimneys; describe sunlight; other ships—mostly coming back—Austrangen—Oslo, L.S.T. boats, our boat—the President—remember the Arcturian—300 ft steel built 3146 passengers, who'd turned by separate engines, independent; later, a tiny Peruvian ship, the S.S. Wanks, red and white Peruvian flag, looked as though they were black circus tents erected on the deck, so small and wee. Gigantic coal tipple. S.S. Sea Scorpion, an almost eyeless coast of bridge, enormous, white Murnauesque facade, football boat; S.S. Cearaloide, this white and black funnel, list to starboard, against wharf; tiny little Honduran freighter (probably from Tela) with what looks—when we return—like a candle burning in its bow scarcely larger than a yacht: so small she could be carried on the back of the other, or, like an embryo, in her womb. The very word yacht was obscene to use of a deep water boat; tremendous ship, raised by floating dry dock, S.S. Noonday; get Margie descriptions of sun, describe the various attitudes of crew at rest on Sunday, first at 4, then later, at teatime: The English second mate on the bridge and the purser on the saloon deck, Brazilian likewise and so on, S.S. Georgianna—Tela, Honduras, multi-ochre ventilatored and ochre funneled with black top, wide ladders to climb rigging: ratguards; Mississippi sunset, wild dark blue cloud shadows cast upwards raying on the blue sky by silverlined black clouds above orange setting sun; Merchant Prince, London, bound for Dublin, the various crowd at rest— later they've gone below for tea; low black ship, yellow funnel with D. in a white square or yellow and black top to funnel white line along the black at deck line, British ensign, Merchant Prince, London, S.S. Ocean Vanity, Glasgow, lumber, cottonseed, petroleum products, carbon black, a green ship with a checkerboard on her funnel and barrels on the fore-deck—bound for Dublin; bales of cotton on the wharves, standard bales and higher densely bales for compression into the cargo. Mahogany stacked for loading; marine legs, for grain; level covered with asphalt pavement, crude cottonseed oil refinery, cloud like a hugh mountain peak, Tio Corrientes, Buenos Aires, with tall towering old fashioned masts, and a nondescript flag, colors fading one into another like a dish-towel; a green ship with a checkerboard on her funnel and barrels on the foredeck bound, again, for Dublin, most American ships recognizable by funnels which are small and squat, as if wearing a beret; copper and jade powder room, the golden Petal Powder Room, the Plaid Powder Room, etc.

At the Ursuline convent hundreds of smashed glass sacramental candle vases in a corner, among dwarf palms, and the debris behind of pruned bushes.

The end: Kilroy had been there even on the convent wall.

Copper model of the noble Robert E. Lee

Grand Moonlight Excursion on the steamboat Robert E. Lee from foot of Canal Street Mon May 29, 1882, 6:30 P.M. Benefit of Church Mission School. Admit one adult. Price one dollar.

Extra: Lee arrived at St. Louis at 11:20, Time out from New Orleans, 3 days, 18 hours, and 19 minutes. Natchez not in sight. Natchez old time—3 days, 21 hours 58 minutes.

Newspaper extra: Issued in New Orleans when result of race was known.

Through the bayou by torchlight, wonderful blazing picture of steamboat among the Spanish moss. The double funnel and noble pennants of Robert E. Lee. European better didn't agree race with Natchez was fair. Tennessee Belle. Blazing night passage of U.S. gunboats down the Mississippi River April 16, 1865.

The cemetery, western sun in one's eyes going down Basin St. drifting through the evening sunlight past voodoo square, where a policeman with wheel on his arm (looking as if he'd been at St. Cats Cambridge) is chatting under the magnolias, and a man is selling hot roasted peanuts, and there is a palace— Arts, Dancing, Architecture—Poetry—Music—facing it, the trams running down the middle, and the lone railway carriages; the cemetery, kneeling images against a rose sky, a little plane above, bowed little images, and a bearded man with keys: the sexton . . . Names on graves: Eulalie Aarang and, on in front of one of the tombs in the wall, an open bottle of Spanish Grandee Giant Olives . . .

We nearly get shut in . . .

The grotto, the peace: and Christ, with his spreading arms at the end of Dauphine (?) St.—or is it St. Peter?

The crew drunk our ship won't sail till Boxing Day.

Mem: The Haitian Consul with doves, and before going to the bank, in the pub, the man with d.t.'s, saying unearthly the word "Oh" but whinneying it, like a horse; the secret manhole underneath the bar.

Hangover on Christmas morning: the sense of *slowness*: pleasure in other people's hangovers, the negro waitress standing

outside the kitchen chewing gum, who seems to be talking,
though in fact she is saying nothing; passing the church the
essence, sunny, remote, of Oaxaca; the sense too of personal
filthiness; in love with my wife but she doesn't realise it—I shall
go to church, and hope we don't get lost in the cemetery—

N. O. Ameta Famille C. O. Lafferranderie

Louis Antoine Peychard

Adeline Cossé, Epouse D'Abraham Brown, décédée le 11
Septembre, 1866, a l'age de 43 ans

Elenora Brown. Romaguera etc.

S.S. Donald S. Wright.—what looked like a great "iron perpendicular centipede" on the foremast was "a telescope mast"
for raising the antennae (that did not telescope) named after
collapsible masts on English ships going up Manchester Ship
Canal: jumbo booms—booms for carrying greater weights
than the others—booms are derricks, jumbo booms with their
tops encased in mackintoshes standing upright parallel with
the mainmasts; gadget looking like a berreted funnel on foremast was crow's nest: the motor lamps were just floodlights—
don't have clusters down hold: things like mackintoshed tennis
rackets on bridge were blinker-lights; lamp in metal case on
foremast yard-arm blinker: berret on funnel, through which we
saw Orion, was not berret, but some kind of dismantled contraption to put over the funnel when they were loading ammunition: supernumerary mast head and funnel, mate didn't know
name of—called antennae mast, when he wanted bosun to do
anything to it; this mast was something special to get the antennae out of the way of the high bauxite shoots.

Dec. 30, sighted C. Cruz in Cuba in afternoon, believed I
could see some of the Caymans over to starboard. Second mate
very important with binoculars. Later Jamaica could not be far
to starboard—

Chief steward tells us very good sailors and captains come

from the Caymans, most of them Banks: they steer by the stars and one of them nearly rammed a submarine.

Sinking sun gliding along horizon.

The moon: lovely leewardings of Melville; her undinal vast belly moonward bends of Crane.

We round the Cape of the Cross and head toward the Windward Passage.

It was as if we are having a real rebirth this time.

We stand in the wind on the bridge and watch Cuba and the moon, relishing everything.

Towns in Jamaica: Savanna la Mar—Falmouth—St. Ann's Bay.

Blue Mountain Peak 7,388 ft.—could I have seen this? In Jamaica. Utterly impossible I think.

Towns in Cuba: Sancti Spiritus—Santa Clara—Holguín—Guantánamo

After dinner we go up on deck again—First mate says:

"You people love the wind."

My God, it is at last true again, too!

He shows us into the wheelhouse: smallish wheel, a finger touch does the trick, controlled hydraulically—it's too damn complicated: Mate gets himself into trouble by taking us down to chartroom, in short leaving the bridge with no officer in one of the thickest sealanes in the world—and we are a slow ship who has to give way to others and the skipper has 200,000 cargo on board. I suppose he wanted to show off, but I should have known better too. Margie goes to apologise to skipper, I wait for Mister Mate to come off watch to apologise to him. I have not heart to apologise for I feel partly responsible; explain psychology of this. Margie after apologising to skipper comes back with his German binoculars, and we go up on bridge, ship is pitching like hell, and we stagger around, watching the stars, afraid to break the binoculars: the wonder of the Pleiades—

now about fifty of them as big as Sirius: the great moon: stars
changing color—wonderful, wonderful night. We turn in at 12,
planning to rise at 4, wake up at 2, again at 3, but get up at 4,
see ship is still crashing into the seas, see the Southern Cross—
the other had been merely The False Cross—the Southern
Cross appeared tilted in the sky, as if an invisible priest were
holding it to ward off evil: to bed again at 5 but up at 7 into
blue sea-drenched morning.

We approach Hispaniola. Exciting names in Haiti: Mirebalais,
Léogane, Miragoâne, Petit Goave, Ile a Vache (Island of the
Cow), C. Tiburon (Cape of the Shark) Jacmel.

Wireless operator has written down radio symbols of weird
places, viz: Port-au-Prince: H H H, Guantánamo: N A W,
Baranquilla: H K A. Some place between Martinique and Cas-
tries, St. Lucia, it seems, S U F, Port of Spain, Z B D, Maracaibo: Y V J, etc. and weirdest of all Y N E against a port
strangely called Bragman's Bluff in Nicaragua.

The Donald S. Wright is bound for Puerto Cabello in
Venezuela after taking Bauxite in British Guiana.

But her way getting there is curious. After Port-au-Prince she
goes through Jamaica Channel round to Ciudad Trujillo,
thence to La Ceiba in the Lake of Maracaibo, thence to British
Guiana (skipping Morawhanna) down The River Essequibo
(can it be?) to get her bauxite—she is only allowed a partial
draft in this river, so then she goes back with about 1200 tons
of cargo or so to Trinidad, Port of Spain, to which the rest of
the cargo of her bauxite has already been transported on a
barge or barges from which it is loaded on board by people
with shovels: then the whole amidships has to be battened
down and with the heat fearful and maddening she proceeds to
Pto. Cabello and hence home to Mobile. This so far as I can
gather.

The wicked steward says enigmatically at breakfast, re Haiti, "You'll get no protection there. General Smedley Butler's dead."

"You been there."

"Been every country in the world—been at sea 27 years."

Another glorious morning; Haiti sighted on the morning of New Years Eve. Rounding the Cape of Our Lady.

Haiti right in the sun, mysterious, folds of hills, gigantic shadows on waves, like shadows of rain, and sheets of silver, and blue, blue.

Man at the wheel going off duty—little mate in shorts says: "Lee, what's your course?"

"Huh?"

Has to be asked this twice, then: "100"

"Lee, will you bring me a cup of coffee?"

Has to be asked this twice: shuffles off

Get what first mate says about winds.

Sailing between two coasts—Cuba and Jamaica, wind doesn't get a chance to grip on the sea, there is one long lovely lilting swell. Heat rises, etc.—low pressure areas—reason for storms. Don't understand it myself.

The American flag bravely flying at stern as we approach Haiti: against white clouds its blue is scarcely more dark than the sea, its stars scarcely less bright than the stars last night.

Rolling into Port au Prince—the mountains, Haiti in sunlight—the bow wave leewarding into silver as far as the land—opposite Jéremie.

3rd mate at 11:30 phones down to get engineers to turn water on, "The engineers are rather inefficient."

Cheery 3rd mate in shorts waxes poetical.

—at lunch, am unable to ask steward to put our iced tea in icebox—why? Fear of being ridiculous.

Île de la Gonâve to port, Haiti to starboard: woke to a vast flat blue broiling misty calm, as if sailing into the widespread jaws of some sea-animal, Conradian.

the crew busy themselves on the derricks, playing about somewhat foolishly on the yard arms of the mizzen.

Île de Gonâve, weird desert, Haiti like an abstract Scotland, sense of sailing on and on and in and into some strange infinite vague mystery.

mysterious almost motionless black sailed boats put out— barren mysterious hills and mountains, seemingly endless, easy to believe anything may go on there.

English 1 bell at quarter to is 2 bells at ten to.

Apologise to first mate: tension while he goes down again to chart room: "Some old skippers think their chartroom's their cathedral."

Have not heard word "bloody" once.

More accurate account of Donald S. Wright itinerary: Ciudad Trujillo, Puerto Cabello (Venezuela) then north to Curaçao, then to Aruba, Maracaibo, Lagunillas, in the Lake itself, then right over to Dutch Guiana, Surinam, to Paramaribo. The other ships are not barges but smaller ships that shuttle between Paramaribo and Trinidad and have to be backed down jungle overhung river, another river that empties in Paramaribo. They take a limited amount of bauxite back to Trinidad and get the remainder from one large barge, an empty husk of a ship large as the Donald S., into which the smaller ships have put the bauxite. Two sort of railway lines and contraptions with shovels go up and down either side of this barge and unload into chutes and hence into the hold of the Donald S. and hence home.

Further encouraging remarks on last night re Haiti.

—What are your impressions of Haiti, steward?

—No good. Have you ever been there before?

—No.

—Agh! No good. You won't like it there. You'll get out quick. Won't be long before United States will have to take it over again—too much trouble.

—Why, what's wrong?

—Ah, all them niggers and halfbreeds running round. I was there with General Smedley Butler, under his command, 37 months. They got a dictator there.

—Isn't that in San Domingo?

—Same thing here. Nothing but a voodoo, that fellow... We're the first ship there since October. We boycotted them. Too much trouble.

Other opinions:

Nothing fit to eat there. They got a funny way of cookin'. Don't know what it is at all.

Can't swim out above your waist. Place is full of sharks. Barracudas too.

Main engine room emergency stop (on our door).

In Officer's lavatory: Emergency Crash Panel. Kick Out.

New Years Eve. Arrival at Port au Prince. Apparently a town of the dead. A few feeble lights gleaming. Something that might be a tram, then stops. Something that might be half a hotel. We drop anchor. Lanterns hoisted, our riding lights. Blow whistle to no avail. Drop gangway. In the gloom, on the foredeck, sailors tell stories of drunks and fights, hopefully. Skipper goes up topside to fish, with little pieces of salami. "I love to catch fish, dogfish, catfish, anything." A native sailing smack comes by without any lights at all, slipping by, slowly, noiselessly, with a sinister black sail. A few roman candles half explode feebly and soundlessly in one corner of the dark abyss of the town and people look at them with yearning. A strange New Years Eve but I am full of good resolutions and we of dear duckery. "A black republic."

356 THE VOYAGE THAT NEVER ENDS

Contrast of the veiled mystery of approach and this darkness.

The noise of waiting at night for custom's officer to come aboard is the noise of an electric fan in a hot ship's cabin...

Customs officer does not come. Nobody comes. Not even ship agent.

The poor purser, all slicked up.

The Captain takes off his shirt and puts on a singlet and retires to cabin with a cup of tea and a cheese sandwich.

And we prepare to celebrate New Years Eve reading O Henry Memorial Prize stories of 1919 from the American Merchant Marine Library association, eating nuts and drinking icewater.

FROM **OCTOBER FERRY TO GABRIOLA**

CHAPTER 11: ERIDANUS

THEIR HOUSE, LIKE THE VENETIAN PALACES, WAS BUILT on piles, on government-owned Foreshore land down an inlet over on the mainland, in the tiny village of Eridanus; they had two rooms, oil lamps, a gold rush cookstove, outside plumbing, a small boat painted yellow, the color of the sun, with a red rim around the gunwale and red oars. In the mornings reflections of the sun on water slid up and down the time-silvered cedar walls; seagulls came onto the porch, demanding their meals, taking crusts from their fingers. Like the fishermen, the Llewelyns paid no taxes, and behind the cabin, which had been sold to them lock, stock and barrel for $100, were forty acres of forest to wander in: sometimes at night curious raccoons came right into the house, and in spring, through their casement windows, they watched the deer swimming across the water, above which hovered, in the hot air of late summer, an endless wayward drift of fireweed-down.

Sometimes too, in the summer evenings, bears stood down on the beach and crunched cockles.

The Llewelyns drew water from their own well: and at the head of a trail through the forest so precipitous it made the trees growing along the dusty main road look three hundred feet high, was a store where they bought their food. Hidden away down below in the little bay of their own within the larger bay, they enjoyed almost complete freedom and privacy, peace and quiet; they swam and sunbathed and if they wanted to sing at the tops of their voices at four o'clock in the morning, or Ethan play the clarinet wildly as the early Ted Lewis himself—it was the flute in Virgil's *Eclogues*—no one would hear them save maybe a heron croaking eerily by on some moonlit fishing trip.

Old Indians on a neighboring reserve said where they lived no two winters seemed the same. The Llewelyns' first had remained mild as spring, or like an extended Indian summer, until spring itself arrived, when snow fell, and the pent-up season spent itself in a week's wrath amid the very buds bursting into bloom. The winter before that, living in the city only fifteen miles away, though they kept physically warm, they had thought dreary beyond measure. But last winter had been tempestuous. Then, the life could be terrifying: at flood tides, in gales and snowstorms, the tumult from sea and forest appalling. The ferocious winter climate of Ontario, whose meanest houses had nightlong-burning Quebec stoves, seemed nothing to that of "Canada's Evergreen Playground on the Shores of the Blue Pacific." Their thin little house was not much more than a summer cabin, without an overnight heater, and almost without insulation. Snow, and of an awe-inspiring new intensity, fell. A new Ice Age descended. The trail became impassable. They wore gunny sacks over their boots, got lost in the dark, and went to search for each other through the forest with lanterns. But rarely when they were together did they ever feel their isolation. Those tempests or mishaps were rare that did not bring them finally some sense of peace, however childlike.

Ships got lost too, in the narrow inlet. In thick fog they heard them—vessels without radar, sometimes no doubt only long tugs or fishing craft, at other times freighters one imagined ancient and benighted, under romantic flags, Liberia or Costa Rica or Peru, and whose crews called out in Greek—trying to find their way through the fjord by the echo of their foghorns from either bank. This also was like getting lost in the forest: it was as if you went ten steps, then stopped; so you advanced in the inlet if you were a lost ship, so many revolutions of the engine, or sometimes for a period of time. Then you stopped and sounded your whistle and listened for the echo. If the echo came back quicker from one side it meant you were closer to the rocks on that side and you steered away. But if the two echoes synchronized you were in midstream and safe. So, in thick fog, if they heard some craft trying to get her bearings in this way, and she sounded too close inshore, Jacqueline and Ethan stood by on their porch and shouted. Or at night they held lanterns aloft, their gigantic shadows were cast on the fog five fathoms out, high over the sea, weaving and bending. But in a snowstorm there is no echo. Then the ships steered by dead reckoning. And the Llewelyns imagined the horror of steering by dead reckoning, blind, in the storm. For now the snow was bringing on the night and such a storm as shall yield no echo. You couldn't stop. If you stopped you were lost. You couldn't even wait for the tide. Again with lanterns the Llewelyns kept watch, to shout a friendly answer to questioning hail. Perhaps they did not help much but it felt as if they were helping. They seldom locked their front door and they rose at sunrise.

The Llewelyns (and still, in the bus, going to Gabriola, Ethan thought like this, or thought he was thinking like this) had lived by the inlet for more than two years as squatters; they'd gone there in May 1947.

But toward the end of this last summer a loud campaign for the eviction of everyone in the hamlet and the destruction of their cabins started in the Vancouver newspapers, their editors having discovered after a quarter of a century, and in the absence for a few days of suitable headlines concerning sex crimes, or atomic war, that by their continued existence at Eridanus the public were being deprived of the usage themselves of this forest, together with its half-mile of waterfront, to say nothing of the beach, as a public park.

In one sense the reverse was true. The cottages remained, for large sections of the year, mostly uninhabited; and those scattered folk who lived in them the year round were as good as unpaid forest wardens of what was not only a valuable stand of government-owned timber, but, unspoiled as the whole place was, with its paths and old cow trails, and older corduroy roads, here anyone was free to walk beneath the huge cedars and broad-leaf maples and pines, a sort of public park already, the difference being that few troubled to avail themselves of its wild graces, nor had its trees been decimated, or yet begun to commit the slow melancholy mass suicide of those great trees in parks that cannot endure living near an encroaching civilization.

Nor were their poor cabins "eyesores," as was cruelly maintained. Many of them, like the Llewelyns', were beautiful in themselves. But even had they not been so, the hamlet of Eridanus, overtowered by trees, was invisible from anywhere save the water itself whence, with those trees behind, the mountains higher, behind that, and its tall-tackled fishing boats near at hand, swinging at anchor, those despised cabins appeared as nearly the only visible landward creations of man that were *not* eyesores. Seen in this way they preserved, collectively—so blended with their surroundings were they, and setting aside what they might mean to the heart of anyone living there, nearly all such their own builders—a very real and unusual beauty.

And how its existence or nonexistence could be of less interest to the inhabitants of a distant city, whose proudest boast was its own possession of one of the largest and most spectacular public parks in the world they were simultaneously agitating to have replaced by two eighteen-hole golf courses and a parking lot for two thousand motorcars the better to observe the wildlife, it was hard to see.

Nonetheless if one has to be threatened with eviction, to be threatened for the sake of a park is perhaps best. Unfortunately Ethan's legal mind warned him that even this public park, the thought of which with its concomitant hot-dog concessions and peripheral autocourts and motels supplanting their heaven was unbearable enough, might be a charitable chimaera, held up before the eyes of the public by civic chimaeras (in the sense that the former may be considered a foolish fancy, the latter as related to the sharks) whose real object it was to put a railway through, build a subsection, an oil refinery, an industrial site for a pulp mill, a totem pole factory, or a dehydrated onion soup factory.

For, on the opposite bank of the inlet some three miles distant, progress was already making its second greatest onslaught on Vancouver since the Canadian Pacific Railway had been finally joined there in the last century. A Shell oil refinery, with its piers on the inlet, had been remotely visible citywards when they arrived. No doubt it had been there since long before the war. But this had been gradually and stealthily enlarged during the last years, a pyre of oil waste, visible once rarely and only at night, now burned night and day, had become two pyres, and there were rumors of yet further expansion, more refineries, preparations for a pipe line to be run through from Alberta. Not till now had these things whispered a terrible *perhaps* to themselves. For the boom was not quite yet, and from that opposite bank, essentially, more than an age still seemed to separate them.

Just the same, Ethan thought, having once before in his experience been rendered homeless by what men were pleased to call progress, then by nature herself, in a conflagration where a little more progress in the shape of a competent fire brigade might certainly have helped (the schoolchildren were getting off the bus at the farther end of My God Bay, by another store, with a bit of bay this time glittering blue through the trees, and outside which, leaning across the aisle, Ethan caught sight of another headline from the local paper saying MY GOD BAY LITERARY SOCIETY COMMEMORATES EDGAR ALLAN POE'S CENTENARY HERE—he looked again; it was so).

The Greyhound started again with a jerk, rallying to it the soul's cry of "*No cede malis.*" Had not this threat of eviction begun to make him suffer as though under some ultimate and irreversible judgment?

Happy, they indeed had been, like spirits in some heaven of the Apocalypse or in some summerland of spiritualists, spirits who had no right to be where they were, which was their only source of doubt, when they doubted it.

But the reverse of their bliss was nothing like infelicity. It resembled terror, a great wind, or a recurrent suspicion of a great wind, the Chinook itself. What he felt dimly they repressed then was anguish on a greater scale than two human hearts were meant to contain, as though their own heart had been secretly drawing to itself some huge accumulating sorrow: alien sorrow, for which there was no longer scarcely the slightest shred of sympathy to be found in the so-called liberal thought of which they imagined themselves the enlightened partakers. Steam, trade, machinery had long banished from it all romance and seclusion.

Once or twice they had thought of calling their cabin the Wicket Gate, after the gate in *The Pilgrim's Progress* Evangelist showed Christian he must pass, in order to reach the Celestial

City, or Paradise. The wicket gate that had been made by the blacksmith to prevent his children falling down on the beach. But why call it anything?

Often it seemed a magical thing to them that it had been sold to them by a blacksmith, some species of magician or alchemist himself. Once or twice he came out to visit them, took a cup of tea, chopped some wood vigorously as though he were at home again, then went away swiftly. Once he sat for a long time without moving on a big fir trunk washed up on the shore, with his back toward them, so motionless for a moment they thought he might have died or had a stroke. Perhaps he felt sorry he had sold it to them, or was thinking of the time he had built it?

As a bird wandereth from his nest, so is man who wandereth from his place. Now they understood the meaning of this proverb—with what hunger they always returned to it, saw the pier they had built waiting below the bank, the tide already coming in, their eternal baptistery.

Ah, but it was their own place on earth, and how tenderly they loved it. How passionately—gladly would Ethan have laid down his life for it. But what was it that gave them this life so free and dear, that gave them so much more than peace, what was it that made it more than an ark of timber? Ah, it was their tree, door, nest, dew, snow, wind and thunder, fire and day. Their starry night and sea wind. Their love.

CHAPTER 17: A HOUSE WHERE
A MAN HAS HANGED HIMSELF

—AND HOW THE WIND BLEW AND THE BIRDS SANG, AND
the sun shone, that day on the way home—on the way
home?—the goddam golden robins all waking up again in the
wind and sunshine and starting singing after their siesta, as if
they too knew that the liquor store toward which Jacky and he
were hastening, to get there before it shut, opened at five
o'clock, the empty gin bottle now bobbing in the lake with an
absurd motion, and an absurder message in it scrawled by
Jacqueline, "Good luck to whoever finds me" (Ethan found it
himself a fortnight later); the golden robin that was the Baltimore oriole and knot expert, and master builder, at its complex
work of nesting, whistling in its rich contralto; they had seen
the two orioles making their nest together earlier in the afternoon, the Llewelyns themselves the watchers on the threshold,
watching them weaving happily their wonderful nest of fibres
and plant down and hairs and string (rebuild, *we* shall rebuild),
the female thrusting a fibre into the nest and then, this was the
wonderful part, reaching over to the inside and pulling the
string through with her little beak, tugging with all her might
to make everything all "a'taunto," solid and tight, he hadn't
fully appreciated this either till they'd got to Eridanus, but that

was what the birds had been doing (their bus went rushing over a bridge crossing a swift river with the sign: *This is the River Amor-de-Cosmos. Drink Grape-up!*—and "I shall build a house myself, or with Jacqueline's aid, even if I need a book for that too," Ethan thought, while the same Mounted Police car they'd seen before choired past in the opposite direction:—no), she would make no mistake, that little bird, and so to make certain she would thrust in another fibre, or the male would, and that was what they were doing now, having resumed the work after the siesta, repeating exactly the same process, though now they had nearly finished, so that looking at their work, this small while later, Jacqueline and Ethan could see how their little home was all so knotted and felted and quilted together that though it was tossing wildly in the lake breeze (that bore to them with a scent of grasses, over the deserted golf links down the thirteenth fairway, the charred creosote smell of their own burned house), it looked as if it would last for years, and they imagined it tossing there for years, braving all the tempests of the storm country, seeing beyond too, through the trees on the right by the twelfth green, the boarded-up house of the matricide, one of Ethan's former clients, dead by his own hand before he was arrested or brought to trial; the daffodils and dandelions growing together in the overgrown garden—where someone was standing, after all, some faint Maria Chapdelaine motionless there—a man who claimed to have seen a polar bear kill a walrus in one blow by banging it on the head with a block of ice, an action that seemed unfortunately to have impressed him too much; his house forlorn as Cézanne's painting "Maison de Pendu" seen the day before yesterday in the art gallery at Ixion (which was on the fifth floor of the Department of Mines and Resources): a house where a man has housed himself: a house where a man has hanged himself; and now the windy whistling empty golf links themselves with their blowing spiny spring grasses and sand dunes and stricken stunted thorn bushes like Wuthering Heights: "I lingered round them, under that benign sky, watched the moths fluttering among the hare-bells"—the course! but ah, what further hazards lurked before them there, what roughs and bunkers and traps and dog-legged approaches, and dongas and treacherous blind (and nine-teenth) holes, and final, it was to be hoped too, bright fairways; and the ecstasies of bobolinks twittering and bobolinking in the blue, bobbing on the links, or bringing rushes of rollicking song downwind, like imagined tintinnabulating harebells, like tinkling bluebells, darting over the "moat" of the old fort—the bastion now the out-of-bounds at the short fourth: "*Ein fester Burg ist unser Gott,*" Ethan said (observing at this moment that the old *Noronic*—"Bask in the warm breezes of sunny Lake Ontario on the boat deck of Canada's favorite pleasure boat" —was halfway to Toronto) and where, among what appeared cunning contracallations, they found an antique long-lost golf ball of forgotten make named the "Zodiak Zone"; the blithe bobolink, friend of hay and clover: the merry bobolink that was also called (ex post facto knowledge too) skunk blackbird, *le goglu,* Dolichonyx oryzivorus; the bobolink that said clink.

CHAPTER 21: GO WEST, YOUNG MAN

A ND SASKATCHEWAN AND SASKATCHEWAN AND SAS-
katchewan: said the train: and Saskatchewan and Saskatchewan and Saskatchewan. And Manitoba and Manitoba
and Manitoba. Five thousand miles at thirty miles an hour.
Five hundred miles of prairie were ablaze. Beyond the Great
Divide, they looked down on the wild beauty of lakes and
ravines and pastures of British Columbia with all the boundless
and immeasurable longing in their gaze of two children of
Israel shading their eyes before a vision of the Promised Land.
And when from the Rockies they had descended through the
Fraser Valley, the first thing they saw of Vancouver was, from
the train window at Port Moody, across the water on their
right, a swift-flowing inlet, a fisherman's shack, built on piles,
blazing...

LETTERS

TO CONRAD AIKEN

5 Woodville Road
Blackheath, London S.E. 3
[Winter, 1929]

I have lived only nineteen years and all of them more or less badly. And yet, the other day, when I sat in a teashop (one of those grubby little places which poor Demarest loved, and the grubbier the better, and so do I) I became suddenly and beautifully alive. I read... "I lay in the warm sweet grass on a blue May morning, My chin in a dandelion, my hands in clover, And drowsed there like a bee... Blue days behind me Reached like a chain of deep blue pools of magic, Enchanted, silent, timeless. Days before me Murmured of blue sea mornings, noons of gold, Green evenings streaked with lilac..."

I sat opposite the Bureau-de-change. The great grey tea urn perspired. But as I read, I became conscious only of a blur of faces: I let the tea that had mysteriously appeared grow clammy and milk-starred, the half veal and ham pie remain in its crinkly paper; vaguely, as though she had been speaking upon another continent, I heard the girl opposite me order some more Dundee cake. My pipe went out.

> ...I lay by the hot white sand-dunes.
> Small yellow flowers, sapless and squat and spiny,
> Stared at the sky. And silently there above me,
> Day after day, beyond all dreams or knowledge,

Presences swept, and over me streamed their shadows,
Swift and blue, or dark...[*]

I paid the bill and went out. I crossed the Strand and walked
down Villiers Street to the Embankment. I looked up at the sea
gulls, high in sunlight. The sunlight roared above me like a vast
invisible sea. The crowd of faces wavered and broke and
flowed.

Sometime when you come to London, Conrad Aiken, wilst
hog it over the way somewhere with me? You will forgive my
presumption, I think, in asking you this.

I am in fact hardly conscious myself of my own presumption. It seems quite fated that I should write this letter just like
this, on this warm bright day while outside a man shouts Rag-
a-bone, Rag-a-bone. It may not even interest you, my letter. It
may not be your intention *ever* to come to London even to
chivy up your publishers.

While on the subject of publishers I might as well say that I
find a difficulty bordering upon impossibility in getting your
"Nocturne of Remembered Spring." Have you got a spare
copy of this in Rye that you could sell me? If you have, it would
be a good excuse for you to write to tell me so. You could also
tell me whether you are coming to London any time, you
would have any time to see me. Charing X is only a quarter of
an hour away from here. But perhaps this letter has infuriated
you so much that you have not read this far.

te-thrum te-thrum
te-thrum te-thrum
Malcolm Lowry

---

*From Aiken's "The House of Dust."

TO CONRAD AIKEN

5 Woodville Road
Blackheath
Tuesday night
[Postmarked March 13, 1929]

Sir. (Which is a cold but respectful exordium.)

It has been said by no less a personage than Chamon Lall, once General Editor of a quarterly of which you were an American Editor that—sorry I'm wrong. It has been said by no less a personage than *Russell Green* (and I don't say that it is an original aphorism because one of his others "Sentimentality is a name given to the emotions of others" is sheer Oscar Wilde) that the only criterion of love is the degree of impatience with which you wait for the postman.

Well, I am a boy and you (respectfully) are a man old enough to be my father, and so again I may not talk of love in the way that Russell Green intended, but all the same, I may here substitute love for—shall we say—*filial affection* and, to apply the aphorism, since I wrote to you, my attitude towards postmen has completely changed. Once they were merely bourgeoisie beetles carrying their loads. Now they are divine but hopeless messengers. The mirror opposite the foot of my bed reflects the window to the right of the head of my bed (set between two mysterious green curtains) and this window—I cheat myself that this is good for my health—I keep open all night. In the mirror I can also see the road behind me when it is light. Early yesterday morning, it must have been about dawn, when I imagined that I could actually *see*, in the mirror, a long and never ending procession of postmen labouring along this road. The letters were delivered and among a great pile for other people was one for me from you.

I cannot remember what you said. You were pleased that I

ended off my letter to you with *te-thrum te-thrum, te-thrum te-thrum*; but I can't remember anything else except your hand-writing. Of course it was, as I realised bitterly when I woke up, merely a rose-festooned illusion. You had no intention of writing me. You didn't like the way I asked if you would have time ever to see me in London when you might have *time* but hardly time enough to trouble about having a lunch on someone you'd never seen. I perhaps didn't make it clear enough that I'd go anywhere within my reach from Pimlico to the Isle of Dogs if only there was half a chance of seeing *you*. And then it is possible I should have sent a postal order in anticipation for "Nocturne of Remembered Spring" because even if you hadn't got it I take it even though you would have found it a nuisance you would have sent the postal order back which would have meant at least a cautious letter of some sort. But I'm wandering from the point.

The point is this.

I suppose there are few things you would hate more than to be invested with any academic authority. Well, this I shall say. Next October I am going to Cambridge for three or four years to try and get an English Tripos and a degree. Until October I am more or less of a free lance and a perpetual source of anxiety to a bewildered parent. The bewildered parent in question would be willing to pay you 5 or 6 guineas a week (I should say six personally, but tactily) if you would tolerate me for any period you like to name between now and then as a member of your household. Let me hasten to say that I would efface myself and not get in the way of your inspiration when it comes toddling along, that my appetite is flexible and usually entirely satisfied by cheese, that although I can't play chess and know little of the intricacies of gladioli, I too have heard the sea sound in strange waters—sh-sh-sh like the hush in a conch shell—and I can wield a fair tennis racket.

All I want to know is why I catch my breath in a sort of agony when I read:

> The lazy sea-waves crumble along the beach
> With a whirring sound like wind in bells,
> He lies outstretched on the yellow wind-worn sands
> Reaching his lazy hands
> Among the golden grains and sea-white shells.*

And I want to be in Rye at twilight and lean *myself* by the wall of the ancient town—*myself*, like ancient wall and dust and sky, and the purple dusk, grown old, grown old in heart. Remember when I write like this, remember that I am not a schoolboy writing a gushing letter to Jeffrey Farnol or somebody. (Remember, too, that you must respect me a little for having such an intense admiration for your poetry.)

I know you are a great man in America and that you have your own school of followers, but to me—in the dismal circle in which I move nobody had ever heard of you, my most intellectual moments, such as they are, being spent entirely alone, it was as though I had discovered you and I like to preserve this absurd idea in my childish mind and give myself a great deal of unearned credit for having done so. Well, to continue, I won't weary you by eulogizing what you know yourself to be good (good is quite stupendously the wrong word but I don't want to appear to gush, you understand.)

I know almost before you reply—if you do reply—that you are either away or that you would not have the slightest intention of acting for the shortest period of time as my guardian and for tutor, but at any rate do you mind reading this letter sympathetically because you must have been pretty much the

---

*From Aiken's "The House of Dust."

same as me in heart when you were a kid. And I do want to learn from you and to read your earliest and most inaccessible works and perhaps even your contributions to the *Dial*. I go back home (here is my address—Inglewood, Caldy, Cheshire) next Monday. Nobody reads at home: the only paper we take is *The British Weekly*; there are few books in the house more exciting than *Religions and Religion* by James Hope Moulton (although a careful searcher might find in a somewhat inaccessible region Donne, Chatterton, *The Smell of Lebanon*, Crabbe's *Inebriety* and *Blue Voyage*) and although I have had a certain amount of youthful success as a writer of slow and slippery blues it is as much as my life is worth to play anything in the house—that doesn't worry me so much—but when they see me writing anything serious they don't exactly discourage me but tell me that it should be subordinate to my real work. What my real work is, heaven only knows, as the only other department that I have had any success in, is in writing seriously and that success rarely meant acceptance but quite often sincere encouragement from people whose opinion could hardly be taken to be humble.

But I don't want to worry you with anything I've written and indeed after reading this rackety incoherence you would probably be extremely averse to being worried in that way. Look here, you don't hate me already, do you? (hate is too dignified a word).

Now if you are in London any time between when you receive this letter and Sunday (inclus) could you let me know, because you see we have put things on somewhat of a business footing?

I could meet you anywhere in London. And anytime. Between now and Montag. If not write to my address in the dismal swamp.

Klioklio,
C. M. Lowry

TO CONRAD AIKEN

8 Plympton Street
[Circa June 14, 1931]

My dear Conrad:

It was very good of you to write me about the tripeos: as for that I can't tell as yet, but we did our best—we did our best. I wrote a fairly good essay on Truth and Poetry, quoting yourself liberally not to say literally, and Poe and the Melody of Chaos; I was all right on the criticism paper, and I think I bluffed my way through on Literature from 1785 to the present day—I knew my Keats better than I thought I did, for instance—on the whole I have nothing to complain about from the papers (which I'll try and get together and send you), and if I have failed, and that's on the cards, I was more stupid at the time than I thought.

Meantime I have been leading a disordered and rather despairing existence, and you can probably guess at the reason why I was incapable of replying promptly. Your telegram, however, brought me to my senses and made me feel rightly ashamed of myself.

My d. & r.d.e. is due to a complexity of melancholy reasons none of which are either particularly complex, melancholy, or reasonable, and I have made up my mind about only one point in this business of living which is that I must, and as soon as possible, identify a finer scene: I must in other words give an imaginary scene identity through the immediate sensation of actual experience etc. This, you say, I may have already done in some part, and is becoming with me a desire for retrogression, for escaping from the subtle and sophisticated: that if it is not deep-rooted in honest transmission at all and has nothing to do with really wanting more experience and to rub off more prejudice, to use more hardship, load myself with finer mountains and strengthen more my reach, than would stopping home among books (even though I shall reach Homer!) but is nothing more than wanting alternately to kill Liverpool and myself: that I am in *truth*—although occasionally straining at particles of light in the midst of a great darkness—"a small boy chased by furies" and you can sympathize with me as such. Well—if t'were so t'were a grievous fault—

I prefer to think sometimes that it is because I really want to be a man rather than a male, which at present I'm not, and that I want to get from somewhere a frank and fearless will which roughly speaking does not put more mud into the world than there is at present. Nonsense.

Then I must read—I must read—I must read! Dostoievsky and Dante: Donne, Dryden, Davenant and Dean Inge.... Again, nonsense, but then at the moment I despair of all literature anyway. If I could read Homer—however much he may have roared in the pines, I'm sure I should hate him: Donne means damn all to me now, Herrick is terrible, Milton I can't read and wouldn't if I could: all Restoration comedy and most all Greek tragedy is a bore...Tolstoy? My God what a bloody awful old writer he was!

Well, there is Melville and Goethe, you say.

Well, there was the story of Hamlet, I said, and fell into silence—

(By the by, "Experiment" was reviewed in the *Times Lit Sup* of a week or two back, side by side with a review of Martin Armstrong's collected—or are they selected?—unaffected, undetected and well-connected poems. I can't remember whether the review was a favourable one or not, I rather fear not—of my own contribution it remarked that it was a kind of prose fugue, with recurring themes, consisting of the rough talk of sailors or something, "effectively contrived"—I can't remember it in detail but I felt quite pleased. I haven't sent you a copy of it because the punctuation, length of dashes and so forth, was all wrongly done and I was sure it would give you a pain in the neck to look at: this is a rather selfish reason, for as a matter of fact the rest of the paper, in my opinion, is well worth reading. So I might send you a copy after all!)

I am delighted to hear that a novel is under way: it is really quite intolerable that I should have been so long sending you the tone dream—

Here it is however....

It occurs to me also, and with some horror, that I have not paid you the £4 I owe you. This has not been because I could not afford to pay it but simply because I have wasted my substance in riotous living—I have just put it off, and off, and there is no doubt whatever but that you could do as well with the four pounds as I could do well without it, but as I write this it so happens I have only a farthing in my pocket: moreover I can never think of the peculiar circumstances under which the debt, or ¾ of it, was accrued, without terror, inchoate flashes of nightmare—and perhaps this procrastination is due in a very small part to the fact that to pay the debt means writing about the circumstances and therefore remembering them. Ho, I am not Mr. Sludge the medium, nor was meant to be.... But I wish I knew where the hell that three pounds was all the same.

The reason why I have a farthing, and not a halfpenny or a penny or a half crown, in my pocket is a peculiar one. The other night I was walking outside a Fuller's Cafe, the windows looked something like Selfridges and not very different from any of the other modern buildings erected all over London, or Cambridge, except perhaps in size—all the windows were filled with chocolates or chocolate-coloured cakes—I was in despair, when suddenly I caught sight of myself in the shop window and saw myself murmuring: Can he warm his blue hands by holding them up to the grand Northern Lights? Would not Lazarus rather be in Sumatra than here? Would he not rather lay him down lengthwise along the line of the Equator. . . . When at that moment a small boy suddenly came up to me, a small and very grimy urchin, and said, "Would you like a farthing?" So I replied, "Well why not keep it—it's good luck to have a farthing. Besides I haven't got a penny to give you for it." And he said, "ho, I don't want it, I've given my good luck to you." He then ran away. Strange!

7 A.M.

I am King Elephant Bag
I am King Elephant Bag
from de rose pink mountains.

I enclose you a letter from one Edward O'Brien, all the more mysterious because he failed to take any notice of my reply. . . . Moreover his letter miscarried to *me*—it pursued Noxon half round Europe—I sent him hopefully my biography (in cameo) as it appears at the back of the letter, at the same time giving away that I was an English writer, not an American. If you have any notion what O'Brien means, meant, or intends, if anything, could you let me know sometime if your brain will function in that direction? I never submitted him any story, and the only story he can have read from *Experiment* is the one about the mickey,* all of which improves the joke.

I can assume only that he did mean to publish the thing in the 1931 volume, American, and have already informed the old man on this score to counteract in part the effect of my (possible) failure in the exam which gawd forbid. O'Brien either ignored or didn't receive a couple of replies so I sent him a wire asking him if he could give me some information "as was going

---

*English dialect word for "parrot," in an ur-version of *Ultramarine*.

to Peru," and received the answer: "O'Brien in the Balkans—O'Brien." Which seems to me funny. Still, I would like your advice. It is a nice point.

And it's that story, you know, in all its pristine beauty, Conrad, full of "stop it, he muttered's," and "they growled's" and "they howled's" and "there, are you better now's," far away, yo hai's

long ago, yo ho
Malc

TO JOHN DAVENPORT

Hotel Francia
Oaxaca de Oaxaca, Mexico
[December, 1937]

S.O.S.   Sinking fast by both bow and stern
S.O.S.   Worse than both the *Morro Castle*
S.O.S.   and the *Titanic*—
S.O.S.   No ship can think of anything else to do when
S.O.S.   it is in danger
S.O.S.   But to ask its closest friend for help.
C.Q.D.   Even if he cannot come.
John:

My first letter to you was impounded by the police here. It contained both congratulation for you and Clem and commiseration for myself.

Better so, because it was a letter nobody should read. Commiseration = Comisario de Policía.

I have now destroyed this letter but with it also myself. This letter might be prettier too.

No words exist to describe the terrible condition I am in.

I have, since being here, been in prison three times.

No words exist either to describe this. Of course, this is the end of introversion. If you cannot be decent outside you might as well have a shot at being decent in.

Here I succeeded but what shots will be needed now even God would not care to know.

Everywhere I go I am pursued and even now, as I write, no less than five policemen are watching me.

This is the perfect Kafka situation but you will pardon me if I do not consider it any longer funny. In fact its horror is almost perfect and will be completely so if this letter does not reach you, as I expect it will not.

At any rate an absolutely fantastic tragedy is involved—so tragic and so fantastic that I could almost wish you to have a look at it. One of the most amusing features of the thing is that even an attempt to play Sidney Carton has resulted in a farce. I thought he was a good man but now my last illusion is destroyed. It was not that he was not good so much as that he was not allowed to be. Excuse me if I speak in riddles but the eyes of the police are polyagnous—is it polyganous? Perhaps polygamous. Finally—I cannot play second fiddle to Harpo Marx. Ah, how the police will try to puzzle this out—they will think I mean Karl! For obvious and oblivious reasons I cannot write to my family; for reasons so obvious they are almost naked I may not write to my wife. I cannot believe this is true; it is a nightmare almost beyond belief. I looked around in the black recesses of what used to be a mind and saw two friends— yourself and Arthur Calder-Marshall. I also saw something else not so friendly: imminent insanity. I have no conceivable idea how you could help me; or anyone else, unless it is by sending money that will be inevitably ill-spent. I can only send greetings from death to birth and go to pray to what in Mexico they call "the Virgin for those who have nobody with."

There is a church here for those who are solitary and the comfort you obtain from it is non-existent though I have wept many times there.

Another complication is that never in my whole life have I been to a place so fantastically beautiful as this, and, in spite of all, it would be difficult for me to leave. It is absolutely as fantastic as the aforementioned tragedy with which I am involved. The people are lovely, gentle, polite, passionate, profound and true. I hope the policemen who read this will believe it. Even they, with reservations, are the same. But—well; just but....

Incidentally I smell.

Nobody but the Oaxaquenians will say a good word for me.

The Spanish detest me; the Americans despise me; and the English turn their backs on me.

If I were able, I would turn my back on myself.

Or wouldn't I?

I scent—(or might if I did not smell so badly myself)—some integrity in all this.

Like Columbus I have torn through one reality and discovered another but like Columbus also I thought Cuba was on the mainland and it was not and like Columbus also it is possible I am leaving a heritage of destruction. I am not at all sure about this but in a Mexican prison you have to drink out of a pisspot sometimes. (Especially when you have no passport.)

But, even without this, I am in horrible danger: and even with it.

Part of this, of course, is imaginary, as usual; but for once it is not as imaginary as usual. In fact danger both to mind and body threatens from all sides.

I am not sure that the danger is not ten times as bad as I make out.

This is not the cry of the boy who cried wolf. It is the wolf itself who cries for help. It is impossible to say that this is less of a cry than a howl.

What is impossible is to eat, sleep, work: and I fear it may rapidly be becoming impossible also to live.

I cannot even remotely imagine that I am writing these terrible words, but here I am, and outside is the sun, and inside— God only knows and He has already refused.

I cannot see Jan now. But for God's sake see she is all right. I foresaw my fate too deeply to involve her in it.

I would like to see you. Whether you would like to see me is up to you. At such a time it is probably impossible, and with such responsibilities as yours: but I fear the worst, and alas, my only friend is the Virgin for those who have nobody with, and she is not much help, while I am on this last tooloose-Lowrytrek.

Malc

TO CONRAD AIKEN

[January, 1938]

Dear old bird:

Have now reached condition of amnesia, breakdown, heartbreak, consumption, cholera, alcoholic poisoning, and God will not like to know what else, if he has to, which is damned doubtful.

All change here, all change here, for Oakshot, Cockshot, Poxshot and fuck the whole bloody lot!

My only friend here is a tertiary who pins a medal of the Virgin of Guadalupe on my coat; follows me in the street (when I am not in prison, and he followed me there too several times); and who thinks I am Jesus Christ, which, as you know, I am not yet, though I may be progressing towards thinking I am myself.

I have been imprisoned as a spy in a dungeon compared with which the Château d'If—in the film—is a little cottage in the country overlooking the sea.

I spent Christmas—New Year's—Wedding Day there. All my mail is late. When it does arrive it is all contradiction and yours is cut up into little holes.

Don't think I can go on. Where I am it is dark. Lost.

Happy New Year,
Malcolm

TO JONATHAN CAPE

24 Calle de Humboldt
Cuernavaca, Morelos
Mexico
[January 2, 1946]

Dear Mr. Cape:

Thank you very much indeed for yours of the 29th November, which did not reach me, however, until New Year's Eve, and moreover reached me here, in Cuernavaca, where, completely by chance, I happen to be living in the very tower which was the original of the house of M. Laruelle, which I had only seen previously from the outside, and that ten years ago, but which is the very place where as it happens the Consul in the *Volcano* also had a little complication with some delayed correspondence.

Passing over my feelings, which you can readily imagine, of involved triumph, I will, lest these should crystallize into a complete agraphia, get down immediately to the business in hand.

My first feeling is that the reader, a copy of whose report you sent me, could not have been (to judge from your first letter to me) as sympathetic as the reader to whom you first gave it.

386 THE VOYAGE THAT NEVER ENDS

On the other hand, while I distinctly agree with much this second reader very intelligently says, and while in his place I might have said much the same by way of criticism, he puts me somewhat at a loss to reply definitely to your questions re revisions, for reasons which I shall try to set forth, and which I am sure both you and he would agree are valid, at least for the author.

It is true that the novel gets off to a slow start, and while he is right to regard this as a fault (and while in general this may be certainly a fault in any novel) I think it possible for various human reasons that its gravity might have weighed upon him more heavily than it would weigh upon the reader per se, certain provisions for him having first been made. If the book anyhow were already in print and its pages not wearing the dumb pleading disparate and desperate look of the unpublished manuscript, I feel a reader's interest would tend to be very much more engaged at the outset just as, were the book already, say, an established classic, a reader's feelings would be most different: albeit he might say *God, this is tough going*, he would plod gamely on through the dark morass—indeed he might feel ashamed not to—because of the reports which had already reached his ears of the rewarding vistas further on.

Using the word *reader* in the more general sense, I suggest that whether or not the *Volcano* as it is seems tedious at the beginning depends somewhat upon that reader's state of mind and how prepared he is to grapple with the form of the book and the author's true intention. Since, while he may be prepared and equipped to do both, he cannot *know* the nature of either of these things at the start, I suggest that a little subtle but solid elucidation in a preface or a blurb might negate very largely or modify the reaction you fear—that it was your first reaction, and might well have been mine in your place, I am asking you for the moment to be generous enough to consider beside the point—if he were *conditioned*, I say, ever so slightly towards the acceptance of that slow beginning as inevitable, supposing I convince you it is—slow, but perhaps not necessarily so tedious after all—the results might be surprising. If you say, well, a good wine needs no bush, all I can reply is: well, I am not talking of good wine but mescal, and quite apart from the bush, once inside the cantina, mescal needs salt and lemon to get it down, and perhaps you would not drink it at all if it were not in such an enticing bottle. If that seems beside the point too, then let me ask who would have felt encouraged to venture into the drought of *The Waste Land* without some anterior knowledge and anticipation of its poetic cases?

Some of the difficulties of approach having been cleared away therefore, I feel the first chapter for example, such as it stands, is necessary since it sets, even without the reader's knowledge, the mood and tone of the book as well as the slow melancholy tragic rhythm of Mexico itself—its sadness—and above all establishes the *terrain*: if anything here finally looks to everyone just too feeble for words I would be only too delighted to cut it, but how can you be sure that by any really serious cutting here, especially any that radically alters the form, you are not undermining the foundations of the book, the basic structure, without which your reader might not have read it at all?

I venture to suggest finally that the book is a good deal thicker, deeper, better, and a great deal more carefully planned and executed than he suspects, and that if your reader is not at fault in not spotting some of its deeper meanings or in dismissing them as pretentious or irrelevant or uninteresting where they erupt onto the surface of the book, that is at least partly because of what may be a virtue and not a fault on my side, namely that the top level of the book, for all its *longueurs*, has been by and large so compellingly designed that the reader does not want to take time off to stop and plunge beneath the surface. If this is in fact true, of how many books can you say it? And how many books of which you can say it can you say also that you were not, somewhere along the line the first time you read it, bored because you wanted to "get on." I do not want to make childish comparisons, but to go to the obvious classics what about *The Idiot? The Possessed?* What about the beginning of *Moby-Dick?* To say nothing of *Wuthering Heights.* E. M. Forster, I think, says somewhere that it is more of a feat to get by with the end, and in the *Volcano* at least I claim I have done this; but without the beginning, or rather the first chapter, which as it were answers it, echoes back to it over the bridge of the intervening chapters, the end—and without it the book—would lose much of its meaning.

Since I am pleading for a rereading of *Under the Volcano* in the light of certain aspects of it which may not perhaps have struck you at all, with a view to any possible alterations, and not making a defense of its every word, I had better say that for my part I feel that the main defect of *Under the Volcano,* from which the others spring, comes from something irremediable. It is that the author's equipment, such as it is, is subjective rather than objective, a better equipment, in short, for a certain kind of poet than a novelist. On the other hand I claim that just as a tailor will try to conceal the deformities of his client so I have tried, aware of this defect, to conceal in the *Volcano* as well as possible the deformities of my own mind, taking heart from the fact that since the conception of the whole thing was essentially poetical, perhaps these deformities don't matter so very much after all, even when they show! But poems often have to be read several times before their full meaning will reveal itself, explode in the mind, and it is precisely this poetical conception of the *whole* that I suggest has been, if understandably, missed. But to be more specific: your reader's main objections to the book are:

1. The long initial tedium, which I have discussed in part but will take up again later.

2. The weakness of the character drawing. This is a valid criticism. But I have not exactly attempted to draw characters in the normal sense—though s'welp me bob it's only Aristotle who thought character counted least. But here, as I shall say somewhere else, there just isn't *room*: the characters will have to wait for another book, though I did go to incredible trouble to make my major characters seem adequate on the most *superficial* plane on which this book can be read, and I believe in some eyes the character drawing will appear the reverse of weak. (What about female readers?) The truth is that the character drawing is not only weak but virtually nonexistent, save with certain minor characters, the four main characters being intended, in one of the book's meanings, to be aspects of the same man, or of the human spirit, and two of them, Hugh and the Consul, more obviously are. I suggest that here and there what may look like unsuccessful attempts at character drawing may only be the concrete bases to the creature's lives without which again the book could not be read at all. But weak or no there is nothing I can do to improve it without reconceiving or rewriting the book, unless it is to take something out—but then, as I say, one might be thereby only removing a prop which, while it perhaps looked vexing to you in passing, was actually holding something important up.

3. "The author has spread himself too much. The book is *much too long* and over elaborate for its content, and could have been much more effective if only half or two thirds its present length. The author has overreached himself and is given to eccentric word-spinning and too much stream-of-consciousness

stuff." This may well be so, but I think the author may be forgiven if he asks for a fuller appraisal of that content—I say it all
again—in terms of the author's intention as a whole and chapter by chapter before he can reach any agreement with anyone
as to what precisely renders it over-elaborate and should therefore be cut to render that whole more effective. If the reader has
not got hold of the content at first go, how can he decide then
what makes it much too long, especially since his reactions may
turn out to be quite different on a second reading? And not
only authors perhaps but readers can overreach themselves, by
reading too fast however carefully they think they are going—
and what tedious book is this one has to read so fast? I believe
there is such a thing as wandering attention that is the fault neither of reader nor writer: though more of this later. As for
the eccentric word-spinning, I honestly don't think there is
much that is not in some way thematic. As for the "stream-of-
consciousness stuff," many techniques have been employed, and
while I did try to cut mere "stuff" to a minimum, I suspect that
your reader would finally agree, if confronted with the same
problems, that most of it could be done in no other way: a lot
of the so-called "stuff" I feel to be justified simply on poetical
or dramatic grounds: and I think you would be surprised to
find how much of what at first sight seems unnecessary even in
this "stuff" is simply disguised, honest-to-God exposition, the
author trying to proceed on Henry James' dictum that what is
not vivid is not represented, what is not represented is not art.

To return to the criticisms on the first and second page of
your reader's report:

1. "Flashbacks of the characters' past lives and past and present thoughts and emotions...(are) often tedious and unconvincing." These flashbacks are necessary however, I feel: where
they are really tedious or unconvincing, I should be glad to cut
of course, but I feel it only fair to the book that this should be

done only after what I shall say later (and have already said) has been taken into account. That which may seem inorganic in itself might prove right in terms of the whole churrigue-resque structure I conceived and which I hope may begin soon to loom out of the fog for you like Borda's horrible-beautiful cathedral in Taxco.

2. "Mexican local colour heaped on in shovelfuls... is very well done and gives one an astonishing sense of the place and the atmosphere." Thank you very much, but if you will excuse my saying so I did not heap the local colour, whatever that is, on in shovelfuls. I am delighted he likes it but take issue because what he says implies carelessness. I hope to convince you that, just as I said in my first letter, all that is there is there for a reason. And what about the use of Nature, of which he says nothing?

3. "The mescal-inspired phantasmagoria, or heebie-jeebies, to which Geoffrey has succumbed... is impressive but I think too long, wayward and elaborate. On account of (3) the book inevitably recalls... *The Lost Weekend.*" I will take this in combination with your reader's last and welcome remarks *re* the book's virtues, and the last sentence of the report in which he says: "Everything should be concentrated on the drunk's inability to rise to the occasion of Yvonne's return, on his deliri-ous consciousness (which is very well done) and on the local colour, which is excellent throughout." I do not want to quib-ble, but I do seem to detect something like a contradiction here. Here is my mescal-inspired phantasmagoria, which is impres-sive but already too long, wayward and elaborate—to say nothing of too much eccentric word-spinning and stream-of-consciousness stuff—and yet on the other hand, I am invited to concentrate still *more* upon it, since all this can be after all no-thing but the delirious consciousness (which is very well done)—and I would like very much to know how I can concentrate still

more upon a delirious consciousness without making it still more long-wayward-elaborate, and since that is the way of delirious consciousnesses, without investing it with still more stream-of-consciousness stuff: moreover here too is my local colour, and although this is already "heaped on in shovelfuls" (if excellent throughout) I am invited to concentrate still more upon it and this without calling in the aid of some yet large long-handled scoop-like implement used to lift and throw earth, coal, grain and so forth: nor do I see either how I can very well concentrate very much more than I have on the drunk's inability to rise to the occasion of Yvonne's return without incurring the risk of being accused of heaping on the mescal-inspired phantasmagoria with—at least!—a snow plough. Having let me have my fun, I must say that I admit the critical probity in your reader's last remarks but that it would be impossible to act on his suggestions without writing another book, possibly a better one, but still, another. I respect what he says, for what he seems to be saying is (like Yeats, when he cut nearly all the famous but irrelevant lines out of the *Ballad of Reading Gaol* and thereby, unfortunately for my thesis, much improved it): a work of art should have but one subject. Perhaps it will be seen that the *Volcano*, after all, *has* but one subject. This brings me to the unhappy (for me) subject of the *Lost Weekend*. Mr. Jackson likewise obeys your reader's aesthetic and does to my mind an excellent job within the limits he set himself. Your reader could not know, of course, that it should have been the other way round—that it was *The Lost Weekend* that should have inevitably recalled the *Volcano*; whether this matters or not in the long run, it happens to have a very desiccating effect on me. I began the *Volcano* in 1936, the same year having written, in New York, a novelette of about 100 pages about an alcoholic entitled *The Last Address*, which takes place mostly in the same hospital ward where Don Birnam

spends an interesting afternoon. This—it was too short I
thought to publish separately or I would have sent it to you for
it was and is, I believe, remarkably good—was accepted and
paid for by *Story Magazine*, who were publishing novelettes at
that time, but was never published because they had meantime
changed their policy back to shorter things again. It was however, in spite of Zola, accepted as more or less pioneer work in
that field, and nine years and two months ago when I was here
in this same town in Mexico I conceived the *Volcano* and I
decided really to go to town on the poetical possibilities of that
subject. I had written a 40,000-word version by 1937 that
Arthur Calder-Marshall liked, but it was not thorough or honest enough. In 1939 I volunteered to come to England but was
told to remain in Canada, and in 1940, while waiting to be
called up, I rewrote the entire book in six months, but it was no
damn good, a failure, except for the drunk passages about the
Consul, but even some of them did not seem to me good
enough. I also rewrote *The Last Address* in 1940–41 and
rechristened it *Lunar Caustic*, and conceived the idea of a trilogy entitled *The Voyage That Never Ends* for your firm (nothing less than a trilogy would do) with the *Volcano* as the first,
infernal part, a much amplified *Lunar Caustic* as the second,
purgatorial part, and an enormous novel I was also working on
called *In Ballast to the White Sea* (which I lost when my house
burned down as I believe I wrote you) as the paradisal third
part, the whole to concern the battering the human spirit takes
(doubtless because it is overreaching itself) in its ascent towards
its true purpose. At the end of 1941 I laid aside *In Ballast*—of
which there were 1000 pages of eccentric word-spinning by
this time—and decided to take this mescal-inspired phantasmagoria the *Volcano* by the throat and really do something
about it, it having become a spiritual thing by this time. I also
told my wife that I would probably cut my throat if during this

period of the world's drunkenness someone else had the same sober idea. I worked for two more years, eight hours a day, and had just ascetically completed all the drunken parts to my satisfaction and there were but three other chapters to rewrite when one day round about New Year's '44, I picked up an American review of *The Lost Weekend*. At first I thought it must be *The Last Week End*, by my old pal John (*Volunteer in Spain*) Sommerfield, a very strange book in which figured in some decline no less a person than myself, and I am still wondering what John thinks about this: but doubtless the old boy ascribes it to the capitalist system. *The Lost Weekend* did not appear in Canada till about April '44, and after reading the book it became extremely hard for the time being to go on writing and having faith in mine. I could still congratulate myself upon having *In Ballast* up my sleeve however, but only a month or so later that went completely west with my house. My wife saved the MSS of the *Volcano*, God knows how, while I was doing something about the forest, and the book was finished over a year ago in Niagara-on-the-Lake, Ontario. We returned to British Columbia to rebuild our house and since we had some serious setbacks and accidents in doing so it took some time to get the typescript in order. Meantime, however, this *Lost Weekend* business on top of everything else had somewhat got me down. The only way I can look upon it is as a form of punishment. My own worst fault in the past has been precisely lack of integrity, and that is particularly hard to face in one's own work. Youth plus booze plus hysterical identifications plus vanity plus self-deception plus no work plus more booze. But now, when this ex-pseudo author climbs down from his cross in his little Oberammergau where he has been hibernating all these years to offer something really original and terrific to atone for his sins, it turns out that somebody from Brooklyn has just done the same thing better. Or has he not?

And how many times has this author not been told that *that* theme of all themes couldn't sell, that nothing was duller than dipsomania! Anyway Papa Henry James would certainly have agreed that all this was a turn of the screw. But I think it not unreasonable to suppose either that he might have added that, for that matter, the *Volcano* was, so to say, a couple of turns of the screw on *The Lost Weekend* anyway. At all events I've tried to give you some of the reasons why I can't turn the *Volcano* into simply a kind of *quid pro quo* of the thing, which is what your reader's suggestions would tend to make it, or, if that's unfair to your reader, what I would then tend to make it. These reasons may be briefly crystallized. 1. Your reader wants me to do what I wanted to do myself (and still sometimes regret not having done) but did not do because 2. *Under the Volcano*, such as it is, is better. After this long digression, to return to the last page of your reader's report: I agree:

A. It is worth my while—and I am anxious—to make the book as effective as possible. But I think it only fair to the book that the lengths which have been gone to already to make it effective as possible *in its own terms* should be appreciated by someone who sees the whole.

B. Cuts should possibly be made in some of the passages indicated, but with the same reservations.

I disagree that:

A. Hugh's past is of little interest

B. or relevance

for reasons I shall set forth. One, which may seem odd, is: There is not a single part of this book I have not submitted to Flaubert's acid test of reading aloud or having read aloud, frequently to the kind of people one would expect to loathe it, and nearly always to people who were not afraid of speaking their minds. Chapter VI, which concerns Hugh's past life, always convulsed people with laughter, so much so that often the reader could not go on. Apart from anything else, then, and there is much else—what about its humour? This does not take care of its relevance, which I shall point out: but to refer back to something I said before, I submit that the real reason why your reader found this chapter of no interest or relevance was perhaps that I had built better than I knew in the previous chapter, and he wanted to skip and get on to the Consul again. Actually this chapter is the heart of the book and if cuts are to be made in it they should be made on the advice of someone who, having seen what the author is driving at, has at least an inspiration equivalent to that of the author who created it.

I had wanted to give in the following pages a kind of synopsis of the *Volcano* chapter by chapter, but since my spare copy of the MSS has not reached me from Canada I will simply suggest as well as I can some of its deeper meanings, and something of the form and intention that was in the author's mind, and that which he feels should be taken into account, should alterations be necessary. The twelve chapters should be considered as twelve blocks, to each of which I have devoted over a period of years a great deal of labour, and I hope to convince you that whatever cuts may be made there must still be twelve chapters. Each chapter is a unity in itself and all are related and interrelated. Twelve is a universal unit. To say nothing of the 12 labours of Hercules, there are 12 hours in a day, and the book is concerned with a single day as well as, though very incidentally, with time: there are 12 months in a year, and the novel is enclosed by a year; while the deeply buried layer of the novel or poem that attaches itself to myth, does so to the Jewish Cabbala where the number 12 is of the highest symbolic importance. The Cabbala is used for poetical purposes because it represents man's spiritual aspiration. The Tree of Life, which is its emblem, is a kind of complicated ladder with Kether, or Light, at the top and an extremely unpleasant abyss some way above the middle. The Consul's spiritual domain in this regard is probably the Qliphoth, the world of shells and demons, represented by the Tree of Life upside down—all this is not important at all to the understanding of the book; I just mention it in passing to hint that, as Henry James says, "There are depths." But also, because I have to have my 12: it is as if I hear a clock slowly striking midnight for Faust; as I think of the slow progression of the chapters, I feel it destined to have 12 chapters and nothing more nor less will satisfy me. For the rest, the book is written on numerous planes with provision made, it was my fond hope, for almost every kind of reader, my approach with all humility being opposite, I felt, to that of Mr. Joyce, *i.e.*, a simplifying, as far as possible, of what originally suggested itself in far more baffling, complex and esoteric terms, rather than the other way round. The novel can be read simply as a story which you can skip if you want. It can be read as a story you will get more out of if you don't skip. It can be regarded as a kind of symphony, or in another way as a kind of opera—or even a horse opera. It is hot music, a poem, a song, a tragedy, a comedy, a farce, and so forth. It is superficial, profound, entertaining and boring, according to taste. It is a prophecy, a political warning, a cryptogram, a preposterous movie, and a writing on the wall. It can even be regarded as a sort of machine: it works too, believe me, as I have found out. In case you think I mean it to be everything but a novel I better say that after all it is intended to be and, though I say so myself, a deeply serious one too. But it is also I claim a work of art somewhat different from the one you suspected it was, and more successful too, even though according to its own lights.

This novel then is concerned principally, in Edmund Wilson's words (speaking of Gogol), with the forces in man which cause him to be terrified of himself. It is also concerned with the guilt of man, with his remorse, with his ceaseless struggling toward the light under the weight of the past, and with his doom. The allegory is that of the Garden of Eden, the Garden representing the world, from which we ourselves run perhaps slightly more danger of being ejected than when I wrote the book. The drunkenness of the Consul is used on one plane to symbolize the universal drunkenness of mankind during the war, or during the period immediately preceding it, which is almost the same thing, and what profundity and final meaning there is in his fate should be seen also in its universal relationship to the ultimate fate of mankind.

Since it is Chapter I that I believe to be chiefly responsible for your reader's charge of tedium, and since, as I've said, I believe that a reader needs only a little flying start for this apparent tedium to be turned into an increasing suspense from the outset, I will devote more space to this first chapter than to any other, unless it is the sixth, saying also in passing that I believe it will become clear on a second reading that nearly all the material in I is necessary, and if one should try to eliminate this chapter entirely, or chop up all the material in it and stuff it in here and there into the book in wedges and blocks—I even tried it once—it would not only take a very long time but the results would be nowhere near as effective, while it would moreover buckle the very form of the book, which is to be considered like that of a wheel, with 12 spokes, the motion of which is something like that, conceivably, of time itself.

Under the Volcano

(*Note*: the book opens in the Casino de la Selva. Selva means wood and this strikes the opening chord of the *Inferno*— remember, the book was planned and still is a kind of Inferno, with Purgatorio and Paradiso to follow, the tragic protagonist in each, like Tchitchikov in *Dead Souls*, becoming slightly better—in the middle of our life... in a dark wood, etc., this chord being struck again in VI, the middle and heart of the book where Hugh, in the middle of his life, recalls at the beginning of that chapter Dante's words: the chord is struck again remotely toward the end of VII where the Consul enters a gloomy cantina called El Bosque, which also means the wood (both of these places being by the way real, one here, the other in Oaxaca), while the chord is resolved in XI, in the chapter concerning Yvonne's death, where the wood becomes real, and dark.)

I

The scene is Mexico, the meeting place, according to some, of mankind itself, pyre of Bierce and springboard of Hart Crane, the age-old arena of racial and political conflicts of every nature, and where a colorful native people of genius have a religion that we can roughly describe as one of death, so that it is a good place, at least as good as Lancashire or Yorkshire, to set our drama of a man's struggle between the powers of darkness and light. Its geographical remoteness from us, as well as the closeness of its problems to our own, will assist the tragedy each in its own way. We can see it as the world itself, or the Garden of Eden, or both at once. Or we can see it as a kind of timeless symbol of the world on which we can place the Garden of Eden, the Tower of Babel and indeed anything else we please. It is paradisal: it is unquestionably infernal. It is, in fact, Mexico, the place of the pulques and chinches, and it is important to remember that when the story opens it is November 1939, not November 1938, the Day of the Dead, and precisely one year after the Consul has gone down the barranca, the ravine, the abyss that man finds himself looking into now (to quote the Archbishop of York) the worse one in the Cabbala, the still unmentionably worse one in the Qliphoth, or simply down the drain, according to taste.

I have spoken already of one reason why I consider this chapter necessary more or less as it is, for the terrain, the mood, the sadness of Mexico, etc., but before I go on to mention any more I must say I fail to see what is wrong with this opening, as Dr. Vigil and M. Laruelle, on the latter's last day in the country, discuss the Consul. After their parting the ensuing exposition is perhaps hard to follow and you can say that it is a melodramatic fault that by concealing the true nature of the death of Yvonne and the Consul I have created suspense by false means: myself, I believe the concealment is organic, but even were it not, the criterion by which most critics condemn such devices seems to me to be that of pure reporting, and against the kind of novel they admire I am in rebellion, both revolutionary and reactionary at once. You can say too that it is a gamey and outworn trick to begin at the end of the book: it certainly is: I like it in this case and there is moreover a deep motive for it, as I have partially explained, and as I think you will see shortly. During Laruelle's walk we have to give some account of who he is; this is done as clearly as possible and if it could be achieved in a shorter or more masterly fashion I would be only too willing to take advice: a second reading however will show you what thematic problems we are also solving on the way—not to say what hams, that have to be there, are being hung in the window. Meanwhile the story is unfolding as the Mexican evening deepens into night: the reader is told of the love of M. Laruelle for Yvonne, the chord of tragic love is struck in the farewell visit at sunset to the Palace of Maximilian, where Hugh and Yvonne are to stand (or have stood) in the noonday in Chapter IV and while M. Laruelle leans over the fateful ravine we have, in his memory, the Taskerson episode. (Taskerson crops up again in V, in VII the Consul sings the Taskerson song to himself, and even in XII he is still trying to walk with the Taskerson "erect manly carriage.") The Taskerson episode

in this Chapter I—damned by implication by your reader—
may be unsound if considered seriously in the light of a psychological etiology for the Consul's drinking or downfall, but I
have a sincere and not unjustified conviction that it is very
funny in itself, and justified in itself musically and artistically at
this point as relief, as also for another reason: is it not precisely
in this particular passage that your reader may have acquired
the necessary *sympathy* with Geoffrey Firmin that enabled him
to read past Chapter II and into III without being beset by the
tedium there instead—and hence to become much more interested as he went on? Your reader has omitted the possibility of
the poor author's having any wit anywhere. If you do not
believe this Taskerson incident is funny, try reading it aloud. I
think that wit might seem slightly larger on a second reading:
also the drunken man on horseback, who now appears to inter-
rupt M. Laruelle's reverie, by hurtling on up the Calle Nicaragua, might have a larger significance: and still more on a
third reading. This drunken horseman is by implication the
first appearance of the Consul himself as a symbol of mankind.
Here also, as if tangentially (even if your reader saw it as but
another shovelful of local colour) is also struck the chord of
Yvonne's death in XI; true, this horse is not riderless as yet, but
it may well be soon: here man and the force he will release are
for the moment fused. (Since by the way there is no suggestion
in your reader's report that he has read the rather important
Chapter XI, in which there is incidentally some of the action he
misses, I had better say at this point that Yvonne is finally killed
by a panic-stricken horse in XI that the Consul drunkenly
releases in a thunderstorm in XII (the 2 chapters overlapping in
time at this juncture) in the erroneous, fuddled yet almost
praiseworthy belief he is doing somebody a good turn. M.
Laruelle now, avoiding the house where I am writing this letter
(which is one thing that must certainly be cut if I am not to

spend my patrimony sending it airmail), goes gloomily toward the local movie. In the cinema and the bar, people are taking refuge from the storm as in the world they are creeping into bomb shelters, and the lights have gone out as they have gone out in the world. The movie playing is *Las Manos de Orlac*, the same film that had been playing exactly a year before when the Consul was killed, but the man with the bloody hands in the poster, via the German origin on the picture, symbolizes the *guilt* of mankind, which relates him also to M. Laruelle and the Consul again, while he is also more particularly a foreshadowing of the thief who takes the money from the dying man by the roadside in Chapter VIII, and whose hands are also covered with blood. Inside the cinema cantina we hear more of the Consul from the cinema manager, Bustamente, much of which again may engage our sympathy for the Consul and our interest in him. It should not be forgotten that it is the Day of the Dead and that on that day in Mexico the dead are supposed to commune with the living. Life however is omnipresent: but meantime there have been both political (the German film star Maria Landrock) and historical (Cortez and Moctezuma) notes being sounded in the background; and while the story itself is being unfolded, the themes and counterthemes of the book are being stated. Finally Bustamente comes back with the book of Elizabethan plays M. Laruelle has left there eighteen months before, and the theme of Faust is struck. Laruelle had been planning to make a modern movie of Faust but for a moment the Consul himself seems like his Faust, who had sold his soul to the devil. We now hear more of the Consul, his gallant war record, and of a war crime he has possibly committed against some German submarine officers—whether he is really as much to blame as he tells himself, he is, in a sense, paid back in coin for it at the end of the book and you may say that here the Consul is merely being established in the Grecian manner as a fellow of some stature, so that his fall may be tragic: it could be cut, I suppose, even though this is exactly as I see the Consul—but do we not look at him with more interest thereafter? We also hear that the Consul has been suspected of being an English spy, or "espider," and though he suffers dreadfully from the mania of persecution, and you feel sometimes, quite objectively, that he is indeed being followed throughout the book, it is as if the Consul himself is not aware of this and is afraid of something quite different: for lack of an object therefore it was the writer's reasonable hope that this first sense of being followed might settle on the reader and haunt him instead. At the moment however Bustamente's sympathy for him should arouse *our* sympathy. This sympathy I feel should be very considerably increased by the Consul's letter which Laruelle reads, and which was never posted, and this letter I believe important: his tortured cry is not answered until in the last chapter, XII, when, in the Farolito, the Consul finds Yvonne's letters he has lost and never really read until this time just before his death. M. Laruelle burns the Consul's letter, the act of which is poetically balanced by the flight of vultures ("like burnt papers floating from a fire") at the end of III, and also by the burning of the Consul's MSS in Yvonne's dying dream in XI: the storm is over: and—

Outside in the dark tempestuous night backwards revolved the luminous wheel.

This wheel is of course the Ferris wheel in the square, but it is, if you like, also many other things: it is Buddha's wheel of the law (see VII), it is eternity, it is the instrument of eternal recurrence, the eternal return, and it is the form of the book; or superficially it can be seen simply in an obvious movie sense as the wheel of time whirling backwards until we have reached the year before and Chapter II and in this sense, if we like, we can look at the rest of the book through Laruelle's eyes, as if it were his creation.

(*Note:* In the Cabbala, the misuse of magical powers is compared to drunkenness or the misuse of wine, and termed, if I remember rightly, in Hebrew *sōd*, which gives us our parallel. There is a kind of attribute of the word *sōd* also which implies garden or a neglected garden, I seem to recall too, for the Cabbala is sometimes considered as the garden itself, with the Tree of Life, which is related of course to that Tree the forbidden fruit of which gave one the knowledge of good and evil, and ourselves the legend of Adam and Eve, planted within it. Be these things as they may—and they are certainly at the root of most of our knowledge, the wisdom of our religious thought, and most of our inborn superstitions as to the origin of man— William James if not Freud would certainly agree with me when I say that the agonies of the drunkard find their most accurate poetic analogue in the agonies of the mystic who has abused his powers. The Consul here of course has the whole thing wonderfully and drunkenly mixed up: mescal in Mexico is a hell of a drink but it is still a drink you can get at any cantina, more readily I dare say than Scotch these days at the dear old Horseshoe. But mescal is also a drug, taken in the form of buttons, and the transcending of its effects is one of the well-known ordeals that occultists have to go through. It would appear that the Consul has fuddledly come to confuse the two, and he is perhaps not far wrong.)

Final note on Chapter I: If this chapter is to be cut, can it not be done then with such wisdom as to make the chapter and the book itself better? I feel the chapter makes a wonderful entity and must be cut, if at all, by someone who at least sees its potentialities in terms of the whole book. I myself don't see much wrong with it. Against the charge of appalling pretentiousness, which is the most obvious one to be made by anyone who has read this letter, I feel I go clear; because these other meanings and danks and darks are not stressed at all: it is only if the reader himself, prompted by instinct or curiosity, cares to invoke them that they will raise their demonic heads from the abyss, or peer at him from above. But even if he is not prompted by anything, new meanings will certainly reveal themselves if he reads this book again. I hope you will be good enough not to remind me that the same might be said of *Orphan Annie* or *Jemima Puddleduck*.

II

You are now back on exactly the same day the year before—the Day of the Dead 1938—and the story of Yvonne's and the Consul's last day begins at seven o'clock in the morning on her arrival. I do not see any difficulties here. The mysterious contrapuntal dialogue in the Bella Vista bar you hear is supplied by Weber, you will later see if you watch and listen carefully, the smuggler who flew Hugh down to Mexico, and who is mixed up with the local thugs—as your reader calls them—and Sinarchistas in the Farolito in Parián who finally shoot the Consul. The chord of *no se puede vivir sin amar*, the writing in gold leaf outside M. Laruelle's house (where I am writing this letter, with my back to the degenerate machicolation, and even if you do not believe in my wheels—the wheel shows up in this chapter in the flywheel in the printer's shop—and so on, you must admit this is funny, as also that it is quite funny that the same movie happens to be playing in town as was playing here nine years ago, not *Las Manos de Orlac* as it happens but *La Tragedia de Mayerling*), is struck ironically by the bartender with his "absolutamente necesario," the recurring notices for the boxing match symbolize the conflict between Yvonne and the Consul. The chapter is a sort of bridge, it was written with extreme care; it too is absolutamente necesario, I think you would agree yourself on a second reading: it is an entity, a unity in itself, as are all the other chapters; it is, I claim, dramatic, amusing, and within its limits I think is entirely successful. I don't see any opportunity for cuts either.

III

I think will improve on a second reading and still more on a third. But since I believe your reader was impressed by it I will pass over it quickly. Word-spinning flashback while the Consul is lying down flat on his face in the Calle Nicaragua is really very careful exposition. This chapter was first written in 1940 and completed in 1942 long before Jackson went Lostweekending. Cuts should be made with great sympathy ("compliments of the Venezuelan Government" bit might go for instance) by someone—or by the author in conjunction with someone—who is prepared for the book to sink slowly at a not distant date into the action of the mind, and who is not necessarily put off by this. The scene between the Consul and Yvonne where he is impotent is balanced by scene between Consul and María in the last chapter: meanings of the Consul's impotence are practically inexhaustible. The dead man with hat over head the Consul sees in the garden is man by the wayside in Chapter VIII. This can happen in really super D.T.s. Paracelsus will bear me out.

IV

Necessary, I feel, much as it is, especially in view of my last sentence re III about the action of the mind. In this there is another kind of action. There is movement and swiftness, it is a contrast, it supplies a needed *ozone*. It gives a needed, also, sympathy and understanding of Mexico and her problems and people from a material viewpoint. If the very beginning seems slightly ridiculous you can read it as satire, but on a second reading I think the whole will improve vastly. We have now the counter-movement of the Battle of the Ebro being lost, while no one does anything about it, which is a kind of correlative of the scene by the roadside in VIII, the victim of which here first makes his appearance outside the cantina La Sepultura, with his horse tethered near, that will kill Yvonne. Man's political aspirations, as opposed to his spiritual, come into view, and Hugh's sense of guilt balances the Consul's. If part of it must be cut, let it be done with a view to the whole—and with genius at least, I feel like saying—and let it not be cut so that it bleeds. Almost everything in it is relevant even down to the horses, the dogs, the river, and the small talk about the local movie. And what is not, as I say, supplies a needed ozone. For myself I think this ride through the Mexican morning sunlight is one of the best things in the book, and if Hugh strikes you as himself slightly preposterous, there is importance to the theme in the passage *re* his passionate desire for *goodness* at the close.

V

Is a contrast in the reverse direction, the opening words having an ironic bearing on the last words of IV. The book is now fast sinking into the action of the mind, and away from normal action, and yet I believe that by now your reader was really interested, *too* interested in fact here in the Consul to be able to cope with VI. Here at all events the most important theme of the book appears: "Le gusta este jardín?" on the sign. The Consul slightly mistranslates this sign, but "You like this garden? Why is it yours? We evict those who destroy!" will have to stand (while we will point out elsewhere that the real translation can be in a certain sense even more more horrifying). The garden is the Garden of Eden, which he even discusses with Mr. Quincey. It is the world too. It also has all the cabbalistic

attributes of "garden." (Though all this is buried far down in
the book, so that if you don't want to bother about it, you
needn't. I wish that Hugh l'Anson Fausset, however, one of
your own writers, one whose writings I very much admire and
some of whose writings have had a very formative influence on
my own life, could read the *Volcano*.) On the surface I am
going to town here on the subject of the drunkard and I hope
do well and amusingly. Parián again is death. Word-spinning
phantasmagoria somewhere toward end of first part is necessary. It should be clear that the Consul has a blackout and that
the second part in the bathroom is concerned with what he
remembers half deliriously of the missing hour. Most of what
he remembers is again disguised exposition and drama which
carries on the story to the question: shall they go to Guanajuato
(life) or Tomalín, which of course involves Parián (death). For
the rest the Consul at one point identifies himself with the
infant Horus, about which or whom the less said the better;
some mystics believe him responsible for this last war, but I
need another language I guess to explain what I mean. Perhaps
Mr. Fausset would explain, but at all events you don't have to
think about it because the passage is only short, and reads like
quite good lunacy. The rest I think is perfectly good clean
D.T.s such as your reader would approve of. This was first
written in 1937. Final revision was made in March 1943. This
too is an entity in itself. Possible objection could be to the technique of the second part but I believe it is a subtle way to do a
difficult thing. Cuts might be made here, I guess, but they
would have to be inspired at least as much as the chapter was.

VI

Here we come to the heart of the book which, instead of going
into high delirious gear of the Consul, returns instead, surprisingly although inevitably if you reflect, to the uneasy, but

healthy, systole-diastole of Hugh. In the middle of our life...
and the theme of the Inferno is stated again, then follows the
enormously long *straight* passage. This passage is the one your
reader claims has little or no interest or relevance and I maintain he skipped because of a virtue on my side, namely he was
more interested in the Consul himself. But here the guilt theme,
and the theme of man's guilt, takes on a new shade of meaning.
Hugh may be a bit of a fool but he none the less typifies the sort
of person who may make or break our future: in fact he is the
future in a certain sense. He is Everyman tightened up a screw,
for he is just beyond being mediocre. And he is the youth of
Everyman. Moreover his frustrations with his music, with the
sea, in his desire to be good and decent, his self-deceptions, triumphs, defeats and dishonesties (and once more I point out
that a much needed ozone blows into the book here with the
sea air) his troubles with his guitar, are everyone's frustrations,
triumphs, defeats, dishonesties and troubles with their *quid pro
quo* of a guitar. And his desire to be a composer or musician is
everyone's innate desire to be a poet of life in some way, while
his desire to be accepted at sea is everyone's desire, conscious or
unconscious, to be a part—even if it doesn't exist—of the brotherhood of man. He is revealed as a frustrated fellow whose
frustrations might just as well have made him a drunk too, just
like the Consul. (Who was frustrated as a poet—as who is
not?—this indeed is another thing that binds us all together,
but for whose drunkenness no satisfactory etiology is ever
given unless it is in VII. "But the cold world shall not know.")
Hugh feels he has betrayed himself by betraying his brother
and also betrayed the brotherhood of man by having been at
one time an anti-Semite. But when, in the middle of the chapter,
which is also the middle of the book, his thoughts are interrupted by Geoffrey's call of "Help" you can receive, I claim,
upon rereading, a *frisson* of a quite different calibre to that

received when reading such pieces as "William Wilson" or
other stories about doppelgängers. Hugh and the Consul are
the same person, but within a book which obeys not the laws of
other books, but those it creates as it goes along. I have reason
to believe that much of this long straight passage is extremely
funny anyway and will cause people to laugh aloud. We now
proceed into the still greater nonsense and at the same time far
more desperate seriousness of the shaving scene. Hugh shaves
the corpse—but I cannot be persuaded that nonetheless much
of this is not very hilarious indeed. We are then introduced to
Geoffrey's room, with his picture of his old ship the *Samaritan*
(and the theme is struck remotely again of the man by the wayside in VIII) upon which ship it has been mentioned before in I,
etc., that he either has committed or imagines he has, but was
certainly made in part responsible for, a crime against a number
of German submarine officers—valid at least as any crime we
may have committed in the past against Germany in general,
that ugsome child of Europe whose evil and destructive energy
is so much responsible for all our progress. At the same time he
shows Hugh his alchemistic books, and we are for a moment, if
in a pseudo-farcical situation, standing before the evidence of
what is no less than the magical basis of the world. You do not
believe the world has a magical basis, especially while the Battle of the Ebro is going on, or worse, bombs are dropping in
Bedford Square? Well, perhaps I don't either. But the point is
that Hitler *did*. And Hitler was another pseudo black magician
out of the same drawer as Amfortas in the *Parsifal* he so much
admired, and who has had the same inevitable fate. And if you
don't believe that a British general actually told me that the real
reason why Hitler destroyed the Polish Jews was to prevent
their cabbalistic knowledge being used against him you can let
me have my point on poetical grounds, I repeat, since it is made
at a very sunken level of the book and is not very important

here anyway. Saturn lives at 63, and Bahomet lives next door, however, and don't say I didn't tell you!

The rest of the chapter, and all this is probably too long, takes Hugh and the Consul and Yvonne, meeting Laruelle on the way (I hope dramatically) up to the house where I am now writing you this letter: the point about the postcard the Consul receives (from the same tiny bearded postman who delivered your delayed letter to me on New Year's Eve) is that it was posted about a year before in 1937 not long after she left, or was sent away by the Consul (following her affair with Laruelle but probably so that the Consul could drink in peace), and that its tone would seem to suggest that her going away was only a final thing in the Consul's mind, that really they loved each other all the time, had just had a lover's quarrel, and in spite of M. Laruelle, the whole thing was absolutely unnecessary. The chapter closes with a dying fall, like the end of some guitar piece of Ed Lang's, or conceivably Hugh's (and in this respect the brackets earlier might represent the "breaks")— oddly but rightly, I felt, the path theme of Dante, however, reappearing and fading with the vanishing road.

I believe on rereading this chapter it will seem to have much more relevance than before and its humor will appear as more considerable. On the other hand this is undoubtedly the juiciest area for your surgeon's knife. The middle part of the shaving scene was written in 1937, as was the very end, that much comprising the whole chapter then. The new version was done in 1943 but I had not quite finally revised it in 1944 when my house burned down. The final revisions I made later in 1944 comprised the first work I had been able to do since the fire, in which several pages of this chapter and notes for cuts were lost, and it well may be the job is shaky or forced here and there. This is the first point in the book where I can be persuaded to share your reader's objections, I think, to any extent. Some of it may be in a kind of bad taste. On the other hand I feel it deserves a careful rereading—I say again and again in the light of the form and intention I have indicated, bearing in mind that the journalistic style of the first part is intended to represent Hugh himself. In brief, I could stand even slashing cuts were your surgeon to say, "This would be more effective if such and such were done," and I saw he was taking everything into account. If a major operation by a sympathetic surgeon will save the patient's life, O.K., but, even though I do live in Mexico, I'm damned if I'm going to help him cut out his heart. (And then, when he's dead, "just flop it back in again anyhow," as the nurse said to me having just attended the post mortem.)

VII

Here we come to seven, the fateful, the magic, the lucky good-bad number and the scene in the tower, where I write this letter. By a coincidence I moved to the tower on January 7—I was living in another apartment in the same house, but downstairs, when I got your letter. My house burned down on June 7; when I returned to the burned site someone had branded, for some reason, the number 7 on a burned tree; why was I not a philosopher? Philosophy has been dying since the days of Duns Scotus, though it continues underground, if quacking slightly. Boehme would support me when I speak of the passion for order even in the smallest things that exist in the universe: 7 too is the number on the horse that will kill Yvonne and 7 the hour when the Consul will die—I believe the intention of this chapter to be quite clear and that it is one your reader approves of and I think too it is probably one of the best in the book. It was first written in 1936, rewritten in 1937, 1940, 1941, 1943, and finally 1944. Parallels with *The Lost Weekend* I think are most in evidence in this chapter. One long one that does not appear

and which was written long before the L.W.E. I hoiked out
with a heavy heart, but imbued with the spirit of competition,
then added something else to my telephone scene to outdo him.
I was particularly annoyed because my telephone scene in III
and this one before I revised it, as I have said, were written long
before Jackson's book appeared. Another parallel toward the
end when he had his drink before him he doesn't pick it up will
have to stand: it was written in 1937 anyway. I allowed myself
also in the conversation in the middle with Laruelle a little of
the Consul's professional contempt for the belief that the D.T.'s
is the end of everything and I think if you ever publish the book
you might do me justice by saying that this begins where Jackson leaves off. If there must be cuts here again I say they should
be made by someone who appreciates this chapter as an entity
right down to the bit about Samaritana mia and with reference
to the whole book. There were the usual thicknesses and obliq-
uities, stray cards from the tarot pack, and odd political and
mystical chords and dissonances being sounded here and there
in this chapter but I won't go into them: but there is also, above
all, the continued attention to the *story*. The horseman, first
seen in IV and who is to be the man by the roadside, is seen
again going up the hill, and whose horse, with the number 7 on
it, will kill Yvonne. This chapter constitutes almost the Consul's last chance and if the book has been read carefully I feel
you should have a fine sense of doom by this time. *Es inevitable
la muerte del Papa* is quite possibly just an anachronism, but I
feel it must stand for I hold this a fine ending.

(Notes re local colour heaped on in shovelfuls: this chapter
is a good example and every damn thing in it is organic. The
madman futilely and endlessly throwing a bicycle tire in front
of him, the man stuck half way up the slippery pole—these are
projections of the Consul and of the futility of his life, and at

the same time are *right*, are *true*, are what one sees here. Life is a forest of symbols, as Baudelaire said, but I won't be told you can't see the wood for the trees here!)

VIII

Here the book, so to speak, goes into reverse—or, more strictly speaking, it begins to go downhill, though not, by any means, I hope, in the sense of deteriorating! Downhill (the first word), toward the abyss. I think it one of the better chapters; though it needs reading carefully, I feel the reader will be well rewarded. Man dying by the roadside with his horse branded No. 7 near is, of course, the chap who'd been sitting outside the pulquería in IV, had appeared singing in VII when the Consul identified himself with him. He is, obviously, mankind himself, mankind dying—then, in the Battle of the Ebro, or now, in Europe, while we do nothing, or if we would, have put ourselves in a position where we *can* do nothing, but talk, while he goes on dying—in another sense he is the Consul too. I claim the chapter proceeds well on its own account while these meanings are revealed without being too much labored. I think the meaning is obvi-ous, intentionally so, almost, in a sense, like a cartoon, and on one plane as oversimplified as journalism, intentionally too, for it is through Hugh's eyes. The story on the top plane is being carried on normally however, and while the local political sig-nificance would be clear to anyone who knows Mexico, the wider political and religious significance must be self-evident to anyone. It was the first chapter written in the book; the incident by the roadside, based on a personal experience, was the germ of the book. I feel that some wag not too unlike your reader might tell me at this point that I would do better to reduce the book back to this original germ so that we could all have it printed in O'Brien's *Best Short Stories of 1946*, with luck, in-stead of as a novel, and against this resourceful notion I can only cite the example of Beethoven, who also was somewhat inclined to overspread himself I seem to think, even though most of his themes are actually so simple they could be played by just rolling an orange down the black keys. The chapter is more apropos now than then, in 1936: then there were no deputies—though I invented them in 1941: now there are; in fact one is living in an apartment downstairs. I don't think it can be cut: but if it must be, it should be done with the same reservations I have made elsewhere. As for the *xopilotes*, the vultures, I should add that they are more than merely cartoon birds: they are real in these parts, in fact one is looking at me as I write, none too pleasantly either: they fly through the whole book and in XI become as it were archetypal, Promethean fowl. Once considered by ornithologists the first of birds, all I can say is that they are more than likely to be the last.

IX

This chapter was originally written in 1937 but then it was through Hugh's eyes. Then it was rewritten as through the Consul's eyes. And now—as it must be for the sake of balance, if you reflect—it is through Yvonne's eyes. Possibly it could have been seen just as well through the bull's eyes, but it reads very well aloud and I think is among other things a successful and colorful entity in itself and musically speaking ought to be an exceedingly good contrast to VIII and X. Readers might disagree about flashbacks here—some think it good, others suspecting a belated attempt to draw character and at that a meretricious one—though I feel many of your *feminine* readers might approve. The flashbacks are not here though either for their own sake, or particularly for the sake of character, which as I said was my last consideration as it was Aristotle's—since there isn't *room*, for one thing. (It was, I think, one of your own writers, and a magnificent one, Sean O'Faolain, who put this heretical notion even further into my headpiece about the comparative unimportance of character anyway. Since he is a wonderful character drawer himself, his words bore weight with me. Were not Hamlet and Laertes, he says, at the final moment, almost the same person? The novel then, he went on to argue, should reform itself by drawing upon its ancient Aeschylean and tragic heritage. There are a thousand writers who can draw adequate characters till all is blue for one who can tell you anything new about hell fire. And I am telling you something new about hell fire. I see the pitfalls—it can be an easy way out of hard work, an invitation to eccentric word-spinning, and labored phantasmagorias, and subjective inferior masterpieces that on closer investigation turn out not even to be bona fide documents but like my own *Ultramarine*, to be apparently translated with a windmill out of the unoriginal Latvian, but just the same in our Elizabethan days we used to have at least passionate poetic writing about things that will always mean something and not just silly ass style and semicolon technique: and in this sense I am trying to remedy a deficiency, to strike a blow, to fire a shot for you as it were, roughly in the direction, say, of another Renaissance: it will probably go straight through my brain but that is another matter. Possibly too the Renaissance is already in full swing but if so I have heard nothing of this in Canada.) No, the real point of this chapter is Hope, with a capital H, for this note must be struck in order to stress the later downfall. Though even the capacity of the intelligent reader for suspending his disbelief is enormous I didn't intend that this feeling of hope should be experienced by the reader in quite the ordinary way, though he can if he wants to. I intended somehow the feeling of hope per se to transcend even one's interest in the characters. Since these characters are in one way "Things," as that French philosopher of the absurd fellow has it, or even if you believe in them you know perfectly well that they are ditched anyhow, this hope should be, rather, a transcendent, a universal hope. The novel meanwhile is, as it were, teetering between past and future— between despair (the past) and hope—hence these flashbacks (some of them could doubtless be cut slightly but I don't think I could do it). Shall the Consul, once more, go forward and be reborn, as if previously to Guanajuato—is there a chance that he may be, at any rate on the top level?—or shall he sink back into degeneracy and Parián and extinction. He is one aspect of Everyman (just as Yvonne is so to speak the eternal woman, as in *Parsifal*, Kundry, whoever she was, angel and destroyer both). The other aspect of Everyman is of course Hugh who all this time is somewhat preposterously subduing the bull: in short, though with intentional absurdity—the whole book for that matter can be seen as a kind of gruesome and serious absurdity, just like the world in fact—he conquers the animal forces of nature which the Consul later lets loose. The threads of the various themes of the book begin to be drawn together. The close of the chapter, with the Indian carrying his father, is a restatement and universalizing of the theme of humanity strug- gling on under the eternal tragic weight of the past. But it is also Freudian (man eternally carrying the psychological burden of his father), Sophoclean, Oedipean, what have you, which relates the Indian to the Consul again.

If cuts are made those things and the fact that it is a unity in itself, as usual, should be taken into account. It was finally completed as it stands in 1944.

X

This was first written in '36–'37 and rewritten at various peri- ods up to 1943. This final version was written after my fire, in the summer and fall of 1944, and I dare say this is another obvious candidate for your surgeon's knife. Nothing I wrote

after the fire save most of XI has quite the integrity of what I
wrote before it but though this chapter seems absolutely interminable, indeed intolerable, when read aloud, I submit it to be
a considerable inspiration and one of the best of the lot. The
opening train theme is related to Freudian death dreams and
also to "A corpse will be transported by express" of the beginning of II and I can't see that it is not extremely thrilling in its
gruesome fashion. Passage that follows re the "Virgin for those
who have nobody with" ties up with opening pages of Chapter
I and were written previously, as was the humorous menu section. I can see valid objections though to the great length of
some of the Tlaxcala stuff from the folder: but I was absolutely
unable to resist it. I cut and cut as it was, I even sacrificed two
good points, namely that Tlaxcala is probably the only capital
in the world where black magic is still a working proposition,
and that it is also the easiest place in the world to get a divorce
in, and then could cut no more: I thought it too good, while the
constant repetition of churrigueresque "of an overloaded
style" seemed to be a suggestion that the book was satirizing
itself. This Tlaxcala folder part has a quite different effect when
read with the eyes, as it will be (I hope)—then you can of
course get it much more swiftly; and I had originally thought it
would possibly go quicker still if some experiment were made
with the typesetting such as the occasional use of black letter
for the headings juxtaposed with anything from cursive down
to diamond type for the rest and back again according to the
reader's interest or the Consul's state of delirium: some simpli-
fication of this suggestion might be extremely effective but I do
not see how it can be very popular with you and is perhaps a
little much anyway. At all events I believe there are strange evo-
cations and explosions here that have merit in themselves even
if you are not closely following what is happening, much as,
even if you can't make out what Harpo is saying, the sound of

the words themselves may be funny. Revelations such as that Pulquería, which is a kind of Mexican pub, is also the name of Raskolnikov's mother should doubtless not be taken too seriously, but the whole Tlaxcala business *does* have an underlying deep seriousness. Tlaxcala, of course, just like Parián, is death: but the Tlaxcalans were Mexico's traitors—here the Consul is giving way to the forces within him that are betraying himself, that indeed have now finally betrayed him, and the general plan of the whole phantasmagoric thing seems to me to be right. Dialogue here brings in the theme of war, which is of course related to the Consul's self-destruction. This chapter was finally completed about a year before atom bombs, etc. But if it does so happen that man is now in danger of finding himself in the evil position of the black magician of old who discovered suddenly that all the elements of the universe were against him, the old Consul might be given credit for pointing out as much in a crazy passage where he even names the elements uranium plutonium, and so forth; undoubtedly it is of no interest as prophecy any more, but I can't say it dates! This little bit is, of course, thematic, if you reflect. At the end of this chapter the volcanoes, which have been getting closer throughout, are used as a symbol of approaching war. In spite of its apparent chaos this chapter has been written very carefully and with attention to every word. It, too, is an entity in itself, and if it must be cut I ask that the cutter see it also as an entity and in its place in the book. Though I suggest it is dramatically extremely powerful, regarded in a certain light, I am more disposed to have this chapter and chapter VI cut than any other, if cuts there must be, and if in the case of this chapter it is merely rendered more dramatic and more powerful.

XI

This was the last chapter I wrote and [it] was completed in late

1944, though I had had its conception in mind for a long time. My object was to pull out here all the stops of Nature, to go to town, as it were, on the natural elemental beauty of the world and the stars, and through the latter to relate the book, as it was related through the wheel at the end of Chapter I, to eternity. Here the wheel appears in another guise, the wheel of the motion of the stars and constellations themselves through the universe. And here again appears the dark wood of Dante, this time as a real wood and not just a cantina or the name of one. Here again too appears the theme of the Day of the Dead, the scene in the cemetery balancing the scene of the mourners at the opening of the book, but this time it has tremendously more human emphasis. The chapter again acts as a double contrast to the lesser horrors of X and the worse ones of XII. On the surface Hugh and Yvonne are simply searching for the Consul, but such a search would have added meaning to anyone who knows anything of the Eleusinian mysteries, and the same esoteric idea of this kind of search also appears in Shakespeare's *Tempest*. Here however all the meanings of the book have to be blended somehow in an unpretentious and organic manner in the interest of the tale itself and this was no mean task, especially as Yvonne had to be killed by a horse in a thunderstorm, and Hugh left holding a guitar in a dark wood, singing drunken songs of revolutionary Spain. Could Thomas Hardy do as much? I suspect your reader, who doesn't even mention the very important fact of Yvonne's death, of not reading this chapter at all—and I take this again as a compliment that he was too interested in what happened to the Consul to do more than glance at it. Be that as it may, I feel passionately that the chapter comes off, partly because I came to believe so absolutely in it. Actually someone being killed by a horse in a thunderstorm is nothing like so unusual an occurrence as you might suppose in these parts, where the paths in the forests are narrow and horses when they do get frightened become more wildly panic-stricken than did the ancestors of their riders who thought the horses Cortez sent against them were supernatural beings. I feel that this chapter like all the rest calls for a sympathetic rereading. It is quite short and I don't think can be cut at all and is *absolutely necessary*. Yvonne's dying visions hark back to her first thoughts at the beginning of Chapter II and also to Chapter IX, but the very end of the chapter has practically stepped outside the bounds of the book altogether. Yvonne imagines herself gathered up and swept up to the stars: a not dissimilar idea appears at the end of one of Julian Green's books, but my notion came obviously from *Faust*, where Marguerite is hauled up to heaven on pulleys, while the devil hauls Faust down to hell. Here Yvonne imagines herself voyaging straight up through the stars to the Pleiades, while the Consul is, simultaneously and incidentally, being cast straight down the abyss. The horse of course is the evil force that the Consul has released. But by this time you know the humbler aspect of this horse. It is no less than the horse you last heard of in X and that first appeared in IV, likewise riderless, during Hugh and Yvonne's ride, outside the pulquería La Sepultura.

(*Note*: Is it too much to say that all these chords, struck and resolved, while no reader can possibly apprehend them on first or even fourth reading, consciously, nevertheless vastly contribute *unconsciously* to the final weight of the book?)

XII

This chapter was first written at the beginning of 1937 and I think is definitely the best of the lot. I have scarcely changed it since 1940—though I made some slight additions and subtractions in 1942 and substituted the passage "How alike are the groans of love to the groans of the dying," etc., in 1944, for another one not so good. I do think it deserves more than rereading carefully and that it is not only not fair to say it merely recalls *The Lost Weekend* but ridiculous. In any event, I believe, it goes even on the superficial plane a good deal further than that in terms of human agony, and, as his book does, it can widen, I think, one's knowledge of hell. In fact the feeling you are supposed to get from this chapter is an almost Biblical one. Hasn't the guy had enough suffering? Surely we've reached the end now. But no. Apparently it's only just starting. All the strands of the book, political, esoteric, tragic, comical, religious, and what not are here gathered together and in the Farolito in Parián we are standing amid the confusion of tongues of Biblical prophecy. Parián, as I have said, has represented death all along, but this, I would like the reader to feel, is far worse than that. This chapter is the easterly tower, Chapter I being the westerly, at each end of my churrigueresque Mexican cathedral, and all the gargoyles of the latter are repeated with interest in this. While the doleful bells of one echo the doleful bells of the other, just as the hopeless letters of Yvonne the Consul finally finds here answer the hopeless letter of the Consul M. Laruelle reads precisely a year later in Chapter I. Possibly you did not find much to criticize in this chapter but I believe it will immeasurably improve when the whole is taken into account. The slightly ridiculous horse that the Consul releases and which kills Yvonne is of course the destructive force we have heard of before, some fifteen times, I am afraid, in this letter and suggested first in I, and which his own final absorption by the powers of evil releases. There was a half-humorous foreshadowing of his action in VII, in terms of a quotation from Goethe, when Laruelle and he were passed by the horse and its rider, who waved at them and rode off singing. There still remain passages of humor in this chapter and they are necessary because after all we are expected to believe and not believe and then again to believe: the humor is a kind of bridge between the naturalistic and the transcendental and then back to the naturalistic again, though that humour I feel always remains true to the special reality created by the chapter itself. I am so inordinately proud of this chapter that you will be surprised when I say that I think it possible that it too can be cut here and there, though the deadly flat tempo of the beginning seems to me essential and important. I don't think the chapter's final effect should be depressing: I feel you should most definitely get your katharsis, while there is even a hint of redemption for the poor old Consul at the end, who realizes that he is after all part of humanity: and indeed, as I have said before, what profundity and final meaning there is in his fate should be seen also in its universal relationship to the ultimate fate of mankind.

> You like this garden?
> Why is it yours?
> We evict those who destroy!

Reading all this over I am struck among other things such as that writers can always grow fancy and learned about their books and say almost anything at all, as Sherwood Anderson once said in another context, by how much stress is laid on the esoteric element. This does not of course matter two hoots in a hollow if the whole thing is not good art, and to make it such was the whole of my labour. The esoteric business was only a deep-laid anchor anyway but I think I may be forgiven for bringing it in evidence since your reader never saw that the book had any such significance at all. That is right too; I don't care whether the reader does or doesn't see it, but the meaning is there just the same and I might have stressed another element of the book just as well. For they are all involved with each other and their fusion is the book. I believe it more than comes off, on the whole, and because of this belief I am asking you for this re-evaluation of it as it was conceived and upon its own terms. Though I would be grievously disappointed were you not to publish it I can scarcely do otherwise than this, believing as I do that the things that stand in the way of its appreciation are largely superficial. On the other hand I am extremely sensible of the honor you do me by considering it and I do not wish to be vain or stubborn about cuts, even large ones, where a more piercing and maturer eye than mine can see the advantage to the *whole*, the wound being drawn together. I can hope only that I have made some case for a further look at the thing being worth while. Whether it sells or not seems to me either way a risk. But there is something about the destiny of the creation of the book that seems to tell me it just might go *on* selling a very long time. Whether this is the same kind of delusion, at best, that beset another of your authors, Herman Melville, when he wrote such berserk pieces as *Pierre* remains to be seen, but certain it is in that case that no major alterations could have altered its destiny, prevented its plates from being burned, or its author from becoming a customs inspector. I was reading somewhere of that internal basic use of time which makes or breaks a motion picture, and which is the work of the director or cutter. It depends on the speed at which one scene moves and on the amount of footage devoted to another: and it depends also on what sequences are placed between others, because the way movies are made allows you to shift whole sequences about. I believe that the reader whose report you sent me was at least impressed to the extent that he read the book creatively, but too much so, as if he were already a director and cutter combined of some *potential* work, without stopping to ask himself how far it had already been directed and cut, and what internal basic use of time, and so on, was making him as interested as he was.

But what, I repeat, of the reaction of your first reader? There is a certain disparity in tone between your letters of October 15 (received in Canada Nov. 2) and that of 29th Nov. (received here in Mexico Dec. 31) i.e., in your first one you do not mention any criticisms but simply say that your reader was greatly impressed and that it was a long time since you had begun to read a book with such hope and expectation as in reading *Under the Volcano* and seizing, perhaps too hastily, on this, I can deduce only that your first reader was tremendously more sympathetic towards it??? You also said, "I will send you a cable when I have finished reading it so it is possible you may get a cable before receiving this letter." Of course I now see why you found this extremely difficult or impossible but at that time I waited and waited in vain for that cable as you can only wait in winter in the Canadian Wilderness, unless it is in Reckmondwike, Yorks. When therefore I received your letter of 29th Nov. here on New Year's Eve, with your second reader's report, it produced, together with the sense of triumph, one of those barranca-like drops in spirits peculiar to authors and it is to this I must attribute the time I've taken to reply. Talk about turning the accomplishment of many years into an hour glass— but I never heard of it being turned into a mescal glass before, and a small one at that! However after puzzling my brains, I decided that however your own feelings might lean x-ward or y-ward of the crystallization of reaction, you were putting me, as you had every right to do, on the spot. In short, you were saying: "If this book is any damn good as it is he'll explain why!" I was being invited, I thought, if necessary, to do battle. So here is the battle. For taking such a long time about it I sincerely apologize but it has been a difficult letter to write.

I have now received your second letter with a copy of the report and I thank you for this. On your twenty-fifth anniversary I heartily congratulate you. It seems to me that among other things your firm has done more international good than any other. For myself, my first school prize was *The Hairy Ape*, ourselves being allowed to choose our own prizes when they were books, so with your volume of O'Neill's plays containing *The Hairy Ape*, complete with Latin inscription inside, I was therefore presented by the Headmaster on Prize Day. Those O'Neill volumes with the labels, I guess, sent me to sea and everywhere else, but also for the Melville volumes, the O'Brien books, Hugh l'Anson Fausset, and among lesser known things the strange Leo Steni novels, and Calder-Marshall's *About Levy*, for these and hundreds of other things besides I am eternally grateful. When I was looking in '28 or '29 for some work in England by the American Conrad Aiken sure enough I found *Costumes by Eros* published by your firm and this led to a lasting and valuable friendship. (I believe him indisputably one of the world's nine or ten greatest living writers and I mention in passing that ⅔ of his stuff has never had a fair hearing in England and is probably just lying around somewhere. I believe him to be living now at his old English home again at Jeakes House, Rye, Sussex.) All this by the way.

I have spoken of thinking of the book as like some Mexican churrigueresque cathedral: but that is probably just confusing, the more especially since I have been quoting Aristotle at you, and the book has in its odd way a severe classical pattern—you can even see the German submarine officers taking revenge on the Consul in the form of the *sinarquistas* and semi-fascist *brutos* at the end, as I said before. No—please put all that down to the local tropic fever which just recently has been sending my temperature up too far. No. The book should be seen as essentially *trochal*, I repeat, the form of it as a wheel so that, when you get to the end, if you have read carefully, you should want to turn back to the beginning again, where it is not impossible, too, that your eye might alight once more upon Sophocles' *Wonders are many, and none is more wonderful than man*— just to cheer you up. For the book was so designed, counter-designed and interwelded that it could be read an indefinite number of times and still not have yielded all its meanings or its drama or its poetry: and it is upon this fact that I base my hope in it, and in that hope that, with all its faults, and now with all the redundancies of my letter, I have offered it to you.

Yours very sincerely,
Malcolm Lowry

TO JACQUES BARZUN

Dollarton, B.C., Canada
May 6, 1947

Dear Mr. Barzun:

You've written, to my mind, such a horribly unfair criticism of my book, *Under the Volcano*, that I feel I may be forgiven for shooting back.

Granted that it has been overpraised to the extent where an unfavorable review seems almost welcome, and granted that your review may end by doing me good, it rankles as an even harsher criticism, if just, could never do; and I feel that this is not only unsporting but weakens your whole general argument; people simply won't listen to your very necessary truths if you do this kind of thing once too often.

Ah ha, I can hear you saying, well I can tear the heart out of this pretty damned easily, I can smell its derivations from a mile away, in fact I need only open the book at random to find just what I want, just the right food for my article: I do not feel you

have made the slightest critical effort to grapple with its form
or its intention. What you have actually succeeded in doing is
to injure a fellow who feels himself to be a kindred spirit.

I do not think there was any need, either, to be so insulting
about it. You are intitled to "fulsome and fictitious" and you
can say if you wish (though it is not specifically true and there
is certainly no irrefutable evidence of the former) that I am "on
the side of good behavior and eager to disgust you with tropical vice." But when you say "He shows this by a long regurgi-
tation of the materials found in *Ulysses* or *The Sun Also Rises*"
are you not overstepping the mark in an effort to be scornful?
For while few modern writers, myself included, can have altogether escaped the influence, direct or indirect, of Joyce and
Hemingway, the "materials" in the sense you convey are not to
be found in either of these books. "And while imitating the
tricks of Joyce, Dos Passos and Sterne, he gives us the heart and
mind of Sir Philip Gibbs." What tricks, precisely, do you mean?
A young writer will naturally try to benefit and make use of
what he has read, as a result of which, especially in technique,
what Van Gogh I think calls "design-governing postures" are
from time to time inevitable. But where I found another writer
in the machinery—the writer you are reading at the moment,
Richards has pointed out, is nearly always the villain—I always
did my utmost to sweat him out. Shards and shreds of course
sometimes remain; they do in your style too. But so far as I
know I have imitated none of the tricks of the writers you mention, one of whom at least once testified to my originality. As a
matter of fact—and to my shame—I have never read *Ulysses*
through, of Dos Passos I have read only *Three Soldiers*, and of
Sterne I have never been able to read more than one page of
Tristram Shandy. (This of course does not rule out direct influence, but what about what I've invented myself?) I liked *The
Sun Also Rises* when I read it 12 years ago but I have never read

it since nor do I think I've ever been particularly influenced by it. Where the *Volcano* is influenced, its influences are, for the most part, other, and for the most part also I genuinely believe, absorbed. Where they are not you can put it down to immaturity; I began the book back in 1936 when I was 27 and doubtless, in spite of many rewritings, it carries a certain stamp of that fact. As for Sir Philip Gibbs are you not just being gratuitously cruel? Perhaps if you would really read the book you would see that quite a lot of it is intended to be—and in fact is—funny, as it were a satire upon myself. Nor, I venture to say, do I think that, upon a second serious reading, you would find it dull.

After Sir Philip Gibbs I can almost forgive you for juxtaposing at random two not very good passages from Chapters III and IX as though they were contiguous, as an example of bad reporting. But even if those passages are not so hot, what of the justice of this kind of criticism? I'd like to know what you'd do with the wretched student who loaded his dice like that for you.

The end, I suppose, is intended to crush one completely. "Mr. Lowry has other moments, borrowed from other styles in fashion, Henry James, Thomas Wolfe, the thought-streamers, the surrealists. His novel can be recommended only as an anthology held together by earnestness."

Whatever your larger motive—which I incidentally believe to be extremely sound—do you not seem to have heard this passage or something like it before? I certainly do. I seem to recognize the voice, slightly disguised, that greeted Mr. Wolfe himself, not to say Mr. Faulkner, Mr. Melville and Mr. James— an immortal voice indeed that once addressed Keats in the same terms that it informed Mr. Whitman that he knew less about poetry than a hog about mathematics.

But be that as it may. It is the "styles in fashion" that hurts. Having lived in the wilderness for nearly a decade, unable to buy even any intelligent American magazines (they were all

banned here, in case you didn't know, until quite recently) and
completely out of touch, I have had no way of knowing what
styles were in fashion and what out, and didn't much care.
Henry James' notebooks I certainly have tried to take to heart,
and as for the thought-streamers (if you're interested in
sources) William would doubtless be pleased. And I'm glad at
least it was earnestness that held the anthology together. Nonetheless I shall laugh—and I hope you with me—should in ten
years or so the Voice again be heard decrying some serious contemporary effort on the grounds that its author is simply regur-
gitating the materials to be found in Lowry. I shall laugh, but I
shall on principle sympathize with the author, even if it is true.

Be this as it may. Any other kind of duello being inconve-
nient at this distance, I had begun this letter with the intention
of being, if possible, as intolerably rude as yourself. I even
bought an April *Harper's* to provide myself with material and
sure enough I found it springing up at me, just as to you, from
my work, your ammunition: for did I not immediately find you
lambasting Señor Steinbeck in vaguely similar terms, although
at much greater length, accusing him of almost everything
except stealing his bus from me—you of course didn't know I
had one, it is in Chapter VIII (a crime I may say of which he is
innocent and vice versa) and speaking of his anti-artistic emotion of self-pity, by which I take it you do not of course mean
your *own* anti-artistic emotion of self-pity by any chance?

There is an interesting passage here too:

In the makers of the tradition, that is to say in Balzac,
Dickens, Zola, Hardy, Dostoevsky, down to Sinclair
Lewis and Dos Passos, there is an affirmation pressing
behind every grimness, an anger or enthusiasm of despair
which endows mud with life and makes it glow like
rubies. The energy of mind makes even a surfeit of facts

bearable, while plot enmeshes the characters so completely that the reader is compelled to believe in a fated
existence, at the very moment when he knows that he is
only the sport of the writer's will.

Good: but why, at that rate, are you so ready to jump upon
the affirmation pressing behind the grimness in the *Volcano*? So
ready to jump upon it indeed as soon as you saw it (because it
was in capital letters doubtless) that you quite missed the anger
or the enthusiasm of despair that it was following? Did you not
trample the one to death without even taking the trouble to see
if the other was there at all, without taking *any* trouble, in
short, except to exhume Sir Philip Gibbs from his dull grave in
order to have a cheap sneer at my expense? And if so, why? I
could tell you, but this is as far as my rudeness will take me.

For one thing, I have just got another batch of reviews, all of
them good, and all of them more irritating than yours. For
another, the book is to be translated into French: the very tough
editors, I am relieved to say, think more highly of it than you,
which is something. And for another I just have news from
England that one of my best friends—Anna Wickham, the
poet, if you're interested—has just hanged herself in London.

God has raised his whip of Hell
That you be no longer weak
That out of anguish, you may speak
That out of anguish, you may speak well.

She once wrote. My wife, by a coincidence having bought
me a week ago, in Canada, the only edition of her poems
(praised by D. H. Lawrence—and why didn't you drag *him* in?)
that can have been sold in 20 years, bought them for me indeed
two days before Anna died. So life is too short or something.

And the grammar of this letter is bad. And it will remain so. So, doubtless, are the semantics. And the syntax. And everything else.

With the general tenor of your criticism in *Harper's* I am enormously, as I hinted, in accord. That for instance political books should be read with the historian's scepticism, and with the historian's willingness to see the drama of both sides, that we suffer from intellectual indigestion, philosophic bankruptcy, and adulterated "brews" of one kind or another—be they behavioristic or what-not, that we are being done down by half thoughts, regurgitated unthoughts found in so and so—how true: I might remind you, though, that there are sometimes deeper sources and not everything comes up your own service elevator.

I think I said that the *Volcano* had been over praised and also praised for qualities it probably doesn't possess and I think that one of the things I wanted to say was that that seemed no good reason for you to tear it to pieces for faults it doesn't possess either.

I wish, sincerely, that you would read it again, and this time, because you don't have to write about it, look instead for what may be good in it. It sings, I believe, considerably—the whole thing—in the mind, if you can stand the partial bankruptcy in character drawing and what actually *is* fictitious about it, the sentences like Schopenhauer's roast geese stuffed with apples.

But on the side of good conduct no. I myself savagely reviewed it for a preface for the English edition—though they would have none of it—thus—never mind the "thus" but ending: All applications for use by temperance societies should be accompanied by a case of Scotch addressed to the author. Now put it back in the three-penny shelf where you found it.

Moreover I had even toyed at one time rather lovingly with the notion of having Hugh and Yvonne killed off while too sober and the Consul returning cheerfully and drunkenly to his duties to mescal and the British Crown under a miraculously transformed and benign Poppergetsthebotl.

You might also remember that so far as the latter was concerned I was doing what I fondly believed (in spite of *L'Assommoir*) to be a pioneer work. *The Lost Weekend* et al did not come along until, as always happens, it was virtually finished, and at that for the fifth time. Moreover it will both horrify and relieve you to learn that it was only the third of a book, if complete in itself, most of the rest having been destroyed by fire.

And if you want sources—what about the Cabbala? The Cabbala is only in the sub-basement of the book but you would discover therein that the Cabbala itself is identified with the "garden" and the abuse of wine with the abuse of magical powers, and hence with the destruction of the garden, and hence with the world. This myth may have somewhat confined me: for though one might sympathize with Mephistopheles, Faust is a different matter. But perhaps I cite this only to show you how much more loathsome the book might have been to you had I put this on the top plane. I very much believe in what positive merits the book has, however. (I don't know if Sir Philip Gibbs ever thought about the Cabbala, I have a gruesome suspicion that that is precisely the sort of thing he may have thought about.)

At all events I am now writing another book, you will be uninterested to learn, dealing roughly speaking with the peculiar punishment meted out to people who lack the sense of humour to write books like *Under the Volcano*. So far, I am pretty convinced that nothing like it has been written, but you can be sure that just as I am finishing it—

Sans blague. One wishes to learn, one wishes to learn, to be a better writer, to think better, and one wishes to learn, period. In spite of some kind of so-called higher education (Cambridge,

Eng.) I have just arrived at that state where I realized I know nothing at all. A cargo ship, to paraphrase Melville, was my real Yale and Harvard too. Doubtless I have absorbed many of the wrong things. But instinct leads the good artist (which I feel myself to be, though I say it myself) to what he wants. So if, instead of ending this letter "may Christ send you sorrow and a serious illness," I were to end it by saying instead that I would be tremendously grateful if one day you would throw your gown out of the window and address some remarks in this direction upon the reading of history, and even in regard to the question of writing and the world in general. I hope you won't take it amiss. You won't do it, but never mind.

With best wishes, yours sincerely,
Malcolm Lowry

P.S. Anthology held together by earnestness—brrrrrr!

TO ALBERT ERSKINE

Hotel de la Plage
Cassis, B. du R., France
[Spring, 1948]

Albert the Good,
    Sorry I haven't written.
    Maybe I am a bit herausgeschnissen,
    I don't eat my food and in my bed I have twice geshitten,
    Anyhow I am living here.
    In a comparative state of mundial fear—
    Also give my love to my dear Twinbad the bailer
    I mean dear Frank Taylor.
    This is written on the night of April 18th

Anyway or the other, there is no rhyme
Unless you can think of one above.

Save love
Malcolm

P.S. We encountered a cyclone—four ships lost
Somewhat tempest tossed.

TO DEREK PETHICK

Dollarton, B.C.
March 6, 1950

Dear Mr. Pethick:

Thank you for your letter and I am flattered you are to speak about the *Volcano*. I am also delighted at your interest in it and by your remarks.

While you are not quite right about the *Volcano*, it is none the less an extraordinary piece of perspicuity on your part, for what you say would very largely be true of a book that does not now exist, and of which you cannot have known, the *Volcano* having been designed as the first part of a trilogy—and the third part which I refer to having been totally destroyed in a fire which consumed our house some years ago—we built another house on the ashes, however.

My wife says it would be more true to say that in the *Volcano* the Consul bore some relation to Moby Dick himself rather than Ahab. However it was not patterned after *Moby-Dick* (the book) which I never studied till fairly recently (and it would seem not hard enough).

The identification, on my side, if any, was with Melville himself and his life. This was partly because I had sailed before the mast, partly because my grandfather had been a skipper of a windjammer who went down with his ship—Melville also had a son named Malcolm who simply disappeared—purely romantic reasons like that, but mostly because of his failure as a writer and his whole outlook generally. His failure for some reason absolutely fascinated me and it seems to me that from an early age I determined to emulate it, in every way possible—for which reason I have always been very fond of *Pierre* (even without having read it at all).

But to get back to the key—if any—the *Volcano* has just come out in France, where they say the key is in the Zohar. This discovery is partly due to a misleading preface by myself, written while not quite sober, but there is something in it, so I'll give you a précis of what they say for what it's worth, if I can translate it. This is in a very learned postface by one Max-Pol Fouchet and now it seems I can't translate it but I'll try to give you the gist. Now it seems I can't even give you the gist so I'll have to try instead to answer some of the points you raise in terms of what I think he says, or has some significance in terms of what I think I say—(so far as I can see, while it doesn't make you wrong, it somehow or other gives the book more thickness than even you ascribe to it, or I thought it had).

To take the points in the wrong order: first, the zodiacal significance—in my intention it had none at all, least of all in relation to Melville—I am trying to be honest, so I refer things to my wife when in doubt—the quotation you mention from *Moby-Dick*, Chapter 99, I am conscious of reading now as for the first time—it never occurred to me there was any such zodiacal significance in *Moby-Dick*, for that matter—and the passage now affects me supernaturally if at all, as if it meant something literal for *me*, and it was I who had been tracing the round again.

Though there is some extra evidence, if you like, in Chapter

VII when the Consul is in Laruelle's tower—the Consul remembers a make of golfball called the Zodiac Zone—a lot more evidence in XI (where the intention was astronomical however). The goat means tragedy (tragedy—goat song) but goat—*cabrón*—cuckold (the horns). The scorpion is an image of suicide (scorpions sting themselves to death, so they say—Dr. Johnson called this a lie, but there is in fact some scientific evidence for it) and was no more than that—or was it? for I now see the whole book takes place "in Scorpio"—the action of the book is in one day, exactly 12 hours, seven to seven; the first chapter takes place 12 months later on the same day, so it is also in Scorpio.

Now I'll have to begin at the beginning again. The truth is, I have never certainly fully grasped the fact that *Moby-Dick* was a political parable, though I can grasp the fact that Ahab (in my grandfather's eyes anyhow) is on quite an important plane a criminal. I seem to remember that Starbuck and quite a few of the crew had the same idea too, but it seemed to me that his revengeful élan was shared to the extent that one could scarcely say the whole crew were enduring toil and danger simply to gratify his desire—what about the harpooners? Yes, what about them? I don't feel on very secure ground, but I have never thought of the book before in that way.

I can see that *The Confidence Man* is a political parable; and that "The Tartarus of Maids" is a sexual one. I see the applicability of the pursuit in *Moby-Dick* today all right, but it never occurred to me that it was intended in that way then, unless in the sort of jocular manner that Melville's vast appetite reaches out all over the table and couldn't help stuffing something of the sort in. Now I have written the above it seems not only illiterate, but not what I mean at all, but I'll have to let it stand. But what you say would be in line with much of Melville's later thought.

The *Volcano* is, though, and you are quite right here, quite definitely on one plane of political parable—indeed it started off as such: Chapter VIII was written first, nearly 15 years ago—though I didn't mean it to suggest that the future belongs to those Mexican workers necessarily, or indeed to anybody at all, unless some true charity can mediate, and man's decency and dignity be reestablished. The police are the bloody police of the present, all right, but they are also "Interference"—interference with people's private lives—the stool-pigeon theme works both ways: one should intervene in the case of the man beside the road, Spain seemed a clear case for intervention, etc., or at least Hugh's intervention: it isn't quite as simple, to say the least, as this. And what about the Consul? How much good was it interfering in his case? Well, I meant to redeem the old bird in various guises throughout the trilogy, but fate put a stop to that—but I'll go on trying to tell you more about him in terms of the *Volcano* only, and the beginning of the letter. As a protagonist on one plane (says this French fellow, and I think he's right), he is a Faustian gent. The book somehow assumes—with some philosophic justice—that the ancestor of us all was perhaps a Magician.

The Consul has been a Cabbalist (this is where you get the Garden of Eden). Mystically speaking, the abuse of wine is connected with the abuse of mystical powers. Has the Consul perhaps been a black magician at one time? We don't know. What Max-Pol Fouchet doesn't say either is that a black magician is a man who has all the elements of the world (not to say universe) against him—this is what the Consul meant in Chapter X (written in 1942) enumerating the elements. In Chapter V (in the bathroom) you have a hint of similar dark forces in the background. The implication is that an analogy is drawn between Man today on this planet and a black magician. This, I feel, has to some extent come to have some basis in truth since writing this book. (The Consul implies his war, as opposed to any Hugh might be involved in, is far more desperate, since it is against the very elements themselves and against nature. This is a war that is bound to be lost.) Oddly enough I put neptunium in but abandoned it for niobium (I thought it sounded sadder— it seems to me nobody, in my position at least, dreamed of atom bombs then—and yet you see, here one sat, just the same, dreaming up the swinish contraption without knowing it. I just took the elements out of the dictionary)—this is on page 304. As I say, this part was written in 1942—and by the time the atom bomb fell in 1945 the book had anyway been long on its way being rejected by publishers. I turned to this particular page just now and it gave me an eerie sort of feeling. The Consul has thus turned into a man that is all destruction—in fact he has almost ceased to be a man altogether, and his human feelings merely make matters more agonizing for him, but don't alter things in the least; he is thus in hell. Should you hold the Bergsonian idea that the sense of time is merely an inhibition to prevent everything happening at once—brooding upon which it is pretty difficult to avoid some notion of eternal recurrence —inevitable destruction is thus simply the teleological end to one series of possibilities; everything hopeful is equally possible; the horror would seem to exist in the possibility that this is no longer true on our plane and absolute catastrophe has fallen in line with our will upon so many planes that even the other possibilities are for us gradually ceasing to exist. This, I may say, is not very clear, as I have expressed it, so you better forget it. Anyhow, I don't believe it for a moment. Personally, I have a fairly cheery view of life, living as my wife and I do in the bush anyway. Nor was the book consciously intended to operate upon quite so many levels. One serious intention was to create a work of art—after a while it began to make a noise like music; when it made the wrong noise I altered it—when it seemed to make the right one finally, I kept it. Another intention was to write one really good book about a drunk—it was a blow to me when *The Lost Weekend* was published, just as I finished it. Another intention: I meant parts of it to be funny, though no one seems to have realized that.

FINALLY some odd and interesting things have happened in connection with the book itself (as they did with *Moby-Dick*, by the way—while he was writing it, a whale sank a ship. Disaster struck the *Acushnet*—the original of the *Pequod*). After the war, at the end of 1945, I went back to Mexico again, taking my wife: absolutely by coincidence we found ourselves living in the original of M. Laruelle's tower, in Cuernavaca, now broken up into apartments. It was the only place we could find for rent.

I began the book back in 1936–38, when I was in Mexico. The news of the book's acceptance—both in England and America—arrived on the same day, in February 1946, from different firms in different countries, to this very tower in Mexico, and was brought by the same little postman who is a character in Chapter VI.

There are other, even stranger coincidences connected with it, some of them frightening, and not the least strange being in relation to your letter, which arrived on the same day as the French translation, but also on the same day as the funeral we were just about to attend of a very good fellow, a mystic—one would say if he was a magician he was a white one—who gave me much of the esoteric inspiration and material for the book. On the same day he died, coincidentally some brute shot his old dog (you will find the dog motif everywhere in the *Volcano*. Dog motif indeed—it makes me think it would make a good opera: now we hear the opening chords of the dog motif, by courtesy of Texaco Oil, etc.)...

Finally thank you for your interest in the book—it is rather discouraging very often being a writer in Canada. Somebody put the *Volcano* in the *Encyclopedia Britannica Year Book*

1948–9, ranking it as the work of a Canadian over and above anything then current in American literature, but not one word did I ever hear of that here. In fact, apart from a few kind words by Birney and Dorothy Livesay, all I have heard was from my royalty report, namely that the sales in Canada from the end of 1947–49 were precisely 2 copies. The *Sun* published only a few syndicated lines that called it a turgid novel of self-destruction, not for the discerning (or something) reader. This at least is Melvillean anyway; though it went very well in the States, and was even miraculously a best seller for a while: one month, believe it or not, it even sold more than *Forever Amber*, though it must be admitted *Amber* was getting a bit faded by then. In England it failed but quite honorably; in France they have put it in a classic series, yet another publisher is giving it wider distribution, and weirder still, it is being serialized in the daily newspaper *Combat*. As to the Swedish, Norwegian and Danish translations, I understand they are out, but I have not seen them. Nor, I imagine, has any Swede, Norwegian or Dane.

With best wishes,
Malcolm Lowry

P.S. Hope this doesn't confuse you too much. I remain delighted by your interest—though I didn't want to leave you with the impression that the intention of the book was either completely despairing or that it contained any specific secular hope—finally I had meant to show in the trilogy that any revolution that did not appeal to the whole man, including the spiritual, would eventually abort—least of all is it a sermon against drink, that poor man's symphony, especially in B Minor, though why not D Major too, after all.

P.P.S. I hope you'll come and have a drink with us when you are in Vancouver.

TO CHRISTOPHER ISHERWOOD

Dollarton, B.C., Canada

June 20, 1950

Dear Christopher Isherwood:

It was a high spot indeed in our life when we read your letter speaking of our script* in such generous terms. It would have been a high spot in mine anyway, the day I felt I had written something good enough to command praise from yourself. I've often felt like writing you in regard to your own work; I never thought I'd see the day you wrote me first. I do feel I have known you a very long time, however, through your work and through the eternal Marlowe who broods upon the cross currents of life's relationships.

For the script though, since you like it and where it comes off, my wife must take equal credit, she being the lady named Margerie Bonner who is a writer herself and the author of an extraordinarily good—and so far in destiny extraordinarily hapless—novel called *Horse in the Sky*. I hope enough really constructive commotions went into the making of the script that it will somehow come to a good fruition; one very sincere hope and motivation was that it would be a lucky thing for Frank. How it actually came into being strikes me as very curious indeed. One expects, and indeed welcomes, normal obstacles, but something so astonishing happened to the climate last winter we thought another ice age was upon us. This is supposed to be a fairly warm part of Canada; we built our house ourselves with lumber from an old sawmill, but didn't prepare for temperatures of fifteen below zero inside it, such as we had January and February. Nor had anyone else prepared. Even so, we came off far better than people in the city, not having any

---

*Of F. Scott Fitzgerald's *Tender Is the Night*.

modern conveniences to go awry. The city of Vancouver was cut off altogether for eight days from the outside world and we had stormy petrels flying beneath our windows. What they thought they were escaping from I don't like to imagine, but it was an exciting phenomenon I don't think has ever been recorded before in an inlet, in this latitude at least.

I find myself with so many things to say I am walking round in circles. What I would like to phrase properly, so that it doesn't sound too repulsive or impractical, is that should you ever find yourself in a mood where you feel like taking a rocket ship to nowhere, and have the time, we do wish you'd consider coming up in this direction and paying us a visit. It doesn't take so long by plane to Vancouver, and I think you'd find it interesting. We live in a shanty town, built on piles, in an inlet, with the forest behind, mainly deserted during the week save by a boat-builder, ourselves and a fisherman or two. At first all you see is a bay with shacks called Wy-Wurk and the like. But it is actually the remains of an old seaport of which we have often been the sole inhabitants. Dollar—hence Dollarton—was the ship-builder, but somebody took his ship building and his sawmill away from him and we're all that's left. Windjammers used to come here, and we've shouted to a Norwegian skipper of a passing freighter out of the window, below which there's enough water to float the *Mauretania*. At the week ends nowadays many of the shacks fill up so it is more fun during the week. We have a small boat and there are many islands where one may picnic. It is a wonderful place to swim if you like swimming and the forest is full of birds—we are just now (it is Midsummer's Eve) having spring and summer at once and the weather is marvellous. There is a fine view of the mountains: and also, for that matter, of an oil refinery. We could put you up on a sort of improvised contraption that we rescued from the sea but which is a great deal more comfortable than it looks.

There are no conveniences but when the weather is fine as it is now there are no inconveniences either. We thought it might be a cheery place to discuss Tepotzlan and kindred subjects. The invitation, at all events, is very sincere from us both, but if it is too far, I hope, like Huysmans, you will at least think about it. We asked Frank too but I think he may have been put off by the bears. There are bears. But there are also deer. And ravens. Not to mention many rare wild plants such as the Blazing Star, Love Lies Bleeding, and even the contorted lousewort. And through what wild centuries roves back the contorted lousewort?

Anyhow, here we are, and you would always be more than welcome.

After this travelogue, again thank you very much indeed for your words. All the very best to you from us both.

Good luck!

Malcolm Lowry

P.S. I began to write this letter originally, returning the compliment (which I appreciate) in my own handwriting, such as it is—though I have no pen that works—taking advantage of this to write outside. But a cat spilt coconut oil on it. Then another cat spilt beer on it. Finally it blew into the sea. Retrieved thence it came somewhat to pieces and was, besides, a bit illegible. So I gave in, temporarily, to the machine age.

TO STUART LOWRY

Dollarton, B.C., Canada
—or perhaps I should spell it Dolorton
[October, 1950]

Dear old Stuart:

A towering sea is bearing down upon me. Gulls are balancing in the gale. A black cormorant is struggling low over the waves against the wind. All around me is a thunderous sound of breaking, smashing, trees pirouetting and dancing, as a full gale smashes through the forest. What is this? A seascape—or a suggestion for program music, as for Sibelius or Wagner. No: this is the view out of our living room window, while we are having our morning coffee. What I see is quite unbelievable, even for you, unless you have seen it—and where else would you see, but here, a house that is built in the sea and where the problems—and noises—are those that beset the mariner rather than the normal householder? It is wonderfully dramatic—too dramatic, even for me, for us, in some respects, for we now live under the shadow, at any moment, of losing it. This I've told you before. We only live here by grace of being pioneers, and Canada, alas, is forgetting that it is its pioneers who built this country and made it what it was: now it wants to be like everyone else and have autocamps instead of trees and Coca-Cola stands instead of human beings. In that way, for it has little culture at all, it could destroy its soul: that is its own business, no doubt—what we mind is that it threatens to destroy us in the process, an eventuality that it now becomes my duty to try and avoid. Have I mentioned that this is supposed to be a begging letter, even if addressed to one who can do naught, and is hamstrung even as I? One of those letters that you see, or may see one day, under a glass case in a museum—just as this house that we fear to be thrown out of someone may make money out of one day—for I am the only Canadian writer ever to be placed in the *Encyclopedia Britannica*—a sort of begging letter at least, though I don't know on what moral grounds I am presumed to be begging for what upon one plane of reasoning would certainly seem to have been once at least intended to be mine; begging being something I understand that even the tycoons of Canada may be driven to from their neighbouring country as an alternative to stealing, a practice I am inhibited from less on moral grounds than fear of the consequences and plain incompetence. However, I couldn't get myself in the proper mood of despair, even though, as a matter of fact, there is every reason for it. This proves that I am not really anything so wondrously effete (I am partly joking of course) and imitative as a latter-day Canadian, but simply an Englishman, i.e., a person who, upon overhearing himself pronounced dead, remarks: Bloody nonsense. With that we shall entitle this instead, "business letter," a euphemism that so far it seems singularly unentitled to. There is something wrong with my prose too this morning, but this I ask you to overlook. The foregoing however is my way of saying—even if I can't keep the cheerfulness out, that we stand in the shadow of eviction, and thus upon the brink of what is popularly known as disaster. The other people in the same position are mostly fishermen and may fish elsewhere; that is to say there are fish elsewhere. We however are fishermen of another sort in a place where there is plenty of fish but no place to sell it save very far away, by which time, if it has not indeed gone bad meanwhile, either it tastes so unique it is accorded a civic reception, or it realizes assets that, like the fish, are frozen. Of the more hopeful and constructive side of this later; all this, in my usual direct fashion, you may take to refer to the crucificial position of a writer in Canada, to which you may, though with less justice than you think if you can imagine for a moment that you are not Stuart but the late personality for whom you now stand *in loco* (loco in the nice sense) reply: Well, I didn't tell you to live there! From now on, however, I shall be strictly business-like. First I shall give you— an important item in the technique of such letters even when one understands perfectly well the utter fruitlessness of it—a list of my accomplishments, immediately followed of course by a similar list of catastrophes, during the last years, though on second thoughts I'll spare you some, and on third thoughts shall confine myself to the last year and a half.

(a) Have written and completed in collaboration with Margerie a detailed movie script—adopted from a novel you won't have heard of—upon which we worked, sometimes with the temperature below zero in the house, some fourteen hours a day—it was so cold at one point we couldn't take off our clothes for a fortnight—of which the report, from two of the greatest authorities on the cinema and a now famous Metro-Goldwyn-Mayer producer, was in brief that "it was obviously the greatest achievement in movies, what movies had been all adding up to, and that even to read, that it was comparable with the power of Theodore Dreiser and the titanic mental drama of Thomas Hardy's *The Dynasts*." (I see no reason to be sparing of adjectives; they were not.) The producer is one of my ex-publishers of the *Volcano*, and you may in England see a minor film of his called *Mystery Street*—very well worth seeing.

(b) Succeeded in having the *Volcano* published in translation in Norway, Denmark, Sweden and France—in the first and last countries put into an edition with the classics of the world.

(c) Germany and Italy—now in preparation, which projects had formerly fallen through.

(d) Seen it hailed as the greatest masterpiece of the last ten years in the French translation in Paris. You could get the reviews yourself more easily than I could: but they have appeared everywhere, even in the famous *Figaro*. And there was a wonderful English appraisal of the translation in the *New York Herald Tribune* Paris edition. The publishers are Correa, and a special edition by the Club Livres de France. In fact it has had every honour showered on it there, and many French authors have received the Legion of Honour and been elected to the Academy for less.

(e) Been put in the *Encyclopedia Britannica*. (For how long? Are you comfortable there, Malcolm?)

Well I could go on with these, but I think it's time now for a few catastrophes, sometimes transcended catastrophes.

(a) Operation for a chronic condition of my legs. Successful and expensive.

(b) Continued anxiety—partly responsible for condition when you met me—of thinking one had T.B. Tests showed I have had T.B. at some time or other—when?—and am liable to it: but have it no longer. Have conquered anxiety neurosis on this score.

(c) Ditto and more important, that Margerie had cancer. She does not; but to that diagnosis I am grateful to her brother-in-law. Had she obeyed the dictum of doctors here she would have been treated as if she had so that she had the anguish of thinking she had.

(d) The pound is devaluated.

(e) Because of the success of the *Volcano* my editor, Albert Erskine, is invited to join the staff of Modern Library. You know who *they* are—you brought me up on them! But that leaves me still under contract to the publisher he has left. Erskine wants me to come over to Modern Library, which of course I want to do, but according to the terms of my contract I have to send my next novel to my old publisher and give him a chance to make me an offer first—and they are holding me to this as they are very anxious to keep me. On the other hand the advantages of going into the Modern Library, and keeping Erskine as my editor, far overweigh anything else. Incidentally my other editor became a producer at M.G.M. on the strength of my book. This is a complicated situation, which cannot fail to work to my eventual great advantage, but difficult to explain in a letter. But it is the opposite of an advantage now.

(f) Because of a dispute between the Harbour Board and the

Provincial Government over our land, which we repeatedly tried to buy when we had money, we face eviction for the second time and it blows over.

(g) I break my back and have to wear a brace—the cost this time is not merely expensive, but calamitous. It was right after this (d) happened.

(h) I write to Alderson Smith: no reply. Am still waiting.

(i) I conquer broken back, the brace, but then am faced (sic) with my legs again. I conquer this by exercise and Margie's help. Also I literally owe my life to the way we live—from which we are once more to be evicted, only this time the threat seems much more positive.

(j) The pound falls further yet—or rather does so, in effect for us, because the Canadian dollar goes *up* to equilibrate the American, this it does on a free market and in a state of disequilibrium, fluctuating, in which it not only overtakes but threatens to go still higher than the American, with the result that my monthly income is now little more than $90—that has the purchasing power of little more than a fiver in the old days, and I am not exaggerating. Rent makes sympathetic and contradictory fluctuations of course, but you would be lucky merely to rent anywhere these days for $90 a month, without food—let alone live. I don't know if this aspect of the sheer hardship of the situation has struck you. What it comes down to is that to live on the income alone involves trying to live on somewhat less than the pay of Mary or Sarah, *without* everything being all found. This practically knocks us out entirely, robbing us also of the little margin of profit we had between the American exchange and the Canadian, and between that exchange now at the same rate and the exchange of the pound. Simultaneously prices came down a little, but no sooner have they done that than they go up still further, threatening yet worse inflation, though the pound, despite greater faith in it, remains the same.

450 THE VOYAGE THAT NEVER ENDS

(k) A notice of eviction that seems final, but with just a bare possibility of reprieve in it: but it scarcely seems possible it can last more than a few months.

(l) Margerie ill—with ourselves still in the dark as to what is really wrong with her: x-rays, brain tumor still suspected, treatment that must be continued, begins to put us into the category of the starving. Much may be done with oatmeal. I begin even to think of the saying, "Home is the place where, when they have to, they take you in." But where indeed is that, unless here? Her mother lives 2000 miles away in America, mine 10,000. And we have no friends in Canada save three fishermen in like case, a cat, five wild ducks, two seagulls, and, of course, a wolf.

(m) Naturally, one didn't expect to live on one's income, in the usual sense; though between books, that can become necessary, because if you live on an advance from your next book you're eating yourself, as the French say, literally, and if you get another job you won't write the book—which is one reason why so many writers quit being writers. But in my case the possibilities of work are or were three: teaching, radio, newspaper work. The first requires at least a year's negotiation and a complete rededication of one's life—and probably going to the Prairies, since the English are hated in B.C. The second pays starvation wages and moreover requires a car, while the third not only does that but would be senseless because what I do anyway to attempt to augment the income makes more money and comes into the category of free lancing. In short there is no possibility of a job where we live—short of turning sailor again or working in a sawmill—for taking one would mean abandoning the really practical hope we cling to in regard to our serious work, and also our house: and indeed at the moment we haven't got money even to *move* anywhere else. Even if I could get a labourer's job the cost of transportation would swallow the money we save by living in the house. And writing is a whole-time job or nothing, so it would mean quitting. Margie can't augment matters by getting a job herself because she's not well enough: besides, we do our work together. And for the same reason, however willing to turn my hand to anything, I couldn't leave her long enough in the wilderness by herself. In short it's better to stick to one's guns: only it seems that begging is a standard part of writing, or is about to become so. You may therefore count this as work, for it's my all too valuable time, not counting yours. It may interest you to know that there is a long broadcast tonight or tomorrow night on the subject of Malcolm Lowry, Canada's greatest most successful writer, which we can't listen to because our radio has run down and we can't afford to replenish the battery. The unkindest cut of all. Despite our love I have been warned that for Margie to live another winter under these conditions is very dangerous during the coldest part, so I had thought in all seriousness of applying for a job as tutor at the court of the King of Siam, which requires no courses, save in jazz music—and we may wind up there yet. While we are clinging to the poor house for all we are worth, we are still trying to make enough to live in the city over the nearly impossible months of December and January. (The climate has changed here during the last ten years and winters have been almost as cold as in the east, causing God knows what misery.)

Losing the house under these callous conditions—and they are totally callous and selfish—would be a blow considering all the others—having lost it by fire and rebuilt it ourselves—of such psychological importance that if we had our way we wouldn't live in Canada at all any more. Well, we don't expect our way. The object is to live at all. I have done more for Canadian literature than any living Canadian, and that is beside the point except when I say that despite all this I have made a success of my life and had conditions been equal would have made an assured income for life too—which I may yet do, of course, through the Modern Library or the movie. You could not expect more success of anybody than I have achieved, and both of us have conquered other seemingly insuperable obstacles too (you are not to judge from my health when you saw me—I myself have now never been fitter, exercise and swim every day, etc.) or I wouldn't be writing like this. It is now evening, with a full roaring black gale outside, with the bottom out of the barometer, that is not our barometer but someone's barometer.

Well, why go on. About the only thing we have left is a sense of humour, and the feeling and hope now that what has been undiagnosable in Margie's condition is due to the manifold and obscure results of a hysterectomy: which it may well be: but this in itself is going to require prolonged treatment which at best merely means expense we cannot afford. You get a wrong picture if you think we are gloomy: but the actual situation is some ten times blacker than I've painted it. So I won't paint it. I haven't liked to paint this much. What it all adds up to is this: that while my prospects for the future will eventually add up to an income for life (vide the Modern Library and that you certainly can believe) we are at the moment faced with a financial crisis—which is not caused by extravagance or lack of forethought, by the way—even my trip to Europe will turn out to have paid for itself, for without that, among other things, no French translation, or rather none of any worth, would have come out. This could happen to any businessman only we have no one near enough to appeal to, and no way of floating a loan. It is an acute crisis that should only be temporary, for apart from the new novel and the projected film I have about ten short stories blocked out for which I have an immediate market in New York, having actually a request from 3 or 4 big magazines for my work (there is no market at all in Canada, which is part of the tragedy) and I simply cannot get the freedom and peace of mind to write them properly—even though of course I am not ceasing to try.

And here we come to the age-old pay off to be found in the shrines of every writer under a glass case in the museum—in short, if there is any way, possible or impossible, for you to find any money for me—bearing in mind that there certainly were provisions made for crisis in Father's will—can you possibly look into this immediately for I've put off writing till the last possible moment, hoping it would not be necessary. However in your last letter, with very large foresight, you did say: Hang on till October. Well, I've hung on. If there's nothing can be done, it has been in my mind, terrifying prospect though it is— though I do not consider it abject, and neither would she or you if I could make the circumstances plain—to write direct to the mater—would you advise me about this? But what else in fact am I to do, if all else fails? Damn it, I shall always remember she once gave me a three-penny bit. If of course—and the idea is naturally hypothetical—I did this she would refer it to you and about all I could ask you to do then is to ask her not to refer it to God, or perhaps, conversely, *to* refer it to God.

And all this, the consequence of ceaseless hard work and application. Well, I know you will do your best. Please forgive my writing. I hope the letter was amusing anyway. All my very best love to Margot whom I sincerely hope is in good health, and to Donnie, love and sincere welcome back from his ordeals and travels. In short God bless to you three from us both,

Malcolm

P.S. This letter is going to give me a nightmare tonight. So don't let it give you one. If you can't do anything, advice would be better than nothing, for at worst I can always get them to deport me back to England as a vagrant—something I think ought to be pointed out to the British Government who then might have to buy me a wig—on Father.

TO DAVID MARKSON

Dollarton, British Columbia
August 25, 1951

Dear David M.:

If I said all that your letter suggests to me it would lead us right smack into the primeval forces of creation and twenty years from now I would still be engaged on the 15th volume of a Grundlage der Wissenschaft von Ausdruck and the letter would remain unwritten. So much for what you feared might be the "crudity with which you concocted your questions," concerning which let your mind be at rest; concerning yours of Aug. 9, let it be not only at rest but positively joyful—I am very glad indeed that you wrote it, as it goes without saying I was grateful to receive it, and as for the contents of *this* letter let your mind in advance be at rest too, though in motion—in fact just like the Tao—no psychic or psychological thunderstone is going to drop on your head, though it is to be hoped some manna (which possibly should be spelt mana) may fall, and though by virtue of the dignity of my years I may assume the right of speaking like a parent from time to time, it's not going to be as austere as all that: as a matter of fact this pseudo-copperplate handwriting and semicolon technique will doubt-less be gradually discarded as the letter proceeds—here it goes —as in Haiti, during what has begun as something resembling one's good old starched evening chapel days in England, with Madame, here's your pew, and the meek arrival of the Pres-byter, and the congregation in their best clothes, are discarded the shining Sunday shoes of the Voodoo priest when, the drums having called down the gods from Olympus for the hundredth time, and himself possessed for the hundred and fiftieth, he hurls himself cheerfully into the flames: but first for the muted conversation in the vestry, and as the voluntary plays, my explanation—and my apologies for this—as to how the helpful daemon I promised to return to you got stranded in the chimney pot. . . . First I did write you and here is a précis of what I said.

I began by explaining about the forest fire situation, adding that although one did not have one very near yet you could breathe nothing else and even at a distance these things were enough to give you the horrors. So I would be brief, I said. Yes, Aiken's *Blue Voyage* was an enormous influence upon me, especially since (I made its acquaintance at the age of 18 in England having just returned from my first voyage to sea) not being able to find out anything about its author, I felt that Aiken was my own discovery. Of course the truth was Aiken was highly respected in a small circle in England, but I didn't find this out till much later, coming from a huntin' and shootin' family near Liverpool, who weren't interested in literary matters. Meantime I was not slow in taking up the dedicatory coincidence of C.M.L. either. So much so that in no time at all I was practically of the opinion that the book was not only dedicated to me, but that I'd written it myself, and was thus, though an Englishman, extremely gratified, though I think privately I was damned annoyed, vicariously to receive the Pulitzer Prize a few years later. (Actually C.M.L. was Clarice Lorenz, Aiken's second wife.) I went on to add (in this letter drafted last June) that what I had to say in this regard would be of more use to you privately, as a novelist and as a writer, than in writing the thesis. It would lead me into a vast psychological field, not to say into the realm of the confidential and the intensely personal:

and from the copy I have before me (as the saying is) it's not quite clear whether the subject is broken off at this point because I fear to appear to my discredit in that field if I am to be honest, or whether, in the attempt possibly to offset certain pitfalls that I imagine might confront *you* as a writer, I fear I may create some bran-new ones for you of my own. So at this point we get on to the Cabbala, to answer your question, and the subject is changed.

"Re the Cabbala," I wrote, "and the whole business of the occult, however right I may be about reducing my French preface to the level of some little doppelgängerelle's chatter, I feel bound to tell you as a fellow mortal of somewhat elder years who wishes to be useful, though not, so to say, to sway your mind, unless it be toward A Better Thing, that however much it may be intermediately important or even healthy for you to rationalize such matters, your rationalization is an illusion. As a matter of fact you could with some justice 'rationalize' the Cabbala itself (roughly speaking a system of thought that creates a magical world within this one that so far as I know has no pretense of being anything but an illusion—you may send it flying out of the window if you like, though perhaps it's not wise, it might come back by another one) but you can't rationalize or anything else the unknown depths of the human psyche—at least not in the way you mean. *You* have one, and its operations are to be found working within you too. (Of course you know this, and much more; still, while amassing the "much more," it's surprising what knowledge of one's own, indeed foreknowledge, one can overlook and which has been there all the time, as if waiting to be used. You'll just have to pardon the pomposity of all this.)

One of the clearest answers that comes immediately to mind in regard to all this is the sort of thing to be found in Jung's 20 year old "Man in search of his soul," which I didn't read till the other day, so forgive me if the suggestion seems infra-dig. More or less popular and dry half-gobbledegookery though it is— and I dare say psychologically superseded or out of date in places and what not—you nonetheless might find it soundly full of the wisest kind of speculation if you haven't happened to have read it. To revert, you suggest Joyce would smile at it all. Not so. Joyce—whom I once encountered smiling, however, in the Luxembourg Gardens—was on the contrary an extremely supersitious (if that's the right word) man. His only regret re Yeats' *The Vision*—which you should read too if you haven't even if you can't make those cones work (I got so that I could make just one cone work)—was that he did not use all that tremendous stuff in a work of art. You may call it tripe. There's a certain element of danger, maybe, in calling it anything else. Joyce (who was looking for Aiken's "Coming Forth by Day of Osiris Jones" when he died) even had a superstition, according to one of his biographers, about the name Lowry, which occurs in his funeral scene. No sooner had he given them these names, he delighted to report, than one after the other these names acquired living, or rather dead, counterparts, all of which had one thing in common, they were found to have come to grotesque and tragic ends! I never checked up to see if a stand-in called L. has already let me out but whether or no it is enough to keep one fighting for a happy ending till the day one dies against *that*! More seriously (if this is not serious) you can readily see why, on purely psychological grounds, Joyce might be a superstitious fellow. What goes up must come down, not to say what happens when you throw nature out with a pitchfork. To be superstitious is not indeed to be "mystical" but I let the point rest for the moment.

Likewise I said I'd let Joseph Frank and Mark Schorer rest for the moment, finding that chiefly interesting as having bearing on what you do with the paper yourself: I noted, with a

friendly salute and as it were the purr of a fellow artisan, that if
you have to write a thesis, that you can't bear to write it in a
form not suggested by the substance, or at any rate not without
form itself, thus showing, I would say, the predominance of the
artist in you over the critic: that really means more than
"Schorer's passing on and out," or should I say "The Consul's
passing out and on": my writing is not very clear at this point,
as one might say, gap in the manuscript, after this, and as a
matter of fact much more, not at all interesting; it goes on
about *Las Manos de Orlac.*

Las Manos de Orlac—then—is a preposterous mad (and
bad, though I pretend it was relatively good, which it perhaps
was) movie of the German Ufa Wiene Caligari Fritz Lang Destiny Golden Age, with Conrad Veidt as Orlac: therein, Orlac
was a great pianist who lost his hands in a railway accident,
had the hands of a murderer grafted on by a "Mad Doctor,"
ever afterwards felt—no doubt because he'd played the Sleep-
walker in *Caligari* too—impelled to commit murders; Hollywood made a remake in about 1936 of truly awe-inspiring
badness, but with Peter Lorre imported from the Fritz Lang
Ufa playing the doctor: the surgical sequences were in this version photographed by the Ufa genius Karl Freund so you get 5
minutes of that kind of Grand Guignol anyway, though the
overall effect could not be worse: thematically speaking,
though, the pelado in Chapter VIII—by extension the Consul,
by extension M. Laruelle—gives the clue: the pelado's hands
were covered with blood. So are man's.

Reception: This is a bit complicado; it was a considerable
success—at least for me—even financial, in the U.S., though
not as much as its presence as 5th on the best seller lists for
some months would seem to indicate: it seemed to be most successful in Dallas, Texas, to my delight, and it once was cited in
a best seller list as "one up" on *Forever Amber*, though to do

Forever Amber justice *Forever Amber* had been going on rather
longer, and we were both down at the bottom anyhow by that
time: we waged quite a battle, though, for a while—I imagine
about 15 or 16,000 copies altogether. Here in Canada it sold 2
copies—so far as I can gather—and was panned in the local
paper. In England it was well received but did little better. In
France it was greeted with enthusiasm and shoved into a Modern Classics series, as was the case in Norway; Sweden, Denmark, Italy and Germany have also made translations of it,
though I have no idea of the outcome save in Denmark, where
it flopped, and Germany, where it's coming out shortly, which
of these last countries has taken the most serious attitude
towards it. (I mean Western Germany, of course.) (Mark Schorer wrote two reviews of it—one extraordinarily sympathetic
one in *Vogue* of all places—others demolished it, no less, and it
also made the *Encyclopedia Britannica*.)

I then mention that it was Royal Welsh Fusiliering brother
who'd insisted I be called Clarence after the gent of that name
who was drowned in a butt of Malmsey wine, gave my regards
to your friend Leonard Brown, intimating that if he was Firmin
that was fine, for I bring the Consul to life in a later book and
make him do just the opposite, and all this without even joining
Alcoholics Heironymus, though it must be said he changes his
potation and even goes on a diet of Schopenhauer and vinegar
for a while, and other remedies from Burton's *Anatomy of Melancholy*, even up to and including water which nearly makes
him die of dysentery, and milk which gives him sinusitis, and
tea which gives him an even worse attack of delowryum tre-
mens; and then reverted to Aiken again, adding that I still
thought he was a very great genius, and incidentally a much
misunderstood one, but that it seemed to me that this touched
on a subject so important for a writer launching away that I'd
better write you a letter for your private ear on the subject (gap

in MSS) for it yet remained to be explained how a boy of 18, more or less inexperienced save in one tough aspect of life, namely the sea (a fragmentary thing, but still I'd been a seaman—O'Neill sent me to sea, I guess—looked at it as such, not a passenger), could be drawn as by some irresistible teleological force toward an aspect of the mind or psyche of another much older, totally different in experience and nationality and outlook, and moreover, in *Blue Voyage* at least, with a philosophy and psychological *drang*—save where it touched beauty on the one hand, human misery on the other, expressed and linked through the phenomenal and magical usage of language—that he the boy, did not understand, and had he understood, would have found thoroughly inimical—for sheer lack of sunlight and air and mountains, if not blue water (you might call it pseudo-Freud and the philosophy of the "nothing but")—and then, as it were, stuck there, calmly disregarding among other things that Aiken himself, save in all but a few of his short stories which on the contrary are mostly a reversion of his prosaic and false and influenced side to almost nothing of lasting worth at all, as he would be the first to agree, say *Time* mag. what it may, had, with certain other exceptions, enormously and continuously developed in his poetry (but curiously I didn't know he was a poet at first) beyond that point into a metaphysical and far wiser and wider realm, to a point indeed where he might well serve as master to any writer in the world, in which connection it is as well not to forget the mature, indeed dying, Joyce, looking for Osiris Jones being reborn. (When Conrad sent me some 20 years ago a copy of the latter masterpiece, to my lasting shame I neither acknowledged it nor made any comment. Why should I? What was all this about Osiris Jones? After all it was not *Blue Voyage* and *I* had not written it. Worse still, it never occurred to me he might be hurt, so cruelly abstract is one side of youth. And weirder than all, one might have reckoned without one's own remote influence, even if not literary or direct, but beneficently springing rather—in so far as it sprang, if spring it did—in part from that very shattering and unsolicited faith in his work I had shown! But what did I see in *Blue Voyage*? Certainly something that was beyond my power rationally to see. Nor was I wrong. Perhaps what one might term Operation II of the daemon?) However it is no wonder I stopped the letter here, for the subject is hard to explain indeed, quite apart from which I had not even touched on what seemed to me the essence of the far greater subject that this began to adumbrate—

Then, after a while, I received yours of Aug. 9.

At which point I think it's time to take those shoes off and get into the flames.

(No joke either, if he didn't do it himself first, no one would believe it could be done and then there would be no initiation.)

I'll start with a few assumptions, in fact jump boldly to conclusions, all of them flattering to myself, and doubtless due to my great narcissism—though I won't waste time on this aspect of it—then make a few tangential observations, in the hope that even if inapplicable, they may some day, odds and ends of 2 x 4's though they are, serve well as reliable timber with which to build a bridge should you need one. For no wonder Dante found the straight way was lost. There is no straight way. There is no path, unless metamorphosed. Dante's wood was an abyss. Psychological—for the last time psychology!—as Kafka says—but true. Fortunately Virgil—since we all stand together in this world—was standing near and he had the common sense to make use of him. Dante didn't grow much happier, it is true, but perhaps that was his fault: and at least he finished his book. Perhaps he'd have done better still if he'd pushed Virgil into one of those swamps instead of another of his poor unfortunates and walked over using his head as a stepping stone but that's beside the point. Anyway Virgil was dead. If he'd been alive it might have been a different story. And I ain't no Virgil. Still I shall squelch along upon my feet of clay as well as I can—perhaps they will even turn into some kind of mottled marble in the process. Anyway:

(a) I'm going to assume, as I should, you mean the letter you wrote.

(b) That having written it, you now wish you hadn't: *i.e.*, perhaps you feel ashamed of so expressing your feelings, in fact you may even feel I've misinterpreted it, etc.

To (b) *don't* wish you hadn't written it. It is the best thing you could have done. And you are right, it *is* perfectly healthy. What would be unhealthy would be if you hadn't so simply and directly expressed your empathies on the subject. True—no doubt you could think—eventually you would have forgotten the said feelings, but here comes nature and the pitchfork again: more than that, a book is a much harder proposition than a human being—once truly recognized it is not in the nature of the thing to let you alone, though the source of its behavior is a reciprocal gratitude beyond human understanding, it's liable to turn into a kind of mantra yoga: old stuff I have to talk here, stemming from the last sentence but one—the feelings turn inward and what is worse begin to work against you: worse still, they can even give one a kind of persecution mania, one suspects necrophily in oneself, incipient paranoia, heaven knows what (and on top of that the mind, equally with the heart, is a lonely hunter—I once fell in love with an elephant—and it's certainly no use worrying about the downgoing and morbid "correspondences" of these things, they become ridiculous, when all one is trying to do is *live*, and God how hard it can be at your age: perhaps I am talking about myself, not you—no matter, still I can permit myself to suffer on your account feeling yourself to be misunderstood, or disregarded, or worse, understood coldly and *cleverly* and rationally and "psychologically," and so more than disregarded, when all one has said is something direct and sincere: [gap in the MSS]—well, I myself am extremely happily married, the luckiest kind of person, both in my wife and the kind of life we mostly lead, as one might say healthy—and by God it really is healthy—normal; what a word!—as if happiness were normal today, or this kind of life which has almost disappeared from the world altogether—note: Howard had no means and no words with which to explain to these simple men that business is the only real thing in life, that it is heaven and paradise and all the happiness of a good Rotarian. These Indians were still living in a semi-civilized state, with little hope of improvement within the next hundred years.—*The Treasure of the Sierra Madre*—but there are all kinds of huge life-giving feelings in the world you can't pin down: for prose, for elephants, for the sea, even for the ducks that swim therein: we are all here anyway.)

Well, it is healthy, your identity with the *Volcano* I mean, even though the book may not be worthy of you, though it might be worse (and I cannot say how moving to me, because I won't disguise from you that I'm extremely proud of most of it), but somehow all this must be used for your benefit; in fact it is yours, that's what it's there for. And whatever they say or don't say I think it's a good book probably.

However the full drama of what you have said has not yet emerged. Nor will it be lost on you. Here is the plot of the book lost by fire. (*In Ballast to the White Sea*—once the sort of Paradiso of the trilogy of which the *Volcano* was the first or "Inferno" section—now incorporated hypothetically elsewhere in the whole bolus of 5 books—I think to be called *The Voyage That Never Ends*. It was lost 7 years, June 7, 1944, when our first house went up in flames, not ten feet from where I sit, and written 9–10 years before that, in New York, when I was a little older than you.)

A, the hero of my novel, a young student at Cambridge, of Scandinavian origin, and with a sea-faring experience such as my own, feels such a kinship for a work as you have most generously expressed for mine—a novel of the sea, he has read in translation, by a Scandinavian novelist X. The disorientation of A at the university is much the same as Hugh's at Cambridge in *U.T.V.* and for the same reasons. X's novel is an appalling and horrendous piece of work, a sort of *Moby-Dick* in fact, but a *Moby-Dick* that was concerned less with whales than the fate of the individual living characters of the *Acushnet* (that being the original name of the *Pequod*). Only in this case the more A reads X's book the more identified he becomes with the principal character in that book, Y—who supplies the one note of relief (in X's book)—(it is a book on the side of life though) the more so as the experience of Y—by extension he feels that of X too—closely—indeed supernaturally—resembles his own: not merely that, but X's book uncannily resembles the one A's been trying to write himself, which it seems to have rendered futile. (As a matter of fact it's more complicated even than that but let it pass.)

My hero is troubled, among other things (a stormy love affair with an older woman, the risk of being sent down for pursuing it, the invidiousness of being a man at the University and yet treated as a child, a Dostoievskian brother, the ghoulishness of his contemporaries, the ideology of the English faculty, the feeling of hopelessness that overwhelms him about his choice of a vocation when now he figures he perhaps isn't a writer and so no better than a child after all and so on), by the fact that he can find absolutely no parallel in *literature* to this growing sense as of identity with the character of Y—and the field of X's novel—save a rather minor, if good, but scarcely helpful book by Louis Adamic, a feeble short story by Aldous Huxley, and a sinister German play running in London called *The Race with a Shadow* by one Wilhelm van Scholz, based on an idea by Goethe. All these, with the exception of the last, which is so horrible he can't take it, are almost parodies on the surface of an experience, by which he is bewildered because he cannot believe that it does not represent something universal and so of vital human importance; nor has it got anything to do with the normal experiences of hero-worship through which one passes: Y is not a hero in the usual sense, his experiences are not enviable, he is not even wise—he isn't even physically described in X's book, for that matter, so that he has no features or stature and is quite impossible to picture save as several kinds of person at once; on another plane he seems more like a voice that has commented upon a human experience with honour and an agonizing truth that is unique to A. (Y is not Melville's "handsome sailor" nor Conrad's ugly one—his virtues are simple and such as A's life in England of that period everywhere betrays and even interdicts: loyalty, simplicity, decency, and a capacity to be reverent, in the bloodiest of circumstances, before the mystery of life, and a hatred of falsehood. It would appear also that he has a faith, of a kind, in God, if not strictly according to Martin Luther.) Yet how can it be unique to A, when by God Y *is* A. And what's all this about a hatred of falsehood, when one of the things that most bothers A is that A himself is an almost pathological liar—unable to give any kind of rational account of himself, he invents the most fantastic tales about himself at every point that are so vivid they have a kind of life of their own. (It is important for you to bear in mind that though I, as you may have guessed, am by and large, more or less, with reservations of course, A—though X is not Aiken, albeit an individual too—I am not lying to *you*, even though it might be more comfortable to do so.) X represents the complementary and lifegiving operation of the daemon pleading to II or perhaps—implicit in II too—but without which II becomes satanic. Something like that. My terms are all mixed up, and I realize that like this it sounds more than a little ridiculous. But bear with me. Probably I don't have to explain it. And how can A be A when he's Y? And yet this is not the half of it either. A is no narcissist. He has not caught paranoia. Moreover he is a tough baby, on one side (in my book, or ex-book) almost as extraverted as some character in the *Treasure of the Sierra Madre*, even though that is a side of himself he exploits with women and lies about, but this much is true, his ship has taken him smack through the first bloody Chinese revolution of 1927, etc., though he has only seen tragic glimpses of the real thing and his knowledge of what he has actually been through even so has only just ceased to be about nil. Nor has he some adolescent fixation or crush on X, because if Y is mysterious, X is ten times more so. (About X he can find out absolutely nothing at all, the Scandinavian's novel having been long since remaindered in translation, the publishers non-existent in England, and there is no blurb to tell him a thing—he's bought the book second hand. Strangest of all A doesn't even want to *write* like X. Not at first he doesn't, that is. A has a style all his own, and what A and X have in common—though A sees his whole life in that book—is something different.) A, though he feels like an old man, has either bypassed or not even reached the stage of adolescence. People like Whitman with an all-embracing love of mankind, and also Lawrence, put him off, save when they write about nature. His knowledge of how gruesome man can be is too close, and in Cambridge, on a flabbier plane, closer still. So his brother not being a type he can take into his confidence, and his father being engaged in a gigantic law suit with the Peruvian Government, and his girl friend rapidly growing fed up with him, he sits down and writes to X. In fact he writes letter after letter to X—they formed, intermediately, a large part of the book—but it never once occurred to him that almost any publisher in Scandinavia would forward his letters, if X is extant; he keeps his problem, as the letters, to himself, meanwhile becoming increasingly afraid of his thoughts as his identification with Y—and by extension with X—becomes more complete....

(to be continued)

In order to keep my promise to get this letter off I have to post this right now to catch the Saturday mail—there is one mail a day only, none on Sunday, and the relative time the two stages of the letter must make to reach you are roughly as follows: From Dollarton to Vancouver, 15 miles—24 hours. From Vancouver to Albany, 3500 miles—12 hours approx. So if I delayed you wouldn't receive anything till the middle of next week. I shan't stop writing, however, till the letter is finished, if it ever can be finished. Plot of *In Ballast* has a triumphant outcome. So see exciting installment next week. On back of all pages save page 1 are some bits of the original MSS of *Under the Volcano* my wife and I dug out for you and thought you might like to have: when I say original, some of it is pre-original, dating 11 years or so back, though I can't find any of the pre-pre-original which goes back to 1936 save in typescript; as a matter of fact we can't even find any typescript to speak of; notes down the margin are due to a habit my wife and I have of exchanging MSS for mutual correction: some of the work looks as though one definitely knew what one was doing, other parts look uncertain and as if the author were out of touch, and the style flabby or derivative, other bits are no longer there—but in the main it's as is—sorry it's not in order, but felt it might please you. When I said confidential—of course that I leave to your highest judgment, because it might hurt someone's feelings. But

I didn't mean that you shouldn't speak to your girl about it, if you feel like speaking to her. If you badly want any of it when I'm through for your thesis better let me edit it. In one way it seems like a dirty trick, on second thoughts, even to have voiced a bona fide criticism in these circumstances of Aiken, to whom I owe so much (though Aiken himself I am sure would be the first to give assent that I should write you like this) and you must be wise and see beyond the superficial envy and ingratitude that evinces, the criticism of myself and my own weaknesses it involves.

Sursum corda!
Malcolm L.

(*Intervallo*)
(Is, ah, Señor David Markson in the house? Will he proceed to the cantina—the dirtiest one—next door, where the gringo peon Bruto pelado Señor Lowry is lying seriously ill? Chocolates? Tequila? Cerveza? Gaseosas? Mescal? H'm. Buenos tardes, señor. How's it going, old man? Sorry, it wasn't that I was lying seriously ill, nor that I was ill because I was seriously lying—because I'm not indeed, though I find it difficult indeed even painful to remember certain details of the plot of my chingado novel—on the contrary I'm trying my damnedest to tell the truth, fantastic though it may be—but because, in this intervallo, I have read your letter again, and I perceived, misericorde, hombre, alas, that I had not thanked you sufficiently from the heart—I hadn't mentioned I had a heart—for what you have so generously and above all simply said, and with a feeling, and trust, I was going to say, I didn't deserve: but if that is so, viejo, what the hell is the point of writing this letter? What kind of the hell reflection of yourself would I give back if I didn't deserve it? So, all right, I do deserve it. As certainly you deserve something back of equal sincerity. If I deny myself, I

deny my book, and in denying my book, I deny you. For
equally it is your book. So I shan't do anything of the sort; I
will, on the contrary, affirm it, be proud of it. As I am not? But
how have I answered—and this is what is making me at the
moment sick, hombre—sickness is in that part used to be call:
soul—moreover I hate to think that my silence, however expli-
cable and non-invidious, made you suffer—this forthrightness,
this frankness, this directness? Have I answered it with an
equal forthrightness, an equal simplicity of feeling? Or with a
concatenation of complexities, an evasion of gobbledegook-
eries—in short, for simplicity, have returned: psychology? And
then on top of that have worn a mien of being so unco quid
pure normal healthy and beyond reproach that perhaps it's
unnatural in itself, as if my life, or anyone else's life, had not
been wrested—and does not have to go on being wrested—out
of the Molochian maw of errors often so destructible they
make one's hair stand on end: so you would be wrong to think
that the human being is not there, that he in turn is not sympathetic, or that he regards that life—despite a definite element of
having *come through*—as anything purer or more upright than
a collaboration between Strindberg, Dostoievsky, The Underground Man, a Ouija board, a talking horse, Joe Venuti and a
Houngan: this on the one side, on the other you must feel yourself right to have trusted me, though not for reasons that are at
all easy to answer. Still you *are* right to do so. The decency, the
honesty is here, sprouting laboriously amid the indecency, the
dishonesty. But immediately I say that the shadow of Melville's
Confidence Man seems to fall upon my pen, that emblem of the
worse than worst, warning one away from one's easy interpre-
tations, one's facile optimism, and whose nostrums conceal
who knows what hidden desire for power, even to exploit, even
though on the face of it, it wouldn't be at all easy to see where
he comes in. Very hard for yourself to see, who feel, if anything,

you were exploiting me. Well, on both sides that is a risk one has to take. Simply for fear of error, of being self-condemned, of making mistakes, even ghastly mistakes, of sounding indeed like *The Confidence Man*, I don't think we should shrink from trying to be constructive, or rather to help one another, where we see the chance. And what is even God to do when if you ask for help the ambassador he chooses fails even to attempt to deliver the goods. Clearly His rating, even if unjustly, would go down. Which brings me to what I conceive to be the purpose of this letter. The best way that I can answer your own trust, can show my own gratitude to you as it were, can only be on the basis of the thought: "I wish to God someone had said something like this to *me*," when I at your age said, or worse did not say, "I don't quite know how to say this." I insisted to myself for a while, "Do you have any idea what it means to me?" "Do you realize what I am saying?" I don't mean I have been unlucky in my friends or influences, exactly. In fact, in many respects, considering this and that, I've been a creature of luck all through. The few friends I've made in my life I've mostly kept, and still revere. I have spoken of the help Aiken gave me, sadly needed, because my father—who was by way of being a capitalist on the grand scale—good man though he was, rarely gave me any advice of much pragmatic value, though I'll always bless him for turning me into a good swimmer. But apart from that I often felt myself a kind of item on the business agenda, even, in some respects, an expendable item. It is natural, I think, to eschew giving, as taking, advice. I'm not sure there's any advice per se in this letter. Still there are times when the need for understanding is absolutely imperative. And it has been my experience that it is precisely among people of one's own artistic persuasion that one is likely to find the most crashing disillusionment. At least I often wished, at your age, should I say, or even not say, "Do you realize what I'm saying?" no matter what the subject, that someone older would have the courage to say, "Yes, I think so," and explain it for my benefit, even if wrongly, at least give me something to go on, at least *take the trouble*. But in fact—though there are exceptions as I've pointed out, especially in the good old tradition of poets— by and large these stuffed geniuses, this aristocratic proletariat of peacock, these sanctissima God donkeys, this Jesus man burro, say, like as not, nothing at all. Mean as so many stingy old gold miners sitting on a stake, they seem to think it too dangerous to open their trap, even if, like certain professors I know of, they're being paid to do so. And it's not merely that they fear to give away the source of the mine. It's how to work it— ah no, that would harm their bloody little conception of their own uniqueness. Ah, that contemptuous look that seems to say: "But don't you know that?" Even if they saw their best friend about to fall slap down the abyss, it wouldn't occur to them to say: "I've been there before, brother—in fact I'm there now—let me stand like a caryatid down there, while you step on my head and go round the other way, for you can achieve the same or a better result by doing that." Even if by saying that they would be achieving the only possible human good they were likely to do on this earth, they'd think of some way out of doing it. Still, if I'm not to be worse still, back to this letter. What? Señor Lowry is not in that cantina, but in his shack on the waterfront, drinking a friendly glass of plebeian gin and orange juice with his wife—and I'm not going to drink much of that at the moment, if this letter is to be right, and writing this letter, as from the Charlie Chaplin stove ascends the pungent aroma of frying horse, for inflation has driven us not merely to sharing, but to eating our archetypes too!)

So all this isolates the poor guy more than ever. So he never posts any of those letters, keeps the whole matter to himself. Meantime two other things are going on, on another plane. As he writes the letters he becomes consumed with an absolute passion—in one sense hereditary—to return to the sea. The sea begins to rise within him, haunts his dreams, and this longing that storms in him day and night to return to the sea was one of the best parts of the book—all of which makes it such a nuisance I have to write it again: (Do I hear myself aright? Well, perhaps your letter will one day give me the guts to do just that, not leave it merely buried, as it lies now, as so much exposition) for it takes a curious form: the longing for the sea emerges into a longing for the fire of the stokehold, for the actual torment—masochistic, though it somehow isn't, but above all for the fire (which being so the book could not have had a finer funeral—my wife rescued all *The Volcano*, I one of hers, but we had to let that go) the fire in which he sees himself purged and emerging as the reborn man. Which the absolute integrity decency and as it were purity of the feeling that overwhelms him whenever he reads X's book or writes—still without posting any of the letters—to X, it can scarcely but be pure for X is like an abstraction, but it has none of the evil either of absolute purity on this plane (albeit the White Sea itself is that, is death too) gives him to believe he may turn into. For, largely due to the suppression of this feeling, all is not well with him in almost every other respect. He neglects his studies, starts to drink like a fish, finds his own work increasingly worthless, gets through an exam on Dante's *Inferno* by consulting a blind medium who tells him what the questions will be, at last becomes, in spite of that, so closely identified with X that now when he does pull himself together and write, he can't be sure he isn't transcribing whole sections of X's novel which, whenever he is sober, which is not often, he has to destroy. Meantime he makes the mistake of taking his brother into his confidence who instead of being sympathetic is scornful of the whole business and accuses him of every kind of abnormal tendency under the sun, and several

not under it. On top of this he—the brother—derides X's book
which enrages A to such an extent that inadvertently he causes
his brother to turn all his venom on himself in a Dostoievskian
scene that leads to the brother's death. Shattered and sobered
by this tragedy (there has to be a large gap in the MSS here if I
am ever to finish) A makes a tremendous effort of will, and during the long vacation—he has four months in the summer—
signs on, as a fireman, a Scandinavian timber ship bound from
Preston, near Liverpool, to Archangel, in ballast. (His purpose,
so he thinks, in doing this, is to gather added material for a play
he proposes to make of X's novel, though incidentally he has
arranged with his professor that this play will serve in lieu of a
thesis for the second part of his English Tripos!) One of the best
parts of the book I have to pass over too briefly here: almost on
the point of sailing it turns out that A has to return to Liverpool
according to law to sign on with the Norwegian Consul, this
being impossible with the Captain, and there not being such a
Consul in Preston. In Liverpool he runs into another brother, a
criminal lawyer, who is tight and tries to stop him going: so the
whole weary effort of will has to be made over again. The ship
however does not go to Archangel but to a port in northern
Norway that oddly *has the same name* as one of the principal
characters, though not the hero, of X's novel. Here, seemingly
by coincidence while the charter of the ship is held in abeyance
pending a decision by the shipowners in Oslo, he falls in with a
character in a cafe reading another book of X's. This book
shows that X has been in China at the same time A has and it
turns out that this character, a schoolmaster, has met X. Also
there is a photograph of X in the book—this is the first indica-
tion to A's conscious mind that there really is in existence such
a person as X. I had forgotten to say the most important thing,
namely that while he took no human action at all (posting
the letters would have amounted to that) some principle of

tyrannic yet thwarted force in his feeling has worked against him, *à rebours*: now he does take action—and heroic action at that—mysteriously the thing begins to work for him in a way that alters his whole conception of life and human destiny. This place (where he is in Norway) also turns out not to be far away from the place where his own mother has been buried and he pays a pilgrimage to her grave, the ship meanwhile, for lack of orders—though as a matter of fact the orders are contradictory, paralleling the indecision in A's mind whether to take another job and go on to Archangel or actually try and meet X—being stalled in the fjord, and the crew paid off. Here we begin to get on to the theme of rebirth. On the day of his pilgrimage to his mother's grave he meets a girl with whom he falls violently in love. This love is returned and this in fact is his first real experience of mature love. Meanwhile, quite without his seeming to will it, coincidence after coincidence, obeying a kind of Law of Series of their own, combine to take him to Oslo and result in his actually meeting X, this meeting coming about through the shipowner who has been sending the contradictory messages and X is no easy person to meet, lives under an assumed name, and—though he has become a playwright too—is a figure of great political significance (he is working against the conspiracy of Quisling's Nasjonal Samling, which considering this was written in 1936 is a pretty good piece of clairvoyance when you think they hadn't even got wise to it in 1940, after the event). When he meets X though, X is on the point of going to *Cambridge*—the very place where A has come from—to do some research on Elizabethan drama, but because of a divided vocation, in a state of confusion and despair bordering on A's own original confusion and despair. It is too complex to describe in detail this part of the book—but the resemblances between A and X are almost as uncanny as the differences. The character Y turns out not to be X but an objective projection—though X has been to sea—whom X had imagined as very like A. However X's apartment, books, etc., though they are mostly Scandinavian, is an almost exact replica of A's rooms in Cambridge. X moreover tells A that the *real* name of the ship that had given him his experience is the same as that of the ship that A had used in imagination in *his* book (of which he has proof, having brought some of the more original sections with him to work on in between planning the play.) X gives him permission to make the play, and the absolutely glaring testimony to the existence of the transcendental in the whole business, finally restores to a man like X, who imagined up till then that he had created things out of cold reason whatever he made his characters say or do, restores his faith, which had almost been lost, in his art. Both men are realigned on the side of life. A's action has also resulted in his salvation by his girl; in effect both the life of the imagination and life itself has been saved by A's having listened finally to the promptings of his own spirit, and acted upon those promptings, rather than the analytical reductions of reason, though it is reason too—by virtue of harmony with the great forces within the soul—that has been saved, and on this note the story and the trilogy closes.

Well, what a hell of a plot, you say, a kind of Strindbergian Tonio Kröger, by Maeterlinck, out of Melville. That may be, but the point is that with a few exceptions like the brother's death, etc.—and in a few other minor points—I didn't make the story up. There was an X: I did write, did not post the letters. Some force did work against me when I took no action and then when I took some action, for me. The story of the name of the imaginary ship being the same as the one in fact is true too, and there are a lot of other even more curious things that are true which I haven't mentioned so that altogether one might say, as X did, in fact once wrote: Reason stands still, what do we know? I have said that X was not Aiken. Someday

I will tell you the whole story. (X's full remark was: "Another spiral has wound its way upward. Reason stands still. What do we know?")

Tragedy in real fact comes in, in that after our first house burned down, we took refuge with a friend in Niagara who, not knowing I knew X, or that I had written a book largely about him that had been lost in the fire, was actually engaged in composing a broadcast on his death when we arrived, so giving me that news for the first time too—he had perished six months before the book of which he was the co-hero, also in flames, in a bomber over Berlin, on the wedding anniversary of my wife and self.

Meantime you needn't bother even to find out who X is. One day, as I say, I shall tell you the story. The reason I have mentioned it here is that upon the subject that makes up that story I have brooded, as you could not have known, half a lifetime. A's feeling—I want you to realize—is, in my opinion, above all, first and foremost *creative*. In that book I advanced the opinion that it was one of the most powerful and one of the most unknown—as to knowledge of what it is—feelings it is possible to have, and one of the purest as it were, even if directed at an object of blistering evil—though it is not exactly an object, it is something you share yourself, as you sooner or later discover: and anyway it is one of the most misunderstood: perhaps it is religious in origin or perhaps it has something to do with evolution itself; but it is certainly a *force* and as a force it obliges you to use it, obliges you to make an act of transcending. You have to go on from there. Aiken once told me that he considered it primarily an operation of genius. Genius knows what it wants and goes after it. He told me—this I say in strict confidence, though he did not swear me to confidence on the subject but admitted it freely—that he was once drawn to Eliot's work in the same way. Eliot himself—who owes a good deal to Aiken himself that has not been acknowledged—has called this identification "one of the most important experiences (for a writer) of adolescence." I'd like to know when adolescence stops at that rate. I surmise an identification on Eliot's part with Laforgue. On the tragic plane you have Keats' identification with Chatterton, leading, Aiken once suggested, to a kind of *conscious* death on Keats' part. However that may be, it is a force of *life*. But also it is an operation of the soul. As you have observed—in fact as you have proved yourself—it can be clairvoyant. But it is only a writer, poor devil, who would ever imagine such a thing was unhealthy. I imagine that in the realm of music it is recognized simply and consciously absorbed as a process in composition, e.g. Berg and Schönberg. Leibowitz has pointed out that though Berg followed Schönberg in almost every discovery, adopting all his principles and reaching the same conclusions, he yet remained a great and original composer. Conversely, without doubt (says he), one can become a great composer after having had a bad master, but in such a case the very fact of becoming a great composer implies that, at one time or another, one has resolutely turned against one's master. I don't know why I have said all this, or what it adds up to. I started from an assumption—possibly quite wrongheaded—that you would regret having written me. I've tried to show that you certainly should not regret it. All this reckons without the human element, but since you unfortunately live some thousands of miles away, to write is the next best thing to our meeting, to which I look forward one day. Don't try to reply in detail though—it would be too difficult, if not impossible. But if I have said anything useful use it for your own good. One thing you could do is to look back sternly upon the impulses in operation before, say, you read the *Volcano*, the teleology that drew you toward it. For example I am drawn inexorably toward *Blue Voyage*, a novel which is the work of a poet, though I don't know that. I am also drawn toward the work of X, a novel likewise the work of a poet it turns out, but who is also a dramatist, though I don't know that either. I think both are novelists only. Sure enough, I become a novelist, whatever that is. But since the aim of my psyche seems to have been to make a synthesis of these two factors, and since my earlier passion was the drama, wouldn't it be a reasonable point to call sublime reason to one's aid in the person of someone like Ortega and assume I have some buried capacity as a poetic dramatist? It might. And something similar may be true of you. Anyhow you are much younger than I, and with time to decide what you want to do. And if you like my book that much, let it help you to get things in the right order. Perhaps they are, anyway. But still. Also send me what ever spontaneity you like. I have to work so hard now that I shan't be able to reply for some months save in monosyllables but don't let that put you off again. It is a pity there is so much space between us but perhaps there is not so much as there appears to be. Give my love to your girl and be happy in this order: Health, Happiness, Sense of Humour, Art, Pleasure. My wife sends her love too. Hold that note, Roland!

Sursum corda!
Malcolm L.

TO HAROLD MATSON

Dollarton, B.C., Canada
October 2, 1951

Dear Hal—

I am posting you today under separate cover a comic classic, or at least a masterpiece of nature, or at all events that is the only way of looking at it, at least for me, or I wouldn't have felt justified in writing it, so if you don't think so, don't tell me, at least not just yet. I believe there is some chance some people will think it first rate in its genre though, if it has one, for it breaks all the rules, save that, I hope, of being interesting and amusing; on one plane it is no less than a kind of short short for Titans, a Moby Jumbo, a comic strip for the infant Panurge, of philosophic trend, and I do not need reminding that the magazine designed to accommodate easily such a Pantagruelian fancy, or *multum in colosseo*—for it is longer than the *Heart of Darkness*—is not yet, though it may be that its merit is such that one would stretch a point even to a bursting of the seams, or at least in two installments, to garage the monster.

However of this I am not sanguine, so please hearken unto my further intention. This enclosed new epistle to the Colossians was originally designed to be accompanied at the same time by another novella of the same length, though absolutely opposite in intention, locale, *sturm und drang*, etc., and of great seriousness (though it is a story of happiness, in fact, roughly of our life here in the forest, exultant side of) entitled "The Forest Path to the Spring." So far as I know this is the only short novel of its type that brings the kind of majesty usually reserved for tragedy (God this sounds pompous) to bear on human integration and all that kind of thing: though it isn't my final word on the subject by a damn sight, I'm mighty proud of it.

As a matter of fact this latter is in part an adumbration— though complete in itself—of a novel to be called *Eridanus* which, if things go well and I can get through the necessary ordeals so to speak which permit me to write the whole, will form a sort of Intermezzo or point of rest to the larger work of five, perhaps six interrelated novels, of which the *Volcano* would be one, though not the best one by any means, the novel you suggested I should write some years back, a sort of *Under Under the Volcano*, should be ten times more terrible (tentatively it's called *Dark as the Grave Wherein my Friend Is Laid*) and the last one *La Mordida* that throws the whole thing into reverse and issues in triumph. (The Consul is brought to life again, that is the real Consul; *Under the Volcano* itself functions as a sort of battery in the middle but only as a work of the imagination by the protagonist.) Better still: some years back I was not equipped to tackle a task of this nature: now, it seems to me, I've gone through the necessary spiritual ordeals that have permitted me to see the truth of what I'm getting at and to see the whole business clearly: all that remains is to get myself into a material position where I can consummate the ordeal by the further ordeal of writing it.

To which end this elephant and "The Forest Path" were intended—apart from a kind of practice on a few smaller peaks —to achieve among other things the practical end of getting a contract with Albert; these two would form part of yet another book to be called *Hear Us O Lord From Heaven Thy Dwelling Place* and would consist of:

(1) "Through the Panama." A story in the form of notes taken on going to Europe, partly on a ship in everything but final distress off the Azores; it reads something like *The Crack-Up*, like Alfred Gordon Pym, but instead of cracking the protagonist's fission begins to be healed. 60-odd pages.

(2) "October Ferry to Gabriola." Another novella, a first version of which we wrote in collaboration for you though it didn't come off. This I've completely redrafted and largely rewritten, and it deals with the theme of eviction, which is related to man's dispossession, but this theme is universalized. This I believe to be a hell of a fine thing.

(3) "In the Black Hills." The humorous-tragic short short I wrote which you have and which I take is for some reason unsaleable. While only tiny it's not quite as slight as it looks when contrasted alongside other themes.

(4) "Strange Comfort Afforded by the Profession." Ditto.

(5) "Elephant and Colosseum." 100 pages.

(6) "The Forest Path to the Spring." 100 pages (about).

I could throw in a couple of other short ones, as a matter of fact I could go on completing short stories till all is blue, other things being equal, which they are not, and the point is I want to call a halt, especially if they're not too saleable in the item, as appears the trouble, and I don't seem able to help this, and get on with the novel. *Hear Us O Lord*, etc., is from the old Manx fisherman's hymn that occurs in 3 of the stories.

Of the above mentioned, three of them at least have the intent of being major productions in their class, and Margerie thinks "The Forest Path" contains the finest stuff I've done. What I meant to do was finish the "Elephant" and "Forest Path" simultaneously and this I've almost done but not quite. I should be through with "The Forest Path" in about a month. Though about the same length as the "Elephant" I feel it might sell, on the other hand this wasn't exactly the point so much as the "Elephant" and "The Forest Path" together would constitute (200 pages) something to show Random House and thus perhaps (together with a précis of my projected novels, etc.) give one a chance to survive the winter. I am sending you two copies of the "Elephant" but I feel it would be pointless to show it to Albert by itself, so bear with me till you receive "The Forest Path," for the two of them together have a wholly different effect, maybe quite electrifying, but the circuit won't come off the way I want for Albert with the "Elephant" alone. Perhaps the "Elephant" would be sufficient to get me turned down by Harcourt, Brace. Not that I don't love the "Elephant" myself, and psychologically you can see it as a good sign—my authority is Herman Hesse, the writer to whom I feel I bear most inner resemblance, though I haven't got that far yet, but the plan for the five, maybe six, goes as far as he in invention, maybe further. But more of this later, when you have "The Forest Path."

Meantime try and bear with me. Love to Tommy and yourself.

Malcolm

TO DAVID MARKSON

Hallowe'en
[Postmarked November 1, 1951]

Dear Dave:

The reason I'm long in replying is that I'm trying to secure a contract for another book (stories) before the winter is out. Also I have sprouted Zola's whiskers and have been preparing a public objection to a local injustice where a 16 year old boy was sentenced to hang (in a disused elevator shaft, painted yellow) for a rape he had not committed. Fortunately they reprieved the poor fellow (apparently to please the visiting Princess Elizabeth) but neither the ritual pardon nor the near-ritual murder on the part of our barbarous public, who has now sentenced him to life imprisonment, is something you would leave alone, if you had studied the evidence, the feeble and neurotic protests, the bloodthirsty cries for revenge, and you were the only writer in the community, much as one hates to risk one's position in it, even if one hasn't got one, and what is more does not care whether one has or not.

Apart from that I've been working very hard indeed on other things and have written a story called "The Bravest Boat" I think you would like.

Meantime my wife wrote *Horse in the Sky* under name of Margerie Bonner. Don't even try to look for *Ultramarine* (the thought hurts my feelings) which is not worth reading and which I shall rewrite one day maybe. Did you see Louis Adamic of whom I wrote you tangentially died about a week later? More of this some day. Meantime God bless him—it's Hallowe'en anyway. Let me know news of your thesis. Many thanks for all your words and lots of luck from

Malcolm

P.S. Sunrise next morning, frost outside, tide high, just below windows. Seagulls having been fed. Coffee *being* made. Have you any advice for me re anything good to read? I agree *Miss Lonelyhearts* is an important book, and that Rimbaud had one leg, but where is the sunrise? Where is the frost? Where are my seagulls? Where is my coffee? Where is love? Where is your tennis racket? What has happened to Joe Venuti? They can't all be in the *Atlantic Monthly* or Bill Saroyan. And in fact there's a lot to be said for Bill Saroyan's *My Heart's in the Highlands* anyway. Don't forget that priceless possession, the author's naïveté. I will prepare you a more austere list, though yours can be austere for that matter. I would read Yeats' *The Vision* (second version) for your purposes, though it is scarcely Joe Venuti: of recent books I liked *The Catcher in the Rye* better than *The Barkeep of Blement*, which I am reading with some enthusiasm.

TO ALBERT ERSKINE

Dollarton
Ash Wednesday (with reservations)
[1952]

Dear old Albert:
    This, an interpolated note of affection and gratitude merely, with the knowledge that you have not time to reply. (But also with the intention of explaining a few peripheral things.)

A clean house, at last, even a clean soul, what is more; a full moon over the inlet, the mergansers gone to rest and the mink returned to her hollow tree. Never was anything more miraculously well nor more peaceful in our town—population three— perhaps four if "Kristbjorg" is still on deck: he swears, or swore the day before yesterday, that in the 60 years of his experience he has never seen the sea do anything worse than it has done here: it has cut away about 20 feet in depth of the entire forest sea bank, dropping whole gardens into the sea, not to say houses, while the entire shore has changed from about $^1/_{15}$ gradient to about $^1/_6$ in places, with the corresponding undermining of foundations. "Quaggan's" big float in front of his boathouse—the whole two hundred feet of it—carried away completely: but our pier still stands—absolutely undamaged— as do our foundations, despite the fact that we have four and a half whole uprooted trees terrifyingly *under* our house. Since our pier is made only out of light two-by-fours and 2-inch planking, is now ten years old, and has stood the brunt of the worst furies of wind and sea ever endured here, we have not met anyone yet who has even bothered to think of a material explanation for its survival, though there might be one, namely in its simplicity, lightness, and freedom from top hamper: thus in a terrific sea—and it was overwhelmed, under water when we left—instead of giving way to the sea and lifting from its foundations, it simply and calmly clung to the beach and stayed where it was, the foundation being just slightly heavier than the overall plankings: nearly all professional jobs gave way in this vicinity, for not having recognized whatever principle there is in this; they figured that the heavier and stronger the planking the more weight it would place on the foundations, and hence the foundations would be the securer and the whole safer in every way in any emergency. But it ain't so—wood *floats* and will try and float even if nailed down, and if overwhelmed by water the heavier it is, the harder it will pull at the nails—and all round guess there is some sort of lesson—apart from an image—in this, the more so since the foundations, in this case, simply and contrariwise adjusted themselves to the undermining of the beach, instead of vice versa, and became securer than ever: naturally we are very proud of ourselves. Our subsidiary house was not so lucky as we said, but then we didn't build it; even that has stood up though, minus a pile, it is sagging badly at one end and we have to prop it up.

I have interrupted another longer letter to you to write you this—because of changing circumstances—but will try to supply you with a sort of log. Friday, March 28, two days before we left the apartment, we ran into a typhoon and damn nearly foundered almost in Falmouth harbour—very eerie and dramatic, albeit with a happy outcome—I'll not tell you of it now, though God knows it's worth the telling, it left Margie, who was taking sulfanilamide for a throat, unable to type and almost completely shattered, coming on top of everything else. I can type, but not well enough on her typewriter to transcribe the job I was then doing, which was a letter to Giroux, especially as I proposed to give you a carbon. I was trying to make the point tactfully that while I did not blame him personally, since they had made such a to-do about moral rights, where their or the office boy's moral rights to the *Volcano* came in: so this letter—though almost finished—I had to abandon or leave in abeyance, and since Haas' decision and yours in my favour, the Case is somewhat Altered.

Sunday we came home, by a coincidence "Quaggan's" birthday—which he had celebrated in part by putting hot bricks on our soaking mattress and chopping some wood for us: so we had a warm as well as a happy homecoming. Of course we do the same sort of thing for him when we can and when necessary, each for the other, but I hadn't known the efficacy of hot bricks till then. He had lost our poor cat though (which has gone wild) so you might say—horrible image on second thoughts— we had the hot bricks without the cat. I guess he'll come home though, that is the cat; at least he has been "reported to have been seen."

Monday the 31st we got your airmail letter written to Dollarton saying that things were still in abeyance, but since Monday was a kind of crucial day with Haas so far as I could gather, we (expecting as it happens correctly a wire from you were there good news) felt some gloom and prepared to fight the rearguard action still further: e.g. letters for paying your debt, etc., though we had become in transit confused about the poems, and what to send: so preparing for the worst began to "dig out sails." Margie meanwhile was rallying nobly.

Tuesday April 1st. Your wire came through to the store, eventually, by telephone: it having been sent to the apartment the day before. They said oh well, they thought that was our address, and the note had been put under Number 33 at the apartment. *But the telegram had meantime been lost*, they said. Finally they found a copy of it and phoned it to the store and Margie came whooping through the woods with the best news I ever heard in my life. (Actual telegram, which we now have on the wall, did not arrive till 2 days later, but it was a supreme moment and bless you for sending it.)

Rest of the week—I received the general terms of the contract both from yourself and Hal, who expressed his unqualified admiration for what you have done for me, as I do ten times more, my unqualified gratitude. Hal's letter though went likewise to the ex-apartment in Vancouver, and not here. Though we might seem to be to blame here for not having informed Hal directly of our change of address, this is actually one of the strangest of coincidences, for the general post office had our change of address by postcard well in advance; in addition to the P.O.'s error Hal failed to put the apartment number on the envelope so it was surprising it reached us at all, though it did, if delayed. In the case of your telegram going to the apartment, while we hadn't thought it necessary to inform the telegraph company of a change of address since we had informed you, they simply and inexplicably disregarded the Dollarton address you'd given, as I have explained, so I felt obliged to reply to Hal first.

I told him I was not sure of 2 *absolutely completed* novels and 1 book of tales i.e. three bona fide books, 2 of them novels, in 2½ years, as seemed called for, despite your more than generous terms, for which terms please also express my deep gratitude to Mr. Haas: though I could guarantee *Hear Us O Lord* and *Lunar Caustic* in that time, or even in 2 years plus (as I said in the telegram) the detailed scenario of the whole, albeit this last entails no obligation to yourself, on the other hand I feel it a necessary item: on the other hand this *detailed* scenario of the whole might seem to many novelists to subsume several more completed novels, but it all depends upon what the hell one considers a completed work of art, and it is on this point that I really desire some leeway for consultation with yourself, and advice. It is possible that *Lunar Caustic* could be finished way ahead of schedule, and that "The Ordeal of Sigbjørn Wilderness" both parts I and II would make a novel that could be completed in the remaining time. But *Dark as the Grave, Eridanus* and *La Mordida* are together a trilogy and though they might well be published separately—as will probably turn out to be the best idea—I can't *think* of them at present separately, a problem you will readily see when you receive the material in question: two years hence, if all goes well, with *Hear Us* already published and *Lunar Caustic* in your hands, it might be that in the remaining 6 months I could finish *Dark as the Grave*, say, but I can't quite think that far ahead with any degree of feeling completely honest as to what it is possible to achieve—and naturally I would like to achieve more than I promise. What I am chiefly anxious to do, presented with such generous terms as you have offered me, is to pay my way, fulfill your trust in me and not to let anyone down. So please don't think that I am beginning to hedge or chisel on the contract: the last thing I want to be is a "difficult" author in that sense. On the contrary I really am motivated by a feeling that once I've got going with any luck and God's help I may be able considerably to exceed your expectations.

Re the financial end of it, it is more than generous, as I have said, but since there seemed some possible flexibility in the arrangement, while accepting it gratefully on whatever terms seem likewise most convenient to yourself, I asked Hal that in case of some kind of untoward accident to wife or self I might feel I could ask to apply at some time for a couple of hundred dollars or so in advance, if and only if, I really mean and add now, it seemed absolutely necessary to the fulfillment of the contract, though I qualified this by saying—which is true—that such an eventuality does not seem likely, and so shouldn't necessarily be an item on the contract: the reason is that my whole financial picture seems likely to improve. I had another letter from France that so far as they know that 800 dollars *is* coming through after all without the franc having fallen: and though England is still stalling for time I expect confirmation of similar good news from that quarter. So with your generous lift and these other items I expect not only to pay my debts but to be well in the clear in regard to emergencies. For we do have a hospital insurance scheme. What was nearly tragic for us when we first borrowed money from you was (one) that the premium was compulsory and so high that one couldn't afford to pay the ordinary doctor's bills or buy medicine. As for me, my health is excellent.

The other item was there has been a question of a film of the *Volcano*, with Peter Lorre. Whether this is going to come off or not, I don't know, but if it did, I asked for a few months' grace or leave of absence or something during which I might assist with the script. Naturally one would not expect to be supported by Random House during such a period; I would not want it to interfere with the final fulfilling of the contract, but naturally such a thing might prove circumambiently a factor in paying one's way.

Finally I said if the third book couldn't be within that time a novel I have a collection of poems, *The Lighthouse Invites the Storm*, that could be got in order almost any time: one would not expect this to sell, but if *Lunar Caustic* was going good and more than paying for itself, it could act as a stop-gap.

Finally I have something I hadn't thought of, namely the film we did for Frank, which is still supposed to be secret, though the secret now seems absurd to keep from you, albeit I haven't told Hal its name. Whether or not this would be feasible as a quid pro quo for a third completed book within that allotted period—what with the difficulties of copyright and the joint authorship—I don't know, but its existence is at least an earnest of what one can do. We did it in seven months and have not ever accepted or borrowed any cash on it and indeed it, alack, did not do for Frank what we had hoped: but perhaps that wasn't its fault, and it may yet. And certainly it wasn't Frank's fault. Shall I write to Frank to send it to you? I dropped *Dark as the Grave* to write this—and eventually I had hoped, among other bright results for Frank, it would prevent our getting into precisely the sort of situation we did get into. I enclose some comments by Isherwood, Leyda and Frank himself. It is by no means an ordinary kind of script. The film of course is

Tender Is the Night and I know Frank won't mind my mentioning it. In fact by writing it for him we felt we were in some sort "keeping in the family." The result was just the beginning of our three years' heartbreak: but at least we keep a-tryin'.

I have two hundred more French reviews, panegyrics of the *Volcano*, Teutonic headlines, Norse encomiums, and even caricatures of the author—but perhaps those are now somewhat beside the point, so I am not bothering you with them for the present.

A Happy Easter to you from us both and loads of gratitude and love,

Malcolm

TO HAROLD MATSON

The Caroline Court
1058 Nelson St.
Vancouver, B.C., Canada
January 25, 1954

Dear Hal:

This is in reply to yours of Jan. 11, though I had already begun a letter to you re Random etc. Yes, thank you, we received the January instalment.

The situation as it has arisen with Random House is a complex one which has been brewing for several months and about whose possible onset I had, in fact, repeatedly written Albert. In the light of what has happened I would have finished my letter to you but that I was awaiting a reply before doing so from Albert to an important official letter I wrote him on *Jan. 4th*: moreover I was too deep in work to write any more letters if I could avoid it. There has been no reply, and there being no evidence in your letter that Albert has explained my side of the question to you (I don't mean this in any derogatory sense to him) I'm put in the ungrateful position of having to explain it myself. Since it seems to me I am more in the right than the wrong, and even the object of some injustice, while my gratitude to Albert remains great and we are of course friends, I'd therefore be obliged if you'd keep this confidential—I mean as between Albert and yourself—the only thing not confidential presumably being my official letter of Jan. 4, which I'm including a copy of. You may wonder why I hadn't written you before, as normally speaking I should have, as I said, but now, in any case, I owe it to you, and myself, to give you all the facts and factors, but I want it understood that I do so with no implied disloyalty to Albert. Now I'll be as brief as possible.

I'd intended to complete the collection of short stories and novellas, *Hear Us O Lord*, as the first book, and for this to be delivered, being conscious of my obligation, on Nov. 1. However, when working on the penultimate story I found, as I told you, the material developing and growing and presently I realized I had a full-dress novel on my hands which I was so deeply involved with by that time it would have been fatal to stop. Moreover, this together with the last three novellas, more or less completed, made yet another sort of novel, and in *Hear Us* itself, the stories therein began to take on an interrelated form as a work of art it had not possessed before: and some of these pieces might be publishable by themselves, particularly *Gabriola*. Albert seemed pretty tepid about the stories and I gained the impression, or formed it, it might be better to kick off with a new and finished novel, whether this later would form part of the collection or not. Moreover in this way I saw myself eventually considerably exceeding the terms of the contract. (Meanwhile it is important to remember that I never, consciously, gave either you or Albert the impression—and I think my former letters bear me out in this—that sooner or later I might not choose to go on by myself for a while, without the payments, to gain time, and without the clause which gives me that right I never could have honorably signed the contract, especially after the discouraging experience with Brace. And to this end I have kept hammering away at my English bank to hurry the settlement of the estate and send me the money owing me.)

Meanwhile *Gabriola* continued to develop and grow more serious, and about this time I (we, for Margie was bitten by a dog the same day and was in hospital with me) had my cursed accident. Despite a broken and dislocated leg and ankle I tried to keep on working after the interim in the hospital, as I had even in hospital, but I'd lost the feel of the work, it was a ghastly and painful summer and altogether I'd say this set me back at least 3 months, looking back on it now, and whatever I may have said or felt at the time. You'll remember when signing the contract we suggested there should be some provision in case of serious accident or illness, and you and Albert decided this should be left up to the understanding or whatever of the publishers. I think I ought to point out that no one seems to have taken any account either of this time lost, or that I did not invoke any such unwritten contractual provision, though my accident could scarcely have been more serious, especially coming at that time, and one reason I didn't invoke it was that one's own anticipation of such a thing had seemed too much like clairvoyance, the accident itself too diabolically pat, psychologically suspect to another, though there was really no damn psychology about it, as I should know! However I had and have no intention of using this as an alibi. I merely state I don't find it sporting it should be entirely overlooked when there arose a question of the deadline.

During the summer I wrote Albert two or three letters re the general situation, not losing sight of the Nov. date, and received no reply. (He was away and the letters weren't forwarded.) This was discouraging, but on emergence into convalescence I may have grown too optimistic again (this time to yourselves) about my chances of getting it in on the dot. By the end of September, realising now it might not be possible to have it ready in final and negotiable form, I wrote Albert again and received a reassuring reply not to worry. Finally, in October I think, after I'd delivered an instalment of over 100 pages, Albert wrote saying he'd thought the November date was merely a date I'd set myself, but had looked up my contract and discovered that Nov. 1 was there all right, but that there was a three months' grace period, and *they could not "call me" before February 1*. I felt confident that by February 1, I could have enough in that would put their eye out, even if it were not quite finished.

However, and this is important, having been in touch with my English bank, I felt I would be in a position by February 1 to buy some time—a supposition in which I've proved right, as you'll see—and my intention all along was to show my good faith by buying some time *anyway*, even if *Gabriola* was finished. Had Albert's letter been urgent re the deadline, I should have taken a chance and asked you to call the changes there and then and stop payments, and would have done so anyhow before that, had not the accident taken most of my ready cash.

I hope this makes it clear that I have been extremely conscious of my obligation to Albert, Random, and yourself.

Just before Christmas I received an official letter from Albert written a week before that, saying that the Keeper of the Contracts had questioned him, and that the material in hand seemed to need more buttressing if they were going to extend the payments beyond February 1, the killing tone of which letter made us want to fall out of the window rather than take anything off the Christmas tree. I immediately replied, outlining the novel and saying I expected to have another 140 pages in by

February 1. The personal letter (which of course mollified matters somewhat) further qualifying the situation Albert had sent to the wrong address, was returned to him, sent back to me, and didn't reach us till after the first of January. A stroke of evil luck, and we may have been to blame for putting the wrong number on the envelope.

By this time I'd heard from my bank, promising me some money in a few days. I therefore, on *January 4*, wrote Albert another official letter, with a covering personal one, voluntarily suggesting that they suspend payments at least until I'd finished *Gabriola* and they could see better what I was doing. This letter I enclose. Personally I have a high regard for the work sent in, as I do for *Gabriola* as a publishable entity, but I felt it extremely unfair *Gabriola* be judged on those 159 pages Albert had, and a hundred times unfairer that all the work be judged by it. More of this later.

The immediate point is, Albert must have received this letter by the 6th of January. But now, on the 8th of January I received another official letter, with a covering personal one, saying *they* had decided to suspend payments, and of a chilliness beyond all chilliness. It appeared I had not only laid a Great Auk's Egg, but where, even, was the Egg? Your letter is dated January 11, and I do not understand why Albert has not informed you of having received my letter, written two days *before* theirs, asking them to stop payments, for it makes a serious difference. The reason why I didn't inform you myself I hope you'll now understand. It was all sprung on me at once. Having completely accepted Albert's former reassurance I thought, even after the first official letter, I had until *February 1*. I thought too, even now, my own request to buy time would be well *in time*: as it turns out I was mistaken, but too late as it was. I hope you'll understand all this.

Naturally it is distressing, as well as psychologically mortifying, not that payments should be suspended a while—for that is no more than I have consistently, even wishfully anticipated, could I carry on without—but that it should be done in such a fashion that it carries the direct implication of irresponsibility in this regard on my part, when the fact is I have been writing Albert about it since last summer and even before that. Against this is the fact that Albert has been motivated, amid many troubles of his own, by great kindness and understanding in trying to mitigate just such worry; once having helped so generously to get the boat launched, he didn't want to rock it.

Without losing sight of this for a moment, or that I am sure he thought he was acting in my best interests, all I can say is that in this instance he didn't think *enough* and I shall say this to him. For though I speak only of the embarrassment to him in the letter enclosed, should what has happened happen, what about the worse embarrassment to me? There was plenty of time in the interim to have given me an opportunity to do it myself, which was precisely what I did do, the first moment the final urgency of the situation became clear. Which leaves me with the feeling that they weren't even acquainted with my willingness to do it, if necessary and possible, otherwise what point was there in making it appear something like a punishment, as well as an impugning of the work in question? I don't see that it's even good business. For how the hell did they suppose I was going to finish it at all, since they didn't know I would have the money to carry on? Perhaps they thought discouragement of this kind, all of a sudden, would give them a better opportunity of getting their money back. For bear in mind that, after Albert's letter relieving me of the tension of the November 1 deadline, up to the time of his letter received roundabout Christmas Eve, it was our impression gained from that letter there was nothing in the contract that obliged me to have sent in a goddam page until the deadline, which was

(now) February 1. Who knows what I couldn't have finished by
then hadn't this happened? One consequence has been I've had
to write so many worrying and complex letters that the section
that was actually finished before the New Year is only reaching
its final typing now. And then on top of this to be *judged* by
what I'd already sent in, which so far as I knew I didn't have to
send in at all!

Perhaps I could have laughed this off but on top of this to
receive no reply whatever to the letter cutting myself off seems
a little too much. For I think morally this is where the situation
should stand and I repeat it makes a serious difference. That
finally they did not cut me off. I cut myself off. My letter to
them concerning this is dated Jan 4. Albert's to me the 6th.
What arises to us from this is that if the author is a gentleman
enough to ask the publishers to suspend their payments on his
work, the publishers should be sporting enough to suspend their
judgement on it, if only that some damaging gossip doesn't get
round through the grapevine that might injure one's chances of
selling anything, say, to the Signet outfit.

Of that judgement, which is so far unfavorable, or non-
existent, I'll speak briefly. It is discouraging, but I'm not really
dismayed. *Gabriola* won't admit of any stock responses to it, as
a novel of situation, character, et al. It's probably hard to read,
as the *Volcano* was, and for some people harder, if they're not
to some extent presold on the reward they may have should
they read it. Probably they're quite right that it isn't a "good"
book. It isn't. It doesn't aim to be, but thinks of itself as a classic. (Especially and/or also in conjunction with its fellows.) The
impression arises from the dim view so far taken of it (in my
more humble moments) that I may have made some elementary
mechanical mistake as to the disposition or order of narrative,
but I'm not particularly worried about it since, if so, it should
be easy to correct. The part I'm just sending in, of which you'll

have a copy, should convince you that if the narrative doesn't move horizontally it certainly can move, if in a bizarre fashion, vertically.

For the rest the *Volcano*, when so viewed in bits and pieces (or even—er—not viewed in bits and pieces) might have caused anyone to take a dim view of it. I hate the feeling, though I may be wrong, that Mr. Haas himself rejected the *Volcano*. On my side I'm not impugning anyone's powers of reading, least of all Albert's, who must express his honest opinion, but I can't see it would have been much different of the *Volcano* under these circumstances.

As for the rest ingratitude is not among my vices, and I remain extremely grateful to Mr. Haas and Random House for their financial assistance. Deo volente, they will more than get it back in the end.

The section sent off to Albert simultaneously with this letter which was finished before Christmas brings the final typed *Gabriola* to 206 pages. But for this we should have reached about 350 pages by now. The complete *Gabriola* as it stands now runs around 500 pages. Margie is making you an extra copy of this last section, a story in itself, called "The Element Follows You Around, Sir," and you'll have it in a few days, I hope, though we're snowed in, the planes are all grounded, not even trains are running, and in fact the elements are following us around, sir. I'm very sorry indeed for any collateral harassment any of this may have caused you. With all the very best from us both,

Malcolm

TO DAVID MARKSON

> Dollarton. 3 golden-eyes,
> 2 mergansers, 3 gulls,
> 7 grebes, 1 cat.
> *[Postmarked May 10, 1954]*

Dear old Dave:

I should have written you weeks ago—and indeed I did write, and more than once—but owing to certain auxiliary circumstances.... Yeah. Well, the first auxiliary circumstance was that a pigeon nesting in the airvent head on the apartment roof fell down the said airvent shaft and got trapped in the wall behind our bed, which bed came out of the wall like a drawer. I was going to make the rescue of said bird coincident with the second circumstance, though in fact the latter preceded it; a cut forehead, no more than a scratch it seemed, while messing about with these city chores more unfamiliar than trapped pigeons: but suddenly the scratch had turned into Grand Guignol—I'd severed a bloody artery. Worse to follow: Margerie, on going to the rescue, got trapped in the elevator. I mean that the elevator chose that very moment to stop between floors when her benighted husband was bleeding to death in the bathroom. Pandemonium: save from me, who having let out the third bathful of Lowry gore felt at the top of his form, and even less disposed to holler for help myself than I was to put a tourniquet round the wound in question: I have not, I said to myself, got an artery in my head, so how can I put a tourniquet on it? Perhaps what I meant was any brains but at all events there was a happy ending and we were saved in the nick, on the stroke of midnight, in St. Paul's Hospital, having been conveyed thence at 117 miles an hour by an air force officer who up to then had been slightly drunk in the corridor below when he'd been having an affair with his half-sister. "And did you do this yourself?" asked the midnight interne grimly, to which I replied, "Christ no, it was that bloody pigeon." All went well for a week or so, when someone supplicated our own aid in a manner almost as urgent as we had—or Margie had—the air force officer, though the urgency in this case was more psychological or interfamilial, and implied a journey, through the wet and wilderness—long live the wet and the wilderness yet!—of some seventy miles to a remote island—the very island upon which lives a friend of yours by the way, should you ever need him, and whom I once mentioned to you—and with a couple of cracked ribs, I mean mine, also perhaps suffered as in combat with the holy bird, and growing increasingly more painful, the more so since to reach our friend's house, one has to descend a precipice some six hundred feet in depth and at a gradient— where steps go down—of about 1 in 2.

Back in the apartment of the holy bird (the janitor suggested that despite the rules we might feed the poor thing on the window-sill after its exertions that night) it was to discover that the cracked ribs had succeeded in apparently paralyzing my innards: in endeavouring to remedy this in the approved Gandhi-esque manner—my enema the Douche, as Haile Selassie put it—there was, after many fruitless attempts, suddenly a sound of breaking and crepitous (though alas, not crapitus, had it been crapitus might have been better) enough to awaken the dead, the dead being me, to a sense, again, of the illogical or brute fact: ribs (and I have broken them all before) seemed to me malleable creatures, designed for give and take—and sway and scend and every kind of pressure from the outside: but apparently not from the inside—horrendous thought (one red-throated loon, one foolish seagull trying to steal a fish off one beautiful merganser, burning oil waste in the refinery, the first star—is the scenery outside from the room you know) like those dams in Holland during the floods of yesteryear, the ribcage was giving under the water-pressure, and it wasn't any use sticking one's finger in the dam. Or up one's arse for that matter. This time Margie got her instructions by telephone, nobly—and embarrassing though it must have been (our doctor lives in North Vancouver)—bind sheet tightly around patient to give support: more enema the douche: cascara: 2 tablespoonsful of epsom salts: an infusion of rosemarine: and caper several times boldly about the room, taking deep breaths of smog. And brandy, said I, should be given to the dying. It was, but by Monday night—that had been Sunday—it still hadn't done any good. "If nothing happens by 8, get to the hospital." Our last call was cut off by the cry Emergency! from somebody else: so I made my own emergency this time under my own steam—I mean I walked—nach dem Krankenhaus. St. Paul's again: (the first and last scenes of the whole *Volcano*— *The Voyage That Never Ends*—are supposed to be there too, but this was nightmarish a little: I ought to have been writing this, not living it or dying it, mutters Malc to himself, chuckling thoughtlessly—you oughtn't to chuckle thoughtlessly, old man, with broken ribs under such circumstances, and I warn you not to try it should you ever be unfortunate enough to be in the same position. So our North Vancouver doctor sent an emergency doctor after me, x-rays were taken, drugs given, and suffice it—with a temperature that was now rising much as it does when you go down into the engine-room of a bauxite freighter—

Several mescals later...

FASTING

behind the bed.

And at the foot a picture of the infant Jesus, apparently being instructed, with a view to the corollary of constructing a cross (since there was one above) while he looked rather like Dylan, when absolutely blind tight, being instructed, as I say, by his father Joseph, in the art of what can be done with a hammer and a nail—a truce to this. (unposted)

Our very dear old Dave:

I am terribly sorry not to have (unwritten)

Very dear old Dave:

Extremely sorry not to have written for so long, or rather not have posted any letters to you, especially when you were so sporting to write us para-psychologically suspecting some Lowry misery-grisery, and at that so entertainingly, brilliantly and sympathetically, so often at that point—(unposted)

—to cut a long story short (and incidentally I wrote you another long unposted letter, which didn't mention our troubles, but concentrated on what we thought might be your own, not posted, because of the supernatural idea that perhaps the troubles didn't really exist but stating them might somehow and obscurely beget some of them for you, god damn it, all this when I know very well that all you might have wanted was for a fellow to say oh or shit or something (as you see I couldn't say shit very well, as the poet said when he shouted Fire, having fallen down the sewer)—to cut that long story short anyhow, we are thinking of coming east this summer, in fact with the object of seeing you before we depart for Tel Aviv up the S.S. ΟΙΔΙΠΟΥΣ ΤΥΡΑΝΝΟΣ, though actually we are bound for Sicily, or at least the kingdom of the 2 Sicilies—if not under dat ole King Bomba (who made a law that stopped the trains every night at 6 P.M. making it obligatory that they hold a religious service on board)—there to live, if not in turn like that old Typhoeus, beneath Mount Etna. Previous to this, Prospero-wise, we aim to return to Milan, in which city the Volcano of your own better (or bitter) discovery is shortly to erupt: or fizzle out. We wondered if you could put us up in New York for a few days previous to this, under a bed or wherever, while we were on our way: said request not being made for financial reasons, but rather from love, whatever that entity is. If you want, you can have our house when we're gone if you want to go west though don't swear we won't haunt it and sing hot teleported tunes at you: but more likely you won't want and more likely still you'll be crossing the seas like us or whatever. Actually we don't know exactly what ship we'll be going on from New York: whether a Greek, Egyptian, Israeli, or Italian freighter. Or the exact date. But the Italian Consul is letting us know. As the said Consul remarked to Margie the other day: "This ship for lady-nice—I haf a friend who know the Commandante: the captain: but I must see friend. But maybe wait 5 or 6 day New York. But is friend I will try.... No, it is my privilege for lady-nice and friend-boy, or is he your housebound?"

At all events, you won't be too far away even if you are; but let us know, as we shall: and meantime HOLD THAT NOTE, ROLAND! BLOW THAT HORN! Hold that note! God bless from us both, Margie and me, and from the shack and many mergansers and other wild and profound sea-foul (not written),

Malcolm

TO DAVID MARKSON

Villa Mazzullo
Taormina
[Early June, 1955]

Dear old Dave:

I am terribly sorry I haven't written. Partial explanation is a p.c. that should arrive about the same time as this.

I am struck dumb by your news of Jim Agee's death: something goes fast out of your life when a man as good as that dies, even though people of worth are dying like flies these days, I can only think, to armour the dead.

All my best love to Scipio and Kitty: their wedding invitation, to hand, has arrived just about in time for me to give them a Christening present—please convey my apologies and congratulations (it is terribly hard for me to write at all at present).

Sicily—or at any rate Taormina—is a first-rate disaster: the noise so appalling I have to wear ear plugs all the time, which is causing one to go deaf (as well as blind). I fear you would like it.

Margie sends her love. As do I. I can't send you any good news so get busy and send me some. We depart for England soon. Robert Haas of Random House was here, but by bad luck I missed him. I heard roundabout that he spoke very well of me which I count damned sporting of him since I am 99 years behind in fulfilling my contract.

Our maid's daughter had a child the other day: the father and mother get married next Monday. I am thinking of forbidding the banns: apart from which the *Volcano*, though translated into Italian, is apparently in potential trouble with the Vatican: so it hasn't come out, the only thing that has being our dinner, from the ice box, which a neighbouring cat has learned how to open. Let her have it!

Sursum corda!
Malc

504 THE VOYAGE THAT NEVER ENDS

TO ALBERT ERSKINE

Brook General Hospital
Ward H (neurosurgical)
Shooters Hill Road, Woolwich
London, S.E. 18
[October, 1955]

Dear brother Albert:

I would appear to be here, Margie likewise, but in another ward, F.2; fortunately we can see each other. It is an extremely good hospital, and everyone is very kind indeed, and one eats (I speak for myself, not Margie, who can't eat at all) like a horse: this is a ward more or less entirely devoted to people with brain or skull injuries, or to the post-operative recovery of such, so that the reaper is omnipresent but it is by no means grim for all that, in fact I spend most of my time shirtless on the cricket pitch in the dew. Briefly the news: it was for a time thought possible that sundry past injuries and fractures or what not might have damaged a tricky area of my brain but despite some still perplexing symptoms it seems this isn't so; therefore, though I have been x-rayed and probably will be again to determine whether an operation is necessary, so far as I can tell I'm not going to be operated on, or at least not yet, and even if so the thing would be a minor one. (I'm having one for haemorrhoids, though I hope that's not where I keep my brain.) Touch wood. The most trying symptom has been eyesight, which has been on the blink (sick transit!) since the beginning of the year, and in fact occasionally so bad I thought I was losing my sight altogether, moreover I had dark thoughts that my childhood trouble was recurring on another plane or to blame: not so, it is just, some experts say, the usual weakening of the muscles behind the eyes that can occur at my age. So I am now bespectacled, for reading, which would scarcely be a unique state were it not that the whole thing is so maddeningly inconsistent. Sometimes, especially in sunlight, I see worse with spectacles than without and by electric light print sometimes will blur or black out altogether: then for a while I'll see perfectly again; much the same too with my physical well being: I lost 42 lbs. in a couple of months in Sicily, but back it all seems to have come here in a fortnight, I'm half sorry to say. Needless to say all this has not been too good for work, with poor Margie out of commission altogether quite impossible. This must be only about the third letter I've managed to complete this year, if I manage to complete it and—beautiful petard!—things are not rendered any easier by the fact that I can't read my own ex-handwriting, or only with great difficulty. By the time you receive this we'll both have been in here a month and probably will have at least another month to go. What is wrong with Margie no one as yet has fully determined but she is certainly damned sick, in fact a great deal sicker than I am: both of us take some grave delight in that they are feeding her paraldehyde as a sedative, though her problem is certainly not an alcoholic one (nor is mine, though I must say I feel I could use a paraldehyde and splash sometimes). Both of us have been under medical care a good deal longer than we've been hospitalized and the former doctor forbade me to write (especially on the *Gabriola* theme), supposing this to have been possible, or even think of writing until things were much better sorted out than they were: the present treatment so far as I'm concerned has had as its aim my resumption of the Work in Progress but I have to write off much of the last 18 months as a dead loss, I fear. Today the necessary MSS has been teleported to me again and sits glistering by my bedside in the ward (where my neighbour died last night to the accompaniment of "Wabash Blues") waiting for me to bash into it once more, which I mean to do as well as I can, starting immediately, though things are bound to be delayed, not least

THE VOYAGE THAT NEVER ENDS

because of typing, moreover what with this eye business I have to revise entirely my method of writing and in fact generally reorient myself to it—it's been hard for me up to now sometimes to hold a pencil at all for more than 5 minutes at a time. Needless to say I feel badly not to have delivered the goods, some goods, long ere now, it was a great pity for me we had to sever the umbilical cord with Random House at the time we did: moreover I got very discouraged, not only by the reception but by the lack of a word from anyone in regard to what small things I did publish: both "The Bravest Boat" and "Strange Comfort" have become classics in French and Italian and the latter is in an anthology of *Best English Short Stories* of all time and so on. I have read aloud parts of *Gabriola* with great success too when in Taormina, which may mean something. But a truce to this. Should I kick the bucket, or the project seem really hopeless, it is arranged that the money so far advanced will be paid back to you: as things stand I can keep our heads above water without aid; I don't want to assume failure in advance, to complete things or to engage myself in extraneous projects in *order* to pay you back now. I hope the situation may be still as it was, that the clock was stopped when it was stopped, and that I may have time, no matter how much I've lost or how tardy I am, to catch up now. It would remove a major source of emotional tension (a commodity I'm not allowed to indulge in) if I could feel this were so. I believe I can make the grade though luck has been consistently against me and us so far and I don't have any right to make any promises save that I'm going to TRY, after so long silence and limbo. A letter to Mr. Haas (to whom please convey as much or as little of this as you think fit), who was in Taormina and who was kind and sporting enough to speak well of me there, I heard, though unfortunately I didn't meet him, accompanies this, which please give him if you think it right, and if not not.

Another strange casualty is my English grammar: a total amne-siacal loss, but I don't think a very serious one. All the best love from us both as always, with the utmost affection,

Malcolm

TO HARVEY BURT

The White Cottage
Ripe, near Lewes
Sussex, England
[June 9, 1956]

Dear Harvey:

Thank you from our hearts for the wonderful letter. But to reply briefly and to point since time is so short. I think your young married couple—he the teacher and actor—sound a good thing for the house and the house for them. The impor-tant thing is to have someone who'll both live in it and love it during the summer (I can't think too far ahead) and perhaps part of the autumn and at least drop down to see it during the winter. With this in view I feel the more things of mine, ours— books, for example—that are left there the less desolated it will look, also *feel* from this end, not to say be for you in other ways more convenient: the less desolated it will be from your point of view too. Also one has to make clear they have no actual responsibility for anything of mine, in case some such feeling as this should be a deterrent. As for *My Heart's In...*—well, all this is left to your heart and discretion. You make our hearts feel better about it all, however: and again, thank you from them. There're a few important points to bequeath to any pos-sible temporary successor, I mention, partly because they are even more valid to anyone not living your more specifically Conradian existence on the beach: first, though it may look like

a Pig-in-a-poke (and indeed is—in a spiritual sense) to hang on
to the "mink's house" next door your old one is virtually a
necessity to any married or indeed unmarried couple if their
lives are to be tenable as ours; I'd hate to see that big cedar
come down between the houses or imagine any other horrors
that could happen otherwise. (To me, too, childish though it
may seem, there is the pier, which we built, which I cannot
imagine myself living without, even if it isn't there or myself am
dead.) Then there is the old pier: it can be a delight to a swimmer. Please give it a long counterbracing master building look
at least before you should leave, cast some Harveyian archi-
techtonic charm at it, some spell against teredos, and tell your
descendents to cherish it (even if in its absence). Finally there is
much of love about the place that will surely come to any
lover's aid, especially in such strange seasons as autumn and
winter and early spring: in your most knightly fashion I com-
mend you to pass such words down to whom it may concern,
(even if necessary in the accents of Sir Walter Scott). Finally
there is the question of the MSS. Leave 'em lay where de Lawd
hath flung them. That is to say, use your discretion about this.
Books—again, as I say, largely these will be better, I think,
where they are more or less: wherever they are. All we'd like
ourselves in Europe, if you can somehow manage it, are two
magical books, both in bad shape, and written apparently by
one Frater Achad. One is called *Q.B.L.*, the other *The Anatomy of the Body of God*. They are books about the Cabbala.
Another very small book is a copy of Melville's *The Confidence
Man*, if you can slip that in anywhere: it's scarcely larger than a
pocket book. *The Melville Log* and the Daumier your guests
might like to look at, in fact they might be an added attraction.
It is a blow that Jimmy won't be there, but give him our best
love should you see him: he thinks very highly of you. I reiter-
ate the names of the two possibilities we had in mind, if any-

thing should fall through at the last moment. Gene Lawrence, 2233 McPherson Ave., S. Burnaby. Or Bill and Alice McConnell—Einar will know where they are now.

You say you think you're gaucho. If that means left, as I understand it to do, let's hope we both are so far gauche that we're right. If I'm to understand that it means provincial, you are the exact opposite, in my opinion, as I was reflecting only the other day, treading Raleigh's walk in The Tower of London.

Do they still come homeward? And the mergansers? And—Ah pardon me thou bleeding piece of earth! I would rather have spoken that line (and that we had erected that outhouse) than have taken—perhaps—Dollarton. God bless!

Love from us both,
Malcolm

TO HARVEY BURT

[Circa August, 1956]

Thank you, dear old Harvey, for the more than bravest boat. It is truly a work of art and great kindness, and if I look at it long enough maybe I can forget the poor shack being hurled out of the window, though that was a great work of art too, and heartbreaking that it had to happen, especially after all the love you put into making it.

I am writing without my glasses so the contours of this note may be a little awry. Also I am very tired: I cannot believe our poor pier has been swept away: that pier, that gave so much happiness to many and us, *was us* in a sense; we risked our lives building it, especially on the further reaches you never saw, where there was a 35-foot perpendicular drop on to the granite and barnacles if you made a mistake: nobody could understand how it survived so long, not even engineers, and it was nicknamed "The Crazy Wonder" on the beach. Ramshackle from certain angles though it was, and the handrails puerile (but oh the washing hung out on the line there, like great white stationary birds beating their wings against the gale). Margie and I built it together with practically no tools and I am broken hearted it has gone.

Malcolm

TO RALPH GUSTAFSON

The White Cottage
Ripe, near Lewes
Sussex, England
[April 29, 1957]

Dear Ralph Gustafson:

I'm very sorry to take so long to reply to your letter of March 12 but Jonathan Cape sent it back to Canada again, so that it had to get re-forwarded again from B.C. before I received it.

I'm very honored to be put in the Penguin though whether I qualify strictly as a Canadian is another matter though I like to think I do: under the old law I did, though I still have a British passport, albeit I took out Canadian papers, never decided on any final citizenship, so am classed as a Canadian resident. My wife and I lived there for fourteen years in a waterfront shack on Burrard Inlet which I still have that I loved or love more than my life and wrote—all my best work, as the saying is, there. I left in 1954 because of my wife's health but we hope to return. But I never became a Canadian citizen under the new law: nonetheless I've as much right to call myself Canadian as Louis Hémon had and I even wrote a Canadian national anthem, though nobody's sung it except me. I had a childish ambition—maybe not so childish—always to contribute something to Canadian literature though, and I wrote a book called *Under the Volcano,* which has become fairly well known, but which people seem to think is written by an American. Like all blokes in the throes of an anthology I suppose that you are persecuted by replies from contributors you want saying that they want you to select something else—of theirs—if possible *too,* and I do not want to torment you in this way but I am no exception, thinking I've done some things better than these two, but I'm proud you selected them anyway, though I thought a thing called "Sestina in a Cantina" (perhaps too long) and one called "Salmon Drowns Eagle" that I thought might have been suitable: and A. J. M. Smith printed another in his Scribner anthology called "In Memoriam Ingvald Bjorndal" that I'm fond of: when I say *I'm* fond of, I mean this literally, because very few people have ever expressed their opinion one way or another about my verse so any fatherly advice on the subject, no matter how devastating, will be very welcome to me: sometimes I think I've never been able fully to understand the most elementary principles of scansion, stress, interior rhyme and the like with the result, by overcompensation, that my poems such as they are *look* as though they had a kind of wooden monotonous classical frame: perhaps I have no ear (Birrell on Dr. Johnson: "He knew but one way of writing poetry, namely to chain together as much sound sense and sombre feeling as he could squeeze into the fetters of rhyming couplets and then to clash those fetters very loudly in your ear. This proceeding he called versification") but then I must have some sort of ear because I began life as a would-be composer of hot jazz, and what is more I think a good one. All this is very sad and complicated to me because I think of practically nothing else but poetry when I'm not thinking about my old shack on Burrard Inlet but *like* so extremely few poems of any kind by anybody that it seems to me I am maybe inhibiting myself from writing, either by some serious lack of judgement in regard to my own craft, or some fanatical narcissism or other that makes me set the touchstone impossibly high, as a result of which I am now writing a huge and sad novel about Burrard Inlet called *October Ferry to Gabriola* that I sometimes feel could have been better stated in about ten short poems—or even lines— instead: then again I have good judgement about other people's poetry when I can understand what they are saying, which isn't very often, so please tell me what I should read: I'd like to edu- cate myself as a poet seriously, though it's getting a bit late in all conscience. Tell me of your own recent work: I like much all that I have read of yours.

Two wild western poets came to see my wife and I in the bush on Burrard one stormy night some years ago, and I enclose you some of the recent work of one, which seems to me—the typed ones—damned good. This fellow Curt Lang was scarcely out of his teens and he impressed me mightily as being a type I thought extinct: namely all poet, whose function is to write poetry. His address is Curt Lang, 517 Pine, West Montreal, Quebec. I think the written poem would be better without the *on retina* in the first line, and the final couplet is weak: but the other two have a kind of fury, and the architec- tural one at the end, a really terrifying quality, that seems to me very rare and original in a poet, whatever the merits of his typography or indeed however he means it to be printed: I do think he is worthy of inclusion, even if you have to kick me out, for he is a young bloke who could use and deserves that kind of encouragement in my opinion. (Not that I couldn't or don't, but I'm older.) The work of his friend on that occasion, whose name I've unfortunately mislaid, is also worth looking into: his name is Al something or other, but Curt Lang would put you on to his work which again impressed me by its originality, intricacy and power. He is an older poet who has published a chapbook or so, but both are well worth watching and he too is worth considering in my opinion but maybe you've already made your selection. I've met a lot of writers but I have rarely been impressed by such dedication on the part of anybody as these two, and as for Lang he might well have genius. (I hope these poems will cause you to drop a line to Lang anyway and if you decide to use any of them he could enlighten you as to the typography—or you him, but could you let me have them back eventually because I thought of sending them to Spender or somebody). Re my bad memory, I seem to recollect a misprint, if not two in "The Glaucous Winged Gull." A memory *stronger* than childhood it was meant to be, not *stranger* anyway, for what that's worth. Among your own admirable but lesser-known works did you not once write a story about someone climbing a building printed by Martha Foley in 1948?— horrifyingly good. I can still feel it. If you didn't write it please take it as a compliment that I thought you did.

Sincerely yours,
Malcolm Lowry

P.S. Did you ever come across the work of a man named Norman Newton? He struck me as an exceptionally promising writer, though I have not heard from him for many years.

P.P.S. We are going to live in the Lake District, in Grasmere, for a while not because it reminds one of Wordsworth so much but because if we half shut our eyes we may be able to imagine we're back on Burrard Inlet!

TO DAVID MARKSON

Grasmere
June 15, 1957

Dollarton? That's what we thought but it's Grasmere where
Wordsworth designed the chimney pots and you may see de
Quincey's room (smoking prohibited) in de Quincey's house to
which, on payment of 1/6 you may be admitted on all days save
Sundays as Wordsworth's cottage, which it was for 5 years.
How goes *Swellfoot the Tyrant*? Your letter was melancholy,
but cannot you *use* that very uncertainty as to one's ability as a
strength? O'Neill (see *Long Day's Journey*) thought himself
not much use as a writer too. Have you read *Isaac Babel*? You
should. Do you know which stars are which and what bird is
flying over your head and what flower blossoming? If you don't
the anguish of *not* knowing is a very valid field for the artist.
Moreover when you learn something it's a good thing to repos-
sess the position of your original ignorance. Best love to Elaine
and yourself from Margie and Malc.

SOURCES

The stories "June the 30th, 1934," "China," "Under the Volcano," and "Kristbjorg's Story: In the Black Hills" were first collected in *Malcolm Lowry: Psalms and Songs*, edited by Margerie Lowry (New York: New American Library, 1975).

The stories "Through the Panama," "Strange Comfort Afforded by the Profession," and "The Forest Path to the Spring" were first collected in *Hear Us O Lord from Heaven Thy Dwelling Place* (Philadelphia: Lippincott, 1961).

Nearly all the poems in this volume were first published in *Selected Poems* (San Francisco: City Lights, 1962). The remaining three, "England," "And yet I am of England too; odi et amo," and "Lament in the Pacific Northwest," can be found in *The Collected Poetry of Malcolm Lowry*, edited and introduced by Kathleen Scherf (Vancouver: UBC Press, 1992).

The excerpts in the "Fragments" section can be found in greater length in the following works: *Dark as the Grave Wherein My Friend Is Laid*, edited by Douglas Day and Margerie Lowry (New York: New American Library, 1968);

Malcolm Lowry's "La Mordida," edited by Patrick A. McCarthy (Athens: University of Georgia Press, 1996); and *October Ferry to Gabriola*, edited by Margerie Lowry (New York: World, 1970).

For a larger selection of Malcolm Lowry's letters see, *The Selected Letters of Malcolm Lowry*, edited by Harvey Breit and Margerie Bonner Lowry (Philadelphia: Lippincott, 1965), and *Sursum corda!: The Collected letters of Malcolm Lowry*, edited and with an introduction and annotations by Sherrill E. Grace (Toronto: University of Toronto Press, 1995–1997).